8|07

THE *Lost Diary*
OF
Don Juan

**Center Point
Large Print**

**This Large Print Book carries the
Seal of Approval of N.A.V.H.**

THE *Lost Diary* OF *Don Juan*

An Account of the True Arts of Passion and the Perilous Adventure of Love

DOUGLAS CARLTON ABRAMS

CENTER POINT PUBLISHING
THORNDIKE, MAINE

This Center Point Large Print edition
is published in the year 2007 by arrangement with
Atria Books, an imprint of Simon & Schuster, Inc.

Copyright © 2007 by Idea Architects.

The text of this Large Print edition is unabridged. In other
aspects, this book may vary from the original edition. Printed in
Thailand. Set in 16-point Times New Roman type.

ISBN-10: 1-60285-018-6
ISBN-13: 978-1-60285-018-7

Library of Congress Cataloging-in-Publication Data

Abrams, Douglas Carlton.
    The Lost diary of Don Juan / Douglas Carlton Abrams.--Center Point large print ed.
      p. cm.
    ISBN-13: 978-1-60285-018-7 (lib. bdg. : alk. paper)
      1. Don Juan (Legendary character)--Fiction. 2. Seduction--Fiction. 3. Nobility--Fiction.
    4. Seville (Spain)--Fiction. 5. Large type books. 6. Diary fiction. I. Title.

PS3601.B735L67 2007b
813'.6--dc22

2007006096

Contents

Editor's Note

As an editor at the University of California Press who was responsible for unsolicited manuscripts, I received many unusual submissions, but nothing like the one you are about to read. The cover letter indicated that the manuscript was being sent to me because of an article I published in the *Journal of Spanish Literature*. I had reviewed the few shreds of evidence that Don Juan, the famed seducer of women, was an actual historical person who lived in southern Spain in the sixteenth century. My correspondent claimed that the enclosed manuscript was nothing less than a translation of a diary kept by this very same Don Juan and hidden for "a dozen generations in secrecy." The package had no return address.

The diary was supposedly written in Seville in 1593, during the Spanish Golden Age. King Philip II ruled the largest empire the world had ever known, and by order of the Crown, Seville was the sole port through which all the silver and gold of the Americas poured. Because of its great wealth and decadence, Seville was often called the Great Babylon of Spain. *Galanteadores* (the Spanish word for gallants or seducers) were common at the time, and their success may have been partly the result of the depletion of men caused by wars and colonization. Although the accuracy of historical census data is hard to judge, it was estimated that in some neighborhoods, *half* of all women were widowed or abandoned.

A man's life does not divide evenly into chapters; neither, apparently, did Don Juan's diary. The letter indicated that the translator had taken the liberty of separating the text into parts and even inserting chapter titles throughout. By the dating, it seems that Don Juan often wrote what has become several "chapters" in a single sitting. I must apologize to my scholarly colleagues for these corruptions of the text, which should not be taken as original. Nor obviously should the Glossary and Notes section, which I have added to provide additional guidance to a general reader unfamiliar with the many historical terms and Spanish words remaining in the translation.

Most scholars have maintained that while perhaps based on folktales, Don Juan Tenorio was nothing more than a fictional character created by the Spanish monk and playwright Tirso de Molina. This diary, if authentic, would substantiate the minority opinion, first proposed by the French scholar Louis Viardot in 1835, that Don Juan was an actual noble who lived in the city of Seville and on whom Molina may have loosely based his character. I have had the diary reviewed by numerous experts who could find no sign of obvious forgery; however, scholarly caution has caused me to wait until now to publish this translation. My colleagues have at last convinced me that a judgment about the diary's authenticity is best made not by me, but by the reader.

—D.C.A.
June 2006

THE *Lost Diary*
OF
Don Juan

I write in the naked pages of this diary so that the truth will be known and my fate will not be left to the rumors and lies already whispering through the streets of Sevilla. Many, I am sure, will try to turn my life into a morality play after I am dead, but no man's life is so easily understood or dismissed.

I would not risk inscribing my secrets in this diary had I not been convinced to do so by my friend and benefactor, Don Pedro, the Marquis de la Mota. I argued that nothing I would write could be circulated in my lifetime without my being condemned by the holy office of the Inquisition and burned at the stake. The Inquisitor himself branded this danger into my imagination just yesterday. Perhaps it is this fresh threat, or the ultimatum of the king, that has at last caused me to pick up this quill and ink these words. The Marquis insisted that it is for posterity that I should write this diary, one's reputation being the only true immortality. But it is hardly vanity alone that causes me to write.

Thirty-six years have passed since my birth, or more correctly since my mother left me, a swaddled bundle, in the barn of the Convento de la Madre Sagrada. It is no doubt a sign of my advancing years that I have been persuaded for the first time in my life to consider how I will be remembered. Yet there is another desire that leads me to write in this diary. It is to pass on what I have learned about the Arts of Passion and of the holiness of womanhood. Since I have forsworn matrimony and have no heirs of my own blood, I must look to all who follow as my descendants and try to share with them what I have learned from the women I have been privileged to know so well.

A man's recollections always tend toward self-flattery, so I will not rely on my testimony alone and will instead write, as faithfully as possible, not only the events but the words themselves that were shouted during a duel or whispered during a passionate embrace.

It is this same pride that leads me to begin my account with the most daring seduction I have ever undertaken. My ambition was nothing less than to free the king's chaste and lonely daughter from her imprisonment in the royal palace of the Alcázar—for a night. I knew that if I were caught, it would be my privilege as a noble to place my head on the executioner's block and avoid the shame of the gallows.

A man's ambition, however, like his fate, is not always known to him in advance, and as I left the arms of the Widow Elvira, I had no hint of the danger that I would embrace last night.

A Flicker of Passion

"One more kiss," Elvira said, pulling gently on the sleeve of my maroon doublet as I dressed quickly. I was late, despite having been warned by the

Marquis that my very life depended on my presence at the king's audience. I had every intention of arriving on time, but this resolve melted when I discovered that the young woman in my arms this afternoon had been widowed by the sea. Her loneliness and her desire had not been soothed in all the five years since her husband's death. "Just *one*," she added, her lips now inclining toward mine. I looked at her smiling face, and her black hair, disheveled by our earlier desire. Her clear brown eyes reflected the flames of the candles that encircled the altar of her bed. How could I refuse her?

I held her cheeks with the tips of my fingers and came closer, approaching her face slowly, anticipation being everything. I brushed her lips gently with mine and then tickled the corner of her mouth with the tip of my tongue. I knew not to smother her with kisses so she would have to defend herself from my assault. I sipped the moist nectar of her mouth as she opened her petals to me. Our mouths fused together, her thirst palpable and her breath short. With our tongues and lips, we drank from each other a cordial as sweet as honey. When I pulled back at long last, she hovered in midair, her eyes still closed but her thirst quenched.

I stroked her soft cheek with my forefinger. "I am sorry I cannot give you more than an evening's entertainment," I said, "but that is all that I can give any woman."

"Don Juan, you gave me more than my husband ever did. I'd heard that in your eyes, a woman sees her true beauty for the first time." She swallowed. "It was not a lie."

I smiled and bowed my head, knowing that each woman's soul is a singular treasure. It was while growing up as an orphan in a convent that I first discovered these riches that few men have the privilege to behold. It was in the words as much as the kisses from Hermana Teresa's mouth that I learned to hear the quiet whispers of a woman's joys, fears, and longings.

The clang of the local church bells was like a rod snapping against my skin. My coachman, Cristóbal, knocked on the door impatiently. I knew my opportunity to honor the king and win his protection was quickly slipping through my fingers.

"I am sorry to have to leave so abruptly," I said as I placed my plumed black hat on my head. "Where I go is not nearly as enjoyable as where I have been." She lay back in her bed with a confirming smile. I grabbed my cape and sword before darting out of her house.

Cristóbal was a head taller than I but thinner, and his limbs were askew like those of a scarecrow. He crossed himself nervously, as he always did when he saw me after one of my seductions. "Another widow, my lord?" he said with a wince.

"I suppose you believe the priests—that a widow should live like a nun until she joins her husband in heaven. Let me tell you a secret, Cristóbal. A woman's desire does not die before her last breath."

He blushed and said, "The *audience,* my lord."

14

"What are we waiting for?" I said with a smile, and stepped into the carriage.

"Quickly now!" Cristóbal urged my mare, no doubt worried for my life, but not just my life. A dead man has no need for a coachman.

Bonita knew our urgency just from the force of Cristóbal's rarely raised voice and galloped through the narrow streets of Lebrija, the wheels of the black carriage scraping against the whitewashed walls. Unlike other coach drivers, Cristóbal never used a whip, and he had a way of whispering into a horse's ear that made her do whatever he wanted. While he had this skill with horses, he was terrified of women. He had always had this fear, ever since I first found him in the Arenal, when he was a boy of twelve. He had run away from his family and was looking for work, and I was looking for a coachman but could not afford a full-grown one. I was no more than twenty-two at the time, and I became something of an older brother to him as we grew into manhood together.

The carriage sped along the rough dirt road back to Sevilla, the wheels spinning dust in every direction. After less than two hours of hard riding, I could see through the carriage window the beautiful walls of Sevilla, burned pink and red by the light of the summer sunset. From within the city, the Giralda erupted to the heavens. At the crown of the tower stood a bronze woman, our city's symbol of faith, a cross in one hand and a palm frond in the other. Next to the bell tower, the round moon, one day past full, already rested on

15

the Cathedral like a satisfied woman reclining in her heavenly bed.

Black smoke suddenly eclipsed the moon as we approached a massive crowd gathered on the Prado de San Sebastián, just outside the city walls. The charred scent of burning flesh offended my nose and turned my stomach. I looked around nervously, but there was no other road to take, and Cristóbal knew it was too late to turn back. Bonita was forced to stop, as we were now surrounded on all sides by a crowd watching a hellish spectacle, mouths agape with terror and eyes ablaze with fascination.

Roped to tall stakes were half a dozen men and women. Two stood defiantly, while the bodies of the rest slouched lifelessly. The dead had chosen to confess their heresy and in return received the mercy of garroting before their burning. Beneath them, piles of kindling and logs fueled great bonfires that engulfed them and even reached the crosses atop each stake. Within the flames, I saw the face of a boy, certainly no older than I was when I arrived in Sevilla at the age of sixteen. Whether commoner or noble, all of the heretics wore the *sanbenito* gown painted with devils and flames. Although I did not know their crimes, some were no doubt followers of Luther. One woman had red hair, and this alone may have caused her to be denounced as a witch. Roped and burning on other stakes next to them were the wooden statues that allowed those who had fled or died in the torture chambers to be burned in effigy. Not even in death did one escape the fury of the Inquisition. The ornate statues looked as real as those figures of our lord Jesus paraded during holy week and had been carved by the same sculptors. It was of utmost importance to the inquisitors that the semblances be exact; these artists were so skillful that even tears on the faces of the sculptures looked as if they were falling down their cheeks.

The screams of the still-living victims filled my ears as the flames licked their skin.

"Ride on!" I said to Cristóbal, unwilling to spend another moment in this diabolical place. But we could not move—not only because of the thickness of the crowd but because soldiers of the Inquisition were now blocking our way.

The soldiers wore metal-studded red vests over their chain-mail shirts, wide black leather belts fastened around their waists, and shining steel helmets on their heads. They carried crossbows that were fired with a trigger, making them extremely deadly. Several soldiers approached our carriage. Only then did I see who stood behind them.

"Ah, Don Juan, have you come to see what your future holds?" inquired Fray Ignacio de Estrada. He had deep lines in his cheeks, and his temples seemed pressed into his head as if in a vise. He did not wear the black robe and regal pointed hat with a purple plume that most inquisitors wore. Instead, he wore only the black and white habit of a Dominican friar. He wore no hat, just the bald head and halo of hair favored by any tonsured monk. Around his neck hung a roughly fashioned cross made of olive wood. Although now in his fifties, the Inquisitor still had the broad shoulders of a vigorous warrior of God.

It was this man who was most responsible for the horror that was occurring all around me. While the inquisitors always turned their victims over to the civil authorities to deny responsibility for their executions, everyone knew who demanded that the kindling be lit.

Fray Ignacio has always seen himself as a holy crusader, sending to their deaths all who offend faith or public decency. He had risen quickly in the hierarchy of the Inquisition and was now second only to the Inquisitor General himself. I had known Fray Ignacio since he had been my teacher at the monastery. His lessons did not endear him to me.

"Even the greatest sinners," he added with a smile that was impossible to distinguish from a sneer, "cannot escape the wrath of God forever."

I breathed deeply and tried to hold my tongue. I could not. "Futures are famously hard to predict, Your *Reverence*."

"Not yours, Don Juan," he said through gritted teeth. "As soon as your favor with the king runs out, I will personally see to it that you are punished for each and every one of your sins."

"The greatest sinners are always punished last, *Your Reverence*. Now, with your permission, the king is waiting."

"So am I," the Inquisitor said, but bowing to the king's authority, he flicked his wrist for the guards to let us through. The soldiers and the sea of people parted as Cristóbal nervously coaxed the mare forward. The Marquis had taught me many years ago never to show weakness to an opponent, but as soon as we were out of view, I collapsed back against my seat and sighed in relief. We galloped again, and as we descended a final hill to the city, I could see the welcoming embrace of its gates. Yet across the riverbanks stood the stone Castillo de San Jorge, the headquarters of the Inquisition, like a beast laying siege to our city.

"Quickly now! Quickly!" Cristóbal urged, shaking the reins as we careened through the gates of the city. Bonita raced the remaining distance to the Alcázar, the carriage lurching back and forth on the cobblestones, until at last we arrived at the Puerta del León. After presenting myself, I was permitted to enter through the heavy wooden doors that stood the height of two men. Rushing into the interior palace, I finally arrived at the Salón de Embajadores. Noble well-wishers filled the room, and the whisper of court gossip and political intrigue filled the air. The walls were tiled and plastered in the knotted geometric designs of the Moors. Black marble columns with gold capitals skirted the room, spanned by horseshoe arches. I looked up in awe at the gold dome that glittered like the star-filled sky. It was here in this audience chamber that, long ago, king Pedro the Cruel decided to kill his own brother for falling in love with the princess whom he himself was to marry. I wondered whether I also would be sentenced to death in this chamber.

The audience was coming to its conclusion, and I was called by name to the presence of the Crown. As I walked to the far end of the room, a hush came over the crowd. All craned to hear my reception. I kneeled before our aging King. His green eyes were sharp and suspicious, as always, but his tired and gray-bearded face looked all the closer to the grave. He suffered from gout, which must have made his journey from Madrid unbearable, and his right leg rested on a folding chair that had been given to him by the emperor of China. Only the King's bankrupt treasury, the result of too many wars and an endless empire, could have forced him to greet the treasure ships that were on their way to Sevilla. I knew that the King despised the pretension and deceit of court as much as I did, and he did not try to hide his boredom. Our pious King slouched in the straight-backed mahogany throne that was as austere as he was.

His grown daughter, Infanta Doña Isabel Clara Eugenia, stood behind him. It was an open secret that she was the king's closest adviser and favorite child. Doña Isabel had her father's intelligent green eyes, but her full, youthful face was much warmer. Her brown hair was pulled back tightly into a bun. She wore a black bonnet encircled with pearls and decorated with a white ostrich feather and jeweled pin.

I waited with my head bent forward, as if anticipating the executioner's blade. The orange-and-apricot-scented fragrance of the Infanta's perfume calmed my nervous breath. Ruffling the stilted silence, the enormous figure of the Marquis stepped from the crowd to introduce me. A bear of a man, he had a powerful chest that was the width of two, yet he moved nimbly toward the throne. His size and his speed made my mentor and friend a deadly opponent in a duel. He was dressed in black, like the King, but his fashionable clothes were laced with silver and gold thread. The tips of his waxed mustache pointed up, and his serpentine beard spiraled down. His receding hairline revealed much of his scalp, and his nose and cheeks were red, as always, the result of many fine meals and innumerable bottles of wine. He had once told me that there comes a time in a man's life when food looks more desirable than a woman. I had prayed that for me such a day might never come.

"Your Majesty, it is my privilege to present to you Don Juan Tenorio, your faithful subject."

"The Inquisitor will be the judge of his faith," the King mumbled, sending a twitter of amusement through the crowd and an ominous shiver down my spine. "By the stories that have been circulating at court," the King said, now turning his gaze toward me, "I would have thought that you were some kind of demon."

"Just a man, Your Majesty," I said. "The rumors at court will turn any man into a demon."

I glanced up and saw that the King was unable to

repress a thin smile. He was more a victim of the gossip and pettiness at court than anyone. "I was told," he continued, "that you would announce your engagement tonight." My face must have shown my surprise as I glanced over at the Marquis, whose raised eyebrows revealed that he had not been the source of this rumor. "Was I misled?" the King asked.

"My enemies deceive you, Your Majesty. I have not fallen in love."

The Infanta leaned forward and whispered something in his ear.

"My daughter says that marriage need not have anything to do with love."

"Your daughter has your wisdom, Your Majesty," I said as my eyes looked beyond him to those of the Infanta. Although now twenty-seven, she still lived with her elderly father. Her mother, who had been married to our King at the age of fifteen to unite Spain and France, had died two years after Doña Isabel was born. Even her younger sister and only confidante, Catalina, had been married off to the Duke of Savoy eight years ago. The Infanta no doubt would accept marriage without love, if the suitor had the right title, which I certainly did not.

"It displeases the Crown that you have not partaken in the Holy Sacrament of Marriage," the King said irritably, and then looked away.

"Your Majesty's pleasure is my only concern," I replied, flashing a meaningful look at the Infanta. Her eyes stared back at me over her fan, and her lips opened almost imperceptibly. Twenty-seven years is too long for a woman's undeniable passions to wait for the politics of royal alliances, I thought, as she looked away modestly.

"Then the Crown commands you," the King replied emphatically, "to find a suitable wife. The modesty of the nobility requires it . . . as does our Holy Inquisition. Next month at court, I will hear whom you have chosen."

He held out his hand limply. I kissed it and backed away, recalling the words of the Inquisitor and the inferno I had just witnessed. Our ailing King was increasingly unable to restrain the ever greater power of the Inquisition.

"Thank you, Your Majesty," the Marquis said, speaking for me. "You have the wisdom of Solomon and the patience of Job."

The King bowed his head slightly, forced to be gracious to a powerful marquis. I backed away and was swallowed up by the sea of people who now returned to their gossiping as quickly as they had stopped. I kept my gaze down, uncomfortable among my betters, and hid in the back of the room as countless others tried to ingratiate themselves with the King.

I stood next to one of the black marble columns, furtively looking at the Infanta. In her silver brocade gown, she looked like a matron and not like the maiden she still was. The arms of her dress hung down like the wings of an angel, and her neck was confined by a lace ruff, as were her wrists. Around her waist she wore a jeweled belt, like a girdle, that came to a sharp point, covering her chastely.

Most women can perceive a stare as if it were the whisper of words, and the Infanta was no different. She turned and looked at me, then replied in the secret language of the fan. She held the delicate black lace just below her beautiful green eyes and long black eyelashes, a possible sign that she wanted to see me in private. This was not the first time she had looked at me over her fan during a royal audience. It was only my fear and weakness that had prevented me from answering her.

The Marquis must have seen the exchange of glances and now approached me with the famed courtesan Alma on his arm. "I don't know if the King was referring to his own daughter," he whispered with a mischievous smile, "when commanding you to partake in the Holy Sacrament of Marriage." His eyebrows were arched, as always, his small eyes missing nothing, plotting everything. He saw what no one else could, and he knew me as no one else did. His thin lips, so prized by the nobility for their cold restraint, smiled as he twisted his beard in his fingers.

"You know that matrimony is the furthest thing from my mind," I whispered back, as we stood beneath one of the horseshoe arches.

Alma's black ringlets framed her blue eyes, which always burned like the hottest part of a flame. The beautiful symmetry of her face spread into a smile at my reply. "Matrimony," she ventured, "is not in our dear Don Juan's vocabulary." Although separated by a decade, Alma and I had both been born in the small town of Carmona. She had been my greatest student, as I had been the Marquis's.

"Matrimony had better enter your vocabulary," the Marquis said to me, "if you wish to stay in the good graces of the King. Nevertheless, I know quite well what your interest is in the Infanta, and I know what *her* interest is in you."

"Really?" Alma replied for me.

"Oh, yes," the Marquis whispered. "Poor Doña Isabel is so terribly lonely and longing for companionship."

"And how would you know that?" I asked.

"From a letter that she wrote to her sister," he said even more quietly, then quoted under his breath, " 'How I long to be married, to be made a woman, to know what a husband's tender hand might feel like.' " The Marquis regularly intercepted the royal mail, and I had at one time stolen letters for him as his spy. Although I knew he would have used his false seal to refasten the letter and send it on to its intended recipient, I chastised him for stealing such a personal confidence.

"And what business of yours are the Infanta's fantasies?" I asked.

"It is important for a loyal counselor to the King," he parried, "to know about all *affairs* of state."

The King and Infanta were retiring after their long journey, and the guests were slowly leaving. "This seduction will be worthy of the diary I gave you," the

25

Marquis whispered in my ear, "but please be careful. Your execution would pain me terribly."

The Marquis excused himself, eager to talk with the King as he was leaving.

"I know it is your rule never to 'satisfy' yourself with a virgin on your first encounter," Alma said, lingering behind.

"A self-serving rule that always leads to a second encounter."

"And eternal gratitude," she added, "as pleasure is awakened in her skin before the inevitable pain."

"Indeed, although pleasure and pain are often impossible to separate."

"My point exactly," she responded. "When the Infanta's pleasure has been attended to, perhaps I could relieve your pain." She brushed her fan against my codpiece, sending a shiver through my body.

"I know why you are the greatest courtesan in Sevilla, and it is not only your beauty. You know a man's needs before he does."

"You taught me to read the unspoken needs that are more than skin-deep," she replied. We were the last two to leave the audience chamber, and we continued our whispering as we walked through the colonnades of the Patio de las Doncellas.

"You were a gifted student."

"Shall I keep my morning 'uncommitted'?"

I breathed in the sweet-smelling jasmine blossoms and replied, "I am no longer your teacher, Doña Alma, as the Marquis is no longer mine."

"A teacher always has more to teach."

"Need I remind you that it is also my rule not to buy affections that should be freely given?"

"For you, Don Juan, I would not charge."

"You are most generous, but I seek something that no prostitute or courtesan can offer. Now I am afraid you must excuse me."

I ducked behind one of the double columns. Alma glanced back with an arched eyebrow. I had little time to consider her further, however, as all my senses turned to the dangers that surrounded me. A flicker of doubt lit through my body, and I felt my legs pulling me toward Alma and the rest of the guests disappearing around the corner. My right leg began to shake, as it always did when I foolishly endangered my life.

Several guards passed the paired columns behind which I was hiding. The Infanta's face with her eyes looking beseechingly over her fan came to mind. How could I refuse her invitation? I had taken a vow to pursue the liberty of womanhood, and I could not let her remain trapped in her tower of loneliness.

Out of my sleeve I pulled the leather mask that I was never without. It had served me so well over the years, first when I was a burglar, then when I was a spy, and now in my even more dangerous intrigues. The black band with its two oval eyelets would hide my identity if I were seen before I reached the Infanta's bedchamber. It was not long before all the guests were gone and the courtyard was silent. I moved out into the moonlight that illumined the stone portico. My hands burned with apprehension and anticipation. The warm midnight breeze did nothing to cool my fever as I stepped between the columns. Fortunately, my days as a burglar now served me well, and I was grateful that the cork soles of my boots hushed my careful steps.

As I turned the corner, a flash of moonlight reflected off the rounded helmets and steel breastplates of two royal guards. I froze. Groping behind me, I felt the cool tile wall and tried to flatten my body against it like a shadow. My heart was pounding as if someone were knocking urgently at a door that would not open.

These sentinels were guarding the greatest treasure of the King, his daughter's modesty. In their gloved hands they held ax-topped lances that allowed them to impale and behead intruders. They stared in my direction.

My black boots, cape, and mask hid me in the shadows. The maroon doublet and trunk hose I always wore at night were equally invisible in the dark. Only the silver blade of my sword risked revealing me. The guards headed in my direction. I quickly stepped into an empty room, hiding behind one of the carved mahogany doors. I tried to quiet my breathing when I felt and then saw one of the guards thrust his head into the room. He was so close I could smell the acrid sweat under his heavy uniform and hear his heavy breathing. The door creaked; I knew that he would certainly discover me. I closed my eyes, held my breath, and tried to disappear through the wall.

"I must be seeing ghosts," he said to the other,

backing away. They continued talking. I sighed and began to breathe again. I knew that if I were patient, the two soldiers would eventually be forced to leave. No man other than the King was allowed to spend the night in the palace. Not even the royal Guard could be trusted with the chastity of the King's daughter.

I did not have to wait long before I saw the two guards being escorted out by a third. The moon, half eclipsed by a cloud, winked at me encouragingly, and I continued toward the royal apartments. Soldiers would be stationed outside, and there were still many guardians who could sound a deadly alarm.

The door to the stairway up to the royal apartments was of course locked. I removed my dagger, and once again the skills I had learned in my youth served me well. I pressed the tumbler in the lock and heard the bolt pin slide open.

Gold sconces held tapers whose flames danced and cast apparitions around me. I climbed each step slowly and began to search the halls, following my instincts deeper into the palace. All of my senses were straining for signs of danger and clues to the Infanta's presence. If I opened the wrong door, I could find myself in the King's own bedchamber.

As I crept around a corner, I smelled the sweetness of orange and apricot. It was the rare Ottoman perfume that I had perceived in the audience chamber. The scent grew stronger as I approached a low double door. Like most in the Alcázar, the doorway had the ornate stuccowork and the Arabic script left by the Moors, who had once patrolled these halls when the emir's harem was as sequestered as our King's daughter. There was a round gold handle on each door, and I approached with my hand outstretched, already grasping at my success.

I felt the rush of air and then heard the squeaking hinge as the door swung open. I was caught off balance, stumbled, but then leapt into the room across the hall. Through the crack in the door, I saw the Infanta's dwarfed and feebleminded dueña waddle out of the room. The vigilant chaperone wore a white wimple over her head and a rosary that hung down as a necklace. In her hand she held delicate red leashes, at the ends of which were the Infanta's two small monkeys, one gray and one brown. The gray one had a shock of white hair on its head that fell back behind its ears and made it look like an elderly chaperone.

These clever animals were the King's best sentinels. Their sense of smell was keener than the dueña's sense of sight, and the vigilant creatures stopped at the slightly opened door where I stood nervously. They shrieked and tried to reach inside with their tiny hands. I knew that if the dueña entered the room, my head would be presented to the Infanta like John the Baptist's. Sweat was dripping down my back. I reached frantically into my pouch for a coin, which I thrust into the tiny hand that was groping inside the door. This quieted the monkey momentarily as he no doubt examined his treasure. Every sentinel has his price. The two monkeys immediately started quarreling over the prize and screeching anew at each other.

"Stop that! What did you find? Give me that! Come, you little beasts!" the dueña said, then added, as much to herself as to them, "She doesn't want us to help her, so we won't."

I breathed deeply and calmed my shaking fingers. When I could no longer hear her footsteps, I slid back into the hallway. The dueña's near-disastrous exit had confirmed that this was indeed the room I was looking for. The door handle to the Infanta's room was cold and smooth. I stopped and glanced around quickly to make sure that I had not been seen. I pushed the handle, hoping she had not yet locked it. It yielded to my touch, and I quietly slipped inside.

No One Will Ever Know

Magdalena," the Infanta said, thinking I was her dueña, "I told you to—"

She saw me in her mirror and turned quickly, her face full of surprise and fear. She had already been undressed from her gown, which hung next to her. She wore only her long white chemise and a corset that hid her breasts and pinched her waist. Remembering that she was undressed, she clutched a white bathing robe to her chest. I shielded my eyes until she was covered. The gold-trimmed robe had no sash, so she held it closed with the clasp of her hands.

I took off my mask and asked, "Shall I leave so soon after your summons?" I was referring to how she had held her fan over her face, revealing only her green eyes. It was these same green eyes, luminous and longing for life, that now stared at me wildly. Her earlier gesture at court could have been virtuous or inviting, depending on the intent of her gaze, which I had been required to interpret. I held my breath, waiting to see whether she had called for me or would call for the guards. My heart pounded. Whether I lived or died would depend on whether I had perceived her desire accurately.

"How *dare* you enter my bedchamber," she said in a whisper of royal contempt. It was an outrage and a capital offense for any man to approach the Infanta's bedchamber. Had I been mistaken? My shoulders began to fall, as my fate seemed certain. Yet the fact that she had whispered her reply suggested she was not yet willing to reveal my intrusion.

"My apologies, Your Highness, for such . . . audacity."

"I should call for the guards!"

"And should have me beheaded. But then you would spend another night . . . alone."

"Are you suggesting . . ." she said, but did not finish her sentence or move toward the door.

"You did summon me, did you not?"

"It would be a scandal."

"A woman's desire is hardly scandalous."

"Her desire is a sin."

"The only sin is her loneliness."

The Infanta turned and faced her mirror. I waited anxiously in the silence as she considered what indeed the true sin was. On her dressing table was a single taper that had burned down into its holder. It was nothing more than a blue glowing ember in its golden bed, a thing of beauty as common and as overlooked as a woman's own flickering passion. How easy it is to satisfy a woman; how great are the rewards and gratitude for any man who makes even the slightest effort. But how few are those in this cruel age who seek to understand womanhood, and so my lust finds countless women who yearn for even the most basic kindness.

The outraged nobles and priests ask how it is possible that these women would so willingly give up their husband's or father's honor by giving up their own modesty. Certainly, they would be far more hesitant if my own discretion did not make any actions impossible to prove, but I will tell you the reason for my success, and it is not the reasons that have been given—not wealth, nor title, nor beauty. The only secret I have used to unlock the bedchambers of the women I have known is their own unquenched thirst for life. The greatest power in the world, greater than kings and popes, is the desire of women. Love, the priests tell us, rules the heavens, but does desire not rule the earth? One who understands the workings of desire understands the very secret of life—even the barren life of a king's daughter.

The Infanta turned back to face me and swallowed. "I did not know . . . you would risk . . ." she said breathlessly. I had been right about her desire, and for now my life was spared.

"I could not refuse an invitation to save a woman

from her imprisonment, even if her prison is a palace." She looked down again. "Do you regret your invitation?" I asked openly.

"My father's room is down the hall," she replied, anxiously looking at the door. She kept a safe distance, no doubt uncertain what kind of predator she had invited into her bedchamber.

I walked over and turned the key until the lock clicked shut. "No one will ever know," I said as I pulled the iron key out. It was heavy in my hand. I approached her slowly and handed her the simple straight key with a circle at the end. She clenched the key and pulled her hand away.

I knew I needed to address the fear that all virgins have, especially a virgin on whose chastity the Empire's honor depends. "Tonight I will take nothing from you. Your virginity will remain for your husband alone." With the smallest tip of my finger, I stroked the naked skin of her neck and then held my hand out to her. Ever so hesitantly, she turned her hand over and let the key fall into the palm of my hand.

I kissed her wrist gently, and she exhaled slowly. All the sinews of the hand travel through the wrist to the rest of the body. I drew my fingertips up her forearm to awaken her skin from its sensual slumber. She shivered. There is a way to touch a woman that takes from her like a thief who steals her soft beauty, and there is a way to touch a woman that gives to her, changing her body into a treasure for her to cherish.

I gestured to her bed. Her father's coat of arms was

embroidered on the crimson drapery that concealed the bed on all sides. The two gold-thread lions in the crest glared at me ferociously. I pulled back the velvet, my heart pounding, and invited her to enter. She stepped onto the platform, and I pulled back the red fringes of her silk bedspread, revealing the white linen sheets underneath. I placed the key on one of her pillows.

Tenderly I removed her ivory hairpins and combed my fingers through her long brown locks. She was trembling. She, like all who do not know their own skin, needed a tender caress to coax her into her own desire, so long denied. Even with the danger that waited all around us, I was not willing to treat her roughly in my haste. Introducing a woman to the Arts of Passion is a sacred honor that should never be rushed, the memory of the first encounter remaining always as a pleasant fragrance that perfumes all other experiences, or as a painful bloodstain that can never be removed fully from the sheets.

She kept her robe closed with one hand and used the other to prop herself up on the bed. The corset still held her chest rigid and upright. I cradled her head gently with both of my hands, and brushed the corner of my mouth against her soft cheek. "Have you ever wondered what it would feel like to be kissed by a man?" I whispered, knowing that the imagination always leads the body. My lips floated a breath above hers. She inclined her head and offered her lips as an answer. I kissed her gently, her eyes closing. Her mouth was even softer than her cheek, and my lips quivered with pleasure. As she opened hers slowly, I tasted the sparkling elixir of her tongue.

A single silk ribbon laced together her corset. Slowly, my fingers began to untie the knot that held her corset closed across her chest.

She shivered again and this time recoiled. "I'm chilled," she said.

With my fingertip, I traced a drop of perspiration snaking down her neck. Even with an open window and the cool plaster of the thick palace walls, the room was still hot. Nonetheless, I removed my black cape and wrapped it around her shoulders. Once she was cloaked, I bestowed a small kiss upon her eager lips as I picked the knot that was as secure as any metal lock. My own shirt clung to my back, wet with perspiration.

Finally my faithful fingers unleashed the sinuous ribbon. I gripped each side of the corset with a greedy hand and slowly pulled it apart, the lengths releasing from her neck to her waist. Her lungs filled with air. I pulled the ribbon free and the corset fell off behind her, leaving her body veiled in only the thin cotton chemise. My tongue traced along her neck. At her ear, I breathed, "Have you ever wondered what it would feel like to have a man touch . . ." I did not need to finish; she gasped as my fingertips cradled the under-side of her breast. I circled the tip of my longest finger around her nipple, now swelling through the thin fabric.

Her body awoke with new life, and the cape fell away. I brushed her chemise up her soft, untouched torso, kissing each finger's breadth of newly revealed flesh. I paused only long enough to remove this last hindrance to her full majesty.

She lay back, and my fingers played gently on her skin like a feather in advance of my lips. She clutched the sheets as the dark of her eyes waxed like two full black moons, shining brightly. Holding her gaze, I trailed my kisses back down toward her waist until her body rose heavenward to meet my lips. Her head was now back and her mouth open, as if she might sing, but the need for secrecy stifled any sound in her throat.

All night, by a single candle, we held a vigil to the Infanta's desire as the pleasure that slumbered in her skin awoke. I touched each handbreadth of her body, each toe and each finger a royal gem that I caressed with the tips of my tongue and talons. The first light of morning revealed her new body, the spirit of her passion entwined with her flesh. She was completely naked, but I was still restrained by my clothes.

I looked up at the crucifix that hung over her bed. It was intricately carved from an elephant tusk, and the muscles of the legs, arms, and stomach rippled not with death but with life and beauty. The body resembled the pagan statues of Apollo, and there was not a drop of blood dripping from Our Lord's wounds. A loincloth around His waist was held by a loose string that seemed to be coming undone. Long curls of hair fell to His chest, and His lips formed a beatific smile. This was a crucifix that already promised the resurrection.

Doña Isabel looked at me with a smile of satisfaction.

Although sleepless, her eyes were still wide with the excitement of one who has discovered a hidden wealth. The taper by her bed had also burned low. Its molded form was gone, and the wax had dripped down over the golden holder and hung precariously off the edge.

"When will you return to me?" the Infanta asked.

"As soon as I am invited."

"You are invited—commanded—to return within a fortnight. Promise me?"

"I am honored, Your Highness, but as a libertine, I can make no promises and take no oaths."

"As a libertine? You mean as a shameless seducer!"

"Your Highness, a libertine is more than a mere seducer—although he may be that, too. A libertine is not constrained by conventional morality—"

"By *any* morality—I could have you killed!" she said.

"You certainly could, but then I would never return."

"You are cruel," she said, turning her head away sharply. "The pleasure you have given me tonight will cause me pain every other as I wait for the return of my desire."

"Your desire, Your Highness, is your own. It remains with you always." I raised her downcast chin and smiled.

She favored me with a smile of her own. "If only you were a prince or a duke," she said wistfully.

"I am afraid I am neither. Just a lowly hidalgo with little more than a letter from your father to testify to my nobility."

"I know who you are, Don Juan. All the women of Spain do." I felt flattered. With her forefinger she lightly touched me on one shoulder and then the other. Her expression was serious, as if involved in a momentous ceremony. "I dub you Don Juan Tenorio, Duke of Longing and Conqueror of Lonely Maidens, Wives, and Widows, Greatest Lover in All the Kingdoms of Spain and All the Realms of the Spanish Empire."

"If you know me, then you will know I desire to rule over no land and no lady."

The Infanta swallowed; her throat was dry. I walked over to the water basin and poured her a cup. I returned to the bed and lay down next to her.

She drank slowly. "Could you ever love me?"

"I can love no woman."

"How sad."

"What is sad about not wanting what you don't have?"

"What do you want, Don Juan?"

"What I want cannot be conquered, only cultivated."

"And what would that be?"

"It is simply—"

"Doña Isabel!" shouted the dueña through the door. "I saw a man in your room through the keyhole! I've called the guards! They are coming with your father!"

Doña Isabel and I stared at each other, eyes wide. She threw on her robe, uncovering the key that was still lying next to her on the pillow. I crept out the concealed side of the bed and had started toward the window when I realized my cape was still tangled among the sheets. I reached back inside the curtains and took what was mine. I kissed Doña Isabel good-bye quickly, but she held my hand and whispered, "Soon." I smiled and turned to leave.

"Isabel!" It was the King. The door shook as he attempted to open it. "Open the door!" he shouted to one of his guards. He must have had another key.

"I am in my bed, Father."

I heard the lock open as I quickly climbed out the window onto the balcony. Mercifully, there was a tile roof above the window, where I was able to hide myself.

I heard a great commotion in the room as her father and the Royal Guard entered. I soon saw the gray hair of the King's head as he came out to the balcony, accompanied by the captain of the guards. A glance up would mean my death. They turned their heads slowly from side to side, reviewing the garden for movement. The captain started to look over his shoulder toward the roof. I inched my way back on the old clay tiles and watched in horror as my boot knocked a broken piece off the edge. I closed my eyes and held my breath.

"Did you hear that?" the King asked. "Down there!" They had not seen it fall, only heard it land.

"Search the grounds!" the King said to the captain before their heads disappeared. Both of them had looked down, assuming that a siege always comes from below and not realizing that the greatest threats to chastity come from within.

"Father, please!" I heard the Infanta say. He must have looked inside the curtains surrounding her bed.

"I'm sorry, daughter," the King said apologetically, but then his tone became stern. "Magdalena says she saw a man in your room through the keyhole."

"A man in my room?" I heard Doña Isabel laugh. I imagined her addressing the King and his guards from her curtained bed. Those curtains must have hidden the worry on her face, but her voice sounded calm and confident. Men have little knowledge of the kind of power that women hold. Mastery over their emotions is one of their greatest strengths, and it is far greater than men imagine. "Magdalena, you must be seeing my dreams! In my sleep I had a vision that our Savior visited me and touched my soul deeply."

I was impressed with her poise. The rumors of her strength were true. She was nothing like her sister, Catalina, who already had eight children in eight years of marriage. I knew that this would not be Doña Isabel's fate. She would no doubt one day rule some realm of the kingdom and her husband as well.

"My pious child," I heard the King say proudly. "You are the light of my eyes, without which I am blind." I smiled. I knew that the flame kindled within Doña Isabel was now burning so brightly that its light and heat would someday escape through the cracks in the palace walls.

"Get out!" the King said, no doubt to the guards who remained. "Magdalena!" he said, spitting out her name, and then adding with barely controlled fury, "Make sure you are not imagining intruders before you raise suspicions about *my* daughter."

Now that Doña Isabel's modesty had been preserved, and I saw no one below, I considered my escape. A jump could easily break a leg or two, but there was no chance of retracing my steps through the palace. It was my turn to shiver. Breathing deeply, I leapt.

I barely caught a nearby branch and hung there, sighing with relief.

I heard horses approaching and let go. As I fell to the ground, the pain in my long-ago injury stabbed my leg like a dozen daggers. I limped a few steps and then ran quickly, knowing that the Royal Guard was not far behind. They were closing in on horse and foot as I reached the garden house. Quickly I ducked into the labyrinth. I heard some guards on foot discuss searching it and hurried through its course. Coming to a dead end, I heard them stomping along the soft ground just behind me. I looked around like a trapped animal. As I sensed them turning the corner, I spied a small hole in the hedge. I crawled through it and escaped, but not before the juniper branches had scratched my face and torn my sleeve.

There was still quite a distance between me and the walls of the garden. I had to make my way through the pathways and tunnels of green that were being patrolled by several dozen guards. The King may have been convinced of his daughter's chastity, but he clearly had not called off the search for possible intruders.

The fountains that bubbled up from the ground were strangely peaceful, though my body remained tense and alert. Not far from the wall, I hid in a bush and found myself surrounded on all sides by soldiers. They were stabbing the thick foliage with their lances as they went. I ducked out of the way to avoid being impaled through my chest, then bowels—and then groin. A few more thrusts and I would have been struck or, worse, discovered. My mind raced, searching for some possible escape. My eyes alighted on a fallen orange that lay rotting on the ground. I drew my sword and stabbed at it but could not reach it. As I strained with my arm, I felt my blade pierce its skin. I threw it into a faraway bush. Its noise distracted the guards long enough for me to slip away.

At last I reached the wall that surrounded the garden. There was a giant palm tree beside the wall, and I put the heels of my boots on the trunk and scaled it like a monkey, my hands gripping its rough skin. But unlike a monkey, I needed to brace my back against the wall as I climbed. I heard the sound of more guards behind me just as I reached the top of the high wall and balanced precariously. The drop to the ground was the height of two men, with nothing to break my fall. Looking down the outside of the wall, I saw guards running in my direction. My shoulders dropped in despair. Even if I was able to run after the fall, I was sure to be caught. There was no going back, but I could not go forward. Images of my inevitable beheading flashed to mind. At that moment a red carriage turned onto the street. It approached from the opposite direction of the guards. I waited and waited, praying that it would arrive before the men did. As it passed, I leapt onto its black-studded roof and snaked inside. I fell against the leather seat, facing backward. My rescuer could easily sound the alarm, and so my fate was in the delicate hands of the beauty in the carriage who now stared at me.

Not Every Man with a Mask Is a Burglar

There were two women in the carriage, both veiled. At first I thought they were mother and daughter, although the elegant clothing of the younger and the plain uniform of the older suggested that they were in fact a noble lady and her dueña. The older woman gasped and covered her mouth. The younger drew her head back and released a startled and musical laugh.

"I'm very sorry to disturb you," I said, smiling.

The doña raised her white veil, revealing a shockingly beautiful face. A pinch of cinnamon was mixed into the white milk of her cheeks, as if they had been kissed by the sun. Her shimmering straight black hair was tied to one side like a horse's mane, and at her temples her hair lay flat like the black wings of a songbird. The amused smile playing across her face straightened. Her eyes shone as brightly as two black diamonds and gazed at me, neither provocative nor coy, but penetrating and totally unnerving.

As the soldiers of the Royal Guard began running by, the dueña leaned out to get their attention.

"Please," I said, "my life is not the only one at risk."

It was too late. Several of the guards had noticed the dueña.

"Not a word, María," the doña said under her breath, pulling back the leather curtain just enough so that she could see out but the soldiers could not see in. "Is there a disturbance?"

"An intruder . . . to the palace . . . my lady!" the soldier gasped.

"He . . ." my protectress said, and then looked down, pondering my fate, "will no doubt be found."

"Yes, my la—" his words were shut out as the curtain closed.

"Doña Ana!" the dueña whispered, clearly outraged. "He—burglar!" She pointed at my mask. Her sentence was clipped by fear and by the rough speech of the natives who had come to Sevilla from the Indies. I smiled sheepishly, as if I were the slave and she the noble. I shook my head but did not remove my mask, knowing that my anonymity was still essential.

"Not every man with a mask is a burglar," Doña Ana replied, staring straight at me. "And most burglars, María, do not dress like noblemen."

I smiled. "Thank you, Doña . . . *Ana*?"

"My father is Don Gonzalo de Ulloa, a commander of the Order of Calatrava," she added, knowing that her father's military position might restrain me. "And you are? Or do masked men not reveal their identity?"

"Does a name or even a face reveal one's true identity?" I replied. Under her black veil, María's face was pinched with anger, and her eyes turned from fearful to ferocious. I knew I had to win her over or risk that she would sound the alarm herself. "Your dueña is right that masked men can be dangerous. She is wise to protect such a beautiful lady." I leaned forward just slightly but apparently too much.

Doña Ana pulled a wide-mouthed pistol out from under her seat and pointed it straight at my heart. This was not the first time she had taken aim. "I can protect myself," Doña Ana said.

"I have obviously overstayed my welcome. I won't impose on your hospitality any longer," I said, knowing that we had left the guards far behind. I opened the door and stumbled out as the carriage rode on. I took off my mask and hid it in my sleeve. I stood in the street, staring at the carriage as it disappeared, wondering how this beautiful maiden had escaped my notice until today. I was determined to find out more about her and to ensure that we might meet again soon.

I walked to the shaded alleyway where I had told Cristóbal to wait. He was brushing down Bonita as he spoke to her softly. His black hair descended in long unruly waves to his neck, and his thin mustache and beard made him look like a youth trying to play the part of an adult. His eyebrows were always raised and his brow wrinkled.

The sleeveless jerkin that descended to Cristóbal's thighs needed replacing, as did his breeches. He has never complained about his uniform, however, and only recently about my adventures. Today he was agi-

46

tated, and I could not help eavesdropping on his conversation with my horse.

"When will he become a respectable noble, so that I can become a respectable coachman and you can become a respectable horse and not an accomplice to a thousand scandals? I know you shouldn't complain: he took you in and taught you to be a proper coachman . . . not you, Bonita, but me."

I could not help laughing, and Cristóbal spun around and stood at attention, clearly mortified that I had overheard him talking. "You are not the only one who wants me to settle down and become a respectable noble. The king has commanded me to marry within a month."

"Will you?"

"You know me better than that. I am incapable of love *or* marriage."

He opened the door to the carriage, his shoulders slumped in defeat. I stepped in and sat down. Before closing the door, he gathered the courage to speak directly. "Tell me, my lord," he whispered, holding his face away from me as if I might hit him, "that you have seduced a chambermaid who caught your fancy and not our noble Infanta."

"You know I do not tell tales, my good Cristóbal. A chambermaid's modesty is as important to her as an Infanta's is to the empire. Now, let's go before we are discovered."

"Where to, my lord?"

I did not honestly know. With this crowning intrigue,

I had as a libertine accomplished everything that I had ever imagined. I had proved my skill, had known the affections of more women than I could count, and now had even been welcomed into the royal bedchamber. My passion was fulfilled, as was my ideal. But to live, a man must have a purpose or his life is a rudderless ship. If he lives simply from meal to meal, his life will be empty of meaning. Whatever the purpose I might discover, it would need to be more incarnate than glory in heaven and more important than any human honor on earth. At last I answered Cristóbal. "Take me home," I said, not knowing where else to go.

The rumble of the wooden wheels on the cobblestones was like a lullaby after a sleepless night. The leather shades rocked back and forth, holding out the bright morning sun from the carriage, and my eyelids grew heavy. I rested my aggrieved knee on the seat across from me as we approached the Convento de San José del Carmen. I looked at the heavy wooden door with its brass studs and at its coat of arms above a small door to its left. Three six-pointed stars surrounded a brown-painted cross, and above it was a golden crown. I had used such a small door in my youth, although the fact that it was opened to me was a secret. Through the barred windows of the chapel I heard the nuns singing. I thought of the Infanta's question of whether I could love her and my reply that I could love no woman. It was not entirely true. I had succumbed to the madness of love once before.

I was a young man of fifteen, and my only purpose

at the time was to become a priest. To this day it is hard for me to believe that I was once a pious acolyte and that I wanted nothing more than to become a servant of the Lord. But how could I have not wanted to serve the Lord, having suckled on the love of His angels? It was in the arms of one of His angels that I glimpsed my first vision of God.

The Love of His Angels

*L*ike every son and daughter of Eve, my life began with the anguished cries of a woman, but although born to one mother, I was raised by twenty-four. As an infant, I was left in the barn at the Convento de la Madre Sagrada outside the town of Carmona, and was found by Hermana Marta on her way to milk the goats. As the story was told, Priora Francisca, the short but imposing superior of the convent, had frowned and looked suspiciously at me, an unwelcome male intruder. Apparently I had smiled at her as sweetly as the Infant Jesus himself. Priora Francisca smiled back and took me in her arms. Having at that moment broken free of my swaddling blanket, I began spraying like a fountain and wet her habit. The sisters tried unsuccessfully to stifle their laughter. Priora Francisca said I should be taken to the orphanage, but Hermana Marta showed her my enfeebled leg and said that the overflowing orphanages would have no choice but to let me die. To everyone's surprise, Priora Francisca listened to the sisters' belief that my appearance had been miraculous and begrudgingly agreed to raise me until I was old enough to send to a monastery.

I was passed from embrace to embrace as each sister's heart was opened wide by the dangerous Holy Child thrust into their cloistered life. They stretched the sinews and massaged the muscles of my twisted leg, which in time straightened and grew strong. Despite their selfless labors the sisters would take no credit for my healing and were convinced that this was yet another miracle. When I was no longer an infant fed on goat's milk, I slept in the barn on a cot with a straw mattress, surrounded by the sounds of the goats' bleating, the barn owl's hooting, and the rooster's crowing as it strutted after the hens. As soon as I could carry a pail, I became responsible for collecting the goats' milk for cheese. I also soon began tilling the soil with the help of the convent's old donkey, nicknamed Zambomba, after the Christmas noisemaker, because he brayed constantly.

Zambomba complained as much as he walked, so my work was both slow and noisy—until one day when I fastened a stick to his halter that dangled a turnip in front of his eyes but beyond the reach of his lips. Zambomba was like a racehorse as he chased the elusive turnip. I loved standing on the plow and being dragged around that field until the sun had set and the whole sky was gold like a flat sheaf of rye at the horizon and then blue and purple as it approached the heavens where the first night stars appeared. I felt as if I could reach my hand up high and stroke the long beard of

God that blew in the wind like rippling white clouds.

By the time I was fifteen, Priora Francisca no doubt knew that I should be sent to the monastery. Yet the convent had come to depend on my labor, and she had even grown fond of me. She must have sought forgiveness for this unfortunate indulgence the rest of her life.

At the time, I wanted to become a priest, like Padre Miguel Antonio, who came to serve mass, to take confession from the nuns, and to teach me my lessons. He was the only priest willing to make the long journey to the convent. It was from Padre Miguel that I learned God always sides with the weak, with the widow, and with the orphan. I would also stay up late reading books of chivalric tales that Padre Miguel would lend me. He had "lived" a little before he became a priest, and he had a rather wonderful book collection. However, he threatened to stop lending them to me because I often overslept and ran in late for morning mass.

One day I arrived in the chapel, breathless, and knelt piously at the back, my fingers interlaced like those of the sisters. In front of me were the black cowls of the nuns and the white cowls of the few younger novitiates. There were two oil lamps at every altar, except for that of Nuestra Señora de Gracia, the protectress of the city, who had watched over me as a baby. This altar was always crowded with oil lamps lit by those who desperately needed her protection.

The painted wooden saints were as tall as many of the nuns, and their sad, distant eyes seemed to stare right through me, as did Priora Francisca's. Her left eye had a permanently raised eyebrow that made it look much larger than her right. I often thought that this eye could see my hidden thoughts, a belief that she often confirmed.

Priora Francisca raised her hands from under her flowing sleeves and clasped her fingers together so tightly it was as if she were preventing the world from splitting in two. She buried her face in her hands, and I did the same. Yet I stole glances at the fresco to the left of the altar. It was of San Bernardo praying to the statue of the Blessed Virgin Mary. The red-robed Virgin had a white scarf around Her head and a blue cloak wrapped loosely around Her waist. In one arm, She held the Infant Jesus, and the fingers of Her other hand gently directed a stream of milk from Her breast into the saint's mouth. San Bernardo was dressed all in white and his eyes looked up at Her in a rapturous gaze as his mouth hung open to receive Her Holy Nourish- ment. I knew that with my hands folded in front of my face, Priora Francisca could not have seen my furtive eyes straying. Yet she whispered sternly over her shoulder, "Keep your prayers holy." I knew not what holy or unholy prayers were, but I soon learned.

The nuns' melodious voices rejoiced together in the love of Our Lord. Their harmonies and antiphonies sent shivers down my spine. It was at that moment that I realized there was nothing more beautiful than the sound of a woman's voice. I was entranced by their music and by the pungent smell of burning rosemary as

I stared at the brightly painted body of our Savior crucified on the cross. The shining red blood poured down from the dark, gaping wound in His side, and from His nailed hands to His thin arms, and down the crossed feet to His toes, and even from His knees. Surrounded and loved by the sisters, I learned to worship womanhood, its affections, its beauty, and its graces. They worshiped a man who was the Son of God, but I worshiped these women who were His angels.

My trance was broken when Priora Francisca cleared her throat. I ran forward to serve as the acolyte. Padre Miguel had a high, wrinkled forehead under his wiry black hair, and his face was serious and questioning. I watched him with eyes that did not just see but drank in every one of his words and every one of his actions, to learn about my future as a priest and as a man. When Padre Miguel led services, his expression was warm, his eyebrows danced, and as he spoke, his precise words pressed his cheeks into a hundred smiles. My solemn duty was to hold the gold plate under the chins of the nuns, so that no crumbs of the host would fall to the floor. My hands trembled as I performed this service, but the sisters smiled at me sweetly.

I remember the beautiful light in Hermana María Bernarda's face, although she was too old and hunchbacked to smile. She did not have to bend over to bow to the altar. Priora Francisca had once said that she was in a perpetual state of grace from her infirmity. I also remember the face of the young Jerónima, a novitiate who always had an otherworldly gaze. She was one of the most pious sisters, praying almost unceasingly.

Finally, I came to the newest novitiate, a girl of sixteen named Teresa who had recently arrived at the convent. In her beautiful, melancholy face I could see that she was seeking refuge from some darkness. So captivating were her downcast eyes that I often found myself gazing at her. As I cradled the plate, I tried not to stare at her red lips and the white smoothness of her cheeks, but I could not avoid them. I wanted to touch them, and before I knew it, I was stroking her chin with the edge of the plate. Her black eyes, sparking like flint, flashed up at me, and the gold plate slipped from my nervous, sweaty hands. It landed on the floor with a loud noise, and continued to clatter before finally falling silent. Priora Francisca scolded me, but fortunately there were no crumbs of our lord's body needing to be rescued.

After prayers that day, Priora Francisca sent me into town. Since the nuns were allowed out of their convent only in the event of illness, fire, or war, they relied on me for contact with the outside world. Weekly I took the embroidery and mending into the town of Carmona and while there performed other errands.

It was early July, and in the summer heat it was hard to breathe and my limbs moved slowly. Sheets of fabric were hung from the houses on one side of Market Street to the other to shade passersby from the ferocious Andalusian sun, but there were still precious few who were out during the heat of the day. One, a young peasant girl about my age, teased me to buy her some lemons but I had no money. She giggled and ran off, leaving me and the fruit vendor, who was dozing by his produce.

A traveling French peddler had set up a stall, and I stopped to look at his wares, including a wood-framed mirror. Such vanities were forbidden in the convent, and I had never seen my reflection. I glanced both ways and then looked upon my own face. I was surprised by how much older I was than in my imagination. My black hair was kept long like Our Lord's and tied at the nape of my neck with twine. My eyes were the color of undiluted chocolate, although at the time I had not yet tasted chocolate or, indeed, any such delicacies.

My vain musings were interrupted by another reflection in the mirror. Three strange men had ridden into town. Two were friars, Dominicans dressed in their white and black hooded robes. The third wore the black clothes and tall, flat hat of a jurist. I turned quickly and saw them stop the girl who had asked me to buy her lemons. The younger friar dismounted from his horse. He had long black sideburns. His voice was gentle: "My dear girl, will you help us?" From a leather bag he pulled out a peach and the girl took it eagerly.

Only then was the sweetness of his tone belied by the serpentine menace in his intention. "Children always see things that others do not. Tell me, is there anyone here who has blasphemed the Church or the Sacraments? Perhaps neighbors, relatives, even your own parents?" The girl shook her head as she greedily devoured the peach. "Any who hold to the Law of Moses, the sect of Mahomet or of Luther?" She did not answer, and this time he grabbed her by the arm to get her attention. "*Alumbrados,* are there *alumbrados?*" he said, although I do not know how she would have known who was guilty of this supposed heresy. I have never understood why it is a heresy to believe that one can experience God beyond the Sacraments and the worship of the Church.

The girl shook her head, clearly terrified, and tried to release herself from his grip. But he would not let her go. "Fornicators? Sodomites? *Adulterers?*" He drew the last word out with particular zeal.

The older friar at last came to the girl's rescue. "Fray Ignacio, I doubt this girl would know whether there were *alumbrados* or adulterers."

"Children are some of our best informants, as you know, *Brother.*"

"You are not yet an inquisitor, Fray Ignacio, and even a zealous prosecutor like you would be wise not to go beyond the jurisdiction of the Holy Office," the older friar rebuked.

Fray Ignacio turned to his companion with a silent and chilling stare and then spoke. "My holy brother, we must not rest until all heresies, perversions, and immoralities are eradicated from our jurisdiction." His lips spread into a thin smile. He turned back to the girl, his voice once again falsely sweet. "Would you kindly tell us in which direction lies the Convento de la Madre Sagrada?"

She pointed to the road, her hand shaking like that of an elderly woman.

I did not know why I needed to warn Priora Francisca, but I knew that I did. I jumped on Zambomba and took a shortcut across the fields and away from the main road back to the convent. I kicked and cajoled the donkey until he was moving faster than ever. Perhaps he too could feel the fear driving me. When we reached the convent, I leapt off Zambomba and ran in through the secret door that stood next to the olive tree. It was in the hollow of that tree that I would later hide love notes, always careful to avoid the watchful eye of Priora Francisca.

I had to slow myself and my breath when I reached Priora Francisca's room. I peeked in and saw her in her daily devotions. There was an enormous wooden cross on the wall with three large nails jutting out. As a boy, I had seen her stand on a stool to reach the nails. She would grip the two on top and place her feet on the third, mold her body into the crucifix and then kick the stool away, hanging on the cross in prayer for two or three hours.

"Priora," I uttered through the open crack in the door, still trying to catch my breath. She did not hear me; her eyes were still off in a distant gaze. "The—Holy—Inqui—sition—is—coming."

This startled her out of her trance and she said, with worry in her voice, "The Holy Inquisition?"

"I saw them—in town—ask directions—to the convent."

I placed the stool in front of her, and she stepped down, her hands still red and clenched. "Tell all the sisters to meet me in the chapel," she commanded, "and then you must hide yourself."

I knocked on each door. The sisters were reading or praying by candlelight, their small cells dark even by day. One after the other, they looked at me in surprise, and I whispered under my breath, "Priora Francisca says to meet in the chapel—quickly." There was quite a commotion as I left them to go to the last room, which was at a distance from the others. It was the room of Teresa. In my haste, I opened the door and then, realizing my error, prepared to knock, but what I saw through the crack made my hand and heart stop.

A Vision of God

There was a candle burning on a table in the dark room. By its light I saw her shadow on the wall and then her body sitting on the bed. Her head was slightly tilted back, her eyes closed, and her mouth open. With her left hand she held her habit above her breast. In her other hand she held a sharp pointed piece of metal with which she was cutting into her flesh. She was carving the Holy Greek Letter of Jesus' Name. I was captivated, but when I saw what she did next, I stopped breathing. As she winced in pain, I saw her touch her nipple. She then made a sound like none I had ever heard from one of the sisters, a bittersweet sighing that I would come to believe was holy music.

Some unknown feeling erupted inside me. Just then she saw me and dropped her habit with a gasp.

I stammered, "Priora—in the chapel," and then ran there myself as fast as I could, sweating and breathless. When Priora Francisca saw me, she said, "Go hide in the barn. They must never know you are here." As I left, I heard her say to the sisters, "Do not go telling things about each other or meddle in matters touching the Holy Office. This is a House of God, and everything we do here pleases Him."

The sun was setting, and the three men riding their mules had arrived. I had to step behind a large oak tree to avoid their seeing me. I did not hide in the barn, as I had been told, but listened outside the window while the young prosecutor questioned Priora Francisca and later the other nuns.

"One of your nuns is not a true believer."

"We are all true believers here."

"I do not want to make trouble for your convent, but there is a heretic among you."

"I promise you that the faith of all of the sisters is as strong as my own."

"Then maybe we should question you about your faith, too."

I could not see Priora Francisca's face, but no doubt she would have arched her eyebrow and pointed her stern eye at the prosecutor.

He spent a long time interrogating Hermana Jerónima, who had the words of God on her lips in every reply. The black-clothed jurist must have been the defense lawyer, but his efforts were feeble and unsuccessful. When Hermana Jerónima confessed nothing, the prosecutor told Priora Francisca that they would need to take the girl back to the headquarters of the Holy Office in Sevilla, where "the question" could be applied. Hermana Jerónima wept, as did all the other sisters, and I too shed silent tears for her, without even knowing the dangers that she would face in the torture chamber of the Inquisition.

It was lucky that I was not in the barn, because Fray Ignacio went to get Zambomba to take Hermana Jerónima away, her hands tied in front of her, fingers interlaced as if in prayer. Many years later I learned that her father had argued with another man, who then had denounced the daughter to the Inquisition in revenge. This fact was apparently not discovered until after Hermana Jerónima had been tortured as an *alumbrada*—for seeking mystical unity with the Almighty.

Soon all the lights of the convent were extinguished and the night was silent. Even the crickets were afraid to chirp. All I could hear was the beating of my heart as I lay on my bed that night. It raced as I saw the vision of Hermana Teresa in her room and heard the sweet panting of her voice over and over again.

"What you did was a sin!" a voice said. I bolted up in bed and turned to face Hermana Teresa, who had come through my secret door from the convent. She tapped my cheek reprovingly but her fingers lingered in a way that was questioning, almost tender. She sat down next to me on the cot, and I stared straight ahead, although my eyes tried to see what she was doing. "The Inquisition will come for us someday, too," she said nervously.

"I won't say anything."

With her fingertips she turned my face to hers. Then she leaned forward and kissed me on the mouth. My eyes went wide and my chest felt as though it had opened to the heavens. She laid me down on the cot, and that night I first discovered the thrilling touch of a woman.

It was in her generous and patient arms that my youthful body was awakened to the world of desire. She knew more than a sixteen-year-old girl who was dedicated to the Virgin should, and she confessed to me that the ripening fruit of her desire had been cracked open by callous older hands. But she shared her forbidden knowledge with me through her lips and skin. And so began a yearlong secret affair that was punctuated by her rejecting me, as she tried to stay faithful to her vows, and then, unable to stop herself, returning at night to my cot in the barn. My every thought during that year was colored by her memory, her beauty, and the holy devotions that we shared. I heard her tears and the sweet sighing of her mouth in my dreams.

On the last night of our affair, she said, "What we have done is a sin."

"How can it be? Perhaps it is holy."

"You are the Devil!" she said.

"Then we are the Devil together," I answered as I

took her in my arms, more confident and accustomed to her rejections.

She began to cry into her hands and said, "They will come for us, too."

"I will protect you," I said boldly, putting my arms around her.

"I have tried to cleanse my soul of the sinfulness of my flesh, but I cannot." I kissed away her tears, and she embraced me.

We lay naked in each other's arms, and I kissed her skin as if she were the hem of a holy vestment. I never wanted to stop kissing her. Finally, she put her head on my chest, and we held each other. We must have fallen asleep, for the next morning Hermana Marta discovered us together on my straw cot.

The roosters had not crowed, and Hermana Teresa had not climbed back into her own bed. We were both whipped, and I was sent to live in the Monasterio de San Pablo in Sevilla, having outgrown my innocence. Priora Francisca hoped that at the monastery I could repent the sins that I had committed with Hermana Teresa, and in time perhaps become a good Dominican.

It was to be my special torment that Fray Ignacio de Estrada, the prosecutor and future Inquisitor of Sevilla, was one of my teachers at the monastery. Knowing of my sin, he saw me as a danger to the morality of the other students.

One day I passed by the chapel and heard him praying. I slowed my step and looked in through the door. He was lying facedown, his arms extended like the crucifix above him. On the cross Our Lord's face was contorted in anguish, his wounds gaping and bleeding profusely. I heard Fray Ignacio's voice pleading, almost weeping.

"I beg of you, My Lord, I beseech you—take the Devil from me—take these thoughts and dreams that plague me each waking and sleeping hour. Take the terror of doubt that tortures me like a thousand thorns. I am not strong enough. Why have you brought this sinner into my fold? To mock me? To test me? Show me a sign that I am doing Your will. Let Juan's redemption be my own!"

The door creaked, and he shot a nervous glance in my direction. I ran to our lesson room. The others were gathering, and I waited at the back, dreading his arrival. My leg shook terribly, and I tried not to look at him darkening the door. I felt him enter before I saw him march into the room, his chin up and his black eyes narrowed in fury.

He addressed us through gritted teeth, but his gaze was fixed on me. I tried to shrink down in my seat. "Who can tell me what is the greatest of the seven deadly sins: Pride, Envy, Covetousness, Anger, Sloth, Gluttony"—the final sin lingered in his mouth as he drew it out on his tongue and then spat it through his teeth—"or Lust." He pointed at a fresco that depicted these sins symbolically: a peacock for Pride, a bat over a heart for Envy, a goat for Covetousness, a dog for Anger, a reclining man for Sloth, a pig for Gluttony, and a monkey for Lust. Above these floated the words NO MÁS, urging the faithful to sin no more. I looked at the bright eyes of the peacock feathers, the brown and white face of the snarling dog, and the smiling grin of the monkey. I looked anywhere but into Fray Ignacio's face. He smacked his rod against the table and called on me nonetheless. "Juan!"

Pride, Priora Francisca had once said, is the greatest of these sins because it leads to all the others. Only humility before God can keep us from sin. I answered meekly, as I had learned. "Pride."

"No!" he said harshly before it was out of my mouth, and smacked the rod on the table again. "You should know the answer, since you have committed this sin!" The room was deathly silent, and I said nothing. "Come here!" he shouted. I walked slowly to the front, as if to my own execution. "Tell the others what you did."

I did not answer, unsure of his request.

"What you did with that nun!"

"I fell in love."

"No! What you *did!*"

"We lay together," I said, looking down, ashamed to share our sacred intimacy with the others.

"Lay together? You fornicated with her, did you not? You defiled her soft breasts and poisoned her virginal skin with your touch. You sucked the breath of God out of her lips and violated her like some demonic incubus. Do you deny it?"

I was trembling. "No."

"You have led an innocent soul astray!" he said. He grabbed my hair and yanked my head down to the table, pressing my cheek into the cold wood. Out of the corner of my eye, I could see him raise the rod above his head like an ax. "*Lust* is the greatest of the seven deadly sins! *Lust!*" I watched in horror as the rod came slicing down toward my neck. Then he swung it in an arc so that its full impact cracked against my bony ass. I was thrust forward, but he held my head to the table, my cheek crushed against the hard surface. "How many times did you defile her?"

"I don't—" I could not finish as the rod stung me again, so hard I thought my bones would crack.

"*Again* . . . and *again* . . . and *again* . . ." he said with each blow. There was a ringing in my ear, and I thought I might pass out. The pain too great to endure, my soul began to float above us, watching like an angel from the ceiling. At last he let my head up, the blood from my nose dripping down to my mouth and onto my habit. I could hardly stand and my vision was still clouded. "Your hands!" I heard him shout, as if down a distant tunnel. I held them out in front of me. They were shaking so greatly I thought they might never stop. Suddenly I was returned to my body as I felt the snap of the rod against the soft flesh of my palm. He beat them until they were open sores running with blood. "Next time," he spat out as he finished my beating, "you will not grasp what is God's—and not yours."

I feared further beatings and tried to avoid Fray

Ignacio, but it was impossible for me to forget Hermana Teresa. I felt imprisoned in the monastery so far away from her. At night, when all were asleep, I would escape over the monastery walls, steal a horse, and ride back to Carmona, but she never came to the window to speak to me and closed the shutters against my words. I wrote to her and left my letters in the hollow of the olive tree, but my petitions were not answered and seemingly went unread.

In despair, I went one night to see Padre Miguel, who I knew remained her confessor. I was the last person in line to kneel on the leather cushion beside his confessional. He recognized my voice and face through the lattice screen.

"I love Teresa and want to marry her," I blurted out.

"She is married to Our Lord."

"She would not be the first to leave. I want to take her across the sea, where our love will not be a sin."

"In God's eyes, your love is a sin everywhere."

"Please, Padre."

"Juan, there is nothing—"

Just then we both saw a woman leaving the church with a child in her arms. She stopped to stare at the confessional and then left without a word. I had heard the rumors circulating that she was his concubine, or devil's mule, as the secret wives of the clergy are known. Padre Miguel had taken the missionary's fervor not to the Indies but to the prostitutes in Carmona and the other towns that surrounded Sevilla. He ministered to those who were forgotten or, like the sisters at the Convento de la Madre Sagrada, too far for other priests to visit. Padre Miguel forgot no one. Perhaps he was unable to forget this woman, too.

"Juan, there is nothing any of us can do about the ones we love."

"Please, Padre, will you talk to her? If she says no, I will trouble her no longer. But the silence . . ."

"I will speak with her at the sisters' next confession. Do not worry, my son." There was a smile in his voice, and he came out to embrace me before I left.

Padre Miguel did speak with Hermana Teresa and I saw her one last time, but I was not able to save her. I hear her weeping in my head as if she were sitting beside me as I write, and even now a strange sadness gnaws at me. All day I have spent writing these recollections, and still I do not know the reason why the sleeping memory of Teresa was reawakened by the Infanta's question. Or was it the black eyes of Doña Ana staring at me as Teresa used to, both questioning and knowing, piercing deep into my soul?

I must confess that there is another reason I have turned to writing in this diary. It is not immortality or vanity but simply uncertainty. I will not lie that the threats of the Inquisitor mean nothing to me, but I will never give in to his catechism of tyranny. Those who believe they know the mind of God can serve only the Devil. If necessary, for my beliefs and holy devotions, I am willing to die, but for what, I wonder, am I willing to live?

Afternoon, 15 June 1593

"I see you have taken my advice and have begun writing in the diary I gave you." The Marquis was standing in the doorway. In my trance I had not noticed him. I quickly closed the red leather diary and placed it in my writing desk, which I then locked.

"Nothing of interest, really, just some personal reflections," I replied.

"It is always wise to keep one's personal reflections under lock and key," he said with a knowing smile. "I didn't mean to surprise you. That rather large matron—the one with the mustache—let me in."

"My beloved landlady, Doña Felipa?"

He winced at my affection for a woman who was as large as he was. Doña Felipa, however, had a boundless heart that was even bigger than her ample body. "I assume so," he said indifferently.

"To what urgent matter do I owe the honor of your visit, Don Pedro?" The Marquis always summoned me to his palace and never visited me in my humble apartment.

"You were wise to come to the King's audience last night."

"As always I owe my life and my liberty to you."

"You have earned another month's pardon. We will have to arrange a marriage during that time."

"You know I cannot change what I am."

"Of course not, and I would never want you to, but

decorum will demand a marriage of convenience."

"I cannot. There are already too many lonely wives in Sevilla."

"You will do what you must, as all men do. But we will resolve your marital troubles on another day. This is not the reason for my visit. I could not restrain my curiosity to hear the outcome of your service to the Crown last night."

"Don Pedro," I said with a smile, "since you, of all people, are closest to me, you must understand that I no longer tell tales about my exploits."

"That would make you the only one in all of Spain," he answered sharply. I appreciated his reminder that my reputation had spread so widely, but fame that lives on the lips of talebearers is ephemeral, to be sure.

"A woman's modesty is too important to sacrifice on the altar of a man's glory," I said. This was hardly my belief when I was first learning to seduce women, and like every brash and insecure youth, I was only too happy to crow to the Marquis and anyone else who would listen. Only age and confidence have taught me that privacy is more important than pride. It also happens to be true that actions that are never confessed or proven cannot be punished.

"I was afraid you might not wish to say more." Few people refused the Marquis anything. He looked around at my small sitting room curiously. It was brightened only by a strip of light that spilled through the window. I had opened the heavy wooden shutters just wide enough to let in the evening sun without letting in the heat. "You could use some furniture befitting your nobility, Don Juan," he said. The oak writing desk, a pine writing stool, a leather-backed chair, and a simple round table were my sole furnishings. The walls were bare except for one long Flemish tapestry, a gift from the Marquis himself, and behind which I hid the ladder to my rooftop lair.

"You know my nobility is tenuous at best."

"Be that as it may, I have seen to it that you are still a noble." As was always the case with the Marquis's large, tangled webs, he was beginning along a distant thread.

"I am afraid that there is no money for furniture until the fleet arrives," I said.

"Good news, then, the ships should be here tomorrow. But you never know whether your gamble in the transatlantic trade will pay off, do you? Storms and pirates, theft and duplicity." The Marquis sat down in the leather-backed chair, his chest hiding its frame and his loose black satin sleeves spilling over its arms, which were carved like the paws of a lion. I poured two cups of wine, and when I turned around I saw a purse of gold coins land on top of my writing desk. "I have a . . . proposition for you. Payment for which will be far less of a gamble."

I handed him his cup. "You know I would do—have done—almost anything for you."

"I want you to sell me the pages of your diary as you write them."

I sipped the sharp wine and averted my eyes by staring into its sanguine depth. "I am flattered, Don

70

Pedro, by your interest in my scribbling, but I am not a poet or a playwright who works on commission."

"I am not interested in poetry or plays, as you know, but in the essence of life contained in your pages. I will pay you one hundred silver reales a page."

"That is a fortune for worthless paper."

"And a price I am happy to pay. What do you say? Will you sell me your diary?"

"I am afraid that this I cannot do at any price. I no longer spy for you, and my intrigues must remain my own."

"Who said I would use them for anything beyond my reading pleasure?"

"Come now, Don Pedro. We both know what gives you pleasure."

The Marquis laughed. "Was there anything wrong with my having used your talents for the greater glory of the Empire?"

"*Your* empire?"

"I am a loyal subject of the King, and all I have ever asked of you is the same loyalty."

"You have been better to me than my own father, but a son must eventually make his own way, and my art lives only on unfettered desire, not on conspiring designs."

The Marquis got up to leave.

"Don Pedro, I will tell you what you came to find out if in turn you will tell me what you know about a lady by the name of Doña Ana. She is the daughter of Don Gonzalo de Ulloa."

"The Commander of Calatrava?" the Marquis said with surprise. "What do you want to know about her?"

"Why have I never seen her before?"

"You've seen her?"

"Yes, earlier today, and I am surprised that a woman of such singular beauty has escaped my notice until now."

"Her father has kept her locked away like a nun in seclusion on his hacienda. His farm adjoins my lands near Carmona. I have known her since she was a child."

"What do you know about her?" I persisted.

"Doña Ana is a woman who could make a man forget all others, so a *galanteador* like you would be wise to try to forget *her*."

"You sound almost paternal. Is she a relative?"

"Let's just say it is in my interest to keep her virginal, and I know what your interests are, since they were also once mine."

"Are you planning to give her hand to one of your noble friends at court?"

"I have told you what you want to know, and in return you agreed to tell me what I want to know. Did you succeed in robbing the royal . . . treasury?"

"I . . . am afraid that I failed."

"How unfortunate." He turned to leave, and his long black cape twirled around him. "Your failures were always a source of disappointment to me."

"Your purse," I called after him.

"Buy some furniture with it, so that you are not a disgrace as well as a disappointment."

I closed the door and then unlocked the writing desk and removed the diary to add this latest entry.

I know quite well what the Marquis's motives are for encouraging me to write of my adventures. He wishes to ruin the husbands and fathers of the women who so generously open the doors of their bedchambers to me. However, I will not let him use my intrigues for his own. I am no longer his spy, and I will share my secrets with no one. I will store the diary not in my writing desk, whose lock can easily be broken, but under the loose tiles of my floor, where it will remain undisturbed.

Now I go to take a meal at the tavern downstairs before using the light of the long summer day to ride out to Doña Ana's land. I go as the *galanteador* that the Marquis made me. As my benefactor, he has been right about so many things in life. But in his judgment that any woman could make me forget all others, I will prove that he is wrong.

Evening, 15 June 1593

Like Salt into the Land

*Y*ou do not want to ride in the carriage?" Cristóbal asked as he finished unhitching the horse.

"Tonight I go alone."

"What if something happens?"

I placed a foot in the stirrup and mounted the horse. "I know you worry about me, but tonight Bonita will

73

be the only accomplice to my scandal." He looked abashed at my reminder of his reproval, but I was smiling. "Don't wait up."

Through the Puerta de Carmona I trotted over the arched Roman road that first passed the Monasterio del Carmen and then the town of San Bernardo. From there I galloped across the countryside. Under my thighs I could feel the muscular flanks of the mare tensing and releasing with every stride. My horse's back was wet with life, and I rejoiced in the beauty of every creature that groans and sweats.

Golden fields of ripe wheat covered the hills, and poisonous oleander flowered in white, pink, and red along the riverbanks. I marveled at the beauty of the land around Sevilla, rising and falling like the buttocks and waist of a woman reclining on her side. How sensual and how fertile is God's creation. In the distance behind me I left the wall that surrounded Sevilla like a corset, and the towering Giralda that joined heaven and earth.

As the sun was setting I saw the Marquis's enormous hacienda mounted on the highest hill within sight. It was like a white fortress, and its small, high windows were a dozen eyes watching in every direction. I asked a farmer where the Commander of Calatrava lived, and he pointed me to a small hacienda, also with white walls and a clay tile roof. Next to it was a lone pine tree, and at a short distance, the land sloped down to a riverbed where oaks and olive trees grew. I hid Bonita some distance down the river from the house to make sure she would not be seen. I had left my carriage at home both to increase the speed of my horse and to avoid its being recognized. I didn't tie Bonita to a tree, knowing she would never run away from me, and instead left her free to graze on the plants growing along the rippling water.

I surveyed the area—as a burglar and *galanteador* must—looking to see where all the chess pieces were. The carriage was next to the barn. A few farmhands, dressed in white cotton shirts and green woolen breeches, were finishing their work. I did not see the Commander, who thankfully had been missing from the carriage earlier in the day. Was he away at some battle for the King? In the gathering darkness, I pulled my mask from my sleeve and placed it over my eyes. The pine tree was my ladder, and its rough bark cut into my hands. Someday, I thought, I will seduce someone on the ground floor. I pulled myself up onto the roof and slinked over to where I could look down into the inner courtyard without being seen.

I tried to be patient, calming my pounding heart. I hoped I would not have to wait long, since I felt a strange sense of urgency. Slowly, slowly, I reminded myself. A *galanteador* must always maintain his poise and dispassion.

To a stranger, the fathers of Sevilla must seem as concerned as any Spaniards with keeping their daughters' chastity under lock and key. This preoccupation we inherited from our Moorish predecessors, who sowed their fears like salt into the land. Fortunately,

Christian husbands generally do not seek proof in their wives' maidenhead or the blood of the first night. This is wise because such purity is impossible to prove. The womanhood of so many virgins is already opened before their first coital embrace.

The fathers of Sevilla also conspire in the ruse of seduction, for even as they guard their daughters like dogs protecting the henhouse, they have no interest in sounding the alarm should a fox make his way inside. Their daughters' marriage, and the wealth of their family, is at stake.

I was about to investigate the whereabouts of the Commander when I heard the sound of singing, joyous and life-filled, burst out into the courtyard. Doña Ana was dancing her reluctant dueña in circles.

"Commander not like you dance this way," her dueña said, after succeeding in pulling away.

"But he's not here."

"Soon."

"Then we'd better dance quickly before he arrives," Doña Ana said, trying again to take her dueña's hands.

"Not proper."

"But we have always danced together," Doña Ana replied.

"You are to marry. Nobleman not want country girl with country ways."

"Perhaps you are right," Doña Ana said, and then added, "or perhaps you are wrong. My husband may want a country girl to *show* him her country ways." She laughed, and the sound of her voice was full of mischief and yet had a melody that was like a song.

The dueña covered her mouth with both hands. She threw her shoulders back and, tossing her head, walked into the house.

"Don't be cross, María," Doña Ana said. "I'm sorry. I will try to control myself—" I did not hear what else she said because she too disappeared into the house. As I moved around the roof to see if I could get a better view, she reappeared with a falcon perched on an elbow-length leather glove. This doña was continuing to surprise me. With her long black hair and proud stance, she was a startling sight. The bird was brown, as were the leather glove and the small hood that covered its eyes. Doña Ana removed the blinder, and the bird shook its head and stood taller in its own prideful stance. The falcon then stared in my direction with an unblinking eye. Doña Ana released the leash around its leg.

"Go, Fenix. Fly up and drink the moonlight." The bird flapped its great wings and flew directly toward my hideout. I crouched and moved out of sight as the falcon ascended. When I looked again, I saw Doña Ana standing on the tips of her toes, and I thought she, too, might soar into the night. She watched its course closely and stared longingly in the direction where it had disappeared into the star-bejeweled sky, enraptured by its flight.

I was about to speak when I saw smoke. Doña Ana noticed it, too, and ran back into the house. I climbed to the other side of the building and saw flames coming out of the windows of the barn. The horses were still inside, and I could hear them whinnying in distress. I was preparing to leap down when I saw Doña Ana run out with her dueña and open the barn door. The horses galloped out of the burning building. "Where are Francisco and Pedro? Where is José?" Doña Ana shouted.

"They leave."

"How could this have started?" Doña Ana demanded.

"Lightning," the strangely calm voice of a man spat out as he stepped from behind the white wall with a flaming torch. He wore a sack with two eyeholes over his face. "Tell your father that his daughter is no longer safe here." The man walked with the torch toward the house.

"No, please," Doña Ana begged, grabbing his arm. He shook her off.

I leapt down from the roof and pulled my sword. I held it at the man's throat, stopping him from stepping through the doorway.

"Lightning never strikes twice," I said.

He dropped the torch on the dirt, then drew his sword and lunged at me. I stepped out of the way and struck back. He blocked my blow with the wooden stump of a forearm that was his other hand. My blade dug into his moldy peg and I had to yank it back out. He ran down to the oak trees by the river. I pursued him, and he turned to strike at me. We fought with our swords on the shallow riverbed, trying to keep our footing on the slippery rock. It was not a proper duel but a knife fight between two criminals. Though he was hardly a skilled swordsman, he was quick and cunning. His advantage was the ferociousness of his blows, which were like a torrent beating down on me. I held him off and looked for my opportunity.

"Stop!" Doña Ana shouted. She was standing on the riverbank with a musket in her hands. "Put your sword down or I'll shoot," she said, pointing the gun at my opponent. Cursing, he stabbed his sword into the riverbed, where it glistened in the moonlight.

In the shadows, I saw a figure. "Behind you!" I shouted, but it was too late. Doña Ana wrestled with the man who had grabbed her, but he overcame her quickly and in seconds was holding a knife to her neck. The men were both laughing. "Drop it!" the man behind Doña Ana said to me. He was also wearing a sack over his head. "Or I'll slit her throat." I stabbed my sword into the riverbed as my opponent removed his and held its tip at my heart. Several other men, all hooded, came out of the shadows, holding guns. This was a well-armed and well-planned attack. Two of them took my arms and held pistols to my head.

"Does your father know about him?" the leader with the severed hand said, pointing at me. "Well, your boyfriend's going to watch, and when I'm done, not even he's going to want you." The man holding Doña Ana laughed. I struggled against my two jailers.

The one on my right argued with the leader: "He didn't say anything about that."

"He didn't have to," the leader said, continuing to

approach Doña Ana. "This is what you call the spoils of war." I strained against their grip as they pointed their pistols at my head.

"Leave her alone," I shouted.

"How noble." The leader chuckled as I fought to free myself. I needed a distraction.

At that moment Doña Ana's falcon cried out as it flew back to her. The jailer on my left raised his pistol to shoot the bird.

"Nooo!" Doña Ana shouted, and I knocked the man's gun off target. The gun fired but missed the bird. In the commotion I shook myself free. With one pistol discharged and only one other to worry about, I knew I could take the risk of rebellion. As I struggled over the loaded gun, it fired into the air. It was now useless. I turned and grabbed my sword.

Doña Ana hit the man behind her in the stomach hard with the handle of her musket, and he fell to the ground, clutching himself. The leader lunged at Doña Ana as I rushed toward them. The guard who had protested stood back, unwilling to stop me. I was almost to Doña Ana's assailant when she fired her musket, hitting him straight in the chest. He fell to the ground and the others fled.

"Oh my God," she shouted, kneeling next to him, her hand covering her lips. "I've killed him."

"Masked men *are* dangerous," I said as I turned his limp body over and pulled off his hood. His hair was dark, as were his vacant eyes, and his teeth were rotten. He looked strangely familiar. I wondered if I had known him during my days as a burglar or as a spy.

Doña Ana turned to me with eyes narrowed in curiosity. She no doubt remembered my words from the carriage. "Who are you and what do you want with me?"

I was about to answer when I heard the beating of a horse's galloping hooves. Her father must have heard the gunshots, and he galloped toward us, brandishing his broadsword. "Go back to the house!" the Commander yelled to his daughter. "I'll take care of him."

"Father!" she shouted, trying to explain, but it was too late. I was running for my life with the Commander in pursuit, committed to one goal—killing me. He swung his sword and cut off a branch next to my head and then swung again and this time cut my sleeve. I kept running through the trees and leapt on Bonita. With a hard kick, she lunged forward. If it had not been for the tree that the Commander's horse had to avoid, he would have overtaken us, but by the time he had come around it, we were off at a full gallop. As I looked behind, I saw him in the moonlight chasing us, swinging his sword above his head, his face aflame with fury. I galloped across the hills, heading for a small forest in the distance. He was not far behind, shouting and kicking his horse to go faster.

As we raced through the trees, I was able to duck and hang to the side to avoid the branches. This allowed Bonita to pull ahead. As soon as we were out of sight, I cut to the side and stopped Bonita dead in her tracks. She was panting heavily, and I stroked her sweaty neck gently, urging her to stay quiet. I heard the Commander and his horse still shattering the branches as they galloped ahead. I circled around and skulked along under the branches to the other side of the woods. Once out of the grove, I avoided the road and galloped across a field, the soft ground hushing Bonita's hooves. Once over a hill and at a safe distance, I removed my mask. The warm wind made my eyes water. I raced back to the walls of the city, eager for the safety of their embrace.

Cristóbal greeted me nervously at the door and noted my cut sleeve. "Lightning," I said, and he looked at me suspiciously. He took my doublet off to sew it up, and I went to my rooms to write, as if I were a guilty sinner going to confession.

Doña Ana's question played over and over in my mind. What *did* I want with her? What had brought me to her hacienda? Was it simply another intrigue? I have always picked the low-lying fruit that is bursting with desire, as the Marquis wisely advised. This has been the reason for my great success. I can smell a woman's need like the ripeness of a peach. And yet a woman who pulls a gun on first meeting is hardly easily plucked.

I'd had no choice but to come to Doña Ana's aid tonight and yet I am not a knight errant on a chivalric quest. I am a lustful libertine motivated by the calculated pursuit of pleasure. Perhaps in our cunning schemes the Marquis and I are not so different. It was, after all, his generous and decadent lessons that made me everything I am. But are my life and my purpose just the ones he bestowed upon me? Here in my writing desk is where I store the Letters Patent that he purchased for me from His Excellency King Philip II. I can recite its words from memory because I have read it so many times to convince myself of its authenticity and mine.

By the Grace of God,

To all whom the Presents shall come, Know ye that We of Our Especial Grace, certain knowledge and mere motion do by the Presents advance, create and prefer Our Juan Tenorio to the state, style, degree, dignity, title, and honor of the noble rank of Hidalgo in our Kingdom of Castille.

Given at Our Chancellery under Our Sign Manual and Great Seal this 14th day of January 1577, by command of the King.

It was signed by King Philip II himself, or a very good forger.

I do not know the answer to Doña Ana's first and most obvious question. Who am I truly? I have been so many things. First an orphan and acolyte. Now a noble and libertine. And between the two, a burglar and spy—as truth now compels me to reveal. Do we always have a choice of who we become, or does life, like the throw of dice, determine our fate? Certainly my becoming a thief was partly my will and partly that of the gods. I could never have imagined or even fully chosen what awaited me when I left the sheltered life of the Church.

A Man Is Not Just What He Is Born

On the final night I returned from Teresa's cell, I fled the walls of the monastery forever. With nowhere else to go, I sought refuge among the beggars, prostitutes, and criminals in Sevilla's infamous Arenal neighborhood. I had been given the name and address of a place where I hoped to find shelter—the Taberna del Pirata. I did not know at the time that this was the most dangerous tavern in Sevilla.

A small window in the door opened, and a gun was pointed at my face. I blurted out the password I had been told: "Jesus Christ, Our Lord, who shed Thy precious blood for us, have pity on me, a great sinner."

"What do you want?" barked a faceless gatekeeper.

"I have been told that a woman named Serena lives here."

"Let him in," called a warm voice from behind. It was the voice of a man I would come to love almost like a father. The ruffian begrudgingly let me in, and I was greeted by the broad smile of a man with a round face and curly brown hair. He wore his white shirt with its sleeves rolled up practically to his shoulders, revealing his powerful arms. Over the shirt he wore a simple brown vest, the uniform of the young tavern owner. "My name is Manuel. Serena is my wife."

Serena had long auburn hair and chocolate-brown eyes not unlike my own. She circled around me as if sizing up a new horse before purchasing it. "I don't know, Manuel, he looks awfully innocent to me."

"I tell you the boy has promise. Look at those hands." I hid them behind my back, but Serena took them gently in hers. She was shocked to see how bruised and raw they were from my beating.

"What happened to your hands?" she asked.

"Climbing rope," I said, not wanting to reveal either that I had run away from the monastery or the reason for my beating.

Manuel looked at me with a raised eyebrow. He knew I was lying, but smiled and said, "I like rope-climbers." He offered to let me sleep on their roof for a time, and I soon discovered that this was a tavern in name only. Manuel was "father" to a band of cut-purses, rope-climbers, and other members of the light-fingered gentry, a regular brotherhood of thieves. They were the establishment's only patrons.

Serena had been a prostitute who fell in with the brotherhood, but Manuel chose her for his own. Unlike many husbands of prostitutes who are happy to rent them out for additional earnings, Manuel wanted her to be a proper wife. So she became "mother" not only to the thieves but also to the prostitutes who lived at the tavern, and she obeyed the royal decrees governing their profession with vigilance. She refused to take on any women who were virgins or who were burdened by debts, and every week her girls had to be examined by a doctor, sometimes twice a week, if the doctor was willing to "barter" for his services.

The brotherhood had recently lost one of its members, and I was invited to join their ranks. I refused, although I had consumed only one discarded, half-eaten meat pie in two days and my stomach was clawing at me from inside. I did not want to take food from my hosts without paying, and so at every meal I pretended that I had already eaten.

"I think you'd make a rather good thief," said Manuel as the brotherhood was sitting down for their evening meal. "You have already passed our first test. You walk as silently on the roof as an owl flies through the night."

"I am honored by the invitation, Señor Manuel, but I am afraid I cannot accept."

"Are you afraid of getting caught?" he persisted.

I looked away. I was afraid but that was not my only reason for declining the invitation.

"Speak your mind, boy. One must always speak the truth. Now, tell me, what stops you from joining our happy family?" I was hesitant to offend my hosts and to reveal my true thoughts to the gathered fellowship. A dozen members of the brotherhood and half a dozen members of the sisterhood surrounded me, most staring at me over their bowls of stew. The women all had the adorned beauty of those whose livelihood depends on their charms. "If you join us, you won't have to starve," Manuel said. I had apparently not been able to hide my hungry eyes even if I had been able to control my hands.

"Stealing is a . . . a sin," I finally said, and then stuttered, "It's one of the . . . Commandments."

Their eyes all went wide. A dozen unbelieving faces stared back at me, and everyone stopped eating. It was Serena who broke the silence as she tried to explain the ways of the world. "One's morals, my boy, must be practical. Those Commandments were made by the rich. Everybody steals. Some just make a virtue of it. Does our noble King not use his tax collectors to steal for his treasury?" She wrapped her arms around her husband with genuine affection. "My dear Manuel and the brotherhood are just the tax collectors for the poor."

The brethren laughed at her last comparison, and some echoed her words: "Yeah, that's what we are—the tax collectors for the poor!"

"It's true," Manuel piped up. "We do make regular donations to the sisters who serve the *sopa boba* to the poor hungry wretches too lame to steal." It was this one daily meal that saved countless people from dying of hunger in the city's streets. It was only my pride and anger at the Church that made me refuse to join the line of widows, orphans, and beggars who lined up each day.

"The nobles ride in their fancy carriages," Serena continued as she looked at her stained dress, "treating us with disdain and spraying us with mud from their wheels. But are we not all made from mud? So why should some ride in golden carriages and others walk barefoot?"

"What do you think, my boy? Does my wife not

make a compelling case?" Manuel asked. He stroked her cheek proudly. "She could have been an advocate. She has even argued for members of the brotherhood before a judge."

Serena offered me a bowl of stew that the others were once again eating greedily as they continued to watch me closely. My stomach was grumbling so loud I knew the others must have heard it. I took the bowl and raised it in a toast. "To the tax collectors for the poor!" Everyone cheered. I ate the stew hungrily, its thick, salty flavor coating my tongue and filling my belly.

After I had sworn that even if I were sliced into little pieces I would not "sing" the names of my companions, I was taught to become a rope-climber, burgling the houses of the nobles at night. My skills at navigating the darkness undetected, which I had learned at the convent, proved invaluable. We worked alone to reduce the risk and increase the rewards, although we were sworn to share everything with the brotherhood.

On my first night, Serena gave me a mask. It was made of black leather and was therefore precious, and I took it in both hands as if receiving a sacred vestment.

"It belonged to one of the best rope-climbers in the brotherhood," she told me.

"What happened to him?" I asked.

"Hanged on the gallows," she said with a maternal and reassuring smile. My stomach dropped. I tried to hide the fear shivering through my skin.

When we made our way to the wealthiest neighborhood that night, I knew exactly which house I wanted to target. It belonged to a noble named Don Diego Tenorio, who had treated me with disdain and splashed me with mud from his carriage wheels. When I arrived, it seemed that everyone inside was dreaming in the arms of Morpheus. I was closing in on a pair of silver candlesticks in one of the upstairs salons, but I hesitated. I remembered what I had learned at the convent and decided that I could not break one of the Ten Commandments, regardless of what Serena had said about nobles stealing constantly from the poor. Just then I heard an argument down the hall. Don Diego was drunk and shouting at his young wife, Doña Elena. "How dare you question where I am going!" I felt drawn to see his face and hid behind the door that opened out of the bedchamber. I could see him holding his wife by the hair.

Her head twisted to the side, she managed to say, "I miss you, Diego."

He let go of her hair and then, with the back of his hand, slapped her across the face. "I shall have a hundred mistresses if I wish!"

His wife wept in the room as he stormed out of the house. I watched for a long time, unable to move, as she sobbed into her hands. Hatred for Don Diego burned in my heart, and I vowed revenge. I returned to the salon and took both his candlesticks and four silver cups as well.

After that night, I developed quite a reputation for

being one of the most skillful members of my trade, not only among the brotherhood but also among those who kept themselves informed about such illegal talents. Over the next two years, I perfected the breathless silence that would serve me so well later. Indeed, my nickname in the brotherhood was El Búho, because no one could hear me coming in the night, and I would strike and escape, like an owl, before anyone noticed I was there. I concentrated on the wealthiest of homes, which were also the most heavily guarded, and while I was required to share my spoils with the others, I was able to save a bit despite many losses at the gambling table.

It was at this time that the Marquis came looking for a spy. Manuel, apparently, had procured many for him. For two years I was a letter thief in the Marquis's private postal service and also eavesdropped on important conversations. The Marquis was careful to avoid having even his spies learn the full extent of his stratagems, but I was a thief as well as a spy and learned what none of his other informants knew. I learned about his many treasonous acts against the King, including his aid to the French and his help in the escape of the fugitive Secretary of State, Antonio Pérez. I was little concerned with his politics. But what I wanted was equally scandalous.

Upon returning from an assignment one night, I found the Marquis in his salon, surrounded by young noblemen, his own unholy legion for whom he served as mentor and leader in the libertine life. A handful of prostitutes dressed in pagan costume fed them sips of wine and placed figs, grapes, and cherries in their mouths. I stared at them with envy, wanting to be a member of their fraternity but knowing I had no right and no title to permit me entry into their society.

I looked at their clothes, embroidered with gold and silver thread, and then at my own plain brown coat and green knee pants. Ashamed, I tried to disappear discreetly as I placed the papers that the Marquis had wanted in his ivory-inlaid writing desk. I locked the drawer and turned to leave.

I passed behind the raised dais where the Marquis was reclining on pillows with one of the prostitutes just as she knocked a goblet of red wine off a low table. I have always been blessed with quick reflexes, and I caught the silver goblet, spilling only a few drops. I held the precious cup in both hands and offered it to the prostitute as if it were the blood of Our Lord. I stared into her beautiful eyes, seeing Hermana Teresa's, and we both held the chalice perhaps a moment too long. The Marquis had seen everything, and I averted my eyes when I saw that he was watching. I turned toward the door.

"Leaving so soon?" the Marquis called out. He grabbed the prostitute by the arm and flung her in my direction. "A gratuity for an assignment well done," he added, referring to the stolen letters locked in his desk. Perhaps because she had drunk too much, the prostitute fell on me and then to the ground.

I helped her up, trying not to stare at the low-cut

dress and the cleavage it revealed. "Thank you, my lord, but I do not lie . . . with prostitutes," I said.

His eyes widened in shock and delight. He announced to the gathered crowd, "A burglar with a code of ethics! How intriguing. Come here. I want to know more." He gestured for me to sit next to him. "Tell me, Juan the Burglar, if you do not sleep with prostitutes, you must seduce men's wives, or perhaps their virginal daughters."

"No," I said. "I have done neither." I was not immune to the charms of women. My heart had fluttered countless times for the ladies from all over Europe who seemed to glide above the muddy streets of Sevilla on their cork shoes. Yet I knew no woman would want to marry a poor orphan, and until that day I believed fornication out of wedlock was a sin, as I had learned at the convent. Fortunately, I knew better than to admit this to the Marquis.

"But you could so easily," he said with a glimmer in his eye, "seduce wives and daughters." I looked at him uncomprehendingly, and he continued, "You already know how to steal things of value, and there is nothing more valuable to a man than his daughter's virginity and his wife's fidelity."

I looked down.

"Yes?" he asked, sensing my doubt.

"But why would I?" I mumbled.

"Why would you . . ." he said, his mind clearly searching, trying to find just the right reason. His intuition was flawless. "Why do men seduce women?

Pride? Pleasure? Power? But some have a higher ambition. They are the women's saviors. Think of all those lonely women, neglected and abused by their husbands or locked up by their fathers. They have no one else to look after them. This is the solemn role of the *galanteadores*—the gallant conquistadors of the night." I thought of Don Diego and his poor wife, Doña Elena. My eyes went wide, and I began to nod. "Good, I see you are beginning to understand," he said.

"Yes, my lord."

"Now, tell me, Juan the Burglar, who are you really?" He perhaps sensed that I was different from his other spies.

"I am just an orphan, my lord," I replied.

"A man is not just what he is born. A man is what he wants, what he desires, what he becomes," the Marquis said, as much to the others as to me. "I could see in your eyes that you would like to join our libertine university. Am I right?"

I dared not speak, knowing that such a thought was worthy of a beating. "A servant can never drink with his lord," sneered a noble, who I would later learn was named Don José. His eyebrows rose in a surprised and haughty manner and his black eyes pierced through me like a knife. His head sat on a bright white starched ruff and his black mustache and beard were immaculately trimmed to the tips of his smirking lips.

"In my house, it is talent and not the accidents of birth that make the man. Am I not a younger son whose brother was to inherit everything? Would that have been just? No, it would have been most unjust," the Marquis said to Don José and the other guests, and turned back to me. "Am I right, Juan the Burglar?"

"Yes, my lord," I said.

"I think you might have talent with women and that your talent might be useful to me. Come back tomorrow night at midnight for a private lesson. We will see if you can become more than you were born."

The Education of a Libertine

$\mathcal{I}$ could not sleep all night. I went to the Marquis's door long before midnight and waited until Fernando, one of the servants, let me in and led me to the salon.

In the room was Beatriz, the prostitute whose goblet I had caught the night before. She circled me and eyed me questioningly, as if evaluating the Marquis's judgment. She ran her finger along my neck, and I shivered. "Well, you certainly do respond to a woman's touch." From behind, she whispered in my ear, "Would you like to know how to seduce a woman so that you can feel her touch whenever you want?"

I nodded nervously.

"Every woman, no matter how indifferent and how beautiful, longs for love and admiration. If you show her the consideration that she lacks, she will be yours."

"Consideration?"

"You did this last night when you handed me my goblet and looked into my eyes. Show her that she is more important than anything in the world. Admire her, speak to her with gentle words, and listen to her—"

"Seduction," the Marquis interrupted as he entered the room, "is the oldest battle. Every woman must protect her chastity, and every man must convince her to surrender it. This is the law of Nature."

"Look for the signs of interest," Beatriz continued as she began to act out her words. "Whether a woman meets your gaze, whether she looks a second time, whether she plays with her jewelry, and whether she gives you a backward glance while baring her neck and combing her hair—"

"All women look for one thing in a man above all others . . ." the Marquis interrupted again, but then he let Beatriz complete the sentence.

Her lips were so close to mine that I could feel her hot breath. "Confidence." She drew back, evaluating the effect of this word on me, and took one of my shaking hands between hers. "Not pride or arrogance—just confidence. A woman's life and those of her children depend on a man's skill, so women have always looked for men who exude confidence like women exude perfume."

"How does a man"—I gulped—"gain such confidence?"

The Marquis answered, "He must face his fear." He pulled his sword and gestured for Fernando, who handed me a sheathed sword. I pulled it out a few inches and felt its sharp blade.

"Many men," Beatriz said, "are brave in battle but weak when facing an unarmed woman."

"Enough talk," the Marquis said impatiently, twirling his sword in front of me. "It is time for your first lesson in swordsmanship. If you are going to learn how to enjoy yourself in the arms of daughters and wives, you must know how to defend yourself from fathers and husbands." He nodded at the door. I pulled the sword from its sheath, which I handed back to Fernando. I followed the Marquis nervously as Beatriz blew me a kiss. I felt it land on my lips, and it gave me strength and courage.

The Marquis led me into a secret room belowground with flaming torches on every wall. In the center of the marble floor was a circle with lines cutting across it in some strange symbol.

"Enter the Circle of Honor," the Marquis said. He stood at the far end. Painted across the circle's diameter was the figure of a man holding his outstretched arm above his head. Half of the man's naked body was covered in flesh and the other half was bone. The decaying corpse looked even more frightening than a skeleton as it explicitly linked life and vigor with death and decay. Its feet touched one end of the circle and the tip of its index finger the other. "All men are false and will eventually betray you, but geometry never will," the Marquis explained. "Each one of these lines represents possible movements of attack and their counters. The distance of the circle is the correct starting distance, although your goal will be to enter in close." He raised his sword until its hilt was in front of his face, and then he slashed it through the air. The sound of his salute was like a whip cracking with menace. I tried to mimic his movements.

The Marquis assumed the dueling position, with his right arm holding the sword out straight. "You must stay balanced in your posture, never letting your anger draw you overly forward or your fear draw you overly back." His broad shoulders and powerful barrel chest made the sword look like a dagger in his hand. In his other, he grasped an ornately engraved wineglass. His challenge for himself was not to spill a drop. He moved around the circle, careful never to cross his feet. I raised my blade and followed his two-step dance in the opposite direction. "Point the tip at me, not up. I am not an angel hovering above you." He stepped into a shadow cast across the circle, and I could hardly see him. "Use the shadows, use the sun, use whatever advantage you have. A dead man cannot cry foul." I pointed the tip at him but had a hard time holding the heavy sword. I had no training whatsoever, the nuns having neglected to teach me the use of a blade outside the kitchen.

"Hold your rapier up at all times," he said. I raised it into place again, already perspiring in the hot room. He thrust at me, and I tried slapping his blade with mine. In doing so I crossed my body with my arm, leaving my sword pointing uselessly to the side. He saw my vulnerability and cut my shoulder with his blade. I grabbed my arm and felt the sting before I saw the blood. "That will remind you to always keep your blade between you and your opponent. Try again!" he barked. In this lesson, the Marquis was both my teacher and my opponent. He taught me how to cut with the shoulder, the elbow, and the wrist, and how to keep my arm supple. He also showed me how to use my sword's thick base against the weaker tip of his, and how to always place my blade in a position that threatened my adversary. We fought as if it were a dance, and danced knowing it was a deadly fight. Around and around the circle we went, thrusting at each opening and deflecting each attack. Every time I failed, he pierced my skin ever so slightly. Even after my white shirt was reduced to rags and blood seeped through in two dozen places, I refused to cry out or to favor the wounds with my hand. We fought on for hours. My limbs ached and my eyes stung with salty sweat. Finally, I learned to kill his movement by putting my blade over his, forcing his point toward the ground and gaining the advantage. He nodded with satisfaction.

"The only man," he told me, "who is invincible in a duel is the man who has nothing to lose." What was left of my shirt was soaked with exertion and tinged with blood, but I would not concede defeat. We continued to thrust at each other. I was aided by natural speed and by an intuition of my opponent's emotions and therefore movements. This I had learned from the sisters, anticipating their desires and their demands before they were spoken. The Marquis and I continued to exchange attack positions. Eventually I managed to fend off each of his movements and even went on the offensive. I was amazed to see him take steps away from my sword. A new feeling of vitality filled my veins as I experienced the power of the blade. "That's it, that's it," he said with paternal satisfaction as his glass of wine slipped through his perspiring fingers, shattering on the marble floor. The sanguine fluid exploded in every direction.

I practiced daily with the Marquis and was invited to live in his palace. Not only did he teach me the science of dueling, he also taught me to appreciate and differentiate fifty varietals of wine and three dozen fragrances of perfume. He was particularly impressed with my nose, which he said was generally more difficult to educate than the palate.

Apart from our lessons, I roamed his palace freely and ate with him at his own table. The only payment I made for my tuition was the occasional special assignment he sent me on. The rest of the time was devoted to my studies. He encouraged me to read in both his pious and secret libraries, which together held more than fifteen hundred volumes. "A libertine is not just one who is free from traditional moral codes," he said as we entered the round room that held his clandestine collection of books. "A libertine is a man whose mind is free, who seeks the truth about life and the desires that drive all men. An able body is nothing without an illuminated mind."

One day Fernando brought me the clothing of a nobleman, so I could pretend to be a true caballero. He patiently showed me how to dress. One of the Marquis's tailors had made the clothes to my exact size, but they still felt like a stage costume. The ruff dug into my neck and the stockings made my legs itch. I was beginning to see how uncomfortable playing the part of a noble could be.

During this time I attempted numerous seductions, all without success. Not only did I lack confidence, I had not yet learned when a woman was ripe for seduction. More than once, as I serenaded a beautiful woman with my guitar, a window or balcony door was shut in my face, and once I heard the words *"Agua va!"* too late to move out of the way as the contents of a chamber pot were emptied from above onto my head. Ten thousand turds perfumed our fair and fragrant city each night, so this was one of the great dangers that I and all other *galanteadores* had to endure. But I was determined to learn the Arts of Passion as well as the Arts of Chivalry and liberty that the Marquis was teaching me. And one evening I finally succeeded in my first seduction.

I was walking by the house of the noble Don Diego, whom I had witnessed hitting his wife on my first night as a burglar. This evening his carriage rushed out of the gates, and through its open window I saw that only he was inside. I knew that his young and neglected wife would be left alone, as she was most nights. Perhaps just twenty-four years old, Doña Elena spent the evenings of her young life by herself, reading and sewing, in her large dark house. I had been watching the house and Don Diego's movements carefully. I had also been watching Doña Elena and had hired a *celestina*, one of the many older women who are willing to deliver letters to lovers for a small price.

It was a spring night and the shutters were open. I saw her in the second-floor window, reading by a candle. Placing my old burglar's mask over my face, I climbed up to her balcony using the wrought-iron grating that covered the first-floor window. Not wanting to startle her, I pretended to whistle like a bird. I saw her head turn to listen more closely to the strange song. She looked out the window and, upon seeing me, her eyes went wide. "Who are you?" she said with fear in her voice.

My legs were shaking, and I had to tighten my muscles to keep them still. I swallowed hard, trying to hide my uncertainty. "Ah . . . have . . . have you received my letters?"

She looked both ways to see if we were being watched. "Your letters have been unsigned." I had done so not just out of discretion, but also because I had no title to sign with.

"I am Juan," I said, climbing onto the balcony and removing my mask but unable to look her in the eyes.

"You must leave at once before you are seen, *Juan*." Her words were adamant, but she spoke my name tenderly.

"Do you really want me to leave? Or to come inside?"

"It does not matter what I want."

I did not know what to say until I noticed the title of the book she held against her chest like a shield. It was the first volume of the chivalric romance of Amadís de Gaula. As a boy, I had read all four volumes and innumerable sequels in Padre Miguel's collection. "Do you just want to *read* about romance?"

"You are quite bold for one so young."

"Passion makes me bold." The words were coming more quickly to mind.

She swallowed and looked toward the door. "My husband will be coming home . . ."

"Then we must not waste time with words." I stepped forward and kissed her on the lips, awkwardly at first.

Her body stiffened and then relaxed. She locked the door and led me to her bed. We made love feverishly out of haste and long-unanswered lust. I tried to remember what I had learned from Teresa's body about how to touch a woman. But my long-silenced skin shouted deafeningly with pleasure at the thrill of womanhood. All my senses stopped in a moment of blinding release. It was quick, but she smiled at me kindly—even gratefully.

As we lay in each other's arms, Doña Elena told me about the loneliness she experienced. She began to cry, and as I comforted her, she told me how she hated her husband and her life and that I had brought her the only joy—however brief it might have been—she had known in years. I returned many times to her bedchamber, though not to hers alone. After Doña Elena, there was a second, and then ten and then twenty. So many wives wanted to do more than read their romances.

The New World gold that continues to pour into this city year after year has led to a frenzy of greed, causing men to pursue their fortune and forget the open-chested treasure they leave at home. The husbands' neglect has made women ever bolder. Smoke can slide under doors and through keyholes, and ignored embers smolder the most. Indeed, the only certain promise of a wife's chastity is her contentment, and it is this and only this that has led to my advances being rebuffed by the few fortunate wives I have met.

I found that daughters under a father's watch were as eager for escape as wives suffering from a husband's neglect. Although more nervous and requiring greater tenderness, they too yearned for release from the prison to which they were confined. With them I had to be all the more clear about my intentions—while I might serve as their savior for a time, I would not marry them. As long as secrecy was maintained, there were countless willing maidens who conspired with me to open the gates of their cages.

With a nod and wink at his numerous parties, the Marquis helped me select those who were ripe for the plucking. Few of these women were able to refuse my invitations and their own needs.

Almost two years to the day after I had come to live in the Marquis's palace, Don José stopped me. He remained a protégé of the Marquis, and my rival. I was returning from one of my conquests and was on my way to recount my success to the Marquis.

"You are still nothing more than the Marquis's lackey," Don José said disdainfully.

"We all serve the Marquis, do we not?"

"Not all of us seduce the women whose families the Marquis wishes to destroy." I was prepared to dismiss his criticism as jealousy, but he told me that Doña Elena was a friend of his sister's. The Marquis was blackmailing her to spy on her husband, Don Diego. He had threatened to tell her husband of her infidelity if she did not cooperate. Don José said that Doña Elena was not the only one, that the Marquis sometimes blackmailed the husbands if he thought they would be desperate to keep their cuckolding a secret.

I stormed out of the palace, shocked by this news, which I confirmed with Doña Elena. I resolved that I would thereafter lie to the Marquis and refuse to tell tales to anyone else. It was up to the women to decide whether they wished to spread word of our affairs. I did not return to the palace for over a week, spending each night in a different bed.

"Where have you been?" the Marquis asked accusingly upon my return.

"My apologies, Don Pedro, but I have been busy."

Don José and Don Hernán were visiting and watched the brewing storm. Don José's smile revealed his satisfaction, while Don Hernán's pale face and watery blue eyes looked worried.

"With whom?" the Marquis asked me.

"No one of any consequence to you—servants and slaves," I said.

"I did not teach you the Arts of Chivalry and the Arts of Liberty so that you could throw these pearls before swine!" he shouted. He pulled out his sword and struck it against a table.

"I am forever grateful for the priceless knowledge that you have given me."

"So use it as I taught you," the Marquis said, pointing his sword at me and then sighing deeply. "I am telling you this because I care about you, Don Juan. I do not want you to waste your talents. You have the potential to be the greatest *galanteador* in all of Spain, but you must challenge yourself and not settle for easy targets."

"I am flattered, Don Pedro."

"I am not flattering you! I am telling the truth. You are as good at the Arts of Chivalry and Liberty as Don José and Don Hernán combined."

Don José stood up at this affront and slapped Don Hernán on the shoulder. He reluctantly stood, too.

"If you don't believe me," the Marquis said to them, "then fight him."

"Both of us?" Don Hernán asked uncertainly. Don José was already reaching for his sword.

"Yes, both of you," the Marquis responded coolly.

Don José unsheathed his blade confidently, having been schooled in the art of swordsmanship since his youth. Don Hernán drew his more hesitantly, although his training was no less than that of Don José.

I was nervous but said nothing, eager to show them that I was their equal in skill if not in birth. We maintained the proper fighting measure as we circled, looking for one another's weakness and our opportunity. Don José waved his sword in front of me mockingly. I slapped it aside, and he was quickly on the defensive, stepping backward. I smothered his blade and with outward pressure forced his sword down and around, stripping it from his fingers. His sword clanged on the marble floor. I heard him gasp and then stoop to pick up his weapon. I now watched Don Hernán prepare for battle.

Don Hernán's hair was already receding at his temples. His stringy mustache descended over the corners of his mouth like the tail of a mouse that seemed to be twitching as he held up his sword. Although more tentative, he fought even more skillfully. But I could sense his movements and his fear before he had acted on it. I soon had Don Hernán on the defensive as well. I now felt Don José behind me, wanting to reclaim his pride, and I fought the battle in two overlapping circles. I used my sword to bring Don Hernán in close and swung him around in front of me so that I was using my blade and his to fight Don José. Don Hernán abandoned his sword to me, and with both swords in a cross, I blocked Don José's desperate blow. I put Don Hernán's sword in my scabbard, knowing there was no honor in defeating one opponent with two swords. Don José continued to thrust madly. I enveloped his sword with mine and closed the distance until the tip of his blade was extending beyond me. Hilt to hilt, I trapped his blade under the arm of my leather doublet and pried his sword out of his hand with the thick base of mine.

"Not disappointing at all," the Marquis said. His staccato clapping echoed in the room. "Not disappointing at all." He was half congratulating me and half boasting to the others. I tried hard to suppress a smile, but my satisfaction disappeared as I turned and saw the Marquis holding his sword at me. I added Don José's sword to my leather belt and met the Marquis's blade slowly and deliberately. We exchanged blows, his powerful, mine less so, but now as skillful.

He slashed at me and I leapt over his blade and cut the puffed shoulder of his sleeve. He looked at me, first with disbelief and then with vengeful rage. I had humiliated him in front of his other students. He came at me with fury, and I retreated but used his passion against him. We fought on, he with something to lose and I with nothing. We battled across the room, overturning chairs and knocking down candelabras. The candles lit a red and green velvet curtain on fire, but the Marquis refused to stop the battle. He would let his whole palace burn before giving up the fight. Don José and Don Hernán pulled down the curtain and smothered the flames as we fought on. Sweat ran down my forehead and blurred my vision. I went on the offensive, menacing the Marquis's red face and heaving chest with my blade. He thrust at me with the desperation of a caged animal, and I defended myself against his blows with difficulty. My strength was waning. I knew I needed to try something soon and thought of the old sword-fighting manual I had discovered in the secret library. I had never attempted the move and knew that if I failed, the Marquis would no doubt overcome me. It was my only chance. With our swords locked in clenched combat, I twisted my wrist like a coiling snake. Before he knew what had happened, the Marquis's sword was clanging on the marble floor.

He looked down at his supine sword. "Carranza's coil," he said, recognizing the move with an amalgam of shock and amusement. "You found his treatise."

I saw the flash of metal as he pulled his dagger from his belt. He held it straight at me as if pointing a pistol at my chest. I had seen the dagger hanging around his waist constantly but had never seen him use it. The handle was made from gold and ivory, tapering into a horse's head. The bright steel blade had been engraved with acid and displayed the flower of his family's house. Yet its size was no match for the sword that he had lent me, and I smiled, thinking he might concede defeat. I tried to laugh, but my amusement was short-lived. He turned over the dagger and showed me what was indeed a tiny pistol hidden on the other side, his finger firmly on the trigger. "There are," he said as if possessed by a demon, "only two options in a duel, my dear *Don* Juan—win or die." I dropped my sword. He laughed aloud, and the rest of us, his assembled students, tried to find the humor in his victory with forced chuckles.

Confident in his victory and his display of my talents, he was once again the good-natured mentor as he slapped me on the back approvingly.

"To what do I owe the honor of your knighting me?" I said, referring to his calling me by the titled name Don Juan, to which I had no claim. To that day he had called me only Juan or Juan the Burglar.

"You have proved yourself a true caballero." The Marquis smiled, turned to his writing desk, and opened a drawer. He took out a folded letter that bore the King's own wax seal. I broke the seal and read with amazement the Letters Patent granting me nobility. Well aware of the Marquis's ability to forge letters from the King, I asked, "Is it real?"

"Yes, quite."

"Don Pedro," I said with disbelief and gratitude, knowing that he had changed my life forever. My heart was pounding and I felt the blood coursing swiftly through my veins.

"Our noble King," the Marquis said, "is always willing to give titles to those who are deserving—and are willing to supplement his royal treasury with escudos."

"But why did you spend your escudos on me?" I asked.

"Because you truly *are* deserving, unlike so many of our fat and fetid aristocracy." Don José pulled in his stomach and stood up taller. "Too many of our nobles know nothing of chivalry—like my poor dead brother. But you have earned your title."

"You are better to me than my own father," I said,

kneeling before him. I could not help my eyes watering but tried to stop myself from shedding a tear in the Marquis's presence. I knew he hated weakness, though the feeling I had was not of weakness but of great strength and gratitude.

He pulled me up, shaking his head to indicate that this sign of fealty was unnecessary. "I know I can count on your loyalty."

He waved for Fernando, who brought over a large purple pillow on which were lying a sword and dagger. The swept hilt of the sword spiraled around the handle in a beguiling design that was as beautiful as it was effective in protecting the hand. The handle was made of silver and gold threads that were twisted to improve the grip, and the pommel had fluted swirls. It was no doubt the intricate work of a master craftsman from Toledo. The dagger was equally elegant, in both its matching grip and plated thumb ring to protect the knuckles. Its thick, wide blade tapered sharply to a deadly point, and its serrated edge was designed to entangle an opponent's blade. "These belonged to my brother," the Marquis said. "I want you to have them. I know you will use them better than he did."

"I don't know what to say, Don Pedro. I'm speechless with gratitude."

"You do not need to say anything. Your deeds will be better than any words, and I am sure that you will be faithful and serve me—and your King—nobly."

I gave the blade that he had long ago lent me back to Fernando and returned Don José's and Don Hernán's blades. They took them, Don Hernán bashful, Don José disdainful. I lifted the shining new sword up in front of my face and saluted the Marquis. The sharp blade cut through the air with almost complete silence.

From that day on I did try to serve the Marquis faithfully while safeguarding the reputations of the women who opened their arms to me. He soon grew tired of my increasing number of reported "failures" and found other means to forward his plans. With my title I gradually established my own life, and through the transatlantic trade, I was able to support my independence.

I have written through much of the night in the hope that my past might somehow illumine my future. I have not found my purpose, but I do see in the shadows of memory that I must never again leave my fate in the hands of the Marquis. Tomorrow, as I join all of Sevilla in greeting the treasure ships, I will learn whether my will remains my own. I have gambled everything on a cargo of linen from Laval that went to the Indies, and if I am lucky, I will be rewarded handsomely for my risk. If the cargo was lost, I shall be ruined and will have to return after so many years to the bonded service of the Marquis. Storms and pirates destroy not only those at sea but all of us on land who wait to discover our fate. And yet, strangely, my mind seems as consumed by a woman I have just met as by my long-awaited wealth. It is my sincere hope that Doña Ana's father will bring her to the celebrations tomorrow. Our fair city with gold in her veins is a sight not to be missed.

Night, 15 June 1593

Gold in the Veins of Sevilla

ristóbal and I walked quickly from my apartment down the cobblestone streets of the Barrio Santa Cruz, knowing that it would be of no use taking the carriage. The streets were already teeming with people, as all the tributaries from every neighborhood joined together into a mighty river heading down to the Arenal and the port. The excitement and worry were palpable. Many fortunes would be made and lost on this day, not just my own.

The sunlight was brilliant on the stones of the Torre del Oro, and the gilded dome at the top was like a beacon welcoming the ships. Once used by the emirs to lock up their wealth, this looming tower was now too small to house the gold and especially silver from the viceroyalties of New Spain and Peru that would soon be disgorged from the bellies of the galleons. It had been weeks since the fast sloop arrived in Sanlúcar de Barrameda to announce that the treasure ships were approaching, and their excruciatingly slow progress up the shoals of the river was made all the more treacherous by the hulls of earlier wrecks left there to rot. Prayers have been offered unceasingly and tensions have been high throughout the Empire, and indeed throughout the capitals of Europe. All have held their breath waiting to see if the ships would make a safe landfall or whether English privateers or Moroccan pirates would waylay them.

In front of us the Arenal spread out like a dirt beach from the city walls to the river. It was a scene of chaos, people jostling with mules and carriages going nowhere.

"Move out of the way!" a driver shouted vainly.

A noble lady daintily held up her billowing skirts as she crossed the dry mud, speaking anxiously to her children. "Careful now, come quickly." Barefoot commoners swarmed all around them.

"Cold orange ice! Cold orange ice!" shouted a vendor selling drinks from his pushcart that had just come from the ice pits.

Two caballeros even managed to take offense at being shoved and were engaged in a swordfight. "How dare you refuse to yield to your better!"

"I'll show you who is better—with my sword!"

Not even the arrival of the ships restrained these duelers, who were clearly trying hard to take their minds off their fortunes with a show of outraged honor. I pulled Cristóbal out of the way just in time to avoid his being gored.

Through the stifling summer dust I could see the forest of masts already lined up facing the riverbank, the hulls squeezed side by side. From all over Europe, these ships had brought goods to be sent to the Indies, and the banks were piled high with their cargo—jars of wine and oil, soap, tiles, cloth, timber, and hempen cordage. My nose stung with the smell of salted cod and herring needed to provision these ships, which stood ready to take the New World goods and much of the gold back to the capitals of Europe to pay the King's many debts.

At last there was a great gasp from the crowd as the ships began sailing past the tower. The cannons of the treasure ships fired salvos and the crowd released its apprehension in a deafening chorus of cheers. I patted Cristóbal on the back, and like everyone around us, we embraced. Relief and excitement flooded my body as we continued to shout. The twenty-five bells in the Giralda all began clanging wildly in celebration of the ships' safe return.

Each boat had three crosslike masts on which hung their full square sails, puffed out like the chests of proud conquistadores. Their white flags with red crosses were flapping forward in the wind, pointing to their destination. The rigging spun around the sails and down the decks like intricate spiderwebs. The great war galleys with forty oars on each side rowed along with them. The galleons themselves looked small and fragile. Their high decks rose above the water like unbalanced children's tops. They looked more likely to fall into the sea than cross it, and I reminded myself never to invest in this dubious gamble again. The prized ships were negotiated to shore with the help of smaller boats with three or four oarsmen. Countless small sailing boats—tartans, shallops, and feluccas— darted about, those on board eager to get a better look or to board first. Among them were the black marketeers, trying to exchange cargo before the customs agents came aboard.

As soon as the boats were docked, these agents, looking for taxes, and the officials of the Inquisition, looking for heretical books, inspected the cargoes. Next the whole crowd in one open-jawed stare watched as a dozen wooden carts—each with four strong wheels and pulled by six oxen—were loaded until straining with gold bars. Another two dozen carts were loaded with silver. Each roughly forged ingot was as wide as two fingers, as high as two knuckles, and longer than a man's hand. The wooden wheels creaked under the loads, and the oxen dug their hooves into the hard mud to move the carts forward.

Once the parade of gold and silver was through the city gates, the rest of us were left to spar over the remaining spoils—but these were worth fortunes in themselves. The stevedores and others seeking the chance of a few reales or their share of the booty began unloading the rest of the precious metals, timber, skins and leather, pearls, corals, cocoa, sugar, and countless other goods.

The wealthy were inviting the captains to their homes to negotiate deals, and the rest of the merchants were haggling over price and quantity on the street. Everything and everyone was for sale, and I watched as slaves were marched off to the steps of the Cathedral to be sold as servants and in some cases as secret second wives, or concubines, as they are called in the capitals of the east.

Finally, we reached my ship, the *San Miguel*, where stevedores were already unloading its cargo of leathers and skins. The smell of tar, sweat, and the foul brew of old seawater in the bilge perfumed the air. Huge rats scuttled back and forth over the gangplank as Captain Fadrique Ramírez, standing astride it like the Colossus, beheaded one with his sword. "Two thousand and twelve," I heard him announce with satisfaction. One stevedore was foolishly trying to slink off with a pelt. Captain Fadrique saw him and ran after him with his sword still drawn. He held it to the man's throat as if he were a pirate about to offer the justice of the sea. The man returned the pelt with an apologetic grin, his shoulders dropping meekly. The captain slashed his sword and cut him across the cheek. "That will teach you never to steal from Captain Fadrique!" The man ran off, holding his bleeding cheek, as the captain returned to his lair. I turned to Cristóbal and said, "I'm going to get my gold. Get the carriage and meet me at the Cathedral."

Cristóbal's face was filled with terror. "You are going to get your gold from him?"

"We have a contract," I said, patting my chest. "Don't worry, I'm not stealing from him." Cristóbal's fears were not assuaged and he was only too happy to leave.

Captain Fadrique had lost an eye in a duel but wore no patch to hide where it was sewn shut. His black hat had long lost its feathers. He was more of a buccaneer than a merchant, and at least half of his ship was filled with black-market goods. With wives in half a dozen ports, he admired my gallantry and

116

liked to ask me about the rumors he had heard. I graciously told him nothing more than he already knew by other means.

Introduced to me at the Taberna del Pirata, he had one night made me a proposition that I could not refuse. After he offered me a contract guaranteeing part ownership of the boat and a ten-times return should the voyage survive the dangers of the sea, I had against my better judgment invested my entire remaining wealth with him. I had insisted that our contract conferred part ownership in the boat not only as my collateral for the investment but also as a means of securing a share of future earnings. Under financial duress, Captain Fadrique had agreed to my silent partnership.

I now stepped onto the plank that reached up to the ship's railing, trying to avoid the rest of the stevedores, unloading the cargo like so many marching ants. Once aboard, I made my way to the small door of the captain's quarters. Through the window, I could see him counting his coins and handing one to a colorful green parrot with a yellow neck. I saw him stroke the bird's feathers affectionately. I knocked.

"Who's there?" he barked, placing a fistful of coins in a small chest before quickly closing it.

"It is Don Juan," I said, opening the door without waiting for him to invite me in.

"Ah, Don Juan!" he said in a friendly tone, although the expression on his face told the truth of his feelings. "We did not receive the price we had wanted for the linen," he said, knowing why I had come. The parrot was gnawing on the gold coin, which it grasped tightly in the skeletal fingers of one claw.

Before I could respond, we were interrupted by a thin and breathless sailor whom I had not noticed in the room at first. "Don Juan, is it true?" he said, his open mouth revealing no more than six teeth. "Did you seduce a nun? In the confessional? I heard it in Veracruz. Gave her something to confess, didn't you?"

Out of respect for the sisters who raised me, I do not generally participate in intrigues involving women who have taken up the veil, but this was an exceptional case. The woman was a passionate lady who was fleeing the grief of her husband's untimely death. After our brief encounter, she had returned to the world and had even forgone the habit that widows are expected to wear, choosing instead to love again.

Without taking my eyes off the captain, I answered the sailor. "I am surprised that my missionary work is a topic of discussion in New Spain, but you should know better than to believe everything you hear. I never do." I eyed the parrot, whose black tongue flickered against the coin as it tried to taste it. "Your parrot seems well paid, Captain."

"The slaves fetched a decent price," Captain Fadrique responded, looking down at the chest but not knowing that I had seen its contents through the window. "While we lost on the linen, the slave cargo saved the voyage." He gestured to the porthole, through which we could see the slaves being led out of the hull.

"Slaves are a cruel cargo," I said.

"But a profitable one," he replied with a smile. "We both trade in flesh, do we not?"

"But you enslave it," I said, approaching his table, "while I set it free."

"Ah, but business is different than pleasure, and I am afraid that the price we were paid for the linen was not what we had hoped."

I held out my finger to the parrot, which now held the gold coin in its beak but for the moment had given up its attempt to devour it. The bird climbed on my finger slowly, like an old man whose legs are stiff with gout. Its claws squeezed my finger tightly, digging into my flesh. I tugged the coin out gently. "The price you were paid is immaterial to the price you agreed to pay—four thousand gold escudos, if I remember correctly." I pulled out the rolled contract from my pocket and read the amount. "Four thousand escudos, it was—and is."

"I don't have them," he said slowly.

The garrulous sailor butted in again. "What about the twin sisters—is that true? Last year in Porto Bello, I heard about them. Wasn't that a bit *re-dundant?*" He was smiling from ear to ear, clearly proud of his cleverness.

"Every woman's desire is different, as is every man's skill," I said, drawing my sword swiftly as the parrot squawked and flew around, scattering feathers. I used the tip of my sword not to engage the captain in a duel but to flip open the chest, which revealed his treasure of hastily minted coins. "I just want my fair share," I said. "I can't pass a collection plate around for my missionary work."

Captain Fadrique laughed and then looked at me with a smile that turned quickly into a frown.

"Now, let's see about that payment. I'll take the chest, if you please," I said, keeping my sword close to his face.

He pushed the wooden chest across the table to me. "This is all I have until the slaves are sold."

"I'll take it as a first payment. I will return for the rest."

As I backed out the door, I said, "Always a pleasure doing business with you, Captain Fadrique."

Once down the gangway and ashore, I gave an older boy an escudo and told him to watch the ship day and night. I told him to let me know if it made any preparations for leaving, explaining that I lived above the Taberna Santa Cruz. There would be five more gold coins if he was vigilant. I knew that for this enormous sum, he would not sleep until he had faithfully discharged his duties. I also knew that Captain Fadrique would not leave before he had sold all of the slaves, which could easily take several weeks or a month.

I now joined the procession to the churches, where sailors were giving thanks for their safe passage. "Procession" is perhaps the wrong word, because the whole neighborhood was one long celebration. The explosion of fireworks filled my ears, and the floodgates of rejoicing were released all around me. The dancers and musicians held back nothing; nor did the prostitutes, who had come from every corner of Europe to pick the pockets of the sailors. In the hot summer sun, the city of Sevilla shared its salty sweat, its musty smells, and its joyous song, one serpentine body slithering to the holy Church for its blessing. Happily, it is often hard to remember that this bloated and decadent city is patrolled by the Inquisition. Today it belonged to Bacchus and not the pious.

The heavy chest in my arms prevented me from dancing to the furious rhythm of the guitars, but I knew there would be time to rejoice later that night. I had more than merriment on my mind as I moved quickly through the crowd.

I walked back to the Cathedral, holding the heavy box like a baby in my arms. I looked up at the tower, its bells now silent. In front of the steps, I saw my carriage and Cristóbal, reading as usual. Unlike other coachmen, who spend countless hours idly waiting for their lords and ladies, Cristóbal is never without a book. He has taken my lessons to heart with a passion for reading that I have seen only once before—in myself.

I put the chest in the back and, with my freedom secure, was about to get in the carriage and go searching for Doña Ana. Yet my carriage wheels did not turn even once. If I had relied on my reason and not on my fate, I never would have guessed that I would find her at the cruelest of markets.

*W*ould you pass up this poor beggar, Don Juan? Were you not once as poor?"

In my jealous concern for my treasure, I had not noticed that the brown-robed priest standing next to my carriage was my old tutor, Padre Miguel. He was putting a few copper coins in the wooden bowl of a one-legged beggar, a veteran of our King's endless wars.

"But I am no longer," I said, "and if you continue giving away your coins, you'll soon be as poor as he is." I smiled, and we embraced. It had been many years since I had seen Padre Miguel, who was no doubt in Sevilla to greet the ships with the rest of Andalusia.

"Did I not teach you that to treat the poor without courtesy is to affront the King of Kings?" he said with a reproving smile.

"Yes, yes, I remember," I replied. " 'The one who asks is a messenger sent from heaven to ask you, in the name of God, to give to him.' "

"You remember well," Padre Miguel said.

"How could I ever forget you or your lessons?"

"Then what *are* you willing to give, Don Juan?"

"I now give only to get, Padre." I had not had my coins long enough in my hands to be willing to put them in another's.

"Those are not the words of the boy I knew at the convent."

"I am no longer that boy," I began, but we were interrupted by the call of the slave auctioneer. I looked at the top of the Cathedral steps at the throngs of slaves, largely blackamoors, but also a handful of Moors, and one or two of the Indians that had unwisely chosen to fight against the empire. They all looked broken, their heads and shoulders hanging low. My eyes were drawn to the face of one blackamoor woman whose beauty had been leached from her by hardship. Beauty is not just a quality of face or of skin but of light, and that luster had dimmed in her eyes.

The frantic sound of wailing and crying drew my eyes to a great commotion at the auction block. At the center of the uproar was none other than the Commander, Doña Ana's father. He was pulling a terrified young girl, not older than fourteen, out of the line of slaves. She tried to flee back to an older woman, perhaps her mother.

"He's a bad one," Padre Miguel whispered in my ear, seeing what I saw.

"You know him?" I said as I searched the crowd quickly to see if Doña Ana was there. I discovered her standing next to her dueña, both looking on with pained faces.

"All the Moriscos in my parish know him," Padre Miguel said, referring to the poor souls who despite their conversion from Islam remained outcasts in Christendom. "They call him the Morisco Slayer. You don't want to make an enemy of him, I promise you."

The Commander pulled his sword out and raised it

over his head, preparing to strike the slave girl with the handle. The girl was cowering on the ground and weeping, as was her mother, who was restrained by irons yet trying to come to her daughter's aid.

Just then Doña Ana stepped between her father and the slave. Raising her naked hand to her father's sword, she said, with love more than defiance, "Father, we do not need to separate this girl from her mother."

"We have no need for her mother," the Commander said, and although his tone was stern, it was softened when he spoke to his daughter. "Now, move out of the way while I teach this girl to obey her new master."

"Please, Father, have mercy on this poor girl, who is not yet even my age."

The girl was trembling on the ground, too afraid to move.

"Please, Father, we don't need another slave. María is enough for us."

"I must sell María to buy this one," the Commander confessed. This brought a gasp of panic from the dueña, just as the slave merchant grabbed her by the elbow.

"No, Father! Please, I beg of you. I love María like a mother."

"She is your slave. She has only been your slave, and she will only ever be your slave. But she is old now. We need one who is younger—and more trustworthy." He cast a telling glance at the dueña, one eyebrow raised like a dagger. Was he blaming her for the attack at the hacienda?

"If you love me, let me keep María as my mother. And let this girl go back to hers, who surely loves her as much as you love me."

"María is not your mother! And this girl will learn to obey me or suffer!" he shouted, more insistent than ever, his arm raised and ready to strike.

Impulsively, I stepped forward to block his blow. This time I came to Doña Ana's aid unmasked. "Surely you would not strike an unarmed girl who has given you no offense."

"What business is this of yours?" His cropped hair was just beginning to gray, although his body was clearly still strong. He had a straight military mustache with a black cut of hair going off to either side and an equally straight one down his chin. As I looked into his handsome face, I noticed a scar on his right cheek. He pointed the tip of his blade at me, but I did not draw mine. "Step out of the way, whoever you are, and do not meddle in the affairs of others."

"My name is Don Juan Tenorio, and I seem to have a habit of meddling in the affairs of others."

The crowd laughed, but the Commander was not amused. "So I have heard. Now step out of the way."

I turned my back to him, and addressed the crowd as if an actor onstage. I knew I needed their support to win this battle. "This old dueña is worth nothing to a new master and everything to the maiden she has raised. Would any intelligent slave merchant accept such an unfair barter? Shouldn't he wait until someone can afford to buy mother and daughter? Who will want the mother if they can't have the daughter, too?"

Doña Ana now stepped forward again and, grabbing her father's unarmed hand and the hand of her dueña, held them both to her breast. "Please, Father, reconsider. I beg of you. María will do anything that you ask of her."

The slave merchant handed the Commander back his pouch of coins. The Commander looked at me with menacing eyes but said to Doña Ana out the side of his mouth, "There are no slaves worth buying here." The slave girl, sensing her opportunity, scurried back to her mother's tearful embrace. Choking on his pride, the Commander turned to me and whispered through gritted teeth, "I will avenge this affront."

I bowed my head to him respectfully and cast a smile at Doña Ana. She met my eyes. Her full almond-shaped face was itself a smile, even while her eyes narrowed and her lips pursed into a frown. She quickly turned back to her father. He put away his sword as she thanked him and took his arm. She led him into their carriage by letting herself be led. "Come, María," she said over her shoulder.

"Yes, Doña Ana," her dueña said breathlessly, following them quickly into the carriage before the Commander changed his mind. Although I had helped save her, the dueña frowned at me, once again the vigilant sentinel and obedient servant of the Commander. As Doña Ana stepped into her carriage, she cast a backward glance at me. And as she sat back, I saw the Commander's face, small and bitter and no doubt contemplating his revenge. I knew that he would not wait long for a more opportune and less public moment. I remembered the words of the Marquis: "Honor is more important than life itself, so a Spaniard will never delay the death of a man who has offended him." Such "honor" among my countrymen is not worthy of the name, being merely false pride and vainglory.

"You have made an enemy today," Padre Miguel whispered in my ear.

"I have many enemies, Padre Miguel, but I am blessed to have a few good friends." I patted him on the shoulder. He smiled at me with the fondness of an old and understanding teacher.

Surveying the slave market, he said, "All this misery for gold."

"Unfortunately, we all live and die by it in Sevilla," I said as I placed a handful of gold coins in his palm. His eyes bulged. "Consider it a tithe," I said, "on a recent payment."

Knowing my former livelihood, he asked, "Is this honestly gained?"

"As honest as the transatlantic trade will ever be."

He smiled, satisfied that an officer of the law would not come looking for these coins, and said, "The poor thank you, Don Juan. The poor truly thank you."

We said good-bye, and I rode home in my carriage, a small fortune next to me and a vision of beauty in my mind. Strangely, my stomach was uncharacteristically tense. I wondered about the wisdom of my actions. I had taken a risk for Doña Ana that I had never taken before. My bold actions in pursuit of women have always been under the cover of night. But today I had declared my allegiance in bright sunlight without hiding from her father. Would my gamble pay off, as had my risky investment? What troubled me most was that my actions were prompted by the heated impulses of a lover and not the cool stratagems of a seducer. I know I must regain the dispassion that has always led to my success as a *galanteador*.

After securing my diary and my gold under the floorboards, I will return to the pleasurable purgatory of the Taberna del Pirata. Despite its name, the tavern does not harbor any actual pirates. Many years ago Manuel disbanded the brotherhood as his tavern became increasingly law-abiding. Age makes one cautious, he confessed. However, the tavern continues to give safe haven to sailors, gamblers, criminals, prostitutes, and courtiers like the Marquis who are looking for excitement to jar the numbness of their sated lives. It is there that I can with discretion learn more from the Marquis about the way to unlock Doña Ana's treasure chest. Perhaps I will also soon discover whether my impulsive actions at the slave market were ill conceived or inspired.

Night, 16 June 1593

Taberna del Pirata

A fresh volley of fireworks exploded in the night sky. I looked out the window of the carriage as the red, blue, and green sparks fell from the heavens.

The streets were still teeming with people, but the festivities moved increasingly into the taverns, which glittered with lamplight and shook with laughter. Even at night, the early-summer air was hot and moist in my coach and my fresh clothes already clung to my skin. While our couplings are not limited to this sultry season, we are not so far from the rest of Creation that we do not respond to the sensuality of the summer with our own passion. This, together with the arrival of the fleet, was reason enough for the taverns of the Arenal to surge and sweat and sing with desire.

We arrived in the area called the Corral de las Mancebías, where all the most famous prostitutes resided. These fine ladies attract the most sordid and entertaining crowd. As I descended from my carriage, my nose was assaulted by the putrid stench of rotting sewage. The carpet of rose petals that had been thrown over the returning sailors earlier that day could not cover the ever-present scent of the city for long.

I left Cristóbal to guard the horse and carriage, and he crossed himself as I walked toward the low brick building that housed the Taberna del Pirata. Cristóbal's pious precaution was not completely unfounded. At most brothels one was required to leave one's weapons at the door, a royal decree that was a vain attempt to prevent the fatal consequences of the inevitable jealousies that flared among those patrons who mistook ephemeral lust for true love while in the arms of a prostitute.

"Don Juan!" Margarita said as I entered the courtyard. I kissed her on both cheeks. Margarita had worked at the tavern when I first arrived as a young man. Although she was long past her prime, Manuel and Serena had not tossed her into the street, as was the fate of so many of the prostitutes of Sevilla when they no longer pleased their patrons. Instead, they found a new position for her as they did for all in their extended "family." Margarita was quite skillful with a pistol, as I had seen on more than one occasion, and the weight that she had put on made her an even more imposing presence at the door.

"How are you, Don Juan? How are you?" she said in her deep, throaty voice.

"Never better, never badder, my beautiful Margarita," I replied with a waggish smile as I unbuckled the black leather belt that held my sword and dagger and handed it to her. She took my cheeks in her hand, squeezing them maternally and winking approvingly.

Our greeting was suddenly interrupted by the sound of splintering wood and shattering glass. A fight was in full swing. I smiled. It was good to be home.

Despite the Marquis's generous purchase of my title, my nobility has always been a masquerade, and I have always felt closer to the rope-climbers than the courtiers. Perhaps that is why my mask and my nocturnal life suit me so well. I have always known that any noblewoman who discovered the truth would refuse to marry an illegitimate orphan who had at one time been a common criminal.

I walked up to the door and barely had time to step

aside as a man was punched through it. I waited in the shadows as a Goliath who stood two heads above me lumbered out and picked up the limp body by the shirt with one of his large hands. His victim was out cold, but this did not stop him from punching his unresponsive adversary again, this time knocking him into the street. Margarita and I wisely said nothing as he turned to go back inside, uttering a satisfied grunt. Nothing short of Margarita's pistol would stop this man, and fistfights were not against the royal decree.

I stepped inside and around his back, careful to keep my distance. My eyes adjusted to the dark interior, lit only by the oil lamps on the walls. The old rooms remained as cavernous as a Roman catacomb, but the bodies inside were very much alive, or most of them, at least. The success of the Taberna had allowed Manuel to expand, and he had enclosed part of the street, which was now the central chamber. It had a high ceiling and enormous clay jars of wine along the far wall. The room was filled with tables, some low, with small stools. Others were the proper height for eating and flanked by long benches.

I peered over the heads of the crowd and saw Manuel. He was standing next to one of the tables, which looked as if it had been cobbled together from driftwood. A drunken sailor clung to it as if it were a life raft. A rather ragged-looking black bull's skin with its horns still attached hung on the wall. Judging by its threadbare condition, the skin had no doubt had many owners before finding its resting place here. Next to the bull's skin was a rough print of the Immaculate Conception of the Blessed Virgin Mary. She stood on a crescent moon with stars arrayed around her head. She looked down peacefully and indulgently on her children's merriment in the hot, smoke-filled room.

Ham hocks hung from the ceiling, sweating like everyone else. Hanging along with these legs were strings of onions, garlic, sausages, and even a salted dried fish. On a shelf were dusty jugs of wine that I knew were empty, since only one drink was offered at the Taberna. This red concoction was made from the last press of grapes, to which oranges and lemons were added to hide the fact that the wine's poor quality had been even further watered down. But while Manuel credits his food and drink and the hospitality he provides, it is the prostitutes upstairs that Serena serves who bring most back again and again.

Manuel was laughing, as he often was, joking with the sailors, who listened to him as if to a preacher. To survive the heat of the place, he had his red shirt open to his navel, revealing his abundant chest hair. Around his waist he wore a black apron, on which he was drying a glass. As I made my way toward him, he saw me and began to say my name, but I cut him short with a finger to my lips.

"One never knows," I whispered, "where one's enemies are."

"You have no enemies here—just family."

"Thank you, Manuel. I know the truth of what you say."

It was only after many years that I discovered how a kind and fair man like Manuel had become the leader of the brotherhood, which had counted many far more ruthless members. Serena had revealed to me the story of Manuel's father, Pedro Vásquez de Escamilla, who had been a notorious assassin. He had gone to the gallows with such dignity, saluting the crowd, straightening his mustache, and placing the rope on his own Adam's apple, that his bravery and disregard for death were still the subject of legend. Apparently, this brutal but gallant killer held such respect among the thieves of Sevilla that his son was something of a celebrity. Manuel, however, took after his gentle mother, who had begged him to become a priest and not a criminal like her late husband.

I handed Manuel an escudo.

"Jamón de Aracena," he said, tilting his head to the kitchen, thinking I was paying him extravagantly for a meal. I smiled as my mouth began to salivate at the mention of this choice ham. The meat of these noble pigs melted like butter in one's mouth. The gold coin that I had given him was far more than my payment for the whole leg. I considered it my contribution to the treasury of the now disbanded brotherhood of thieves and to the family who truly did remain at the tavern.

I went to sit at my friends' and my preferred table against the plastered wall with the lantern overhead. From here, with our backs to the wall, we could survey dangers from any approach. I looked up at the balcony, where the prostitutes were calling out and inviting their clients with handkerchiefs. Their white shirts revealed their naked shoulders and were tied across their breasts, loose enough to give a generous impression of what lay beneath. They had flowers in their hair, and their painted faces lit up the room. They were successful, so successful in fact that they made six times more than the doctors who came to treat them. But the doctors did not have to kiss the rotted teeth and smell the rank breath of the sailors, most of whom had some measure of scurvy.

Manuel brought a platter of the choicest carving and a clay mug filled with wine.

"The print is new," I said, gesturing to the image of the Blessed Virgin. "It makes this place look almost respectable."

Manuel smiled. "I am going to get a canvas painting of the Holy Mother for that wall." I had to smile at Manuel's desire to improve his establishment. Noticing my wry smile, he said, "Someday I will be an honorable tavern owner, the kind who would have made my mother proud, may her soul rest in peace."

"Not in my lifetime, I hope. You are already as honorable as any man should be."

"I really would do it," he insisted. "But the money"—he tilted his head toward the prostitutes—"is too good to give up!" We laughed until he had to run off to get a drink for a marooned sailor who was dying of thirst and letting everyone know it.

The Marquis and the other members of our libertine band, Don Hernán and Don José, were just arriving. In the years after the purchase of my nobility, these two noble disciples of the Marquis welcomed me into their fraternity, Don Hernán immediately and Don José more begrudgingly. As my reputation grew, Don José's outright disdain had turned to respect and, ultimately, genuine affection and, I dare say, admiration tinged with envy. I saluted all three of them warmly with a wave, which met nods of recognition across the crowded room.

Tonight I was surprised to see Alma on Don José's arm. Only my friend Don José would bring a courtesan with him to a brothel. Like other Tusonas, Alma played the part of the noble lady. As a member of this highest class of her profession, she wore high-heeled shoes and a flowing gown, both of which were prohibited to common prostitutes. Only the revealing bodice that she would unveil for the right offer was proof of her true intentions. Tonight Alma added to her allure with a cloak of transparent silk, which she used seductively to cover her right eye and reveal her left.

The Marquis walked through the crowd, careful not to rub shoulders with anything that might rub off. Don José was now married, yet devotedly unfaithful, and almost before he had entered the doorway, he was accosted by prostitutes whom he frequented regularly. He was trying to get Alma to join him with one of these.

"I am enough for any man, and more than enough for you, Don José," Alma said, and tossed her head.

Serena arrived to save a situation that could have

turned ugly. "Doña Alma's charms are too expensive for our humble establishment, but not to worry, Don José, we work hard to assist all our patrons with their 'special' needs." Don José was quickly on his way upstairs with a prostitute on each arm. The red and yellow feathers in his hat and his proud strut gave him the appearance of a rooster on his way to the henhouse. Before he could sit and be social, Don José always needed some "assistance." Tonight he was apparently in need of a great deal of assistance. Serena and Alma were laughing together, perhaps at Don José, perhaps at men in general. They certainly knew them well.

Don Hernán had arrived with his mistress, who was holding on to him possessively and darting menacing looks at the prostitutes who were circling. Poor Don Hernán did not seem happy, despite his mistress's constant attention. Endlessly torn between his wife and his mistress, he always seemed to be longing for the one he was not with. He looked even more anxious than usual as he watched the giant sailor threatening yet another patron.

As the Marquis, Don Hernán, and his mistress sat at the long table with me, the Marquis was approached almost immediately by a prostitute named Blanca. She could obviously spy the best-paying customer. He spent more on a meal than the sailors earned in three months at sea. Blanca slid in next to him and rested her hand on his inner thigh.

Manuel quickly brought more mugs of wine and welcomed his noble guests. "What's wrong with it?" he asked, seeing that I had not yet devoured the ham. "Your mother would not be happy," he said, only half joking.

"I am afraid I am an orphan, so I know no better."

"Then listen to your Mama Manuel: Eat up. A man cannot live on wine, women, and song—even you."

As Manuel left, the Marquis said with a grimace, hesitantly sipping at his mug of wine, "I think a man is better living off the women here than the wine."

I tried to do as Manuel had insisted and, forgoing the knife chained to the table for common use, pulled out my own meat knife from my boot. While my folding knife was no different from those carried in the boots of other caballeros, mine was hidden in a secret seam that made it difficult to detect. It had proved invaluable on numerous occasions over the years. The smooth handle was made of carved bone, and I now used the metal blade to put the oily red and white strips of meat in my mouth. I chewed the tender white fat and washed it down with a swig of wine. As refined as the Marquis had made my palate, I still enjoyed the house vintage, even with its musty scent of old oak, earth, and pitch.

"Don Pedro, I was wondering—" I began, prepared to ask him about Doña Ana, but I was interrupted midsentence by Alma, who had joined us.

"Don Juan without a woman in his arms is like the Giralda without a bell," Alma said as she sat down on my lap. I smiled as I remembered the bells clanging in the tower earlier that day. Alma was clearly feeling lonely tonight, without a patron, and was turning to her old tutor for entertainment. She luxuriated on the couch of my body like Cleopatra and flipped her outstretched arm over my shoulder. She curled it around my neck and stroked my face with her fingers, ensnaring me like poor defenseless Mark Antony, who would forsake his country for the charms of a woman. My opportunity to speak with the Marquis was lost. He was on his way upstairs with Blanca but would not be long. His sojourns upstairs were always brief.

"Ah, my cunning Alma, you are right to see the injustice in this situation—or at least the opportunity."

"I know a man with a need when I see him—and a man with skill. You have rung as many bells in your tower as I have in mine."

"I could hardly have done so, since your bell tower rings out the watch every hour on the hour." Don Hernán and his mistress laughed, and Alma sat up and pretended to be offended.

She moved her face close to mine, so close I could feel her hot breath. "What you have lacked in quantity, you have made up for in quality."

"My dear Alma, but your church is much more lucrative than mine, for you know that I am not paid nor do I pay for affections." I have always believed that a woman's affections can be genuine only if they are surrendered willingly. Favors that are bought must be their counterfeit.

"For another chance to chime with the great Don Juan, I would not charge."

"But that would be stealing."

"Consider it charity."

"My poor underserved Alma, I am not a priest but a gambler, and what challenge would it be to seduce a woman who must by her chosen profession lie with any man willing to pay the right price?"

Her eyebrow arched as she turned her head to the side. She was obviously offended at my stating the pecuniary truth about her affections but took it as a further challenge. Two guitars and a tambourine began to play as if in accompaniment to our repartee. "What is it about you that has made you so irresistible to women?" she said, studying me closely. "Is it the gentleness of your face and your long, curled eyelashes . . ."

". . . that make a woman think that she is looking in the mirror of her own desire?" I said, completing her thought.

"Or is it your full, ripe lips . . ."

". . . that a woman knows will allow her to taste the sweetness of her own pleasure?" I had often lamented my full lips, the mark of slaves and bastard children.

"Or is it the light that shines in your eyes . . ."

". . . that illumines the hidden folds of a woman's soul?"

"Yes, that's it," she confirmed.

"This, my inquisitorial Alma, any man can possess. While he can do little to change his physical form, the burning flame of his eyes is wholly dependent on the passion of his soul."

"Someday I will have you again, Don Juan, you can be sure of it."

"Your persistence is a virtue, but virtue does not always win over vice."

Alma threw her head back indifferently and stood up. "Eventually, I will win. A woman always does." She let the music caress her body as her head rocked back and forth in time and her arms rose above her head, her hands clapping in rhythm. The tempo of the music began to quicken. The crowd clapped and snapped their fingers along with the driving pace. As if possessed, Alma began to dance the *zarabanda,* the dance that had been banned by royal decree ten years ago for its lasciviousness. But nothing was banned at the Taberna del Pirata, and the crowd responded with shouts and cheers of appreciation. A large circle spread around her. To have the opportunity to watch a courtesan as beautiful as Alma dance the *zarabanda* was a rare privilege for all present, including me.

The priests decry the *zarabanda* as the last stop on the Road to Perdition and warn that it was created by the Devil with the Limp. But I say desire is older than humanity, created on the sixth day with the animals, and it has a power that is greater than our ability to control it. It is this power that the seducer draws upon as the sorcerer uses his spells. Before monogamy, before marriage, before Church, and before King, there was seduction. Women as well as men long for its embrace and need the fire of lust that was stolen from the gods to survive in the bitter cold of life.

Alma's hips began to swing from side to side as her arms snaked above her head, and then her body was one wave rising up from the ground and cresting at her fingertips. As the tempo increased, she began to spin, her hair whirling around her, as if she were in a trance of her own pleasure. The music slowed, as did Alma's movements, which accentuated the sensual, slithering beauty of a woman's body. Then she raised her hands above her head gracefully, with her fingertips touching, forming a full moon. She twirled quickly and then slowly as she circled the room and finally stopped in front of me. She held out her hand and beckoned with her delicate fingers. I laughed and waved her away but she held out her hand insistently and now the crowd was clapping and pounding the tables to the feverish rhythm of the guitars and tambourine. I tried to wave her off again, but she insisted, beckoning me with the red-painted nails of her skillful fingers. Alma and the crowd were not to be denied.

The Marquis had just returned with Blanca and was frowning at the idea of a noble dancing in public for peasants. As I looked at his raised eyebrows, I took her hand. No title or rank would rob me of the pleasure in dance. She pulled me into the middle of the room. I matched her stance, raising one arm above my head and resting the fingertips of the other on my hip. As the guitarists began to pluck the strings, we marched around each other, stamping our feet into the ground. Together we pantomimed the dance of seduction—the rejection while inviting, the invitation while rejecting. I clapped my hands above my head as I circled around her. She approached. Her eyes looked into mine, our lips almost touching. I felt her warm and panting breath on my face like a summer wind. She drew back, and I seized her hand. She spun like a spool into me and we held each other's waists as we circled together with increasing speed, matched by the meter of the guitar and tambourine. The room became a whirling blur of lights and sound. The rhythmic clapping reached a crescendo, the beat as rapid as the heart of a breathless woman. Then it stopped abruptly and we separated. I offered her the forward dance steps one last time, and she accepted, extending her hand. As I approached, she rubbed her thumb and forefinger together—the crowd exploding in laughter—to make it clear that this dance was about commerce and not courtship. It was my turn to reject her with backward steps, which brought a playful slap and more thunderous laughter.

Our dance was overtaken by three prostitutes, Inés, Leonor, and Blanca. They were not to be upstaged in their own theater and stepped onto one of the long tables so that all could view them. They wore the ankle-length dresses that distinguished them from the proper ladies and courtesans like Alma. The guitars and tambourine sang out with even greater joy for these local goddesses. Their dresses had two rows of fringes that shook as they did. Their breasts danced against the fabric of their low-cut bodices, and their hips undulated to the quickening music. The smooth curve of their calves and the promising fullness of their thighs disappeared into the folds of the fabric. In their hands and around their necks they thrust their scarves back and forth wildly as one followed the other in these improvised dance steps. Alma sat at the other end of the table, her head turned away and her chin raised.

As I watched their ebullient display of breast and thigh, I marveled at the beauty of their womanhood, of all womanhood. Woman is the masterwork of God, the last of Creation and endowed with the divine power to create new life. As if to confirm the truth of these ruminations, the women picked up their skirts and revealed their legs up to the miraculous curve of Creation. They wore nothing underneath, which must have aided them in the many watches of their work. If it had not been for their skillful handling of their skirts, they would have revealed everything—but good shopkeepers know not to give away the store. Just the suggestion of what lay beyond the folds of their dresses and the curve of their hips was enough to have the men gripping their chests and pulling out their hair.

The hips of the prostitutes vibrated like a bell that had been rung frantically to announce a fire in the city. Abruptly the music stopped. Inés stepped down and threw her scarf over my neck and pulled me back into the corral. The other two followed and threw their scarves over me as well. The music burst out anew with a feverish rhythm. Their scarves descended around my waist as I raised my hands overhead. We spun together like a wagon wheel until the spokes gave way and they whirled into the grateful crowd. Undaunted, they returned, placing their hands on my shoulders. Inés, the ringleader and troublemaker, clawed my chest to my waist as she slithered her body down. The others followed her until they were all bowing before me, as if I were a sultan. I pulled them up one by one. It was my turn to prostrate to their divinity, and I squatted before them with my hands clasped devoutly. Inés and then the others each raised a leg and placed their sharp heels against my chest. They pushed and I fell backward, rolling across the room into a standing farewell. The sound of the crowd was deafening as I sat down next to Alma.

"They have no artistry," she said, disapproving of the lewdness of the prostitutes' dance.

"This crowd doesn't have the stamina for art."

I had hoped that this might be my opportunity to speak with the Marquis about Doña Ana, but to my surprise, standing next to him was an unfamiliar man whose presence would make any such conversation impossible. He wore an old soldier's uniform, a large-brimmed hat trimmed with feathers and pulled low, and a cape covering his leather doublet. His outfit gave him the unmistakable look of an assassin.

Secrets Never Stay Buried

"May I present Señor Ignacio Álvarez de Soria, formerly the Commander of Calatrava's closest lieutenant and confidant," the Marquis said. The man was stone-faced, but his eyes darted around the room to see if anyone had heard his name. It did sound vaguely familiar. It was clear that, assassin or not, he had, like so many soldiers, turned to a life of crime to supplement his paltry pension. The Marquis handed him a pouch of coins, which brought the first smile to the man's face. He raised his hat slightly and nodded in gratitude before leaving without a word.

"That man," whispered the Marquis, knowing that I would be curious, "has just revealed to me where all the Commander's secrets are buried."

"No doubt you will have them dug up," I said.

"There is no need. Secrets never stay buried."

I worried about what evil plan the Marquis had in mind for the Commander and possibly even for Doña Ana. I had seen him ruin more than one young maiden to get to her father. "What are Doña Ana's secrets?" I asked, trying not to sound too interested.

"Doña Ana's secrets?" he said with interest. "I said that he knew where the *Commander's* secrets were buried."

"Are they not the same?" I answered quickly.

"Well, yes, it is true that the sins of the fathers are always visited on the sons . . . and daughters."

"And what would those sins be?"

"Well, I am afraid you were too busy dancing with the prostitutes to hear them."

"Just harmless entertainment."

"Disgraceful," the Marquis replied. "I think the King would be dismayed to hear that you have been dancing with prostitutes instead of heeding his command."

"You know I cannot obey his command."

"You have no choice."

"Then I must flee."

"Our Most Catholic King rules half the world."

"Then I must flee to the other half."

The Marquis shook his head in disappointment. "You were once loyal to your King—and to me."

"You know I remain loyal."

"Really? At one time I would have sent you to discover the Commander's secrets, but you are now too busy dancing with your *prostitutes*."

"Only dancing, Don Pedro."

"Well, let us say it is fortunate that the Commander's *loyal* lieutenant had gambling debts needing repayment."

"A gambler? But he so cleverly dresses the part of an assassin."

"Oh, he is an assassin."

"Are you planning to kill the Commander?" I asked directly, unable to hide my interest.

"Your concern surprises me," the Marquis said.

"I just wonder what strategy you had in mind," I said, pretending once again to be his faithful lieutenant.

"To take a man's honor is worse than to take his life, is it not?"

"This *is* what you taught me," I said.

"And you learned quite well." I thought about my dishonoring of the Commander that afternoon and realized I had not learned so well. Again my stomach tightened, and I questioned my earlier actions, but now

146

I also feared the danger that the Marquis's ambitions might pose for Doña Ana.

Serena arrived at our table, having escorted Don José downstairs from his long sojourn in the company of his assistants. An experienced proprietor, Serena knew a satisfied customer when she saw one, and as she let go of Don José's elbow, she said, "only the best for you, Don José."

"Who needs fine wine when you have such fine women?" he replied. Alma's pursed lips revealed that she was still smarting from his earlier rejection.

"Tell Don Juan," Serena demanded, "since he does not think that my girls are good enough for him. Don Pedro has ruined him."

"Me?" the Marquis said. "Do I not frequent your girls regularly?"

"Don Juan," she said, "stealing a woman's chastity is not the only pleasure in life."

"It was Manuel, you forget, who taught me to steal. The Marquis just taught me what was worth stealing." Everyone laughed except Serena, although she smiled graciously.

"When," she continued, "are you going to get married, have a family, and then, like every other husband in Sevilla, enjoy the finest pleasures of lordly life with my girls?"

"You are not the only one who wants me to marry," I said, raising an eyebrow and looking at the Marquis.

"Tell him, Don José," she persisted, "tell him about my girls."

"They are the finest of the fine, the choicest of the choice," Don José said with a grin.

"But there is one girl who is finer than them all," said Manuel as he approached and grabbed his wife around her full waist. He brushed back the gray strands of hair that had escaped her bun and gave her a kiss that made all of us seasoned libertines blush.

"I'll see you later when all these youngsters have gone to sleep," she said with a knowing backward glance. She rolled up the sleeves of her white shirt and smoothed the plain maroon vest and green skirt over her mature woman's body. She let out an expectant sigh and went to recruit some more customers. There was a true smile on Manuel's lips as he watched her go. Unlike the dust, smoke, and dirt that settled on everything in the tavern, his countenance retained a youthful shine, as did hers.

"Tell us," Don José finally said, breaking the long, respectful silence that had followed this marital intimacy. "How do you do it? All these beautiful young women around and still you only have eyes for your wife."

"My lords," he replied, as if he were a diplomat who had just been consulted on a vital affair of state, "happy marriage is the greatest wealth a man can possess, and one that a peasant can have as easily as a king." Always the merchant, he added, "This wealth can be yours for only a handful of reales."

"Surely that price is too high," Don José responded.

"No knowledge is worth more to a man's happiness,"

Manuel insisted. "A handful of reales is a bargain, if you've seen what a living hell a bad marriage can be."

"'Happy marriage' is a contradiction in terms," the Marquis said bluntly.

"There's no hope of happiness in my marriage," Don José said, placing a handful of reales on the table. "But my question is hardheaded—how does a healthy, full-blooded man such as you stop himself from eating up all of his own . . ." He searched for the right word in his limited vocabulary and settled on "*profits*."

"The answer, my lord, is simple, though not easy— if it were easy, we'd be out of business." We all looked at him eagerly. "To be faithful to one's wife, a married man can look but not touch."

"Ah," I said, "then may the Blessed Virgin Mary forever save me from the temptation of marriage," which brought a good round of laughter.

Don Hernán, however, was still brooding, now without his mistress, who had gone to reapply her face paint. "As Don Pedro said, marriage is no guarantee of happiness," he admitted. "Nor marriage and a mistress. My wife is jealous of my mistress, and my mistress is jealous of my wife and wants endless proof of my love."

"Is that why you are fighting the bulls tomorrow?" Alma asked. One's devotion to a woman was a common reason for men to brave the bulls.

"Yes," he said morosely. "I don't know. Perhaps I should end it. My wife has given me three good sons, and she loves me. She really does."

We all stared at poor Don Hernán. He was living in the wrong city at the wrong time in history. In Sevilla everything has become a gamble and every man puts his coins down on more than one card. The riches that pour in unceasingly have devalued money, marriage, and the very meaning of life. To be faithful to one's wife seems like an unnecessary penance to almost all men—with the seeming exception of Manuel. This is no doubt part of my reluctance to marry. I am not willing to wed a woman just to be unfaithful and untrue. I have seen repeatedly what endless suffering such duplicity inevitably brings.

"Don Juan," Don Hernán asked miserably, "how do you keep all of your women happy?"

"Like a priest is married to the body of the Church, I am married to the body of womanhood, in awe of every woman and beholden to none. In short, I marry none of them." The obviousness of this answer brought more laughter.

"Surely," Don Hernán insisted, "you must feel something for the women you seduce."

"A libertine," I replied, "must feel everything in his skin and nothing in his heart." The Marquis was looking on with admiration.

"How," Don Hernán continued, "can you feel nothing in your heart?"

"You must build a fortress around it and never lower a drawbridge for any damsel. You, my friend, have let two women into your castle and their jealousy will destroy it—and you."

"Don't you care about any woman?"

"Caring about every woman means that you care about none more than the others."

"I cannot have any woman, like you, Don Juan, so I must care about the two I have."

"There is one woman Don Juan cannot have," said the Marquis mischievously.

All eyes turned to the Marquis. "And who could withstand the charms of Don Juan?" Don José asked incredulously.

"Doña Ana."

"Who?" Don José asked blankly.

"The beautiful and virtuous Doña Ana, daughter of Don Gonzalo de Ulloa, a Commander of the Order of Calatrava."

"How could she resist the advances of Don Juan?" Don Hernán said dubiously.

"She is a woman who will give her heart to no man," the Marquis said, back to his intrigue with the Commander. He was issuing the challenge. I now realized that his previous warning had just served to goad me on. I played along.

"It is not to a woman's heart that I appeal," I said as everyone laughed. "I speak first to her mind, the organ so undervalued by most men, and through her mind to her loins, which have a will of their own, just like a man's."

"Doña Ana's mind is incorruptible."

"It was you who taught me that no woman is incorruptible."

151

"Every rule is proved by its exception," the Marquis replied. "Doña Ana's mind is indeed incorruptible, but everyone has a secret with which you can possess their soul."

We all drew back as we took a breath, trying to absorb the devilish meaning of his words. I knew that the Marquis was purposely playing with my earlier concern for Doña Ana, and I refused to let him orchestrate my emotions or my actions. He was trying to use me to ruin Doña Ana or her father, whether with proof from this diary or some spy who might be watching her window. I refused to fall into his trap. I excused myself and told the others that I needed to go.

"Don Juan?" the Marquis said. "I hope to see you at my house tomorrow for the *holy* feast and to review the *holy* procession." The feast day was one of my favorites, but I could not suffer the procession, which the Inquisitor would use to demonstrate his power.

"I am honored by the invitation, Don Pedro, but I have no interest in watching the Inquisitor swagger through the streets." The eyes of my companions widened at my brazenness.

"You should be more circumspect in your references to the Inquisitor," the Marquis replied. "In his eyes your heresy is not just that you indulge in fornication out of wedlock—"

"Along with every noble in Spain," Don José said, coming to my aid.

"—but that you claim your indulgence is not a sin."

I let his accusation linger in the air and then came to

the defense of mankind. "As long as desire is banished from the Kingdom of heaven, there will always be a long line at the Gates of Hell."

"I do hope you'll change your mind—at least about the party," the Marquis replied. After a long pause, he added more soberly, "Doña Ana will be there." I bowed and said good-bye to my friends, to Alma, and to Serena and Manuel. I left the tavern not to indulge in a woman but to abstain from one. Yet having grown up in the Church, I have never liked fasting, and so was grateful for the feast that awaited me on the carriage ride home.

A Thousand Nights with a Stranger

As we rode by the Cathedral toward my lodgings, I saw in the waning moonlight a blackamoor woman. As I looked closer I saw that it was Fátima, a slave from Mozambique who had arrived with the Portuguese. We had met when I was attending a masquerade party at the home of her mistress, Duchess Cristina. Fátima was serving the guests dinner, and I followed her back to the kitchen for my dessert. Although the seduction was unsuccessful, I did succeed, after much insistence, in convincing her to tell me about her life. It turned out to be far more interesting than those of the nobles gathered that night.

A mature woman, perhaps my age or older, Fátima had been separated from a husband and two sons for over a decade since she was sold into slavery. She was given the baptismal name of María but clung to her own name proudly and answered only to it. As the carriage approached, I could see the suffering in her face as well as the long neck and proud head that refused to be bowed.

Her high cheekbones descended gracefully to her full lips. "A beautiful queen should ride in a carriage," I said as we came alongside her. She kept walking right past us but flashed a nervous and guarded glance over her shoulder.

"Don Juan!" she exclaimed, her face lighting up like a flame that scattered the shadows around her.

"At your service, Doña Fátima," I said, opening the door and extending my hand. She smiled. I clasped her hand and pulled her in.

Cristóbal knew to take the long route to her house, which gave us a chance to get reacquainted. I looked at Fátima sitting proudly on the cushions of my coach. These enclosed coaches have been the source of great controversy since they became fashionable on the streets of Sevilla. Their comfort and privacy allow them to become moving bedchambers, which is why mine has served as my very own cloud of Zeus.

"What brings you out into the dangerous streets of our city at this hour?" I asked, unable to restrain my curiosity.

"I was escaping a greater danger."

"What do you mean?"

She hung her head and said, "He tried to rape me."

"Who? Duke Octavio?"

"No. He is away, as always, in Naples with his mistress, leaving the chief steward free to . . ."

"What did you do?"

"I cut him."

As she spoke about her ordeal, I gave up all hope of seduction. "My carriage is at your disposal."

"I have nowhere to go," she said, her eyes darting at me and then away. If she returned, she would have to face the chief steward again, but to run away was far more dangerous.

"Will you be safe?"

"I don't think he will try again," she said with a triumphant smile.

"Cristóbal, take us to Duchess Cristina's."

I settled back into my seat, trying to be content with my role as Good Samaritan, though I could not help noticing the long column of her neck, the graceful slope of her chin, and the redness of her lips, which glistened in the light of the carriage lantern.

Fátima reached inside her blouse and pulled out a small square pouch made of cloth. It hung around her neck by a fraying string. "This holds my husband's spirit," she said, cradling the amulet lovingly in her palms. "It has kept him close to my heart for eleven years and three months." She turned her face to me slowly and there was sadness and desperation in her voice. "I'm starting to lose him, Don Juan. I can no longer feel his skin or remember his touch. Not even in my dreams."

I heard her unspoken request and took her hand in

mine. Although her fingers were chapped from washing and callused from working, they were still long and graceful. I kissed the sensitive skin at the center of her palm, where some say they can read one's fate in the broken lines. Her future I had no knowledge of, but whatever it might be, I was determined to add just a few more moments of joy.

Her soft hand pressed against my face and her fingers felt my rough cheek. I gently stroked her neck as she closed her eyes and did not resist my hand.

"Take us home, Cristóbal," I barked. What this daughter of Eve needed could not be given on a hasty carriage ride.

We held each other, and I kissed her face and lips slowly. Her breath quickened. The carriage finally stopped, and we raced up the three flights of stairs to my apartment and then up the ladder to my rooftop observatory. She ran to the edge like a girl and smiled as she looked down at the dancing and laughing that still filled the plaza below. The sound of the guitars echoed around the square and rose up as if played for our amusement alone. We looked over the terracotta roofs to the heaven-kissing Giralda. The moon was a halo around its crown. The balcony where the bells hung at its summit was alight with glowing lanterns in honor of the ships' safe return. As Fátima stared in wonder at its beauty, I stared in wonder at hers, the raven-black skin of her face aglow in the moonlight.

"Doves," she said as she heard them cooing, and turned her head to look at the wooden cage.

"Messenger pigeons," I said, but neglected to mention that I used them for my lovers to send me notes. While these messengers only allow notes to return home, they are more reliable than the lovers' mail, since there is no chance that the notes, once in flight, will be intercepted.

I opened one of the small doors of their home and let her hold a white dove. "Set it free," I said.

She looked uncertain but I encouraged her. Smiling, she threw the bird up into the welcoming night sky, and her outstretched arms stayed poised in midair as if she too had taken flight. I touched the tips of one of her wings and drew my fingers down its length. Her arms floated down slowly.

She turned to face me, and I touched her lips with my fingertips and traced down her neck to her chest. As I reached her heart, she grasped my hand and pressed it into the flesh between her breasts. Two tears streamed down her face but she was smiling even more deeply, her head rocking from side to side gently. I cradled the back of her neck with one hand as she clung to the other, which was resting on her chest. Then she pulled my hand slowly over to her breast, and I grasped it whole as if it were a sacred chalice. She arched her body back, pushing her chest toward me, and I kissed her neck and then her mouth. I stroked her body through her white blouse and green skirt, and she sighed and ran the outstretched palms of her hands down my face and chest.

"Come with me," I said, pressing her hand and leading

her up another small ladder to a walled lookout, built to see whether ships had arrived at the river. From it, we also saw the crenellated wall of the Real Alcázar, its peaks looking like the points of Poseidon's trident. We could even see the Torre del Oro down by the river, where the Moors not only stored their gold but would also observe the stars in the sky.

The vista that I was interested in tonight was not the river of commerce, or of stars, but the river of Fátima's desire. We fell down into each other's arms. I had placed my cape underneath us and there were many silk pillows that allowed us to recline in the fashion of the Moors.

We were both in a fever, but I went slowly, the goal being to prolong the delirium. Fátima's skin had the taste of salt and of the lemon rind that she must have used to perfume herself. It was as enlivening as a street vendor's refreshment. I slowly undid her buttons, pausing after each one for her to take a breath. She revealed her small breasts timidly, and I sat looking into her eyes and smiled. She relaxed and let her blouse fall away, and I held up my hand as if touching her through the ether. She quivered. I could feel her heat even before her skin. Restraint is the defining strength of a true caballero, since any boor can thrust but only a skilled swordsman can tarry.

She approached my lingering fingertips until my hands and lips moved slowly over her neck and chest, and then around her waist and thigh, as her skirt slid down her legs.

I undid my own clothes with one hand while keeping the other on her body. I brushed her skin with my fingertips and gently drew my nails down. How many are the poets who have compared a woman's body to a guitar, but what they neglect to reveal is that every stretch of skin has its own sound, and strumming them all together makes the most beautiful music ever created. In the end, a woman offers her beauty in exchange for a man's skill, and her body is revealed in equal measure to his ability.

Our tongues were lost in each other's mouths. My fingers trailed down her back and graceful buttocks and around to her womanhood. Shuddering as I stroked her, I felt the riverbed of her desire moisten, but I did not enter her until her banks were overflowing. When I finally did, her eyes and mouth opened widely, and she swallowed several short breaths of life. She pulled me toward her so that our cheeks touched and our eyes stared past each other, hers across a continent and mine, strangely, across the countryside. Doña Ana's face floated to mind and her laughter echoed like madness.

It startled me from the practiced rhythms of lust, but I shook her from my head and continued to focus on Doña Fátima's beautiful face and melodious song. For an entire watch of the night I plucked music from her body, the rhythm fast and then slow, as the tension rose ever higher. At last she panted and I heeded her whispered request. Her body stiffened as we both felt the Supreme Pleasure pulse through us. We relaxed into the pool of our gratification. I feathered the softness of her thighs and buttocks. They were moist, and I knew that pleasure filled every inch of her body.

She turned onto her side and lay there completely within herself. Her eyes were closed, and a subtle smile played upon her face. As I lay beside her, I gently drew my fingertips along her. Her thigh rose like a gentle hillside and then fell steeply to her waist. Although the moon had now set, her skin was aglow, luminous as the moon itself. I could feel the light emanating from her soul. When a woman feels the fullness of her pleasure, her soul rises up above her body. It is for this reason that there is nothing more beautiful than a woman whose desire has truly been satisfied, for there is no physical form as radiant as the soul that dwells inside every woman. The priests tell us that the body is like a thorn to the soul, but I have seen the truth—it is only from the body that the soul blossoms, and our soul cannot be separated from it in life. My hand tingled as I felt this holiness surrounding her skin.

Through pleasure Fátima's body had been transmuted into a substance more precious even than gold. I drew my fingertips over her skin and felt her soul palpably. As I caressed her, I thought of one of the alchemical texts I had read in the Marquis's secret library. Its author had recommended putting base metal out under the full moon, conjecturing that moonlight was the subtlest form of matter and the most substantial form of spirit. He had come close to understanding the deep power of the Divine Creator but had mistaken the heavenly body above for the womanly body below. Is not the river of a woman's desire the very elixir of life? Through her gates can one not find eternal life, which is nothing less than the divine act of creation?

As the first light of morning started to glimmer in the distance, I kissed her, and she opened her eyes. Together we dressed. "The Duchess speaks of you constantly, wondering always about your return," she said as she finished buttoning up her blouse. "I now know why," she added.

I placed a dove in a small cage and handed it to her. "Give this to the Duchess. Tell her you saw me in my carriage and that I gave it to you for her. Perhaps in her anticipation, she will be lenient on you."

She smiled at the gift and perhaps also at knowing that her mistress would never suspect she and her slave had had the same lover. We descended the ladder to my living room and then to the stable, where I had to rouse Cristóbal from his hammock. He startled awake and fell out onto the floor. We tried to muffle our laughter.

"Cristóbal, please take Doña Fátima home."

"Yes, my lord." I knew he would drop her off discreetly down the street from her home. Cristóbal was always trying to protect the reputation of the women who were making mine.

As she stepped into the carriage, I smiled and bowed my head respectfully. "I hope I have helped you to forget your hardship, Doña Fátima, if only for a few pleasurable moments."

The smile vanished from Fátima's face. "My hardship?" she said. "I can never forget my hardship, not even for a moment."

"Surely skillful hands and lips can replace pain with pleasure, if only briefly."

"I am grateful, Don Juan, for your kindness to a slave like me, and your skill is even greater than the rumors. But in my mind you were my husband, the father of my children."

"Then he too must have had skill."

"Not like yours, but there was more pleasure in one kiss from the man I loved than a thousand nights with a stranger."

I was trying to understand how her words could possibly be true. She must have seen my incomprehension, for she answered the question I did not ask. "My husband was not just skillful with his hands. He was skillful with his heart."

As I stared through her, I imagined her back in her village in Mozambique, her husband holding her hand and kissing her lips while her children laughed and tried to squeeze between them. And then my reverie ended.

I knocked on the door of the carriage and Cristóbal encouraged Bonita. I watched the wagon wheels start to spin. As I looked down, I saw the amulet lying on the cobblestones.

"Wait!" I ran after the carriage and handed it to Fátima.

She clutched it to her chest and smiled at me. "Thank you, Don Juan."

I knocked once more lightly on the carriage door and Cristóbal rode on again.

As I slowly climbed the stairs to my room, I thought about Fátima's comments. I caressed them in my mind, uncomprehending and yet intrigued. I had seen the suffering love causes. And yet I had known the great pleasure of which she spoke. But what troubled me even more than Fátima's words were Doña Ana's apparition and her laughter in my head. To lie with one woman and think of another was a betrayal of the Libertine Code that I had learned from the Marquis. There was only one way I knew to put out the fires of lust that Doña Ana had awakened.

Fortunately, I will not have to wait long to continue her seduction. I will suffer the Inquisitor in the procession and go to celebrate our lord and the holiness of his flesh.

Morning, 17 June 1593

Corpus Christi

I dressed in my most festive daytime attire, a rose-colored doublet and hat and salmon breeches. My hat was plumed by a large green ostrich feather that crested and sloped down to my shoulder. I always wore light colors by day and dark maroons and blacks at night, when it was advantageous to blend into the shadows.

Cristóbal took me to the Marquis's palace, which overlooked the Plaza de San Francisco, where the procession came to an end and where the bulls would be fought later that afternoon. The Marquis had invited me and others to his house to watch from his balcony.

As I descended from the carriage, the heels of my leather shoes crushed the sprigs of rosemary that had been strewn over the cobblestones. Their pungent fragrance entered my nostrils and reminded me of the perfumed scent of womanhood, which still lingered on my fingertips from the night before. The rosemary only partly succeeded in masking the equally pungent aroma of horse droppings left by the many carriages that had abandoned wives and daughters into the safekeeping of the Marquis. While the prominent men of the city were preening their feathers in the procession, most of their wives, and their daughters who were close to marriageable age, would be left defenseless on the Marquis's balcony. My interest today, however, was in only one daughter, and from what I had seen, she was hardly defenseless.

The Marquis's palace was an enormous brown stone edifice with three curved balconies and many large windows surrounded by decorative columns. Two guards stood at the door, and over their clothes they wore the sleeveless blue tunic that bore the Marquis's coat of arms, with a castle and lion embroidered in gold. Their ruffs were stiff and their gloved hands held decorative spears, the small blades worthless in an attack. Without turning their heads, they smiled at me, knowing that I was friend, not foe.

I stepped through the stone archway and past the

enormous green wooden doors with their golden nipple-shaped studs. As I did, I left the bright light and blazing heat of the late morning behind. The entryway was dark and cool, like a cave. The few rays of sunlight slanted humbly and powerlessly on the floor. Overhead were ornately painted wooden beams.

Immediately I felt at home, having slept in one of the palace's twenty-two rooms for two years. During that time, I could only begin my studies, but then continued for ten more years after I left, unearthing all of the mysteries and heresies that had been left out of my pious education at the convent. Still, at the end of a decade I had read only half of the fifteen hundred volumes in the Marquis's two libraries. In translation, I read many books written by the Moors and the Hebrews. I do not know how anyone could possibly hope to understand the burning heart of a Spaniard without learning the culture of the Moors that we inherited in this land, or without learning the religion of the Hebrews, which had been the Faith of the Mother of God, the Apostles, and even Our Savior himself.

The large wooden doors of the Marquis's mansion were often kept open to the street, but the wrought-iron gate separating the entryway from the courtyard was locked, as usual. I wrapped my hands around the cold metal bars, as if a prisoner. Through the gate I could see the central patio and the Roman tiles that had been brought from outside the city. They depicted the many seductions and disguises of Zeus. In the center was a fountain that refreshed and cooled the air, and around it a trellis of white carnations and red roses.

I rang the bell and waited for a servant to open the gate. I saw the blue and gold uniform beset with jewels descend the stairs before I could see the face. I smiled as I recognized Fernando, who had remained devoted to the Marquis all these years and had been promoted to chief steward. When he saw me, his eyebrows jumped up and his mouth widened in a mischievous grin that suggested he had been keeping up on my adventures through the gossipmongers at the *mentideros*. It was to these lie parlors that people all across the Empire increasingly flocked to learn about the quite different conquests of the conquistadores and the *galanteadores*. Fernando opened the gate quickly, and we embraced warmly.

The Marquis honored me by coming to greet me, leaning over the balcony of the courtyard. He wore an ornate blue and gold doublet and breeches, the colors matching those of his servants. His clothes were much more ornate, and his sleeves puffed out fashionably. His stockings sloped down to his square-toed satin shoes, which made even his enormous legs look delicate, like those of a dancer. His ruff was larger than usual, which is becoming the fashion, and it made his head look as if it were resting on a large banquet platter.

"Well, well, you changed your mind after all! Come quick, you don't want to miss the *holy* sisters." As I came up the stairs, he embraced me warmly, as if I were the Prodigal Son.

"My apologies, Don Pedro, I had important business to attend to."

He raised his eyebrow. "I know your business quite well, since it was once also mine. If you will reconsider my offer—I'll make it thirty gold escudos a page—then I can look forward to reading who she was."

"Thirty pieces of gold. Judas only received silver. But I am no Judas and could not possibly betray my saviors."

He laughed but was clearly not pleased with my intransigence. Offer what he might, I would not sell my diary for three hundred escudos a page.

We walked past the chapel, which was always dark except when the prior from the Convento de San Francisco came for his obligatory monthly chess game. At these times the Marquis would leave the door open wide and have a candle lit within for good measure. The Franciscans had long ago taken up residence in the enormous convent that bordered the square opposite the Marquis's house.

We joined the others on the balcony. The noble ladies were arrayed in satin, velvet, and silk, all woven with gold thread. Many wore small hats. Their transparent veils had just the opposite effect of their modest intention and gave them an aura of allure and mystery. Each beautiful pair of eyes looked at me modestly from behind a fan. The Marquis had feigned illness to avoid walking with the nobles and prominent merchants in the procession. My guild of *galanteadores* had no banner or position in the parade. I smiled as I reviewed the assembled ladies, though I did not see Doña Ana.

My attention was drawn reluctantly to the procession, as the ladies all began pointing and laughing. Into view came the *gigantes* and *cabezudos,* the first with their giant bodies and the second with their enormous heads. They made obscene gestures with their large hands, which made the whole crowd laugh in delight and the ladies around us giggle and blush. It was good to know that even the Inquisitor could not stop the people from celebrating Our Lord with some good-natured merriment. Blessedly, the endless guilds and nobles had passed in their somber march, and I could witness the culmination of the procession—including the scandalous part to come.

From our height on the second story, over the arcade that surrounded the square, I saw the green carpet of rosemary that marked the route. The crowd stood like the banks of a river, leaving a narrow channel though which the procession marched and danced. I wondered how I could ask the Marquis about his plan for Doña Ana's family without confessing my interest.

The noblemen who had finished their part in the procession started to arrive, just as the nuns dancing the *zarabanda* came into view. It was indeed the same dance Alma performed in the tavern the night before, although less revealing to be sure. While their habits showed no skin aside from their face and hands, their movements were no different, if less experienced. They performed the toe-out, toe-in glides well, but truly excelled at the massive hip gyrations, the shaking of their bosoms, and the snapping of their fingers, which they did with admirable zeal. The Marquis was clapping in approval and laughing. He informed me that he had been involved in getting permission from the archbishop for the unusual exception to the ban on this dance being performed anywhere in public.

"It's a blasphemy," said a man's voice one balcony over as we watched these sisters and their holy fertility dance. I was not scandalized or in fact surprised, given how many take up the veil these days for less than pious reasons. Convents are filled with the younger daughters of noble families who cannot afford the enormous dowries that are demanded of them. These poor women are locked up without any concern for their wishes or their desires—and to dance the *zarabanda* during the fiesta is probably the closest they come to living the normal life that they long for.

I turned to the caballero who had been so quick to condemn the sisters' joy as a blasphemy. It was then that I saw his face and the scar on his cheek. It was the Commander. I looked around the balcony, trying to find Doña Ana, certain that she would be there. Just as I saw the profile of her beautiful almond-shaped face, the Marquis noted my gaze with satisfaction.

"*That* is Doña Ana," he said. "Is she not the most beautiful woman in all of Sevilla?"

"There are so many beautiful women in our fair city. I don't know how anyone could choose."

At that moment, the enormous *tarasca* arrived. The

serpent moved on hidden wheels and was covered in scales. It had a large belly and six grotesque breasts, a long tail, red eyes, and a mouth that opened and closed, revealing sharp teeth. Surrounding it were red devils and demons with pointed horns and pitchforks. On top of the giant creature were a drummer and seven colorful tumblers who formed a pyramid four men high. The top tumbler was balancing on his head precariously. Out of the beast's mouth a three-pronged tongue stuck out and was at that moment scaring a peasant who stood in the crowd. The tongue then knocked a straw hat off the peasant's head, which caused a roar of laughter from the crowd and even those on the balconies above. My eyes, however, were repeatedly drawn away from the jugglers and clowns to gaze at Doña Ana and her long black hair, which was laced with white flowers like a bride's. Her teeth sparkled between her red lips, and her singular laugh, full of life and music, sent shivers down my back. She must have noticed me staring, because she stole a glance in my direction but looked away quickly.

After the jugglers came the floats. On the first was a ship and a lighthouse—the coming of Our Savior's truth. In the ship sat a young man and an old man, each draped in blue robes and holding a cross and a globe, the Father and the Son. Between them flew a dove, the Holy Spirit.

The second float depicted Adam and Eve in the Garden of Eden. They enacted a pantomime of the Fall, and even from this distance the snake's temptation of Eve and Eve's temptation of Adam were quite clear. As Eve offered the fruit to Adam, the Marquis turned to me and said, "The Carmelite is right—in Sevilla, the Devil has more hands to tempt us with."

I looked past him to Doña Ana and nodded in agreement.

The third float was of the Castillo de San Jorge, the headquarters of the Inquisition, with smoke coming out of its fake cannons.

"What, Don Pedro, if you don't mind my asking," I whispered as we continued to watch the procession, "is the offense that the Commander has committed that causes you to seek your revenge?"

The Marquis paused and then said, "Does one need an offense?"

Following the floats was a throng of men flagellating themselves with leather whips. Bright red blood streaked down their naked backs. While some were no doubt sincere in their penitence, it is not unusual for these same zealots to whip themselves in front of a beautiful woman so that their blood bespatters her. For many this is a great courtesy and a sign of love's true devotion.

"Don Pedro, may I speak—" The Commander did not finish, since he recognized me and stiffened as if preparing for combat. His jaw jutted out and his eyes narrowed.

"Commander, do you know my friend Don Juan?"

"I'm afraid so, and I am surprised to hear that he is a friend of yours." He turned away and the Marquis followed him, but not before he leaned back and said, "You really do have a way of ingratiating yourself with people."

I saw that Doña Ana was also gone. I looked through the halls and discovered her and her dueña heading down to the garden, whispering. I considered following but was distracted by the loud voice of the Commander. I decided that it might be important to eavesdrop on the conversation in the library.

"I appreciate your friendship, Don Pedro, and your family's kindness over the years, but I cannot agree to what you ask."

"Every man, Commander, has a price."

"My honor and that of my family cannot be bought."

"Ah, Don Gonzalo, I am so sorry to hear that. I had hoped that you would not force my hand, but you leave me no choice." I saw through the crack in the door that the Marquis had turned his back on the Commander. "Information has come to my attention that might be somewhat *compromising* to you and your family."

"I have nothing to hide."

"I think you do. You see, Commander, the man who buried your wife told me . . . there were two bodies buried in her coffin."

I thought I saw fear on the Commander's face. Just then the Marquis came toward the slightly open door. I hid against the wall, but I heard him say, "Now shall we discuss our deal?" as he closed the door. I tried to walk around to the window that opened out of the room onto the courtyard balcony, but when I did, I saw that Doña Ana's dueña was there, also trying to eavesdrop on the conversation. Perhaps such actions were what made her untrustworthy in the Commander's eyes.

While I was eager to hear the importance of the revelation about the dead—a murder perhaps?—I was even more interested in the revelations about the living that I hoped to discover in the garden. Finding Doña Ana unchaperoned was a rare opportunity, and I hurried downstairs, my blood coursing through my veins with the thrill of the hunt.

After searching through the large garden I finally came to the Marquis's siesta room. This room was my favorite, and as always my eyes were dazzled by its bright yellow walls, covered with marble carvings depicting many erotic scenes from the pagan myths. On both walls were pillowed benches, their armrests curved like the handles of a Greek lyre. The ceiling was an extraordinary grid of cedar beams, within which were gleaming stucco stalactites painted gold.

There, through the arched stucco window, I saw her with her back to me. My heart jumped, and I walked toward her, my footsteps muffled by the Turkish carpet. Doña Ana was facing a pool of water behind which was a gigantic fig tree, its knobby trunk too wide for a man to wrap his arms around. Its branches shaded the pool and reached right to the window through which I could see Doña Ana straining to grasp a ripe green fig that was just out of her reach. The enormous swollen fruit was almost as large as her fist. I stepped up on the tiled window bench that lay between us and, pulling my sword from its scabbard, sliced the branch so that the fruit fell into her hand.

Startled, she turned to look at me. "How like a man to sever what can so easily be plucked," she said, her tone hardly grateful. She discarded the fig and its branch on the window seat between us.

"But it was out of your reach."

"I have never needed your help."

"My apologies. I was simply trying to win your favor and perhaps have a moment to speak."

"You think that I would be so bold as to speak with you publicly like this?" she asked, looking at the garden, which could have hidden a hundred ears.

"Then shall we speak in private?" I asked, gesturing to the siesta room.

"I wouldn't speak with a man like you anywhere."

"What is a man like me *like*?" She looked away without answering, so I answered for her. "Do not the same passions, the same cruelties, and the same kindnesses live in the hearts of all the sons of Adam, whether hidden as in Abel or revealed as in Cain?"

"Not every man has a reputation like yours."

"Reputation or rumor?"

"What is the difference?" she asked in a harsh, indifferent tone, turning her head away.

"One is true and the other is only . . . mostly true."

She tried to stop herself from smiling but was only partly successful. However, her expression was soon stern again, and I knew that this seduction was going to call for a different approach. "I am sorry for my intrusion yesterday."

"You made an enemy of my father."

"I was trying to make a friend of his daughter."

"Your efforts were in vain. I have no interest in your *galanteador* game."

"Yes, you are right, Doña Ana, it is a game, the most pleasurable diversion ever invented." She turned her back to me but did not walk away. "I think you are just scared."

"I'm not scared of you or your game," she said, turning back to me. Although she had said that she would not speak to me, her pride prevented her from remaining silent.

"I might be scared if I were you."

"Indifference is not the same as fear."

"Indifference? Did I misread your gaze at the slave market?"

"If you took it as interest, yes."

"I felt as if you were looking right through me."

"I was curious."

"Curious?"

"Curious to know what kind of a man would choose the life that you have chosen."

"A man who worships women."

"An idolater?"

"If you are to believe the preachers, perhaps."

"Well, I have no interest in idol worshippers, for I shall marry a man who worships only love."

"Passion is a form of love, is it not?"

"*There* is your passion," she said, pointing to one of the marble wall sculptures. It was the seduction of Leda. "The passion of the *galanteador* is merely lust." Zeus had taken the form of a giant swan equal in size to the beautiful queen of Sparta. The swan held Leda's neck with his beak as he mounted her from the front, his webbed feet spreading her thighs and his wings beating against her naked back. Leda was looking down, and her face did not reveal whether she was a willing accomplice in this portrayal. I was impressed that Doña Ana did not blush at this carnal work of art, which the Marquis had to smuggle into Spain to get past the censors of the Inquisition.

"You are not embarrassed by the pagan imagination?" I asked.

"I grew up on a hacienda," she said. "I know how all animals behave." She sat, perhaps from the heat, or perhaps forgetting herself. My legs were facing the room and hers were facing the garden, maintaining a minimal degree of modesty on the window seat.

I smiled but pressed her further. "Perhaps a true passion exists that is not just lust. There, perhaps." I pointed to a sculpture of a nude Aphrodite, reclining on a couch, her eyes closed and her head thrown back in obvious carnal satisfaction.

"That is but a dream," Doña Ana replied. "The true passion of which you speak could occur only in marriage, for without love, there is only lust, forever fleeting and empty." She nodded with finality and victory as we sat in the intimacy of silence. I reached for the fig and branch that separated us. The ripe fruit came off easily in my hand as I recalled the words of the Marquis and wondered why I did not simply move on to one of the ladies upstairs whose desire was ready to be plucked. I pulled open the green skin, revealing the pink and moist center. I offered her half, and she looked away.

"You seem to know quite a lot about lust . . . for a maiden." I split open the tender pink interior of my half of the fig and approached it slowly and sensually.

She gasped and stood up, offended. "I have a suitor, Don Juan," she said disdainfully. "He has risked his life for me. You risk nothing but your vanity."

"Some masked knight-errant, I suppose?" The words were spoken before I had considered them. My heart ached at the sight of the worried surprise on her face. I searched for other words, but there were footsteps on the path. I got up and hid behind the wall.

"Your father going to whip me if find out," her dueña whispered urgently. I saw Doña Ana look nervously in my direction. "He is suspicious already."

"My father is always suspicious, but he need not worry. His will is my own."

"The Commander speak to Marquis about your marriage." At the mention of her marriage, my heart skipped a beat. This seemed strange, since wedlock had never proved an obstacle for me before. Indeed, when women discover the loneliness and isolation of marriage, they have far less to lose in opening the doors of their bedchamber to me. Yet I felt an urgency to seduce her at the first opportunity.

"Did you hear to whom I would be married?"

"No. He not say. Now come. Procession almost over."

As I heard them walk away, I gave one backward glance at Leda and Zeus. Their illicit union had given birth to Helen of Troy. Doña Ana was certainly as beautiful as the pagan queen. Would her beauty also lead to heartache and death?

I returned to the balcony, from where I could see that the procession was finally coming to an end. *Los seises,* the dancing choirboys, marched in their red and yellow doublets and white hose, their plumed hats in their hands, like miniature members of the royal guard. The Marquis came and stood next to me. He continued to review the procession and commented, "You were talking to Doña Ana in the garden."

I said nothing.

"My spies, as you well know, are everywhere."

"My, my," I replied with a smile, "you are behaving like a jealous husband. I'm quite surprised at you, Don Pedro."

"Doña Ana is no good to me if her chastity is compromised. Is that clear?"

"I thought you were issuing me a challenge last night at the tavern."

"It was not a challenge but a warning."

"You seemed almost to be boasting about her chastity."

"She is chaste and will remain so. Is that clear?"

"So you have plans for her. May I ask what they are?"

"My plans are my own, but I don't want them interfered with."

"Her father does not look happy about these plans," I said, nodding at the far balcony, where he stood with his daughter, his face a bitter scowl.

"Everyone has a price when the hardship is great enough, and in the Commander's case he has already lost favor with the King, which is very, very bad for a military man." The Marquis's puckered lips, shaking head, and false sadness told me who was behind the Commander's loss of favor.

"Your cruelty is stunning, Don Pedro," I said, which made him smile with satisfaction.

"But my cruelty is pale in comparison to the Inquisitor's," he said as the most feared man in Spain came into view. The Inquisitor was dressed simply in his habit, but unlike the other religious men and women who had already passed, he was sitting in a chair under a scarlet and gold canopy and supported by four men. Next to them a soldier carried the green standard of the Inquisition. My stomach tensed as I saw the detestable symbol—the ornate crown and simple green cross with an olive branch and a sword, the symbols of mercy and justice, on either side. I had seen little mercy, and its justice was nothing more than violence and persecution. The Marquis must have noticed my disdain. "You do know why he hates *galanteadores* so much?" the Marquis continued. He took great pains to discover everyone's past, believing he could thereby control their future. He had, however, never discovered the truth about mine.

"He was one," I said as the dutiful student.

"You are right that converts are often the most zealous crusaders—but in this case you are wrong. His *father* was one, and all his life the poor Inquisitor has had to endure the rumors and stigma of his illegitimate birth."

Surrounding the Inquisitor was a wall of his soldiers, wearing their red vests and round helmets and holding their deadly crossbows. The crowd knelt faithfully as the Inquisitor and his personal army passed. Everyone knew that failure do to so would place one under suspicion.

At that moment Alma arrived and joined us on the balcony. She stroked her hand down the front of the Marquis's doublet. "I just love men with big crossbows."

"Alma," the Marquis said, "I'm so glad you could join us."

"Even a courtesan has to observe certain Holy Days," she said.

"Look there," the Marquis said in a serious tone, pointing to a man in a simple white garment who was dragging his feet slowly in front of the monstrance. The giant silver tower rose up behind him, its ornate columns and archways glittering in the bright sun. Behind this last float, and after an escort of two dozen purple-robed canons of the Cathedral, came the Archbishop. His embroidered stole was gold, as was the staff he carried in his hand, but his presence was unimpressive after that of the Inquisitor, who, while lacking these symbols of power, had it nonetheless.

"Who is the penitent?" I asked, unable to see his downcast face under the tall pointed white hat that added to his shame.

"Some country priest who was accused of being an errant thinker—an *alumbrado*," the Marquis whispered to me.

"What was the real reason?" I asked.

"Having a lover," the Marquis replied.

"That is common enough," I said.

"The Inquisitor is using him as an example. He's furious that his public decrees have had little effect on the immorality in his jurisdiction. When they tortured him," the Marquis now whispered, *"he had them cut off."*

"No!" I said in disbelief, instinctively covering my loins. "I didn't think the tribunal permitted that." I had never heard of this being one of the Inquisition's many punishments.

"Fray Ignacio is a zealot," the Marquis said with disgust.

"Who told you?" I asked, not wanting to believe him.

"Fray Ignacio," the Marquis admitted.

"Sometimes I'm shocked at the company you keep."

"It is important for me to be on good terms with all who wield power and influence. As you know, that priest is not the only one the Inquisitor would like to use as an example." He looked meaningfully at me. I knew all too well that it was only because of the Marquis's protection that the Inquisitor's soldiers had not come for me in the night. I watched the procession leave the plaza on its way back to the Cathedral and saw the Inquisitor and his soldiers disappear.

With the procession over, the servants called us for the afternoon meal. I sat on the right hand of the Marquis at the opposite end of the table from Doña Ana, who sat next to her father. My sport was to watch her without her father seeing me.

The meal itself was sumptuous, beginning with *ensalada real*. This favorite of the King contained various kinds of fruit, vegetables, sugared almonds, and preserved cherries. After the salad came the deviled eggs, and then fish, salmon and *dorada*. Next were the oysters and the shrimp. No one ate these with more relish and desire than Doña Ana. Indeed, it was more enticing to watch her eat than to eat myself. I gazed, enraptured, as her tongue came out of her mouth and her lips drew in the juicy flesh of the oyster. All the while she let out a quiet coo of pleasure. She had not lost her country ways completely. I was not the only one who was captivated by her. When she looked up, she smiled with embarrassment. When her eyes met mine, she quickly looked away. I am always amazed at our willingness to eat casually in public, given how secretive we are about our other bodily appetites. The act of ingestion is as intimate and, when truly enjoyed, as sensual. Alma was smiling, having witnessed our glances.

Next the servants brought out the meat dishes, ten in all. There were partridges and pigeons and then a chicken hash that was covered with slices of bacon and sausage with roundels of lemon and pimiento and garlic. *Olla podrida* with its thick pork stew was served along with a type of *manjar blanco,* containing thin slices of chicken simmered in a sauce of milk, sugar, and flour. When I lived with the Marquis, I watched the cooks preparing all of these dishes and knew that, like the subtleties of music that are appreciated only by another musician, the subtleties of the palate were appreciated only by one who knew how the dishes are prepared. Next came duck, rabbit, veal, venison, and an entire roast pig.

Each dish Doña Ana ate with equal satisfaction until, unable to contain himself, her father leaned over and whispered in her ear. She took her napkin and dried off her hands, which were dripping with juices, and then dabbed the corners of her mouth delicately.

At last dessert was served. First I saw the purple shimmering skin of cherries and the rough red flesh of strawberries. And then confections—fruit pastries, egg yolks preserved in sugar, and various kinds of almond cakes, and finally cheeses, olives, and bonbons of anise. As she ate these, Doña Ana forgot herself and was once again groaning with even more joy. The rest of the guests looked at her as if watching an actress onstage surrender to an uncontrollable passion.

I found myself quietly moaning along as I began to lick the side of a green melon slice that was wet and tender. Not to be left out, Alma began to moan with pleasure as she sucked in an exceptionally large strawberry. The Marquis looked up from the fruit pastry he was devouring silently. He looked at me, then Alma, and then his eyes settled on Doña Ana, who was lost in a pomegranate and its countless seeds. I stopped my groaning as I waited for his response. He either did not want Doña Ana to be embarrassed or for us to have all the pleasure, so he began to groan and grunt as well. The strawberry filling of his pastry dripped down his chin and narrow beard like blood.

Once their host had joined in this savory song, the rest of his guests dared not offend him. They too began to express their enjoyment with sounds of pleasure and satisfaction, gobbling up the rest of the almond cakes, cheese, and olives. Doña Ana looked up with delight at this chorus. Only the Commander disapproved of the pagan feast. Shoving his chair back, he grabbed his daughter by the arm and said, "The bullfight is about to begin." He stared at me sternly, as if I had instigated this licentiousness. Or had he too noticed my furtive glances?

Full of food but with my desire not yet sated, I went up with the others to the balconies. I positioned myself where I might watch the beauty as well as the bulls. My loyalties, however, were now divided, because I knew my friends Don José and Don Hernán would be among the toreadors. I worried about my reluctant friend Don Hernán. Last month three toreadors had died, and there were then only half the number of bulls there would be today.

The Bullfight

The plaza had been barricaded and a booth with a blue canopy set up in front of the convent to shade the King. Next to him were the mayor and other dignitaries, both secular and religious, including, of course, the Inquisitor. Some years ago the papacy had forbidden clergy from attending bullfights, especially on Holy Days, but it had had to reverse the decision, since few ever heeded it. Fortunately for us, the Inquisition is quite fond of bullfights and recognizes that such an event is a fitting sacrifice to our Savior.

A fence made out of rough-hewn logs had also been set up to protect the countless spectators. Those who could afford it stood in the shade under the gallery, while the rest stood in the sweating sun. After the King had taken his seat, Don José, Don Hernán, and the other champions were presented. As usual all of them had had more than a little to drink during the afternoon meal. Their intemperance always improved the bulls' chances of goring one or more of the toreadors, and their horns had of course been sharpened to make them as deadly as possible. Over his noble attire, each champion wore a red tunic, which would attract the bulls' attention, and on his head a black hat with an ostrich feather. Don José's plume was blue, Don Hernán's red. Around their waists, they wore their swords and daggers. Don Hernán had also donned a red scarf around his neck, a sign to his mistress that this heroic deed was for her. For a moment I wished that I were fighting, to impress Doña Ana, but this desire was fleeting. I did not long for the bullfight, in which one risked one's life for ephemeral honor. I preferred to take my chances in the pursuit of real pleasure and not false pride.

After saluting the dignitaries, the toreadors took their lap of honor on their horses and then the two dozen bulls were released. The toreadors wasted no time planting the steel tips of their spears into the bulls' flanks and breaking them off with a twist of the wrist. I watched as Don José came alongside a bull and, arching backward, skillfully pierced it with his spear. He lodged another and then another, and I cheered for him with great enthusiasm.

Streaks of blood were flowing down the black backs of the bulls. People were talking, and I found myself aggravated at this obvious sign of disrespect for the danger the toreadors were facing. Men were selling lemonade and strawberries to the crowd, and a dozen cats had been released into the ring to add to the carnival. The crowd laughed as one of the lackeys ran from a bull and jumped into a barrel, and then even more when another jumped into the fountain. He climbed up the statue of Hermes as if the bull might leap into the fountain to gore him.

I tried to concentrate on the confusion of bulls, horses, and men unfolding in the square. I was thinking Don José might actually win, having lodged more blades than any other, when I was distracted by Don Hernán. His bright red scarf was blowing in the wind, and he was not faring as well. The enormous bull that he was confronting had jostled him from his saddle. Honor demanded that he right this wrong.

He bravely dismounted and approached the bull with his sword drawn to kill it. He faced the bull, which was the largest in the ring, a beast of terrifying size, with a massive neck and horns that were each two hand-breadths wide. I have always marveled at how the spectators root as much for the bull as for the toreador, wanting to see the bull fight back before its inevitable death.

The sharp blades that covered its back like a crown of thorns had driven the bull into a vicious mood. It charged him, and Don Hernán got nervous and tried to move out of the way—but he was not quick enough. One of the bull's horns gored him in the shoulder and knocked him to the ground. The spectators held their breath, showing their true allegiance, yet no one could come to his aid, as honor demanded. My heart pounded as Don Hernán valiantly raised his sword again and the massive bull charged anew. My poor friend was already badly wounded. He was not even fast enough to move out of the way as the bull gored him a second time, once again knocking him to the ground. I clenched my fist, praying, "Please, Madre

Santa, have mercy on Don Hernán," but he did not get up.

"Papá!" I heard a boy's voice cry, and then I saw the child, no more than eight or nine, crawl under the barricade. He was running to Don Hernán's side while the bull turned. The crowd to a person was standing and breathless The bull beat the ground with its hoof and headed toward the young boy, certain to gore him, too. There was no honor that required a small boy to die with his father.

Where were the guards? Where were the other toreadors? They were all facing other bulls, and no one was coming to the boy's aid. Without thinking, I jumped down from the balcony to the roof of the gallery and then to the ground. There was no time to heed the pain in my leg. I ran as fast as I could.

The boy stood frozen. The bull was closing in. Its deranged eyes and deadly horns were bearing down on him, about to take the boy with his father. It was no more than a few feet from him. I desperately pushed Don Hernán's son out of the way, both of us toppling to the ground. We escaped the bull's charge by only a breath, but I had no time to catch mine.

The bull turned a tight circle and headed straight at me as one of the toreadors swept the boy onto his saddle. The beast's tongue was hanging out and saliva was dripping from its mouth. It made a low, menacing bellow, like some deranged Minotaur. Rivers of blood glistened on its back. I looked to my side and saw a barrel. I crawled inside just as the bull's horns battered the wooden shell. The barrel would have rolled away if the horns had not gored right through the boards. I looked in horror at the sharpened blades. Frantic and not thinking, I snuck out of the barrel. The bull saw me and pounded the barrel on the ground until it shattered. There was nothing between me and the bull, and instinctively I began to run. The bull was so close that I could feel its hot breath on my back, and its enraged bellow shook my body. Don José came to my side, but with the bull closing in again, there was no time to climb on his mount. He started to gallop away, and I ran alongside. The bull chased us in a wide circle. It then leapt up, its forelegs off the ground, bucking its head, certain to gore me or the horse with its two curved daggers. There was no hope of escape. I barely had time to draw my sword from my scabbard and face the bull. This time, stepping aside to avoid the bull's horns yet staying in close, I thrust the sword into the bull's massive neck. The immortal bull took my sword but did not die. Don José stood up tall in his stirrups and plunged his sword like a harpoon into the bones of the neck. Together, our blades severed the vulnerable nape of the neck, which brought the ferocious beast to a sudden stop. It fell to its knees and rolled over, dead.

The crowd was howling with relief and joy. I looked up to see them standing and applauding wildly. I was still stunned and shaken from this unexpected duel with the Minotaur but tried to smile. I raised my hand to acknowledge the crowd, and they applauded all the louder. I noticed that the toreadors were hardly pleased with my receiving so much attention—except Don José, who was applauding the loudest of all. I gestured to him, since we had overcome the monster together, and as we sheathed our swords, we held each other's hand high in triumph.

Entering the fray had been some unfamiliar reflex, perhaps as old in our breasts as the reflexes of passion, but if I had known the accolades I would receive from the women present, I might have had reason to choose the danger willingly. I did not have time to acknowledge the applause any longer, for we had to help our friend Don Hernán, who was still alive, although badly wounded. We left the ring with him on a wooden stretcher, the thunderous applause unabated. Women threw flowers and scarves at us, but I was uninterested in these trophies and tried to comfort my friend.

"I'm going to die," Don Hernán said. His face was pale, and the light in his eyes was dimming.

"Just hold on. The doctor is coming."

"No, I'm going to die. I'm not afraid, Juan. Ask the Marquis to look after my wife and children. They are everything to me."

"I promise."

"I made a mistake, a terrible mistake. Tell my wife, please," he said, choking on his blood and tears. "Tell my son, when he is a man, of the mistake his father made. Tell him that to be . . . a man . . . is to choose." He coughed more blood while I tried to deny the truth of his words. Both of us knew the signs of approaching death. I heard a crowd coming as we waited in the shade of the gallery in front of the Marquis's palace, sweat pouring down our faces, Don Hernán's mixed with a trickle of blood from his mouth. At last the doctor and his attendants came to our side. From behind them came Don Hernán's wife, fighting her way through the crowd, her blue dress dragging along the dusty ground. When she saw her husband, she released a soul-rending howl of grief. They placed Don Hernán in a long carriage and rushed him to his house, where he could be examined by the doctor.

I looked up at the balcony of the Marquis's house and saw his large red face looking down. The others stared on silently, and I searched for Doña Ana. She did not look away but stared into my eyes, her gaze once again piercing me deeply.

Cristóbal was standing in front of my carriage, by the door. I needed to clean off the dust and the blood that covered my clothes. I told Cristóbal to take me back to my apartment. Through the window, I could hear him talking excitedly the whole way, recounting to me every moment as he had seen it. As the fear drained from my body, so too did my strength. I sank into the seat, only half listening to his wild and improbable tale.

Once home, Cristóbal filled a bath for me. He scrubbed my back and limbs, which ached from the terror that had pumped through them. I stayed in the cooling bath for what seemed like hours, my body relaxed but my mind still troubled. I rubbed my sore leg as my mind drifted to Don Hernán in my arms and his puzzling words. But what troubled me most was why I had entered the ring at all. Something deeper than thought or reason had taken control of my body. Surely, honor and heroism were partly to blame, as these are never far from a caballero's heart, but there was something else less familiar and more worrisome that had changed the scales of loss and gain.

Through the window the dark of night was starting to vanquish the day. Cristóbal lit three candles in the room. Their golden light reflected off the bathwater. An urgent knock at the door sent Cristóbal to see who it was.

"He's in the bath," I heard him say.

"I need to speak to him."

"You'll have to come back."

"This can't wait," Alma said, barging through.

I got out of the bath and pulled a towel around me. Her bright yellow dress and veil raised my spirits for a moment until I saw her red, terrified eyes. Through her tears Alma revealed to me the identity of the poor penitent whom the Inquisitor had paraded in front of the monstrance as an example. My chest collapsed as I heard his name.

Sins of the Flesh

*P*adre Miguel," she said desperately, her love for our mutual friend from Carmona as great as mine. The holy priest who had been my tutor also had been her parish priest. "He was the only one who ever accepted us," she said, as much to herself as to me. She was referring to the *conversos* of Carmona and Padre Miguel's unwillingness to exclude anyone from God's love, not even the converted Jews.

"Where is he?" I demanded, dressing hastily.

"He is being held at the Castillo de San Jorge," she said.

I quickly finished dressing and grabbed my cape.

"Where are you going?" she asked, already knowing the answer. "You can't just walk into the castle of the Inquisition," she said in horror. "You'll risk your life to free him."

"It is no doubt because of me and our friendship that he was made an example."

"You can't blame yourself. How do you know?"

"I know the Inquisitor."

"Then it is a trap. They will arrest you and throw you in a cell forever."

"That is a risk that I must take for our dear Padre Miguel," I said. I sped down the stairs, Alma and Cristóbal trailing behind me.

Cristóbal's voice was trembling. "Please, my lord, don't make me go there. People never return who enter those gates."

"I will go alone by horseback."

"Then I will go with you," Alma said bravely, if with some uncertainty. Perhaps she was thinking about her parents, who had no doubt been tortured in the Castillo before they were killed.

I stopped on the stairs and turned to face her. I pulled

off the cloak that hung over her shoulders and chest, revealing the low-cut bodice of her otherwise modest dress. "Dressed like a courtesan? We will both be safer if I go alone."

"Please, Don Juan," she said with renewed worry in her eyes, "please be careful." I smiled and nodded, emboldened by her affection.

Cristóbal saddled my horse, and I galloped through the streets as fast as my mare could carry me. The Puerta del Arenal was crowded with people and wagons, but I could not wait and kicked my stirrup irons into Bonita's panting flanks. We galloped through the carts and the crowd, scattering hay and turning heads. I rode like a demon down the riverbank as the sun set red in the sky.

The horse's hooves clattered against the wooden planks of the floating bridge to Triana. My fists clenched tightly around the reins, and I looked at the fortress ahead of me. Eight stone towers clawed their way toward the sky. The castle was a vestige of the past on the banks of a city that had tried in vain to turn from those dark days of death to the light of discovery. Jutting out from its crenels were small wheeled cannons to stop anyone, like me, who might consider freeing a prisoner. But I knew of a weakness that all impregnable fortresses have. I galloped past the main gate, outside which several guards were posted, and arrived at a back door on the other side.

There I dismounted, roped my horse, and approached the guard, whose stern bearded face looked out from under his round steel helmet. His chain-mail shirt was from the age of the Crusades, as were the steel knees that covered his leather boots. He saw me and nervously pointed his crossbow at my face. In the man's eyes I could see the hunger of his children. I waved two gold escudos in front of him, which got his attention. I nodded to the door. He hesitated, deciding between his duties. After a glance in both directions revealed no one, he opened the large wooden door. I dropped the coins in his hand. The poor pay of soldiers is always the weakness of any army, even the Army of God.

"The penitent, where is he?" I asked, adding another coin.

He pointed to the tower directly above us.

"There will be more if my presence remains a secret."

I entered and walked carefully, alert for other guards who might not be so easily persuaded. To bribe entry was one thing; to be found inside was quite another. I pulled my mask out of my sleeve and put it over my eyes. The massive stone walls blocked out what remained of the twilight except for a few high cross-shaped windows that still glowed red. Torches flamed on the walls, marking my path.

Searching anxiously for a stairway to the tower, I was startled by a pitiful scream. Instinctively, I hid myself. I doubted that Padre Miguel, his punishment already inflicted, would be tortured again, but I knew there was no end to the Inquisitor's cruelty. To make sure it was not my friend, I looked through a small barred window in a nearby door. The torturer's enormous body blocked the victim's face, yet I could hear the poor wretch choking on the water being poured down her throat. The water torture used a cloth placed into the mouth to draw the water into the stomach. An earthen jug spilled water like an endless fountain. The victim would no doubt feel as if he were drowning. Next to them I saw a seated clerk waiting to write down the confession and a doctor whose solemn role was to make sure the victim was cognizant. A confession had to be a sincere act of faith and not a cry of delirium. The presence of the doctor, however, did not always ensure that victims survived the question.

My eyes were drawn to the other fiendish instruments of torture arrayed around the room. The pulley and rope dangling overhead were used to raise victims above the ground with their arms tied behind their backs. Victims would be allowed to fall until just above the ground, their arms wrenched sharply from their sockets. Below this was the most common torture of all, the *potro*. This simple but fiendish rack used ropes to pull the prisoner's limbs and slowly dislocate each and every joint.

"You are accused of witchcraft! Confess the truth and you will know God's mercy," an angry voice shouted. It was a voice that sounded very much like the Inquisitor's, but I could not see his face.

"I am—not—" I heard a weak voice sputter and cough.

I closed my eyes in pity as I hurried past the closed door, the screams from other rooms still echoing down the hall. I squeezed my fist in vain protest, knowing there was nothing I could do for her or the dozens more locked in other cells, tortured on other racks. There was only one victim of the Inquisition's cruelty whom I had any hope of saving, and I continued on to the tower where he was imprisoned. I saw a door that did not have the barred window of the other cells. By its look and location, it promised to be the stairway up. Down the hall I heard the approaching voices of guards. I pulled urgently on the iron handle of the door and discovered it was locked. I took out my meat knife and inserted its tip into the lock, trying to reach the spring. The guards were closing in. I shut my eyes and tried to listen to the sound of the lock, their footfalls now just around the corner. It clicked, and I yanked the door open and closed it just as quickly. Resting against its solid timbers, I breathed again as I heard the guards pass.

I climbed the circular stone steps three at a time in my haste. "Padre?" I said through the door as I picked another lock.

"Who is it?"

The lock opened and I slipped inside. Padre Miguel was kneeling and weeping, his hands clutching his rosary.

"Padre?" I said breathlessly as I took off my mask.

He stared at me with disbelief, as if I were an angelic vision. There was a distant look in his eyes. "Juan?"

"I've come to help you escape."

"There is no escape for me, my son."

"I can take you out the way I came," I said. I took his arms in my hands, gripping the rough brown fabric of his sleeves.

"No, my son, my prison is my sin."

"What is sinful about your love and devotion to a woman?"

"I was married to the Church, and I betrayed that vow."

"How many are the archbishops and even popes who have fathered children?"

"I cannot excuse or condemn the sins of others, but I can repent for mine."

"You are just a man. Lust cannot be denied."

"It must be denied. It must be conquered, or we are as the animals."

"We *are* animals! We are not angels!" I said in barely controlled fury, the years of anger coming to the surface. It was this attempt to separate our souls from our flesh that had driven me from the Church. I breathed deeply and tried to help Padre Miguel up. "Come, Padre, before it is too late."

He smiled and put his hand on my arm with warmth but also with resignation. "It is already too late for me, my boy."

My shoulders dropped, but before I could accept my defeat, I heard a loud creaking of hinges. The door to the room opened slowly. The white-robed Inquisitor stood in the doorway, flanked by two guards. A smile spread across his face as he realized his good fortune.

"I came personally to give confession to the penitent and how does God reward me for my kindness? He sends me the greatest sinner of all."

I tightened the muscles of my leg to keep it from shaking. I heard Alma's voice in my head, begging me to keep silent, but I was never able to hold my tongue. "It is you who need to confess your sins for what you have done to this holy *padre*."

"I knew that your sexual perversity could not be far from such a tragic case, Don Juan. Are you here on a pastoral visit for the debauched?"

"I thought the penitent's crime was errant thought."

"Ah, you come as an advocate. Well, every prisoner is entitled to one—including you. Seize him." The guards grabbed my arms and held them firmly as I resisted.

"Most reverend and magnificent lord," Padre Miguel begged, walking on his knees and kissing the ring on the hand of the Inquisitor. "I need no defense. My guilt is undeniable." He was trying to save me, but I knew his words would fall on deaf ears.

"I know, I know," the Inquisitor said to Padre Miguel, patting him on the head and then turning to me, needing to prove the righteousness of his cause as he always had. "First comes the errant thought of the mind. And then is the errant action of the body. The two are inseparable. Ours is a jealous God who does not suffer infidelity from those who have vowed their love to him. You never learned the lessons I tried to teach you, did you?"

"Please, Juan," Padre Miguel begged. "Go now, while you still can."

I turned to the Inquisitor. "You couldn't beat it into me, could you?" I spat out through gritted teeth.

"Your penitence and your salvation were my responsibility, as is the penitence and salvation of every sinner in my charge." The Inquisitor opened his white robe and then lifted up the hem of the white lace garment he wore underneath. As he did, I saw dozens of thorns that he had no doubt had the sisters sew into the fabric. "Each of these thorns is a sinner in my care. It can be removed only when that sinner repents or is *relaxed*." He drew the final word out ominously, suggesting the threat of death it contained. "Every moment of my life I feel the thorns scraping against my skin, and I know that I can never rest until they know God's mercy." He pointed to one of them. "This thorn, Don Juan, is yours. It has tormented me longer than any other—since the day you came to our monastery after your sins led that holy sister to eternal damnation."

"No, Your Reverence, I did not cause Hermana Teresa's damnation. *You* did."

"The Devil never takes responsibility for his deeds."

"Then take responsibility for yours! Hermana Teresa believed that you would return for her next."

"What are you talking about?"

"With so many murdered, it must be hard to remember them all. *You* killed Hermana Jerónima— she was innocent!"

He looked down, remembering across the years, and

his eyebrows rose. Only after she had died in the torture chamber, where they had tried to extract a confession, was her innocence proved. "The Will of God is not always for us to know."

"But yet you are willing to be his Executioner!"

"The Will of God for you, Don Juan, is quite clear. If you didn't have such powerful friends," he said with disgust, "I would castrate you now." He closed the yellow nails of his claw into a fist. "Get rid of him. God's Will cannot yet be done."

The two large guards lifted me practically off my feet and marched me back down the tower stairs and through the hall. I saw two other soldiers carrying a stretcher with a body. It was no doubt the victim I had heard being tortured. As they passed us, I saw the face of an elderly woman, her long gray hair flowing down her shoulders. Her eyes were vacant, and her mouth hung open. I tried to breathe as the blood of outraged horror pumped through my hands and feet. The guards threw me out the door, startling the watchman on the other side. I got on my horse and galloped furiously around the castle. The standard of the Inquisition hung on either side of the entrance to the bridge. My fury and desire for revenge unanswered, I drew my sword and slashed one of the banners, cutting it in half. I rode back across the river toward the walls of Sevilla before the Inquisitor could change his mind and come looking for me. As I rode home, I wept for Padre Miguel, and I wept for the girl he had long ago helped me to see on that last fateful night.

After I had gone to Padre Miguel's confessional and he had agreed to speak to Hermana Teresa, each hour of waiting was a month, each day a year. Finally Padre Miguel arrived at the *monasterio*. Fray Ignacio looked at him suspiciously, no doubt because he was a visitor of mine. When we were alone, Padre Miguel told me, "She has agreed to write you a letter. She says she will leave it in the usual place tonight." He had no idea about the hollow in the olive tree, but he knew that I would understand.

I climbed one final time over the monastery wall as the sun was setting, and "borrowed" a horse. The night was cold but I rode feverishly, crouched up on the saddle, too eager to sit. The horse and I were both covered with sweat. I slowed down only when I arrived at the convent wall. As I dismounted, my steed snorted. I tried to calm him with pats of my hand and the soothing sounds of my voice. I pushed open the secret door, its wood rotten and the lock still broken. Her letter was in the hollow of the tree that still held all of mine. By the light of the full moon, I began to read her note, my heart beating ever faster.

I have tried to forget you. I have tried to cleanse my anguished soul of my body's sinfulness, but I could not. I have broken my vows and defiled my body. The Inquisitor will come to punish my sin if I do not punish myself.

I dropped the letter and ran to the locked door of the convent. I banged on the wood door without stopping until Priora Francisca herself opened it. "Juan, you are forbidden from—"

I did not have time to speak and pushed past her, shaking off her knotted hands as she tried to hold on to my wrist. I ran to Teresa's cell, shouting her name, as the nuns all peeked out of their rooms. I tried to open the door, but there was a chair propped against it. I shouted, "Teresa!" and threw my shoulder into the door several times until it burst open.

Teresa was lying on her bed, her arms draped over the side and streaks of blood dripping down her chest and arms where she had carved her skin with a knife. A pool of blood on the floor collected each drop that fell from her arm. I rushed to Teresa's side and cradled her head. My heartbeat was deafening as I stroked her cheek, just as she had once stroked mine. I begged her to live. The cage of my chest and the very soul it contained felt as if they were being crushed.

Her eyes were distant but there was still a shard of life in them, as she recognized me with a smile. She whispered, "Pray for me, Juan . . ." There was terror in her eyes. "I didn't mean . . ." Her eyes began to close.

"No!" I shouted. I picked her body up, but her eyes

looked at me vacantly. "We must go to Doctor Pablo. He will heal you, he will save you . . ."

I carried her past Priora Francisca and the other nuns, crowded in the doorway, their hands clasped over their mouths. I hurried out of the dark convent, clutching Teresa's body to my chest, but tripped on the rocky ground. A great pain, as if something had been severed, shot through my knee when we tumbled together to the ground. I turned Teresa over anxiously, but she was already dead. Weeping and moaning, I looked up at the full moon. I gently rocked Teresa's body back and forth all night. I could see no soul leaving her body, no redemption, no salvation.

As the sun rose, Priora Francisca urged me to go. She and several other nuns took Teresa's body and covered it with a blanket. I stood with difficulty. The weight of her body in my lap had somehow masked the pain, but now that I tried to walk, I could do so only with a limp. At last I was able to pull myself into the saddle and ride back, my leg dangling. I dug out the last tears from my eyes and vowed that I would never again weep for a woman. I kept that vow until tonight, when I wept fresh tears for Teresa as I climbed the stairs to my apartment, where Alma was still waiting. She once again proved that a woman knows a man better than he knows himself.

hank God you are safe," Alma said when I opened the door to my apartment.

"I failed."

"What happened?"

"Padre Miguel's mind is imprisoned along with his body."

"You saw him?"

"They have killed his soul."

She threw her arms around my neck and wept into my chest. I held her and stroked her hair softly.

"What can we do?"

"Nothing."

"Can we go to the Marquis?"

"How can you free a man from himself?"

"Where are you going?" she asked as I took a jug of wine from the table and headed for my bedroom.

"To numb the pain," I said, and I drained a third of the jug in one draft.

"What about the Marquis's masquerade?"

"I'm not going."

"You must. A messenger from the Marquis has just left. The masquerade is being held in your honor."

"My honor?" I said with disbelief.

"For your victory over the bull today."

"There has been no victory today."

"You cannot afford to offend the Marquis, even less now." She wrapped her cloak around herself and

205

walked to the door. "You must go . . . and besides, Doña Ana will no doubt be there."

"What difference would that make?"

"A woman always knows even what a man will not admit to himself."

She closed the door behind her as I thought of Doña Ana and smiled. Seeing her and hearing her laughter might indeed distract me from my pain—although somehow I suspected that going to her tonight might cause me even more.

The Masquerade Party

The church bells had already struck eleven times when my carriage pulled up at the Marquis's mansion for the masquerade. The celebration was fully under way in the enormous state salon; unlike the smaller gathering earlier in the day, the room was now filled from one wall to the other with people. I stood off to the side, hiding behind my leather mask. The other men also wore black leather or wooden masks. The women's faces were hidden behind white masks tied with satin ribbons or held up with delicate wands.

I melted into the tiled wall and surveyed the room, looking for Doña Ana. The light from the hundreds of candles in the chandeliers shimmered and cast their glow over the entire room. A large wooden screen inlaid with mother-of-pearl was supposed to separate the men from the women. But since this was the Marquis's party, he had placed it strategically so that there was hardly room for the women on their side and they inevitably spilled over into the company of men. The Marquis was a master at such stage setting, and he would stand back to watch the drama unfold. Once the floodgates between the two sides of the room had been opened, the men and women socialized, separated only by their masks, which helped more than hindered flirtation. Tonight, however, such intrigue did not excite me.

"Don Juan!" Don José and his wife recognized me behind my mask. I smiled, trying to be gracious to my compatriot from the bullfight. As his wife peppered me with questions, Don José's eyes darted constantly around the room, noticing all the lovely ladies. His wife, who had been imported from Vienna, clung to his arm nervously and no doubt jealously. Her beautiful golden hair fell in ringlets behind her mask. With my identity revealed, I soon found myself accosted on all sides by women and men wanting to congratulate me on my performance that afternoon. On another occasion I might have enjoyed their admiration. Yet at that moment I wanted only to be alone. My efforts to excuse myself, however, were prevented by the Marquis joining the crowd. Even with his eyes covered by a comic wooden mask, his large frame and well-fed form were unmistakable.

"An impressive show this afternoon," he said, and then he whispered in my ear, "Your conquests in Sevilla will be all the easier after such a display."

"What news of Don Hernán?" I asked.

The Marquis raised his mask, and my stomach

dropped. "He died a few hours after the bullfight from his wounds." And then, not wanting to turn his fiesta into a funeral, he said to the gathered crowd, "our noble friend Don Hernán died for honor and for passion. We should celebrate his life."

"There was neither honor nor passion in his death," I said and pushed through the crowd to be alone.

The Marquis caught up to me, taking me gently by the arm. "You did what you could. That's all any of us can do."

"He begged me to ask you to look after his wife and children."

"Of course they will have my protection." What the Marquis lacked in sentiment, he made up for in dedication to those he saw as his own. We could say no more about Don Hernán because Doña Ana and her father were just arriving. She held a mask to her face, but the Commander had no time for such frivolity. Judging from the Commander's downturned lips and glowering eyes, it was clear he was here against his will. I noticed that the dueña was not with them tonight. Recognizing the Marquis but not me, Doña Ana smiled graciously. Her father's face remained stone. The Marquis pretended not to notice and said, "Commander, I wonder if I might have another word with you in my library. It concerns your land holdings."

"I cannot leave my daughter unchaperoned."

"It will only take a moment, and I am sure my noble and trustworthy friend here will chaperone her until we return."

"Who is he?"

Before I could answer, the Marquis said, "My loyal lieutenant."

"If I am not safe in the Marquis's house," Doña Ana asked, "where in the world *am* I safe?" She glanced at me knowingly. Perhaps she did recognize me, not as myself but as the masked knight-errant at her hacienda.

"A young woman is not safe anywhere in the world," the Commander replied.

"I have heard that Doña Ana is quite capable of defending herself," the Marquis said pointedly.

"I will be all right, Father."

Soon the Marquis and the Commander left, but not before he had looked back at his daughter and especially at me. As they disappeared into the library, I asked, "would you like a refreshment?"

"No, thank you," she said. The darting of her eyes and how she moistened her lips revealed that she did suspect she had seen me before.

Remembering her fondness for the night air and the moon, I asked, "would you like to drink . . . the moonlight?"

She looked surprised and intrigued by my request, as if deciphering another clue. She nodded and smiled. "Yes, please. I find the pleasantries of these parties to be stifling."

"No pleasantries, I promise."

She let out a few bars of that song of her laugh, and my heart seemed to rise up in my chest.

I escorted her to the balcony, my hand tingling as I

held it near her back, even without touching the blue fabric of her dress. A slight wind had kept all the others inside, and we alone braved the night air. The wind swirled around us and fluttered the white flowers in her black hair.

As we gazed out at the moon, I could not help looking at her. She was no longer holding her mask up, and I could see the oval shape of her face and the black eyes that were brighter than two full moons. Doña Ana looked even more beautiful than she had earlier in the day, although she wore little of the cosmetics that had become so fashionable. Her skin was soft and unadorned, and her lips glistened in the moonlight even without a layer of wax.

Looking heavenward, she said, "I thought you offered to drink in the moonlight—not to drink in me."

"My apologies for staring, Doña Ana. I will try to control myself."

"You are the man who entered my carriage and who saved me that night, aren't you?"

"You saved yourself."

"I am sorry about my father."

"He was trying to protect you."

"There is not much time. Soon I will be . . . Please tell me who you are."

I raised my mask, and her face dropped. Seeing the disappointment in her eyes made me feel as if I were falling from the balcony.

"I should have known it was you. I am afraid modesty, Don Juan, compels me to go."

"Perhaps charity will compel you to stay."

"I do not know what game the Marquis is playing."

"I do not know, either. Perhaps he wants to see if I *am* his loyal lieutenant."

"Loyalty is not your strength, or so I have heard."

"I think you are mistaken," I said, looking down.

"I'm sorry," she said. "I saw your loyalty this afternoon—and your bravery."

"Don Hernán—the toreador—is dead."

"I am so sorry . . . that poor boy." We looked down respectfully for Don Hernán's soul, which was on its way to heaven, or wherever the souls of men who are unfaithful husbands but loving fathers dwell after death.

"I really should go," she said, perhaps wondering whether my words were just another attempt to seduce her.

"Please don't go," I said. I did not want to lose her company, which was all that was holding back my sadness. I could not look at her as I spoke. "It would comfort me greatly if you stayed. I lost two friends today."

"Two?"

"One to death and one to dogma."

"I have seen you come to the aid of others three times," she said, no doubt referring also to the slave market.

"Do you forgive me for interfering?"

"Yes."

"At the hacienda and the slave market, you no doubt

know, I had an ulterior motive. I wanted to seduce you. The bullfight was an unfamiliar impulse."

"A charitable one."

"Perhaps. As I said, it is unfamiliar."

"Why do you seduce so many women, Don Juan, and marry none?" she asked, returning to the curiosity that had prompted her first gaze.

"I am driven by my own desire, it is undeniable, but I am also driven by the heartache and loneliness of the women who surround me."

"Perhaps it is your own heartache and loneliness that cause you to flee from one woman's arms to the next."

"Perhaps," I said, bowing my head to her impressive insight into human nature.

"Or perhaps it is fear that one will discover the man behind the mask," she added more confidently.

I took my mask off my head and placed it on the balcony railing, and smiled at the truth of her statement. "None of us are truly as brave as we pretend," I confessed.

Her face was quite close to mine. "Yes, it's true, but some, I imagine, find their courage, while others, the cowards of love, just die alone."

"Some man will be very lucky to win you as his wife."

"How many women have you said that to, Don Juan?"

"Including you?" My lips were drawn toward hers as I whispered, "One."

"Oh, your mask!" she exclaimed, reaching for it as

the wind blew it off the balcony. She lost her balance, and I had to grab her arm to prevent her from falling off as well.

Once she was safe, I said, "Don't worry, the masquerade is over for me tonight."

"Thank you," she said, "for saving me . . . again."

"Thank you for saving me from my sadness tonight." We looked into each other's eyes. I still held her arm, as if she or I might fall from our dizzying height.

"So, my dear Don Juan, I see you have watched Doña Ana carefully." The Marquis had come onto the balcony without my noticing, the Commander by his side. I let go of Doña Ana's arm.

"I was just hearing about the death of your friend," Doña Ana said quickly.

"Yes, of course, bullfighting is a dangerous game, and in this case, I'm afraid the bull won."

"What is the meaning of this, Don Pedro?" the Commander asked, gesturing at me, clearly angered to discover that it was I who was the Marquis's loyal lieutenant.

"Don Juan saved me from falling off the balcony," Doña Ana said before the Marquis could answer. "We owe him our gratitude, Father." The red-faced Commander was unconvinced.

"Commander, this is not a time for accusation but for celebration," the Marquis declared. "I want Don Juan to be the first to know that you have agreed to give Doña Ana's hand in marriage . . . to *me*."

Doña Ana's wide eyes made it clear that this was

news to her as well. "Yes, my dear, I am delighted to say that your wise father has consented to our engagement."

Doña Ana forced a gracious smile with her mouth, but her worried eyes revealed the truth. I felt as though I had been run through with a sword, but I too tried to smile. The Commander's face was without expression. "It is time for an heir to the house of La Mota, and I can think of no more beautiful a vessel for my offspring than you, my dear Doña Ana. Let us return to the party and have a toast to the heir of La Mota."

After the toast, I left the party directly. I reached my carriage and saw my mask on the cobblestones. I picked it up and tucked it into my sleeve. As the wheels of the carriage creaked on the stones, I vowed to give up my efforts to seduce Doña Ana. Even a *galanteador* must have a code of ethics, and she was now promised to my mentor and closest friend. Yet the more I reminded myself of this fact, the more her face danced in front of me like an apparition, and the more her laughter echoed in my head like madness. I had thought that writing about the events of today and our encounters might exorcise her from my mind. I was wrong.

It is already morning and Doña Ana still haunts me like a ghost. There is, however, one way I know to forget a flesh-and-blood woman that has never failed me.

Morning, 18 June 1593

214

More than two weeks have passed, and I have tried valiantly to forget Doña Ana in the only way I know how—to burn away her memory with the skin of other women. Ten, to be exact. Yet I have known no relief. As a libertine, I have always lived for the pleasures of the moment. Lust is an impulse that flickers like a candle and goes out, but the light and warmth it sheds while it burns have been everything. To worry about the coming darkness is as futile as brooding over one's own death. It is only the worshipful fantasy of love, with its daughters, regret and hope, that causes the sinews of one's soul to be stretched on the rack between past and future.

The cruelty called love uses the same pious beliefs and unrelenting methods as the Inquisition, constantly interrogating the heart for a purity of faith and devotion that is impossible to maintain. We are not angels who sit in heaven all day, singing praises to our beloved. We prowl the streets like animals, looking for our next meal and the scent of another. Fidelity—whether to God or to love—is not in our blood.

How easy it has been for me to move on from the beauty of one woman to that of another. This does not mean that I have grown tired of the women I have known. My quest for more of life and more of womanhood has simply led me on to new encounters. Many have returned again and again over months or years, though they have never lingered longer than the last kiss we shared. But Doña Ana, without so much as a kiss or a caress, will not leave me in peace. Her voice and face encroach increasingly on my affairs.

On Sunday the Marquis even commented on my strange lack of interest in two Frenchwomen, refined and alluring daughters of a diplomat, whom he was certain I would seduce. He wondered whether I would seduce one or the other or both. He loves to put the cat among the pigeons, but I had no appetite, not even for the chase. He asked me what was wrong and whether I was ill. I told him nothing.

What vexes me most is that this strange passion I feel is different. Usually, my passion is hot and intemperate and won't rest until quenched by the cool plunge into the river of carnal pleasure. But this longing is simply to see Doña Ana again, to talk with her, and to hear her laugh. How could my desire be satisfied by a glance or a distant voice? Yet this would be enough.

As if to taunt me, her father has moved her to their house in the city, which stands only two streets away on Calle Susona. The street is named after a Jewess who fell in love with a Christian. When she heard that her father was involved in a planned uprising, she feared that her lover might be killed and warned him. He alerted the authorities, and her father and the other conspirators were arrested and executed. Susona converted, but not to marry her beloved; she ended her days alone in a convent. She left instructions that after her death, her head was to be displayed outside her house. This horrible relic of love can still be seen in its niche in the brick wall where it was given a permanent resting place. Is there not far greater danger in love than lust? For in love, one has much more to lose than merely one's life.

Last night, as if possessed by a demon, I tied on my black leather mask and climbed the ladder to my rooftop observatory. I had no interest in pausing to pay homage to the towering Giralda, the night stars, or the waning moon. Anxious and eager, I set out, traveling by rooftop to avoid detection. Blessedly, the streets of the Barrio Santa Cruz are close enough that one can leap across them. It was the Moors who first built their houses in this fashion to shade the street from the unrelenting heat of the Andalusian sun, and the Jews who built this neighborhood continued the tradition. Only in the new neighborhoods are there wide promenades that make it impossible to travel across the sky.

After flying over the final divide, I perched on a nearby roof in the shadow of a palm tree. From there I could look into the small square and down the Calle Susona. By the lamplight, I could see the skull, still displayed in the wall as a warning. Out of loyalty to the Marquis, I did not dare speak to Doña Ana, but my heart raced when I saw her shadow behind the drapes. A shadow! How can one be moved by a shadow? But this was enough to justify my journey. Yet I returned to my rooftop all the more consumed by Doña Ana.

As if to relieve me of my feverish ruminations, on my breathless return, I received the dove from Duchess

Cristina, who requested that I visit her that very night. *My husband,* she wrote in the note that she had attached to the leg of the dove, *has left me for four months, once again forcing me to live the life of a nun. As he attends to his lover, I am left alone without joy or tenderness. Come back, Don Juan, through my window, as on that first summer night when you brought the rain to quench my thirst.* So last night I answered Duchess Cristina's need with my own.

Born into one of the most powerful families in Spain, Duchess Cristina had her marriage made practically before her birth. She was married to an Italian duke named Octavio to solidify a political alliance, but her husband spent all of his time in Naples, where he had a lover. Through thirty-five years of marriage, four children who had survived, and a dozen grandchildren, Duchess Cristina had endured his long affair. She and I forged our own alliance one night during a party at the palace of the Countess of Lebrija.

When I first saw the Duchess, I was struck by the daintiness of her white-gloved hands and the restraint with which she held her fan. She was well trained in the rigid pose of the nobility. She fluttered her fan with the speed and imperceptible movement of a sparrow's wing, though it did not succeed in cooling her from the heat of the summer night. Hanging from her other glove and wrapped around her forearm was a gold chain with a cross. From the cross hung a wilted red rose, a sign that she had abandoned flirtation.

Her hair was gathered into a tight bun at the nape of

her neck, and she wore a black lace veil over her hair, which gave her the appearance of being in mourning. I could see the great beauty in her mature face that was impossible to hide. Age takes its toll on all of us, but the lines that were beginning to engrave her soft skin were like an intricate silver setting for the jewels of her blue eyes. Although her expression was as unchanging as a court portrait, the tiny droplets of perspiration on her brow told me she was not a painting. Her white cheeks had a delicate flush, which was not rouge but the natural heat seeping through her skin. Her neck was tethered with a pearl necklace, and her full bosom rose and fell with sighs as she endured the boredom of the party. She had a look of unanswered longing that drew me to her as a rooster is drawn to a hen, because they both need each other.

The greatest misstep in the dance of courtship is to believe it is our charm or beauty that is ultimately in question in this ancient fertility rite. Seduction and passion are simply life longing for life. They have little to do with our fears and faults. When we discover this Divine Secret, we realize that we are far less than we ever feared and far more than we ever imagined. Life uses us for its own satisfaction, and when we surrender to its will, we become a part of every kiss, whether or not it is made with our lips, and of every caress, whether or not it is made with our fingertips.

I approached her as she walked to the table of drinks. "May I?" I said. "You must slake your thirst in this heat." I held a small goblet by the bottom of the stem, and the gold glinted in the candlelight. With blue eyes she looked at me, both prey and predator, nervous and hungry. She took the goblet, careful not to touch my fingers, but said nothing. She looked at me over the rim of the cup as she drank, never breaking our gaze, her head tilted down, her eyes looking up.

"Is your husband here?" I asked boldly.

"He is in Naples on court affairs," she said, but she was a terrible liar and could not even convince herself to believe her words. I later learned that the affairs keeping her husband away almost continually concerned a servant whom he had loved from youth but could not marry because of her ignoble birth.

"How long has he been gone?" I asked.

"Six months," she said, still not taking her eyes off me.

"You must miss him a great deal."

At this she just nodded, unable to speak the lie.

"Six months is a long time to go without a dance," I said, and she smiled and did not say no. I took her hand, and we danced *la volta,* the latest amusement from Italy. It was here, with one hand on her waist and the other pressed against her palm, that I saw her body relax into its womanhood. The sight was beautiful to behold.

That night I had my carriage follow hers at a discreet but noticeable distance. I was pleased to see that she left her window open, a bold invitation that I happily accepted. Now an expert at balcony entrances, I climbed from the roof of my carriage over the wrought-iron railing onto her tiled landing. I wondered why anyone would want to enter by the front door.

Tonight I answered her letter once again, arriving on her balcony in the hope that I could prove to myself that flesh is flesh and skin is skin. Her bedchamber was larger than I remembered, and by candlelight I could see that it was filled with new art and objects. On our first night together it had been bare, but now there was hardly an inch of wall or ground that was not covered with Turkish rugs, ornate furniture, or large Roman urns filled with flowers. She came out from behind a wooden screen wearing a silk robe and fanning her face. The black hair that was starting to reveal silver threads wafted in the gentle air.

"I prayed that you would answer the dove," she said.

I took off the black mask that ensured I would arrive unrecognized.

She opened her robe to reveal her breasts and turned her head to the side modestly. Her breasts looked like two shooting stars descending in the heavens. She had confided in me that despite the decorum of her nobility, she had chosen to nurse her own children. She hid this scandal even from her servants. Her wet nurse and I were the only ones who knew the truth. I now stared at the bright pinkness of her large, well-suckled nipples, startling against the cloudlike whiteness of her skin. What a miracle that this source of life-sustaining nourishment is also such a source of joy. Do we need any further proof that God created us for pleasure and celebrates our desire? I approached and stroked the side of her breast tenderly with my fingertip. Her skin seemed pale in comparison to Doña Ana's, and once again I was distracted from the feast before me. My hand fell away.

"What's wrong?"

For the first time I admitted my distraction: "I am somewhere else, with someone else."

I thought she might be disappointed, but she simply smiled and took a white mask that was hanging from the screen. It had a small feather descending on either side. She placed the ribbon over her head and the mask over her eyes.

"I can be someone else. Who do you want me to be?" she whispered seductively in my ear, circling around my back. She took the leather mask in my hands and went to put it back over my face. "And you can be someone else, too."

I stopped her hand, having never made love to a woman while wearing my mask. "I cannot be—"

"Please," she begged, "be Octavio."

I was incredulous. "Your husband?"

"Yes."

"After his neglect, his affair?"

"A woman's heart always dreams that her husband will be the man he could be and not just the man he is." She put the mask over my eyes, and this time I did not resist her. "Only a woman's infelicity causes her infidelity," she said as she kissed my mouth. She closed her eyes and no doubt imagined that she was kissing her husband's lips. There was an ache in my chest. It felt intolerable to pretend to be someone else. But I tried to surrender to the fantasy.

I kissed her back, biting her lip gently and closing my own eyes. I imagined Doña Ana's full lips and her beautiful eyes staring at me. Duchess Cristina led me to the silk pillows that lay on her carpet, and I lost my hands in the folds of her flesh, rounded and softened with age. I sucked on those beautiful pink nipples and played with her womanhood.

I kept my undergarments on even after I had disrobed, because a woman does not relish the sight of a man's nakedness as he relishes hers. I have always remained sheathed until a woman is ready and wanting me fully. Tonight I also knew that this loincloth would give me time to rise to my full powers as I heard the sounds of a woman's satisfaction, which are the world's greatest aphrodisiac.

I nipped at her gently with my teeth as she gasped for air and let out a sigh. I drew my mouth back from her breast and looked at her smile below the mask. For the masquerade to continue, I would need to avoid looking at her face. I kissed my way down her body to the banquet below as she took a goblet from the bedside and dripped red wine on her belly. The sharp taste awoke my appetite, and I proceeded downward.

I held her buttocks before me like a chalice. I began with my tongue fluttering as gently as the wings of a butterfly landing on the bud of her desire. As she arched her back and offered herself, I drew her flesh into my mouth like the dripping meat of cracked lobster. I used my tongue to awaken and my lips to sip, and she lashed from side to side. Some complain about the fragrance of the banquet of womanhood, but flesh does not smell like flowers, and this is the aroma of life, which sweats and screams with creation.

As I tried to assuage my deeper hunger, the Duchess tossed from side to side, spilling the red wine on the white marble floor. Then she needed something more and pulled me up by my hair. I obliged her, and we rolled across the floor together as if tossed by a storm, our bodies rising up like a wave and crashing on her bed. To know a mature woman is to know more than her body. It is to know the foundation of her need and the hungers that drive her. It is to know her dreams and her secrets. It is to know that a dance is a fight, and a fight is a dance, and that passion and compassion beat in the same breast.

A woman can dance and fight long after a man, so he must never try to overpower her desire. He cannot. A woman's passion is nothing less than the sea that tosses a man's ship, and to weather the storm he must use skill and humility to ride her waves, having given up his own course and dragged down his sails, letting the sea take him where it will. For a sailor who knows that there is nothing to fear, this is the greatest adventure of life, as he lashes himself to the mast, knowing that his surrender is his strength and the chance for his redemption.

I tried to hold on to the fantasy as we rocked back and forth, until she moaned into my ear, "Yes, yes," and in a spasm of pleasure called out, "Yes, Octavio, yes," before her body went limp. Mine soon followed. I had not finished but was done. To make love to a fantasy was the second betrayal of a libertine.

I collapsed next to her and rolled onto my back. I pulled off my mask in disgust and heard Doña Ana's words in my head: "Perhaps it is fear that one will discover the man behind the mask." The masquerade was over for me tonight. Duchess Cristina curled alongside me and placed her soft cheek on my chest. She fell asleep in my arms, and although I longed to leave, I did not want to awaken her. Let her dream, I thought. Let her dream of dear Octavio, home at last.

Although my arm was wrapped around her chest and drew her tighter, I felt quite alone, and my mind raced as I argued with myself that I could not possibly love one woman, having known the holiness of all women. Over and over I saw the face of Doña Ana. Blessed sleep soothes all worries, and I was soon lying in the arms of Morpheus. But my sleep was neither long nor blessed, as I was awakened just before dawn by some restless demon. For as long as I can remember, when I've slept in a woman's arms, I have never been awakened by the sun on my face. Instead, I am always cast out of bed in the dark by some inner calling that forces me to wander like the fugitive Cain. I was extricating myself from her still-sleeping body when I heard a voice.

"Abuelo?" said a small boy, thinking I was his grandfather returned from Naples at last. Anxiously, I

looked around, grateful that the candles had burned out and the room was dark. He was tugging on my hand persistently. *"Abuelo?"*

I shook Duchess Cristina's shoulder, but she was completely unresponsive, snoring contentedly. As I moved my chest out from under her head, her face fell against the pillow without waking. I felt a small hand brush against my cheek and knew I had no choice but to seek help elsewhere.

I pulled on the Duchess's silk robe, which reached only to my knees. I tied the silk belt closed and took a very deep breath. I picked up the boy without speaking and felt the weight of his small body clinging to me. I thought of Don Hernán's son and his love for his father and held the boy closer. I carried him upstairs to the servants' quarters. I followed the lovely scent of Fátima's skin to her door and knocked, waking her. She lit a candle, but the boy was resting his head on my shoulder, his eyes closed. I pointed to him anxiously, and Fátima understood immediately. She took the Duchess's sleeping grandson into her arms, and I experienced a strange feeling of sadness as my arms emptied. Before I left, she held up the oil candle and said, "let me have a look at you." She laughed at my outfit and added, "So you have discovered the joy of children."

"Joy? You mean horror? I already have enough trouble sleeping."

"I saw the truth on your face. To give love to one who needs it is a far greater pleasure even than to receive it."

"Perhaps after the boy is back in bed, *you* will give love to one who needs it." I smiled, hoping once again to lose the persistent ache in my chest. Doña Ana's presumptuous words echoed back: "Perhaps it is your own heartache and loneliness that cause you to flee from one woman's arms to the next." I shook her away.

"What you want," she replied, "is not love, my lord."

"I'll settle for whatever you are willing to give," I said, touching her cheek.

"My husband, thanks to you, is back with me," she said, looking down at her heart, where the amulet rested.

"I'm happy to hear it." I sighed. "Perhaps someday you will be reunited with him and your sons once again." She smiled gratefully in anticipation of that day.

I returned to the Duchess's bedchamber, where she was still immobile in the pool of her pleasure. Dressing quickly, I went to the balcony window. As I left the way I had come, I looked at the force of nature that lay on her sheets. I marveled at how this woman had managed to contain the storm of her desire within her black dress and white gloves. Holding her delicate fan, she had seemed the model of regal restraint, but once the window was opened, a typhoon was released that left clothes scattered, wineglasses spilled, and her fan irreparably broken.

As I record these futile attempts to forget one woman with another, I know that women have used me for their own purposes as surely as I have used them. Yet

227

this mutual exchange now seems empty of true passion. I want a desire that is more than mere abandon,
an aching embrace even more enduring than any
blissful release. Did this require love? And how could
it possibly be even more pleasurable to give this love
than to receive it? In the garden Doña Ana had told me
of her need for such love, but the Marquis is incapable
of giving it. Will her infelicity lead to her infidelity? I
try to shake these musings from my mind, knowing
they will lead only to betrayal. Today I must go
hunting with the Marquis as his devoted and loyal lieutenant. And yet the only quarry that I want is further
news of Doña Ana.

Morning, 7 July 1593

The Truth

*W*hen I arrived at the Marquis's stables, I
found that he and I were the only two members of the hunting party and that our expedition was
hardly the innocent sport that I had been led to believe.
"Where are the dogs?" I asked.
"We won't need them today," he replied.
"And the muskets?"
"We won't need them, either."
I took a pistol and placed it in the saddle holster of
the horse he had given me to ride. "For the highway
robbers at least," I said. He bowed his head in consent
and smiled. The Marquis mounted his favorite horse, a
white stallion, and I mounted a chestnut mare.

We trotted out of the city through the Puerta de Carmona toward his ancestral lands and the village closest to the convent where I had been raised. It was also in the direction of Doña Ana's hacienda, although I was not going to mention this.

"Yah! Yah!" the Marquis shouted, and kicked his horse as we raced across the countryside. We galloped over hills covered in a carpet of red poppies, and through armies of silver olive trees. Yellow sunflowers hung their enormous heads sadly, like mourners. Sheep grazed on the abundant thyme and rosemary in the shade of the cypress and oak trees that dotted the horizon.

We passed the ruined walls of abandoned hilltop towns and broken watchtowers on cliffs—reminders of the age of chivalry, when Christians and Moors would clash with lances and scimitars. Even more ominous were the crosses sticking out of piles of rocks that marked the graves of those killed by highway robbers. I was wondering if the Marquis's decision to ride unescorted was wise, when a motley band of half a dozen highwaymen raced toward us from behind one of the ruins. I kicked my horse, urging it to move faster, but to my disbelief, the Marquis slowed. I pulled my pistol with one hand and held my reins with the other as they came alongside us. I was shocked to see the leader of the band dismount and kneel before the Marquis as if he were a squire.

"Your Lordship," he said in a gravelly voice that unmistakably belonged to the man who had protested against raping Doña Ana the night her barn was set on fire.

"You are the new leader, I take it?" the Marquis said, clearly knowing these men.

"Yes, my lord, after Alvaro was shot."

"How dare your band of brigands attempt to violate a noble lady!"

The ruffian spoke with fear in his voice. "It won't happen again, my lord, you can be sure—"

In one swift movement the Marquis pulled his long pistol from his saddle and shot the man. His body lurched backward from the force of the bullet and fell to the ground, blood seeping through his white shirt. "I am sure of it," the Marquis said as the rest of the men looked on with wide eyes and open mouths. The Marquis kicked his horse and was soon trotting away.

Shock and disgust must have been visible on my face as I came up alongside him. "What if that was not the man who tried to—"

"Of course he wasn't the man. He was just an example. Doña Ana shot the one who tried to attack her . . . with the help of a masked caballero." The Marquis did not wait for my reply or excuse and kicked his horse brutally into a gallop.

Again we raced across the hills of wild wheat, red poppies sprinkled throughout like spots of blood. We rode past the Marquis's hilltop fortress and on to Doña Ana's hacienda. In the distance, I saw another rider approach at a full gallop on what looked like a brilliant silver horse. As he came closer, I could see that the horse and rider were partially covered in metal armor that shone so brilliantly in the sun it was practically blinding. The approach of the military has always made me nervous, but the Marquis did not slow down until we were no more than ten lengths apart.

Only then did I recognize the cross of the order of Calatrava painted on the cape covering the Commander's armor. We pulled back our reins and brought our horses to a halt, and they stood there snorting and shaking their proud manes. On his steel-covered horse, the Commander was an imposing sight. Metal covered the horse's black head from its eyes to its nose and strips of metal and mail covered its neck. The pieces of armor on its body were riveted one to the next. The Commander's velvet and steel saddle rested on a yellow and red blanket made of silk. On his left arm was strapped a shield with the shell of Santiago. The Commander sat upright on his horse with a vigilant stare that transformed into rage as he recognized me.

He drew his enormous broadsword from its sheath and held it above his head, as he had the night he chased me across this same countryside. I doubted that he recognized me from that night, but my offense at the slave market was enough to justify his fury. I wondered whether the Marquis had brought me here to die. "I will avenge my honor," the Commander said, and kicked his horse, which caused it to leap at mine. I quickly drew my thin rapier and was barely able to restrain his blow, my horse moving nervously to the side.

"Commander! No!" the Marquis shouted, trying to stop the attack. He was trying to control his horse, which was turning in circles, preventing him from coming to my aid. "Stop!" he shouted, with a voice that held fear as well as fury. The Commander's blows were relentless, and I could hardly hold them back with my rapier. My hands stung with the force of his metal on mine. Finally, he knocked me from my horse. My horse reared up, and I worried that in his fury the Commander might behead my mare. In the commotion, I rolled under the bellies of our horses and appeared on the other side. The tip of my sword was now at the Commander's neck, his face torn between surprise and fury. I took my sword away quickly and this act of mercy, while not ending his anger, ended the battle.

"Commander, Don Juan is my loyal lieutenant."

"A man who sleeps with other men's wives is an enemy to all men. And you should know, Don Pedro, that not all lieutenants are loyal."

"We are here, Commander, not to do battle but to complete our alliance. Do you accept the price I offered for your hacienda?" the Marquis said, gesturing to the square white house with its clay tile roof.

The Commander looked down. It was clear that he had lost in this alliance with the Marquis, as everyone did. "Yes," he spat out, still seething.

"Consider it," the Marquis said, "a dowry, only one in which you receive gold in return." Perhaps he was trying to help the Commander pay off his debts, but the

232

Marquis always got more than he gave and was no doubt adding to his landholdings. He had once told me that land was the only true wealth. "God made the earth," he said piously, "and he is not making any more."

The Commander yanked his horse around on its hind legs to leave but was stopped by the Marquis's imploring voice. "Commander?" The military man stopped and stared at the Marquis as his horse moved restlessly. He said nothing. "Have my letters and my visits made any impression on her? Has she started to love me?" This great big beast of a man seemed tender and vulnerable before his feelings for Doña Ana. Perhaps it was not just for an heir that he was marrying her.

"Love is not part of our deal."

"Talk to her, Commander, please."

The Commander nodded slowly and begrudgingly but then spun his stallion around violently, forcing its neck with the reins. With wild eyes, the horse reared up on its hind legs, its long mane hanging down, and galloped off. This harsh man knew no tender words that would convince his daughter to love the Marquis. If the Marquis's own letters were having no influence, her father's orders would have little more. I thought of the way she had forced a smile the night of the masquerade party, trying to hide her true feelings.

Looking back at the Marquis, I was shocked by the revelation of his feelings for Doña Ana. Whatever his understanding of love might be, he wanted it from her, needed it from her, desperately. The Marquis watched the Commander's dust trail disappear before he spoke. "How she slipped into the locked chamber of my heart I do not know. And now I will do anything not to let her escape."

"Why do you choose to marry a woman who does not love you when many would do so happily?"

"There is no other for me. There has never been any other. I watched Doña Ana grow into womanhood as a farmer watches his fruit, and have waited years for her to be ready to pluck."

"A man cannot force a woman to love him."

"She will love me—or suffer for it." I knew that the Marquis meant what he said and had myriad ways to make a person's life miserable if he wished, especially if he controlled her life and freedom as her husband. The Marquis had two favorite books in his libraries from which he often took inspiration, both by Italians, Niccolò Machiavelli's *Il Principe* and Dante Alighieri's *Inferno*. Inspired by the latter, he was quite capable of subjecting Doña Ana to each and every one of the nine circles of hell, while she, unwilling to submit, would struggle and suffer as long as she had breath in her lungs.

The Marquis said nothing more but spurred his stallion and rode at a breakneck gallop. I followed just behind him. My fingertips were throbbing against the reins as I realized that I needed to warn Doña Ana. She was in real danger if she denied the Marquis even feigned affection. I rode alongside, trying to keep up, but as I approached, he sped faster. It was clear that he was racing me back to his stable, and I accepted his challenge. We raced through a grove of orange trees and along a riverbed, the horses' hooves gliding over the water and then splashing down into the shallow stream in an explosion of speed. First he was leading and then I. As I inched ahead, I heard him growl and beat his horse on. We came onto the main road, the horses' hooves pounding against the hard-packed dirt, the dust kicking up in all directions. The rows of grapevines that bordered us on both sides blurred into one rolling carpet of green.

As we approached the city gate, I was once again leading. I looked back and saw possession in his eyes. He would not accept defeat. I began to slow as we came upon the gates, but he galloped right through them, scattering the crowd. Now I was caught in the battle, and I followed him in heated pursuit. The stakes were clear—Doña Ana was the prize. I was trailing his horse by a length as we galloped past the Cathedral, parting a crowd of clergy. We jockeyed around carriages and down the busy streets. Our horses' hooves clattered on the cobblestones, the loud noise and force of the beasts chasing away all in our path. Vendors and buyers scrambled out of the way quickly, while those less fortunate fell with their goods in the attempt.

As we entered the Plaza de San Francisco, I spoke to my horse. I whispered to her of her beauty and power and told her that these must win the race. Impossibly, she flew with renewed strength, no doubt also sensing the approaching stables. We pulled up to the Marquis's saddle and then pulled even, and then were ahead by a handbreadth. I looked over at the Marquis's face—his eyes ablaze with fury and his teeth bared—and I knew that to win would be unwise. Restraint, I reminded myself, is the defining feature of the true caballero. I pulled slightly on my reins, my horse fighting me not to lose, and the Marquis galloped into the stable first.

We dismounted, both as winded as our horses, but the Marquis managed to say, "In life—some win—and others—lose." I smiled and acknowledged my defeat to him with my hand. My mind was already elsewhere. I began to leave the stable, the smell of horse sweat and hay in my nose.

"Don Juan?" the Marquis called me back. "Doña Ana and I will enter into holy matrimony on July the fifteenth. By then you must tell the King whom you wish to marry. At last both of us will surrender to the *Sacrament* of Marriage." He pronounced the word "Sacrament" with a chilling sneer. I nodded and tried to smile before turning to leave again. "I trust you have not forgotten about the King's ultimatum," he persisted.

"Of course not, my lord," I said. But presently I was preoccupied with Doña Ana's fate more than my own. I knew what must be done next, for once wronged, the Marquis never forgave. I had to warn Doña Ana, and for her safety I would need to do so as soon as night had fallen.

Afternoon, 7 July 1593

Knowledge That Could Lead to Our Ruin

After I had returned from "hunting" and had written in my diary, Cristóbal informed me that the famous assassin Ignacio Álvarez de Soria had swung from the gallows earlier that day. He said in disbelief, "I saw him with my own eyes at the Taberna del Pirata the night the ships arrived." He must have noticed my face drop. "Did you know him?"

"I met him once—that night, actually." Having got what he wanted, the Marquis clearly did not wish anyone else to know about the other body buried in the coffin with Doña Ana's mother. It was no doubt he who had made sure no one would. Who, I wondered, had the Commander killed and buried with his wife? Had he not killed many?

As I waited until the cover of darkness, I washed the dust and sweat away, changed into fresh clothes, and went downstairs to the tavern to take my afternoon meal. I convinced Cristóbal to join me, though he continues to protest that a coachman should not eat at the same table as his lord. I've tried to tell him that there are many hidalgos who in their poverty have become servants, but he insists on maintaining propriety.

"Put the book away, Cristóbal," I had to say as he read at the table. He did not hear me. "Cristóbal!"

"Yes?" he said, looking up from his book finally.

"There is a time for reading, and there is a time for living."

He reluctantly closed the book.

We were waited on by Colette, the beautiful niece of Doña Felipa. She had come from France with her father, pulled, like so many, by the city's wealth. On their arrival her father had caught the fever from the Indies and was now quite ill. Colette cooked and waited tables all day and took care of her father all night. Her black hair was braided hastily and her full cheeks sloped down to a dimpled chin. She had thick eyebrows, like a man's, but these only accentuated the feminine gracefulness of the rest of her face.

"How is your father?" I asked, knowing that compassion often leads to passion.

"He is not well, my lord. He has been taken to the Hospital de las Cinco Llagas," she said, purposely leaning over me to pour my cup of steaming chocolate. I returned the compliment by inhaling the fragrance of her body from her torso to her neck. The scent of her sweat was mixed with the aroma of chocolate brewed with vanilla and cinnamon.

I saw that Cristóbal was gazing at Colette. It was the first time I had seen him stare at any woman, and I was pleased by his interest, which is the mother of boldness. I watched him watch her as she walked away. When she glanced back at us, however, his shoulders sank and his gaze dropped to his plate. I tapped on his chest with my palm to get him to sit up straight, not only like a proper coachman but like a true caballero. How is he ever going to win the affections of a woman if he stoops like a broken man and stares down, never showing her the heart in his chest or the soul in his eyes? I have tried to teach Cristóbal to be proud. Yet the heart is much harder to teach than the head.

As I left two silver coins on the table, Cristóbal looked at my overpayment with surprise and dismay.

"Interested?" I asked as we walked to the carriage.

He shrugged indifferently, but I could see the lie in his face.

"You are interested in her, aren't you?"

"She is the only woman in Sevilla whom you haven't yet ruined for another man's love," Cristóbal said boldly, and then, thinking better of it, added, ". . . my lord."

I laughed. "So it is love, is it?"

He did not have a chance to deny it, because Colette had followed us, running out to the carriage.

"My lord, you have forgotten your reales," she said, holding out the coins.

"That was for you, Colette."

She threw the coins at my chest. They bounced off my leather doublet and fell to the ground. "I am not a prostitute who can be bought." Her heavy eyebrows were arched with the indignation of a woman who is certain she has been wronged.

"Who said anything about a prostitute, and since when are prostitutes paid in advance?" I asked.

"That is much more than the price of your meal."

"My coachman, Cristóbal, insisted that we leave it for you. To buy medicine for your father."

Cristóbal looked shocked at this white lie. Perhaps to

hide his face, he stooped and picked up the coins. He slowly held them out to her. She gave him her hand. He smiled with embarrassment as he dropped them into her palm, and she smiled back timidly with gratitude, and no doubt with embarrassment at her outburst. Cristóbal looked away quickly, but as she left I saw him watch her disappear, her green skirt flowing and the white shirt clinging to her shoulders, wet from the afternoon heat. When she was at the door, she turned and looked back. This time Cristóbal was not able to hide his eyes before they looked into hers.

I got into the carriage, shaking my head and trying to understand his terror of women. With his light brown hair and pale blue eyes, Cristóbal is handsome enough. Even the small scar under one eye gives him a sense of mystery and intrigue. I've told him that scars add interest to the body. They convey that one has faced dangers and lived to tell of them. But he still covers his face with his hand instinctively. His mother, he explained, had beaten him for not defending her against his drunken father. It is perhaps because of his father that Cristóbal refuses to drink, which I guess is an admirable quality in a servant, and especially a coachman.

"Take me to the Alameda de Hércules," I told Cristóbal, "by way of Calle Susona." I wanted to see the various windows of Doña Ana's house and plan my return that night. As we rode by slowly I saw that her carriage was not there and all the curtains were drawn.

As we rode on through the Plaza de San Francisco, I

glanced out the window, still trying to distract myself from Doña Ana. I looked at the line of professional beggars, war amputees, students, widows, and men without work, all awaiting the convent broth. I was about to let the leather curtain fall when to my surprise I saw what seemed to be Doña Ana's red carriage parked in front of the entrance to the church of the Convento de San Francisco. "Stop!" I said, and got out without waiting for Cristóbal to open the door. "Go back to the tavern and give Colette a ride to the hospital. Your concern for her father will win her heart." My own concern was to keep my carriage from being seen, but I knew that we could also aid two women at once.

"I . . . I . . ." Cristóbal stammered.

"Fear is a thief, Cristóbal. Don't let it steal your life."

"But, my lord—"

"I'll tell you one more time as plainly as I can. If *you* don't live your life, who will? Do you understand?"

"Yes, my lord."

As Cristóbal rode back to Colette, I hurried through the crowd to the church, trying to be inconspicuous. I was pleased to see that it was indeed the same red carriage that I had slipped into on our first meeting and into which the Commander and Doña Ana had stepped at the slave market. Looking around to make sure I had not been seen, I entered the church.

I dipped my fingers into the pink marble font and instinctively crossed myself with the holy water. I had not been inside a church in many years. I was careful to walk quietly and to hide behind the massive stone columns. Doña Ana and the Commander were standing in what must have been their family chapel. The engraving on its wall read CAPILLA DE SANTA MARÍA MAGDALENA. I moved closer and could see that Doña Ana was crying.

"Why, Father, why did you give my hand to the Marquis? Do you not love me and want me to be happy?"

The Commander was clearly moved by his daughter's plight but answered sternly, "I had no choice but to accept his marriage proposal."

"Why? There must be other wealthy nobles to whom you can marry me."

"It is not because of the Marquis's wealth that I have consented to the marriage, although it is true that his gold will allow us to keep this chapel where your mother is buried and where I will join her." He looked down tenderly at a white marble sculpture of a pious woman kneeling and reading a Bible. "She will be my sentinel as I enter eternal life."

"Please do not speak of your death, Father. I could not bear to lose you, too."

"A soldier lives between life and death, and his grave must always be ready." The Commander turned to his own tomb. On top of the stone coffin I could see the carved marble body of a man. The Commander touched its face. "So lifelike, don't you think?"

"I don't know how you can spend the Marquis's gold on your tomb while selling your daughter like a whore."

The Commander spun around, and with the hand that had been touching his own marble face, he slapped his daughter's cheek. I had to restrain myself, knowing that nothing would be gained by coming to her aid just then. He realized his mistake instantly, and as she held her cheek, he spoke to her with the first measure of tenderness I had witnessed. "I never should have raised you with such spirit. It will only cause you to suffer all the more in your marriage."

"Then why did you consent, if not for his gold?"

"The Marquis has knowledge . . . knowledge that could lead to our ruin."

"What does he know?"

"It is not important what he knows, just that he knows," the Commander said with a tone of finality that Doña Ana did not dare challenge. He knelt down at his wife's tomb. "Your mother's candle is burned out. I must go and get another from the devotions seller."

"Can we not send María?"

"It is my duty and my privilege to buy a sacred candle for your mother. There are so few ways that I can honor her now . . . where *is* your dueña? She should be here watching over you."

"She is praying in another chapel."

"Why is she not here with you?"

"She never comes to my mother's chapel."

"María!" the Commander shouted, his voice echoing throughout the large sanctuary and the small chapels of the silent church.

243

The dueña arrived quickly. She wore a black sash tied maternally under her breasts that made her white dress billow out as if she were pregnant. She wasn't wearing her veil, and I could see clearly that she was from the Indies. Her older, bronze face was beautiful under her braided gray hair, but her eyes were filled with fear and worry, perhaps for Doña Ana, perhaps for herself in this land of her conquerors. "Watch over her, as is your duty," the Commander said, and left. I hid myself behind the column to make sure he did not see me.

After he was gone, Doña Ana said, "I know my father told you to stay here, but I want to be alone with my mother."

I could see the dueña's insulted face, as if she had bitten into a lemon. "I wait in the carriage. You tell Commander why."

As she left, I knew this was the moment, but I did not know how long it would last. I approached Doña Ana slowly as she was sobbing into her hands.

"Doña Ana, I must speak with you." She looked at me in shock and tried to dry her eyes. "There is no need to hide your feelings. Perhaps I can offer you the kindness that you showed me at the Marquis's."

"You must go before my father returns."

"I must warn you before I go. Your happiness, if not your life, will be in danger if you do not return the Marquis's love."

"*I* cannot lie about love."

"Your marriage will break the hearts of many men in

Sevilla, but you could not have a better protector and benefactor than the Marquis."

"Whose heart will be broken?"

"Too many to name, but in love, as in life, some win and others lose."

"I am not willing to concede defeat."

"You could not ask to marry a more powerful man aside from the King's own son."

"Title and social rank mean nothing to me."

"The Marquis will provide you with every comfort."

"I care not for *comforts,*" she said scornfully.

"Is it his age that repulses you?"

"It is the emptiness of his heart. You saw how he felt nothing for his friend," she said, stopping to look away, but then whispered, "Your friend who died in the bull-fight."

I now understood for the first time from her words that Doña Ana felt something for me. My chest swelled. "Is there another whom you love?" I asked boldly.

"I have never met a man who did not lie about love," she said, staring back at me.

It was my turn to look away. "If you will not accept the Marquis's affection, then you must escape his wrath by fleeing Sevilla."

"I have nowhere to go."

"You will not be safe here."

"A woman does not have your choice to live without marriage unless she is a nun or a prostitute, of which I am neither."

"Then I beg you to return the Marquis's love. It is genuine."

"But mine would never be, and unlike some I cannot counterfeit my affections." I knew she would never give the Marquis what he wanted, and I saw her falling into the circles of hell that he would create for her. I wanted to tell her that my affection was genuine, but I heard her father's footsteps and had to hide behind his tomb.

"Where is María?"

"I wanted to be alone with my mother. I sent her to the carriage."

"You are never to be unchaperoned! Go to the carriage immediately!" She went obediently but not without a furtive glance in my direction.

I listened as the Commander replaced the candle and knelt in prayer. His words were not to God but to his wife. "Catalina, my soul, are you listening? What have I done? It was my love for you that . . . I miss you every day. Our daughter is better never having known love than having to suffer its loss." He was silent. I was moved by his affection for his wife and for his daughter. What cruelty that so few find love and that those who do are often denied it by death. How strange love is—why does it grace some and curse others? "Will she ever forgive me?" the Commander continued. "I fear for her. I beg of you, please watch over her. I beg of you, my love."

I heard the Commander slide the bolt of the chapel as he left and realized that I might be locked in. My fear was relieved when I heard him call out to the priest, "Padre! Will you lock the chapel?"

"With pleasure, Don Gonzalo, I will do so immediately. Are you happy with your tomb?"

"The Italian sculptor did a miraculous job. You were right to recommend him . . ." As I heard them continue to talk, I left my hiding place and glanced quickly at the Commander's tomb. It was him as a much younger and quite handsome man, his head, with long hair and a mustache, resting on a pillow. Even the flutes of his ruff were carved intricately out of white marble, as were his armor, his hands, and the sword that he held on his chest.

As I went to leave I glanced at the equally lifelike sculpture of his wife. Her face was round and smooth, like Doña Ana's, although the white marble had a deathly pallor. Her mother did not look much older than Doña Ana herself. I slid the bolt open and edged silently out the door. As I backed behind the column and looked once again at the gentle face of the statue, prayerful words came to my lips for the first time since I was a boy: "Please protect her from the Marquis." I shocked myself with this act of piety, having so long ago lost all faith.

I heard the priest's and the Commander's footsteps and hid behind the column.

"I am sure you will not let my wife's candle burn down again."

"My apologies, Don Gonzalo, I will see to it personally."

I left the church and saw Doña Ana's red carriage drive off. I walked home and was pleased to see that I had arrived before Cristóbal. I took my diary from under the loose tile in the floor to record these events, and when I sat down at my writing desk, I discovered that the lock on my desk had been broken. Someone was eager to read this diary, and if he could not buy it, he was willing to steal it. Fortunately, his spies had not found it in its true hiding place.

Despite his suspicions, the Marquis need not worry. My loyalty is not in doubt. His cruelties may lead to his damnation, but his kindness to me has been my salvation. Without the Marquis, I would still be a common rope-climber. He has given me everything—my skill, my nobility, and my purpose. I must return his devotion to me with my own. I also know I can offer Doña Ana no more than my warning. I could never offer her the True Passionate Love for which she longs.

I must confess, however, that I write with more certainty than I feel. It is the first time in so many years that my emotions overwhelm my reason. Doña Ana says she is unwilling to concede defeat. Am I? Fortunately, Alma returns from Carmona tomorrow, and I am sure that in her skillful hands the truth will be revealed, for no one could better challenge the illusion of love with the reality of lust.

Evening, 7 July 1593

$\mathcal{J}$ walked down Calle de las Sierpes. The corner apartment where Alma lived and worked was on the second floor, across from the Monasterio de San Pablo. It was here that she ministered to the needs of her faithful. The windows to the balcony were opened wide, and the white cotton curtains blew outward into the street like a woman tipping up her skirts. I smiled expectantly, knowing that the two years since Alma's apprenticeship with me would only have heightened her already quite extraordinary skill.

"Don *Juan?*" said Lenora, her dueña, as she opened the door. Alma had a false dueña who helped her play the part of the great lady. All of the most expensive courtesans had them.

"Is Doña Alma . . . *available?*" I asked, knowing she might be entertaining a patron of her arts. In the short time since she had come to Sevilla, she had climbed to the heights of her profession. She was rightly considered the finest courtesan in all Sevilla, and her rates were commensurate with her reputation. Since she began charging for her affections, I had, as is my rule, refused to lie with her. Yet today I was willing to make an exception, knowing that if anyone had the power to banish Doña Ana's laugh from my ear and her face from my eye, it was Alma.

"She has just arrived from Carmona—"

"My timing is impeccable, then."

"—and is in the bath," said Lenora, holding up a brown sea sponge that she had been using to soap Alma's body.

"Will you let her know that I am here and ask whether I should go or stay?"

"Yes, my lord." She disappeared into Alma's room. I looked around at the bookshelf and noticed more than a few medical textbooks. I ran my finger along the spine of the one on surgical amputations and smiled.

"My lady would like you to join her . . . in the bath." Although Lenora's real job was not to protect Alma's modesty but to help her sell it, she could not stop herself from blushing at her lady's forwardness. I, on the other hand, was not surprised at all, just delighted that the invitation was still open. I held out my hand for the sponge, and Lenora dropped it into my hand with a conspiratorial smile.

Alma's perfectly proportioned face was as youthful as ever, though her eyes looked older and perhaps wiser. Her irises were bright blue and circled dark pupils that glowed as if there were candles lit within them. They reflected her mind's passionate quest for knowledge and experience. Her long black ringlets spilled into her bath, covering her full breasts. Her skin was shimmering under the soapy water, and my body was already responding to her beauty.

"I wondered how long it would take you to come back to my bedchamber," she said as I sat down on the stool behind her, taking her dueña's place. "Will you join me for a bath and tell me what adventures you have had since I left?" I began to sponge her body, rubbing the rough fibers up her arms and along her neck, but I remained silent.

Most women do not want to know anything about the others. In truth, the rumors heighten their curiosity and draw them like moths to the flame. But in the moment of their immolation, they prefer to believe, even if briefly, that they are the only one, or that they will be the last. So many embark like missionaries hoping to convert an unrepentant sinner. They ignore my clear confession that I will worship each goddess, like the Ancients, who knew that the whisper of the divine was everywhere.

Alma, however, is unlike any woman I have ever met. She seeks carnal knowledge as devotedly as I do. She calls me her teacher, as I called the Marquis mine. My lessons only turned her back to hearing her own desire, but like a scholar of the Arts of Passion, she wanted to know about each and every possibility of the flesh. It was this pursuit that caused her to leave Carmona and come to Sevilla against my stern advice and warning. But if anyone is to blame for her corruption, I am the one.

I was in Carmona, near where I grew up, because of a conquest that was cut short by the untimely return of a jealous husband. He drew his sword, and I was not quite able to draw mine, which was across the room with my pants. He struck the first blow, which cut my forearm, but once I had drawn my sword, he proved to be a poor swordsman and an even worse coward.

My arm bleeding profusely, I went to my old friend Doctor Pablo. He had been the only man besides Padre Miguel permitted into the convent where I grew up. He would come when the nuns were ill but also to ring the bells of the church on Holy Days. His family was descended from conversos. The prejudice of the town toward his impure blood forced him and his kind to live apart, despite his being one of the most pious men I have ever met. His bloodline was not significant to Priora Francisca; she knew he was the best doctor in the town of Carmona. But his true passion, even more than healing, was service to the Lord through ringing the bells of the convent. Some would say his technique was overly zealous.

He would use the rope to pull himself up so that his feet were standing on the base of the bell as it clanged back and forth wildly. This was very dangerous, and more than one bell ringer had been thrown to his death when the bell flipped over the top. Still, he loved it and would laugh as he swung back and forth precariously. He often told me that one must be a lover of life and that we praise God's creation more with our laughter than with our tears.

"Juan!" Doctor Pablo said when he recognized me. "Look at you!" he added with a great laugh, referring to my noble clothes, and then, seeing my arm, he added with concern, "look at you indeed!" I knew it had been too many years since I had visited the good doctor, and my stomach twisted with guilt for not having paid my respects sooner. Yet he embraced me warmly, blood and all, and led me over to his table.

I apologized to Doctor Pablo for calling so late, but he dismissed my concern with a wave of his hand. His young and beautiful niece looked up from her book with fiery blue eyes. The good doctor had taught his niece to read medical texts, one of which was open on her lap. From my days watching him ring the convent bells, I knew that he had always been somewhat unorthodox.

"My uncle was just teaching me how to remove a limb," Alma said, without the typical modesty of a young maiden.

"I do hope that won't be necessary in my case."

"It is late, Alma," Doctor Pablo said to his niece as she began to help him sew up my arm. "And it is after all the night before your *wedding,*" he insisted good-naturedly.

"Then congratulations are in order," I said, bowing my head. "You must be most excited and perhaps a little nervous." But her face was filled not with joy or fear, only resignation. She nodded graciously and then agreed to go. Before she left the room, she stole one more glance.

"You'd think she was going to a funeral the way she talks about it. The night before their wedding, most girls care only about their dress or their hair, but all she thinks about is sewing up lacerations. Perhaps I have done her a disservice by teaching her the mysteries of the body."

253

"Tell me, my good doctor, how a man who has been married only to his healing practice, and who lives only for ringing the bells of the Convento de la Madre Sagrada, comes to raise such a beautiful maiden."

"It is a sad and shameful story," he said as he continued stitching, "which I share with you in confidence, since you are like a member of my own family."

"My life is a secret, as you well know, and I will certainly keep yours."

"My brother and his wife were denounced to the Inquisition by a neighbor who had seen my sister-in-law lighting candles hidden in the cupboard. They were arrested and taken to the chambers of the Inquisition. They never . . ." He could not finish his sentence but swallowed as he was overcome with the memory. I knew that his relatives must have been discovered practicing their Hebrew religion. Finally, Doctor Pablo continued: "My niece then came to live with me. It has been only a partial home for Alma without a mother. It has also not been easy to arrange a marriage for her, the crimes of her parents being held against the poor child."

"Is the husband someone undesirable?" I asked.

"Not at all. He is the son of a well-to-do furniture merchant, and the boy is devoted to her. They've known each other since childhood, and he has always been in love with her. I think this was the reason his father finally consented."

"She is a beauty."

"God is merciful, or I might never have been able to

marry her off." He chuckled to himself, always able to see the humor in everything. "The greatest obstacle was not the family shame but her blessed stubbornness. It took me a year to convince her to marry him."

"What is her complaint?"

"His greatest flaw is he's 'too familiar.' She says she wants adventure—and, God help her, *passion*. She's been reading too many of those romantic tales. I guess it is my fault for teaching her to read, but I had hoped she would become a nun at the Convento de la Madre Sagrada."

I inhaled quickly through my puckered lips and raised an eyebrow. "There's more passion than one might think behind those cloistered walls."

"You're no doubt right. She is better off as a wife and mother. And, thank God, she has finally consented. After tomorrow, her willfulness will be her husband's problem, not mine."

I raised my arm and admired his handiwork. "It is a shame that she cannot become a doctor. Your family makes the finest ones around. Just look at that stitching. You'd think you were a seamstress."

"I often think that I am little more than a well-paid seamstress—or maybe not so well paid," he said, laughing again. He wrapped my wound up with cotton cloth and told me to keep it clean. I gave him some gold escudos for his troubles, a handsome payment that he was most grateful for. He did not know how much he had given to me in my youth, and my gratitude could not be expressed in a thousand gold coins.

For in the solemn world of the convent, it was he who taught me to face my life with laughter.

We embraced as I thanked him, and he dismissed my gratitude. "Just make sure I see you again soon—and next time without a wound."

"I promise."

As he turned his back to put away his coins and his needle, I heard a noise in the hall. I opened the door slightly, and Alma fell forward from where she had been listening. I saw that the good doctor had not noticed her, and I put my finger to my lips. I would not give her away.

"Shall I show you out?" the doctor called over his shoulder.

"No need," I said. "I can find my way." I led Alma by the elbow down the hall. "Do you really want to know passion?" I asked.

Her eyes were sparkling with clear interest. But then her face dropped, and her excitement was replaced with worry as she looked down. I knew she was thinking about the sword of marriage that hung over her head. "Don't worry," I said, "my instruction takes but one night and is always kept in total confidence."

The lesson was one of the most profound that I can remember, and Alma was a gifted student, a phenomenon actually. She did not have the fear or acquiescence of so many virgins but watched every touch and every gesture as if watching a dissection at the same time as she, the corpse, came alive and reveled in the pure sensation of life. I stroked each part of her body, introducing her to its profound potential for pleasure, and she twisted and writhed as if in a fever, her enjoyment so intense.

I got up to leave before sunrise, but she was still awake and begged me to take her back to Sevilla.

"I cannot take you with me, for I will not marry you or any woman."

"You do not need to marry me, just teach me. Show me the world that you know. I want the life you live."

I was shocked and flattered by her interest in my degenerate lifestyle, but it was impossible. "A woman cannot know the life that I lead unless she is a harlot—"

"Or a courtesan," she interrupted.

"What do you know about courtesans?" I said, more surprised than ever.

"I have read about them. I beg of you. Take me away from here and make me a courtesan."

"You have no idea what you are asking for or what you would be giving up."

"Is not a wife just a courtesan with one patron whom she can neither choose nor refuse?"

I was shocked by her boldness—and her intelligence. "I am sorry, but you do not know what kind of life you would be embracing."

She did not cling to me or beg me further, but in her face I saw a resoluteness that troubled me. It was clear she had made up her mind, and I worried like all professors must that the knowledge they impart may have unforeseen consequences. I left quickly and quietly, passing her uncle asleep at his desk.

I went back to the tavern where Cristóbal and I were spending the night, although it was now practically day. We ate a quick bowl of *gachas,* the tasty mix of flour, cream, and bread warming our stomachs, and then departed at sunrise. As the carriage rattled out of the city gates, the chilly winter air made me shiver. I pulled the blanket up off the floor of the carriage and discovered a stowaway hugging her knees.

"Stop the carriage," I said at once.

We jerked to a halt.

Alma looked at me with those blue eyes, not frightened, not submissive, but with the same determination I had seen in her room. "Start the carriage," she shouted. Cristóbal was no doubt surprised to hear a woman's voice in the carriage, but probably not too surprised, and so he obliged. The carriage lurched forward.

"I cannot take you with me."

"You cannot leave me."

"You are forsaking marriage and children for ephemeral pleasures. A woman is not like a man." Or so I thought at the time.

"I have made up my mind," she said.

"And so have I. The answer is no."

"If you do not take me with you, I will say that you raped me last night."

"But I did not even enter you."

I saw from the look of resolve on her face that she meant to follow through on her threat. Why was she so desperate to escape? Was she fleeing from the stigma of the Inquisition? Could I refuse to give her refuge? I thought of how the Marquis had taught me and given me a new life. I had no more opportunity to consider or argue with myself, since her lips were already pressed against mine, and her hand was on my codpiece. She would be a brilliant courtesan.

"Won't you join me in my bath?" she said again, bringing me back from my reverie. "My dueña can sponge me."

I said nothing but continued to rub her neck and down her arm with the sponge as I looked out at her bedchamber. Her bed was fit for a princess, raised like an altar on a high platform and covered with the finest silk sheets. She had chosen red, knowing that men are not so different from bulls. What she could do with her tongue, her fingertips, and the walls of her womanhood kept men coming back with great devotion. But it was her knowledge of men's hearts, their vanity and their fear, their need for power and the truth of their great weakness, that she used to bring them to their knees like a master toreador.

"You don't need to tell me names, just explicit details," she tried one last time.

Finally, I scraped the sponge along the underside of her right breast and said, "My adventures must be of little interest now that you have so many of your own."

"I am always eager to learn from you, Don Juan. What will you teach me tonight?"

"You were my best student," I said, caressing the

slope of her face with the fingertips of my other hand. She leaned her cheek into my hand. I came off my stool and knelt prayerfully behind her. My hand slid down her neck and cupped her breast. Her chest filled with a quick breath. I squeezed her nipple slowly between my second and third fingers, and she let out a gasp of pleasure.

Then she clutched my hand to her chest and asked, "What about your rule?"

"I have decided to forsake it for a night with you."

"Are you sure that is wise?"

"You seem hesitant. Have your invitations been ill conceived?"

"No, no," she said, trying to reassure me and perhaps herself.

"Is it a matter of compensation?"

"There is no payment that could equal the value of the knowledge that you have given me. I just never imagined . . ." She swallowed as my hand, still in the warm water, stroked her thigh. I came to the side of the bath, my fingers playing with the soft folds of her clamshell and polishing its pearl. She was not breathing and threw her head back, clenching her teeth and trying unsuccessfully to stifle a moan.

Then she rose quickly from her bath like Aphrodite rising from the foam of the sea. Her body was glistening, and her curves sent shivers through me. She stepped out of the water and wrapped a purple robe around her wet body, so that it clung to her.

"I saw him in Carmona," she said.

"Really?" I asked with interest, understanding her hesitation.

She turned and began brushing her long hair in the mirror of her dressing table. "After two and a half years, Tomás still wants to marry me. He has never stopped calling me his Intended." She laughed a little in disbelief.

"He knows about your . . . life here in Sevilla?"

"I have told him everything, thinking it would turn him away, but he says he does not care how many men I have had, as long as he is the last."

"That is true devotion."

"What does Don Juan know about devotion?"

"Nothing," I said. My mind returned to the reason why I had come to Alma's bedchamber.

"I cannot leave Sevilla," she said, arguing with herself, "and the excitement of my life here to become a merchant's country wife in Carmona."

Our conversation was interrupted by the lugubrious march of the Inquisition's faithful soldiers outside the open window. The Inquisitor called on friends and relatives to denounce one another as heretics—including those who were still attached to the Laws of Moses, the sect of Mahomet, and that of Luther—or as *alumbrados,* sorcerers, blasphemers, and readers of banned books. Alma went to the window and closed the doors to the balcony and then the white curtains. I knew that she was trying to shut out her memories, but the voices still drifted through the cracks in the heavy doors. She stood there, clenching the curtains.

I heard the Inquisitor read yet another edict proclaiming that fornication between unmarried men and women was a mortal sin. This heresy, he said, was punishable by a hundred lashes, fines of a thousand maravedis, exile, or worse. Everyone knew what was meant by "worse." I was also sure that his stopping to read the edict in front of the apartment of a famous courtesan was not a coincidence. He could not have known that his favorite fornicator was also inside.

As the sound of the procession droned off into the distance, I stood behind her and put my hand on her shoulder. She turned her head, and I saw tears streaming down her cheeks. "Oh, Don Juan," she said, turning fully and kissing me on the lips as she had done on that first day in the carriage. She practically marched me backward to the bed. "Let us create a soul to replace those that are being chased out by the wicked."

I gave her a knowing smile as I held her chin with my fingers. Since that first morning when I made it clear that I was only her teacher, she had never expressed a desire for me that was anything more. "My dearest Alma," I said. "You know it is my strict rule not to leave any trace of my liaisons beyond the pleasurable memories that may linger." I understood what drove her desire, for Death and Life do an endless dance, and passion is often stoked by the death knell. Inevitably Life wants to replace its own. It was this request that Alma, or the Life calling out from her body, now made. Sooner or later, this longing for Life overwhelms every woman, even the most devoted libertine like Alma.

"Perhaps you will forsake this other rule tonight as well?"

"I am afraid I cannot," I said as we fell together onto her bed, her body pinning mine to the sheet.

"I have always wanted to know how you do it."

"How I do what?"

"How you control your seed."

"Oh, that."

"I often felt the spasms and shudders of your manhood, but you never leaked the sap of your pleasure or went soft." She grabbed my codpiece, and I was already swelling with life. "How do you experience the Supreme Pleasure without releasing your seed?"

I smiled, wondering whether I should tell her a secret that I had never revealed to anyone, not even the Marquis. Her work as a courtesan had given her enough experience with other men to know that this skill was not widely known, if known at all. Yet if anyone was worthy of this knowledge, it was Alma.

"A man's pleasure dances at the edge of a cliff," I began. "As he steps closer and closer, playing with the edge, he can deepen his breath and tighten the muscles in his loins not to fall into its depths. Finally, he can leap off the cliff with the wings of Daedalus, experiencing the Supreme Pleasure, the shiver and shudder of release, without ever losing his seed or going soft. This is the Ultimate Skill and the secret of how a man can learn to fly." As I saw the image in my mind of a bird in flight, I thought of Doña Ana's falcon flying into the night sky. I dismissed the memory from my mind and returned to the topic at hand. I knew it was this secret skill that had allowed me to match any woman's insatiable desire—or so I thought.

It was not just Alma's eyes that were now on fire. She wanted to consume me, and I was happy to oblige. She dropped her silk robe and then tore my clothes from my body as if her fingers were talons. Our love-making was like wrestling as we teased and pleased each other's sensitive skin, turning one another over, restraining and tumbling, seeing who could extract more pleasure from the other. I thought Alma would tear me limb from limb, so great was her hunger. I used my claws to scratch along her arms and thighs and to turn her over and bite at the nape of her neck, which makes a woman arch her back like a cat.

I threw myself into her arms, the old pleasure surging back. Not a fantasy but the raw reality of carnal knowledge, searing and blissful. I was desperate to prove to myself that the title conferred by the Infanta was not mistaken. I would prove—to myself alone—that I remained the Greatest Lover in All the Kingdoms of Spain and All the Realms of the Spanish Empire.

Alma too used me, squeezing the skillful muscles of her womanhood to coax me to release my seed, either mistakenly believing that my pleasure was not complete or unable to resist her body's desire to bring forth new life. As the pleasure became too intense, I withdrew, ceding that round to her. Alma was the lustiest lover I've ever had, and as I had surpassed the Marquis, I knew that she had now surpassed me. The ancient Greeks believed that a woman's pleasure is nine times greater than a man's, but with my Ultimate Skill I had been able to even the score, experiencing the Supreme Pleasure over and over. As long as a woman's desire could last, so could mine. And I was not willing to concede defeat yet.

Pleasuring a woman who knows the full length and breadth of her own desire is different than making love to a virgin or even a mature woman whose passion remains a mystery to her. As I held her hands down over her head, manacled in the chamber of lust, I kissed and tantalized her with my tongue down her face, lips, and neck to her breasts, until she was writhing underneath me. Power is inescapable in passion, and it was this bargain between dominance and submission from which we were extracting great satisfaction. I sucked on her breasts, not like a suckling babe but like a wolf, until she begged me to devour her. There is no greater skill for a true caballero than kneeling at the altar of a woman's pleasure. My tongue and fingers allowed me to bring her to a reckless abandon while I kept my wits about me.

Only then did I dare enter her again. I threw myself into the pleasure of her eager embrace and did not restrain myself, as I would with one who needs tender encouragement. Together we rocked on the sea of desire until at last, tossing from side to side, she threw me over and climbed aboard. As she rode the waves of her pleasure, I coaxed her fingertips to her own shores.

Women hesitate to take control of their own desire but when they do, it is never again at the mercy of any man. As she touched herself and I gripped her breasts, she bucked wildly, the magnificent muscles of her haunch tightening and releasing, like Pegasus flying over the Aegean. Finally, she collapsed on top of me, and I thought she might be done.

Instead she demanded to pleasure me, and I willingly submitted to her touch and tongue. A true caballero must know how to receive as well as to give, for receiving is also a skill. If he does not know how to surrender to his own pleasure, he will always remain the physician performing his passionless exams.

This time, however, as I relaxed my body into her able courtesan's hands, my mind would not remain in this magnificent moment but rushed backward and forward, thinking of Doña Ana. Within short order, I had lost my desire and was as soft as clay in her hands.

This was the third and final betrayal of a libertine, and my heart was racing, as were my thoughts. I got up to pour a glass of wine from the table next to Alma's bed. I could see the potter's wheel of her mind spinning as she tried to make shape of my unusual loss of desire.

"You have been exhausting yourself while I was gone," she said.

I laughed. "No more than usual."

"Then what am I to make of this abrupt loss of your desire?"

"A man's desire rises and falls with the tides, just like

a woman's," I said, hiding behind my professorial role.

"I have never seen Don Juan lose his desire."

Nor had I.

"Don Juan is a man, like all other men," I said, trying to feign calm although my own doubts and accusations screamed in my skull. This was the first time I had ever lost my desire, and the loss had been caused by the memory of another woman, a woman I had not even kissed. Something new and terrifying was happening. While my mind was loyal to the Marquis, my body was loyal only to Doña Ana.

"Perhaps I am losing my skill," she said nervously.

"Hardly," I said. "Your skill is even greater than I remember."

"Do you no longer find me beautiful?" she asked with even greater worry. This is the fear that all women must battle.

"Your beauty remains as stunning as on the day I met you."

"Then tell me about your misadventures while I was gone. I want to learn from them," she said cunningly. It was clear that her interest was more than studious curiosity.

"You know I don't keep a catalog of my trysts, nor reveal them," I said.

"*Who* is she?"

"What are you talking about?"

"You've met someone . . . someone different . . . haven't you? A woman can hide her heart, but a man cannot. It is the doña at the Marquis's on Corpus

Christi. It's Doña . . . Ana, isn't it?" There was practically menace in her voice. But if I could keep the truth from her, perhaps I could keep it from myself.

"Every woman I lie with is different. I do not compare one to the other."

And then, as the truth dawned on her, she said almost to herself, "You are in love, aren't you?" She laughed, amused by the possibility.

I laughed, too, and turned to get dressed, hoping to hide the worry on my face. "Perhaps you are right, Doña Alma. I have just been exhausting myself. Perhaps I just need a good night's rest. Thank you for this evening's entertainment. It has been quite revealing."

"You are, aren't you?" she said, still insisting.

"Love?" I laughed. "Love has always been the furthest thing from my mind."

"One does not love with one's mind," she said.

"A good teacher always learns from his students."

But she would not be put off. "Was it different lying with someone you loved?"

"I have not so much as kissed her."

She seemed quite surprised, almost relieved, by this revelation. "Then perhaps it is nothing more than an infatuation that will vanish the first time you kiss her lips."

"I am afraid I will not have the opportunity to find out," I said. I kissed Alma's hand and left. I stepped into the night, feeling the fatigue of which Alma spoke. My whole body was in a stupor, but my mind was still darting back and forth. Whether my feelings were true love or mere infatuation, my life as a libertine in Sevilla was over.

I now know that I must flee as far from Doña Ana's shadow as I can. The New World is my only hope of escaping her and the ruins of my life as a libertine. It is also my only hope of remaining loyal to the man who has given me everything and could, should he wish, choose to take it all away. I go now to arrange passage for one to New Spain. My first port of call will be the ship of which I still own a share and whose captain still has the remainder of my gold.

Evening, 8 July 1593

A New World

When I arrived at the *San Miguel*, the boy was still standing watch across from the ship, "They will be leaving soon, my lord. They are taking on provisions."

"Good, so will I."

The sailor who had been so interested in my affairs tripped over himself making his way to tell the captain I had returned. I opened the door to the small chamber, wondering whether I would face a pistol. To my surprise, Captain Fadrique welcomed me with a warm smile.

"Don Juan, at last we can square our accounts. I am afraid I underestimated you. Here is your gold," he said, pointing to two sacks on his desk. I opened them and ran my hand through the coins to make sure that they were all indeed gold. I was not disappointed. Then it became clear why his feelings had changed so dramatically. "As a partner and part owner of the *San Miguel*, I need to ask you for another investment."

I hesitated but then asked, "When does your ship leave?"

"We sail in eight days' time from Sanlúcar de Barrameda, and I can again promise you ten times your money."

"How much do you need?" I asked against my better judgment.

"Six thousand escudos," he said.

"I will entertain your request on one condition."

"Tell me."

"That I accompany you and my investment to New Spain."

He cocked his head, surprised by the unusual request, but quickly said, "Granted. We depart in two days' time and will arrive in Sanlúcar de Barrameda six days thereafter. From there we will go to the Canaries to await the remainder of the ships making the crossing to Veracruz."

"I have always wished to see the land of gold."

"It is a land of gold if you bring gold with you."

"I will see you on Saturday."

As I was leaving, he called out after me, "Don Juan . . . don't get delayed by one of your . . . intrigues."

"There will be no more intrigues for me in Sevilla."

"I don't believe everything I hear," he said with a smile, echoing my words from our previous encounter.

I rode home unable to think of anything except Doña Ana. What if I travel to the other side of the world and find that her shadow has traveled just as far? Can a man outsail his own heart? To bring reason back into my life, I must discover what I feel for her and what she feels for me. I know Alma is right. It is nothing more than an infatuation, and the fantasy will vanish the first time I kiss her lips. If this enchantment requires a kiss to be ended, then it is a kiss I must have. Everything that I have known, the life that I have created, even the loyalty of my heart to the Marquis, depends on ridding myself of this torment. One chaste kiss is all it will take, and this alone would not be a betrayal of the Marquis. I will kiss the bride good-bye and let her go to the altar.

I find myself drawn to Doña Ana as if I am a wildly fluttering moth banging against the window, and she is the calm and glowing flame. I will be setting out on a nocturnal flight soon, very soon. If I can arrange to get past the sentinels who guard her bedchamber window, I will go tomorrow night, but first I must have tomorrow to lay my plan. And tonight I must sleep.

Night, 8 July 1593

A Moth to a Flame

I woke up this morning as if there had been a knock at the door, sitting upright and knowing exactly what I needed to do. I was once again the burglar, but the treasure I wanted was nothing more than a farewell kiss.

I scouted out the area around Doña Ana's apartment. As I suspected, the Marquis had stationed a spy on the rooftop, where he could overlook the courtyard with its one lonely and towering palm tree and observe the door and balcony. Fortunately, Carlos was an old colleague from my days in the Marquis's private postal service. He was ten years my senior and now had a large belly and a red nose. He looked even older than his years and was definitely past his prime as a spy.

I pretended that I had been sent to report in. "The Marquis wants to know, what news?"

"All quiet," Carlos said. "I don't know what the Marquis is worried about. I haven't seen anything in a week. I do prefer more active work."

"Don't we all," I said with a smile.

"But the Commander's away," Carlos added with a smile, "and the Marquis doesn't want his soon-to-be bride to play, if you know what I mean."

I laughed. "A woman's chastity is the most difficult thing to guard."

"You should know," he said with a wink. "We do miss you, Don Juan, and that muscatel you used to steal. I miss that, too." Carlos was a drunkard who, fortunately for my purposes, could not refuse a drink.

I returned as the sun was setting with a wineskin, to which I had added a harmless but effective sleeping potion purchased at the apothecary. It was calibrated to give me eight hours unobserved. "For old times' sake," I said as I handed the black bladder of wine to Carlos, "but for after your watch is done. The Marquis wouldn't want you drinking during your watch."

"Thank you, Don Juan! Thank you!" he said, uncorking the skin and smelling its sweet aroma.

"Remember—it's for after your watch."

"Of course, of course, you and the Marquis can count on me." He still remained as deferential as he had been during the days when the Marquis had put me in charge of the other spies. I was now a noble, which made him all the more obliging.

"Now, tell me, have you seen anyone come or go from the house?"

"Just a street vendor selling chocolate drinks. The dueña bought one. That stuff for women is like wine for men. She couldn't get inside the house before she was sipping it down."

"A lonely woman can never refuse the seductions of chocolate," I said, and I waved good-bye. Earlier in the day I had sent Cristóbal, wearing a wide-brimmed hat that covered his face, to sell chocolate mixed with water. I had added an equivalent dose of sleeping potion into the dueña's drink.

I left but quickly hid across the street until I saw Carlos raise the wineskin above his head and gaze heavenward at it. He squeezed a stream of wine into his mouth, its golden elixir glowing in the remaining sunlight. I went home and waited the few hours until midnight.

Trusting my instincts that the time was right, I took my mask, my horse, and a gift for Doña Ana. I did not want my carriage to be recognized and instead rode Bonita the short distance to Doña Ana's house. The horse grazed in the courtyard as I scaled the palm tree with my boots against its bark and my hands holding its trunk. When I reached the roof, I saw Carlos lying flat with the empty skin next to him. I looked into the window of the dueña's room and saw her fast asleep in her sewing chair, her head resting against the wall, her sewing still on her lap. From the roof I lowered myself to the balcony, as I had done so many times as a burglar. Through a crack in the curtains I could see Doña Ana, sitting at a writing desk. Her beautiful black hair was tied in a bun, and she wore a rose-colored dress that revealed her neck and shoulders, which I imagined she might wear only on days when the Commander was away. Over it she wore a yellow cloak with blue stripes, but it had fallen away. She had removed her farthingale, and her dress hung down around her legs. When I knocked on the window, she startled and turned. I saw a look of fear on her face and quickly removed my mask as she came to see who it was. I knew she was not a woman to run from danger, and I stood back to let her approach. She opened the door to the balcony without hesitation. "What are you doing here?"

"I . . . ah . . ." It was as if I were embarking on my first seduction, so slow were the words in my mouth. "I have come . . . to see you."

"You must leave at once . . . before my dueña . . ."

I was encouraged by her own breathlessness. "María is asleep."

"What have you done to her?"

"It is harmless. A sleeping potion to give us—"

"If you have come to convince me to give my heart to the Marquis, you are wasting your time."

"I have not come on the Marquis's behalf, but on my own."

She looked down. "Why do you trouble me at this hour, Don Juan?"

"I have tried—out of loyalty to the Marquis—to avoid you and to deny my feelings, but I cannot. I brought you a gift," I said, and began to unbutton my doublet.

She covered her mouth in shock and looked away. I smiled as I pulled out a small white dove.

"Oh!" she said as a tender smile broke across her guarded face. "How beautiful!"

"It is not like the other pigeons I have. It is special."

Doña Ana looked both ways and then said, "Come in quickly *before you are seen.*" She said the last words loudly and to the street, and I wondered whether she was trying to alert someone that I was there. I knew I would need my kiss soon, to leave a free man. If she was trying to be rescued, she did not act besieged. She led me into her room, where there was a low dais with red and yellow velvet pillows. Behind it there was a large silk drape and a wood-framed mirror. A mahogany door led to her bedchamber. I thought I might get my kiss after she placed the dove in a small cage, but she led me to a larger one covered by a beautiful blanket from the Indies. The design was beguiling. The red, yellow, and green cotton threads were woven into a dozen diamonds overlapping in an unbreakable chain. Doña Ana pulled the blanket off with a flourish of pride. In the cage, her hooded falcon stood silently, his head snapping to the side, listening. "It is only when Fenix's eyes are covered and her sight is blinded that she does not resist her captivity," she said.

"One does not have to remain a captive," I replied.

"I will not live a caged life in a loveless marriage. You can be sure of that."

I leaned over to kiss her lips, drawn to them as the tides are drawn to the moon. The hard sting of her slap across my cheek brought me to my senses. She did indeed know how to defend herself.

"Nor will I live a lie, marrying one man and having an affair with another. The only man who will kiss my lips is the man I choose to marry." She put on her falconer's glove and took the hawk out of its cage. I followed her to the door.

We passed her writing desk; on it lay an open book in which she had been writing. "Is this your diary?"

With her free hand, she closed it. "Just a sad story I am writing."

"Does it have a happy ending?"

"I don't know," she said, looking into my eyes. She opened the balcony door as we stepped out into the night.

"Will you come with me for a tour of heaven from the top of the Giralda?"

"I cannot." She sighed, and I knew that her heart wanted to go.

"Are you afraid to drink the moonlight yourself?" I said. I looked at her and then at the ripening moon.

"I do not have the luxury of fear. I have only desperation left."

"Then come with me, out of your cage, for a night of freedom."

"We might be *seen*," she said, as if hearing the deeper meaning in her words. She looked behind her into the house, took a deep breath, and then pulled off the falcon's hood. "Yes." Fenix flapped her wings and flew into the night. Putting my mask back on, I climbed down and stood on Bonita's saddle to help Doña Ana. She threw her falconer's glove on the tile floor of her balcony and descended to the horse. Growing up in the country had made her a skillful climber, though I was even more impressed that she did not sit sidesaddle but mounted the horse like a man, gripping it with her legs, her long dress straining over the saddle. I felt her body in front of me and breathed deeply. My arms were on either side of hers, holding the reins, which felt lighter, and the leather smoother, than they ever had before.

I encouraged Bonita with words and the heel of my boot pressed softly against her flank. She began to trot and then settled into a steady canter. Speed would be part of our protection, as it would be difficult for people to identify us, but a gallop would suggest an escape. Doña Ana's hair smelled like the jasmine flowers that she wound through it, and wisps blew in my face and tickled my cheeks. Her warm back and soft buttocks moved against me with the rhythm of the horse and made my legs stiffen in my metal stirrups. I slowed down as we approached the empty plaza of the Giralda, the mournful black stones of the Cathedral now silent. It was late, and the plaza was empty.

The swifts were circling above the Cathedral, flying in their erratic loops like bats. The pigeons sitting on the heads of the saints around the arched doorway took flight as we approached. A confused dove flew toward us and then flapped its wings as it backed away.

I dismounted and pulled my meat knife from my boot. With it, I was able to pick the old lock of the door quickly. I helped Doña Ana down as we and the horse all ducked under the low doorway. I helped her back into the saddle and returned to my mount behind her. In one of the books in the Marquis's library, I had read that the tower had thirty-four ramps that the muezzin had ridden up on his donkey five times a day to call out the prayers of Mahomet. Our Christian bells were now rung by a hammer controlled by a mechanical clock that was contrived with gears, pulleys, and ropes. So we had only to avoid the night watchman, and he would not be making his rounds for several hours.

With a gentle prod, Bonita began to walk up the ramps in the dim candlelight. Once we were a small distance up, I squeezed the horse's flanks with my thighs, and she began to gallop. We raced up the remaining ramps until we arrived at the platform at the top of the tower, breathless and holding on for our lives. I will never forget the sight we beheld before us.

A Tour of Heaven

We hid the horse around the back of the square stone wall that stood in the center of the platform and that supported the highest balcony above. I had not taken the time to place my knife back in my boot and still gripped it in my teeth, like a pirate. Doña Ana took the handle of the knife and removed it from my mouth.

"Run, Bonita," I said to the horse jokingly, "she's got a knife." The horse was unmoved, but I ran around the stone wall and raced up the final flight of stairs to the summit, where the highest bell hung silently. Doña Ana chased me and was not far behind. As she came out the top, I held up my hands in surrender, and we both laughed.

Then she saw the view and forgot totally about the knife in her hand. She walked around this heaven-hung balcony slowly, as if she had been granted entrance into the Kingdom of Our Lord, and from here, with the city so far below, it did look as if we were closer to God than to man. I took a deep breath and looked out at the magnificent beauty that surrounded us and tried to still my beating heart.

This highest chamber had a marble railing over which we gazed down at the spires on top of the Cathedral, and at the walls and palace of the Alcázar, and then at the Torre del Oro and the river, which was glistening in the moonlight. From there we turned and saw the city hall and the Iglesia del Salvador. We saw the street sweepers snuffing out the oil lamps on Génova, Alemanes, and Francos streets, where the artisans from all over Europe were living. Finally I pointed in the direction of her hacienda, near Carmona. The wonder on her face disappeared, and her expression grew serious. She looked at the knife in her hand and felt the sharp blade with her thumb, then touched her neck, remembering.

"You were very brave," I said.

"Why did you come to my hacienda that night?"

"To seduce you—and to thank you for saving my life."

"Well, we're even."

"I wanted to know what kind of woman would not be afraid of a masked man who fell into her carriage."

"And what do you want now?"

"I don't know," I said. I raised my fingertips to touch her face but then stopped. I could almost feel her soft skin through the ether that separated our flesh. "You are right to question me, because my motives are not clear even to myself."

"I will not marry a man who does not love me, and the Marquis's dark heart is incapable of loving anyone."

"I tried to warn you at the chapel because I had seen what the Marquis was willing to do to win you. It was he who sent the highwaymen to your hacienda—to scare you into leaving your father's seclusion and perhaps to force you to marry him."

Her eyes were ablaze with surprise and understanding. "His heart is darker than I had even imagined. I am simply a possession, like our land, that he has forced my father to sell."

"I owe the Marquis my life and more." I moved my face closer to hers, eager to kiss her lips just once.

I felt the sharp blade of the knife against my neck. "I am not like the other noblewomen you trifle with. If you break my heart, I will revenge myself and my family."

"You have your father's sense of honor," I said, moving my jaw away from the knife. I reached up and put my right hand around the blade as I went to kiss her again. She pulled back instinctively, and I felt a sharp pain and then the moist blood in my hand.

"Oh, Madre Santa!" she said as she realized what she had done and saw the bloody cut on my hand. "We must stop the bleeding," she said worriedly. She reached down and took the hem of her petticoat, then cut it off with the knife. "I am so sorry."

"It's nothing," I said. She began to bandage my hand with the strip of cotton. "It was my fault. You had warned me, and I did not listen."

"It was an accident," she said. "I didn't mean to—"

"Don't worry. I've had far worse wounds inflicted by

far less beautiful adversaries." I held out my other hand for the knife, which she placed in my palm. I closed it against my leg and slid it back into my boot.

"How did you know how to pick the lock?" she asked. "Are you a burglar? You do look like one." She smiled and raised my mask. I had forgotten that I was still wearing it.

I looked away, wondering whether to confess. I walked over to the other side of the balcony and looked out over the river and the Arenal, where I had fled after the monastery.

"I'm sorry," she said, coming over to me.

"I've never told any woman the truth." I remembered that she was not willing to live a lie. Neither was I. "I *was* a burglar," I admitted.

"A hidalgo reduced to a burglar?" she said incredulously.

"I was not a noble at the time. I owe my title, like so many things, to the Marquis."

"Your parents were not noble?"

My scalp started to tingle, and my palms began to sweat. "Wouldn't you prefer to believe the fantasy, like all the other women?"

"The truth is always more alluring than any fantasy. Please, I want to know the truth. I swear it will die with me."

"The entire *scandalous* truth?" I said, trying to make light of it and my own uncertainty.

"Every *scandalous* detail," she said, raising her eyebrow with interest.

I had a great desire to tell her everything. "I will tell you what I have told no one, not even the Marquis. Not even myself."

She laughed, and the sound rose up and made the stars shake and shimmer in the sky.

I told her about the convent, and about Hermana Teresa, and about the monastery, and about the brotherhood of thieves. Her eyes were aglow with interest, and she drank in my every word with her slightly opened lips. At last she asked, "Did you ever discover who your parents were?" noting that I had left out that vital part of the story. She missed nothing. Again I told her what I had revealed to no living soul.

"I went one last time to Padre Miguel's confessional, telling him that I was leaving the monastery and that I might never see him again. He hesitatingly broke the Seal of Confession and told me the truth about my parents on that last visit. I was kneeling silently on the leather cushion, staring through the wooden lattice, listening to every word, as he told me what he had concealed for so long. Fifteen years earlier, a woman had knelt on the very same cushion. She wept as she confessed that she had given birth to a baby out of wedlock. She could not keep the child and had left him in the barn of a convent for the nuns to watch over because she could not. The convent housed the Virgin protectress of the city, and she had hoped the Virgin might also protect her newborn child. I asked him whether he recognized my mother, and he said that he had."

"Who was she?" Doña Ana asked, unable to contain her curiosity.

"She was a prostitute by the name of Serena."

"Was she still alive?" Doña Ana was as anxious to know now as I had been then.

"He did not know but said he heard she had gone to Sevilla. I asked whether my mother had revealed to him the name of my father. She had. During Holy Week, one of Padre Miguel's sermons on the Magdalene had persuaded Serena to give up her trade. She had embraced the crucifix, which he held out to her, and had even considered the convent for fallen women. But her resolve was weakened by the overtures of a noble whose name was Don Diego Tenorio."

"Don Diego *Tenorio*?" she asked, recognizing the family name as one of the titled nobility.

"Yes. He came to her one night, offering to make her his mistress. Of course, he never did, and left her with child."

"Did you go to him?"

"He would not see me. Finally, after several days of waiting, I stepped out in front of his silver carriage as it was leaving his mansion. The driver was forced to pull the horses up short, so that the carriage jerked and retreated. One of his armed escorts pulled a musket, but I refused to move until I had spoken to him. 'Tell him that it is his son by Serena, the prostitute from Carmona,' I shouted. He did not even open the carriage curtains or speak to me directly. 'Tell whomever it is that the son of a prostitute has many fathers.' He forced a chuckle, which was echoed by his coachmen and escorts. Defeated, I stepped aside and let the carriage pass, the wooden wheels splashing mud on my brown pants and bare feet. His was the first house that I robbed when I became a rope-climber."

Doña Ana laughed. "Did you find your mother?"

"Yes, but this time I was not so quick to reveal my identity, knowing that the past is not always a welcome guest. I searched for a prostitute named Serena, which fortunately was a rare name. Eventually I found her. She was married to the owner of a tavern in the Arenal, although his true occupation at the time was leading a brotherhood of thieves."

"She was no longer a prostitute?"

"No, she was too old to hire herself out, so instead, she procured prostitutes for the tavern, which also served as a brothel."

"What did you say?"

"I asked where she came from and she admitted that she was from Carmona. I never told her or her husband, Manuel, that I was her son, but I did ask her once whether she had any children. Even before she spoke, her fallen face told the truth of Padre Miguel's words, but she pinned a smile to her mouth, as prostitutes so often must, and said, 'Children, my dear boy, were a liability in my profession.'" Doña Ana put her hand on my arm. "It was her husband who taught me the talents of a burglar, and it was she who gave me this very mask."

Doña Ana said, "I wish I could just speak to my

mother. Mine died giving birth to me. But I at least have had a father, and you have had neither father nor mother."

"The Marquis has been like a father to me. It was he who taught me to be a noble and procured a letter from the King—but knowing the Marquis, I cannot swear to its legitimacy. Now you know the truth of Don Juan, no don, no noble at all, really. You also know why I have never revealed my shameful story to anyone." I turned my head away, certain that like all other nobles she would despise a common orphan, a bastard and the son of a prostitute.

She touched my cheek with her fingertips and brought my face back to hers. "The truth," she said, "*is* more alluring than any fantasy."

She brought her bright red lips close to mine, but this time I was going to ask for permission. "May I?"

She nodded as she moistened her lips. They glistened in the starlight. I kissed her gently and then, as she melted into my embrace, I held her tight. Our lips were fused, our breath inseparable. A thousand doves flew out of my chest. We kissed for what seemed like an hour but was perhaps no longer than a minute, and when our lips parted, I looked at her face, her eyes still closed tenderly.

The spell was not broken.

My heart was a church bell rung wildly by a deranged monk. I could not deny it. It was no mere enchantment or even infatuation. I felt love for the first time since Teresa's death, and it coursed through my veins like ice. We embraced as I held Doña Ana's body and soul to my chest. I looked out at the stars and they seemed brighter than I had ever seen them. A new sense of wonder was mixed with trepidation, as I knew there was no way to remain loyal both to the Marquis and to Doña Ana.

At that moment, one of the lower bells of the tower rang out the hour, tearing our embrace apart. The loud noise frightened Bonita, who whinnied loudly.

"What in the name . . . ?" we heard the watchman say as we saw him walk around to investigate on the level below us. He had come early.

"Hurry down the stairs and meet me at the level below," I said to Doña Ana, who did not need to be told twice.

From the top balcony, I leapt down to the horse, landing first on my hands, to protect my knee and my other vulnerable parts. Just as I did, the watchman turned the corner where the horse was hiding. My mounting her startled the horse and caused her to rear up on her hind legs. I compelled Bonita forward with my heels as the watchman ran after me, shouting for the officers of the law: *"Alguaciles! Alguaciles!"* I galloped around the terrace of the tower under the large bells, with him chasing behind. I reached the stairs on the other side and extended an arm to Doña Ana, who took it and helped me pull her on. The watchman was rounding the corner only a few feet back, and he lunged at us. He grabbed Doña Ana's leg, and she slapped his hand, which he hastily withdrew. I kicked the horse's flanks again, and she was only too eager to bolt forward. We galloped out of his reach and started down the ramps.

I thought we might be safe but then heard him ringing a bell as he continued shouting for the *alguaciles*. We galloped furiously down the ramps, keeping our heads low and avoiding the oil candles as we rushed around each corner. It was not the watchman that I feared, but the alarm that he was sounding. At the bottom, we approached the low wooden doorway. I told Doña Ana to duck, and bending to the side, we burst forth just as a constable and half a dozen officers were arriving.

We galloped through their ranks and sped down the narrow and winding streets of the Barrio Santa Cruz. They chased us down street after street, getting closer and closer. My mare was no longer up for the chase. They were nearly upon us. If they recognized my face or, more important, that of Doña Ana, all might be lost. I knew the tortuous turns of the neighborhood better than they did and galloped down one alleyway and then another until we heard their hooves rush by on the Callejón del Agua. My horse's chest and ours as well were heaving, and we struggled to catch our breath.

I slowed Bonita when we entered the small courtyard in front of Doña Ana's house, and brought the horse alongside the balcony. I knew that Carlos and the dueña would still be sleeping soundly, but I tried to be as quiet as possible to avoid alerting the neighbors.

I helped Doña Ana back up onto the balcony, and I

climbed up after her. As I reached the balcony, my stomach collapsed: her dueña was awake and scolding her in her room. She must have only sipped the chocolate, I realized as I hid and listened to the heated argument inside. What I heard was a staggering revelation— I was not the only one who had been living a lie.

A Child of Deception and Cruelty

You want ruin your life?" Her dueña was shaking with fury.

"Will you tell my father?" Doña Ana asked, her tone strangely calm, almost eager.

"Marquis find out he not marry you!"

"That was my hope." Doña Ana shot a glance toward the window but did not seem to see me in the dark, now moonless night. "I had no choice, no other means of protest than to create a scandal," she continued, every word filled with desperation. I knew that what she was saying was only a half-truth. I assured myself that she could not have fabricated her feelings as we stood at the gates of heaven.

"The Marquis destroy our family," María shot back.

"He can do no more than he has already done."

"Yes, he can," María said ominously, and looked away.

"What? What more can he do?"

"I cannot say."

"You must tell me the truth. I command you! Tell me what the Marquis knows!"

"Your father kill me."

"Please, I beg of you!"

"I cannot." María began to weep. "I cannot, my child."

"If you love me, tell me why my life is not my own."

María collapsed onto the dais and held her clenched hands in front of her chest, rocking herself back and forth. "Because my life not my own."

"What do you mean?"

María continued rocking herself as if she were a child.

"My father will never know," Doña Ana said, closing the balcony doors and looking through them. The doors were warped and the seal was poor, and I listened with the ear of a spy as I saw her sit down next to her dueña, her body rigid. *"Please,"* she begged, as tears ran down her face.

María went over to Fenix's cage. She picked up the colorful cotton blanket that Doña Ana used to cover the cage. "Your first swaddling blanket," she said, holding up the worn and rough fabric.

"What do you mean? I still have mine. It is of silk."

"Doña Catalina screaming," María said, her eyes distant. "Her baby take so long . . . two days . . . three days . . . no baby."

"I know my mother died in childbirth," Doña Ana said.

"My baby crying . . ."

"Your baby?"

María continued, as if not hearing Doña Ana. "Midwife hide in room. She scared. She close door and hold it. She say, 'Doña Catalina go to heaven . . . and take baby.'"

"That's impossible," Doña Ana said, but María continued slowly, in measured words.

"Your father throw open door. He have dagger in hand. He want kill midwife. My baby screaming. He shout, 'Shut it up.' I rock baby, but cry louder and louder. He rip baby from my arms. Hold knife to baby . . ." María was choking on her tears, remembering that terrible night. "Then he look crazy. He drop dagger and hold baby. He say, 'My child live. My baby live.' He give me back baby and say, 'You wet nurse—nothing more.'" María was weeping and brushing Doña Ana's hair. "I rock baby and try to protect her, as I always do . . ."

Doña Ana was covering her mouth as silent tears streaked her cheeks. "How can this be true?" she said. "Then *you* . . . ?"

María looked down.

"Why have you never told me?"

"Your father send me away if you ever find out."

"That is why he tried to sell you at the slave market, isn't it?"

"I just tell him I want to go with you when you marry."

"He was afraid you would tell me the truth . . ." María was nodding in silent agreement. *"Then who is my father?"*

María looked down again.

291

"It was him, wasn't it?"

María did not look at her.

"Did you love him?" Doña Ana asked.

María shook her head from side to side, almost imperceptibly.

"He forced you, didn't he?"

María did not deny it.

"So I am a child of deception *and* cruelty."

"He not bad man. I want to hate him, but he give me you."

Doña Ana looked at her with uncertainty. "He *raped* you."

"Man is jaguar."

"That's why you told me all those stories of the jungle?"

"Yes."

"If man is jaguar," Doña Ana said, "then woman must become panther."

"Your father give me this." María pulled out a blue crucifix. I strained to see. I knew I risked being discovered, but I could not stop myself. I wanted to hear everything that was said, not like a spy but like a lover who yearns to know every detail about his beloved. "It from my land. I wear to remind me that he is good man."

"He tried to sell you—away from your own daughter."

"He just want scare me. He never do it. He afraid you find out."

"Well, now I have," Doña Ana said, turning her back on her mother.

"Only Marquis know," her mother said, stroking Doña Ana's hair again, "and he keep wife's secret." I knew the truth of this statement and that to hide the truth he was willing to kill the man who had told him the secret of the two corpses in the coffin—mother and child.

"If he knows, why does he still want to marry me?"

"Because he *love* you."

"He does not know what love is. All he cares about is power."

"If man want wife's love, she have power."

"I can't marry him."

"It best life for you."

"I won't."

"So long I hate not to tell world you my child. But with Marquis, I know you live life of noble and not of slave."

"But I am not a noble," Doña Ana said.

"Both father—and mother—noble. My father *cacique*. I born daughter of chief—of king," María said, her finger pointing proudly to the sky. "And now slave." She hung her head. "But you are no slave. You noble again." Her mother's eyes flashed with triumph.

"And you?" Don Ana asked.

"Marquis promise I go with you."

"As my mother or my maid?"

"You and I know truth in heart," she said, tapping her chest with her fingers.

"I can't do it," Doña Ana said, turning away again.

"You must! You think Don Juan—oh yes, mother

know everything—give you better life? He forget you first time he see other beauty. He never marry you and leave you broken heart. You think man who sleep with wives be faithful to you?"

At that same moment I heard the call of her falcon, I saw it flying back, but I was distracted from the sky by the sound below. It was the red carriage I had feared. Just in time I realized I did not have my mask on and pulled it down over my eyes, but the driver looked up and saw me. "Commander! A burglar on the balcony!"

The Commander stuck his head out of the carriage. For a second time tonight, I vaulted onto my horse and raced through the streets.

"Follow him!"

The Commander's two-horse carriage was in close pursuit, but I could take the turns more quickly, and I tried to lose him through the streets of the Barrio Santa Cruz at a full gallop. Finally, after a circuitous route, I arrived back in my silent plaza and hid myself and my horse behind the wooden door that sealed off the courtyard of the Taberna Santa Cruz and my apartment above it. I ran up my stairs and hid in my unlit room. I could see the Commander's carriage circling around the plaza under the flickering street lanterns. He looked up at my dark windows as if staring directly at me, although I knew that he could not possibly have seen my face. "Take me home!" I heard him shout at his driver, barely restraining the fury in his voice. The Commander left knowing that the man at the window was much more dangerous than any common burglar, for the valuables he was after were more precious than any silver cups or gold coins.

The Commander's revenge will have to wait for another day, but I doubt he will wait long. Yet it is not his challenge that weighs heaviest on my heart tonight but that of Doña Ana's mother. Could a man who sleeps with other men's wives—could I—ever be faithful to Doña Ana?

Early morning, 10 July 1593

The Wager of Love

All night I tossed in my bed, wrestling with myself, knowing that Doña Ana's mother was right. I could not possibly be faithful to one woman after knowing the affections of so many. And even if I could, how then could I betray the Marquis? And even if I were willing to betray him, I had no doubt that he would chase us to the end of the empire for his revenge. What life would I be able to give Doña Ana? Her mother knew the truth. The Marquis's love gave her the power. I could not possibly ask her to forsake everything for the fleeting madness of my love—a love that she might not even share. I heard her say from her own mouth that she had gone with me to the Giralda to ruin her engagement to the Marquis. Was it my feelings alone that I felt in that kiss in the tower of heaven? Surely she knew that only God was watching us there. Still, perhaps her willingness was caused more by her hatred for the Marquis than by her love for

295

me. I had had my kiss, and I now needed to leave the bride forever.

When I finally got out of bed, I was no more rested than I had been the night before. I got dressed and put on my sword, eager to say good-bye to the Marquis and to go to the docks where the *San Miguel* would be leaving that afternoon. As I marched out, I found Cristóbal in the sitting room playing with my deck of cards at the table. He was so engrossed, he did not notice me at first. He was playing a game that he had made up, a game played by one in which he matched suits and numbers. I looked over his shoulder at the colorful red, blue, and yellow picture cards. Among the ones he had laid out in front of him I saw the King of Chalices, as a drawing of Charlemagne; the King of Swords as the Hebrew King David; the King of Coins as Julius Caesar; and the Queen of Chalices as the beautiful Helen of Troy.

"I wonder," I began as he started and the cards sprayed on the floor, "if you will ever learn to play games that are not played alone."

"I'll give my heart to a woman, my lord," Cristóbal said with unusual boldness, "when you give yours."

"Don't wait for me, or you may die alone."

"I'll prepare the carriage," he said, collecting the cards.

"Take my chest," I said, having packed my clothes, my gold, and this diary in the large wooden box.

"Your chest?" he said, surprised and worried by the request.

"My chest—put it in the carriage."

"Yes, my lord."

When we arrived at the Marquis's mansion, I was shown into his study at once. "I was just on my way to find you," the Marquis said with menace. His enormous chest and padded doublet made him look like an angry bear. "The Commander has informed me that *someone* is trying to seduce Doña Ana. He chased a man from her balcony last night." I could feel his heavy inquisitorial stare. It was most certainly his paternal fondness that stopped him from accusing me directly.

"I assume he has some suspicion of who it might be?"

"I do not choose to believe his suspicion, so I will ask if you know who might value my love and his life so little that he would willingly be that foolish."

I chose my words carefully. "I imagine there might be many who would pursue such a beautiful woman, but they would be unwise to cross swords with you."

"Yes, but many men are not wise, nor cautious, when it comes to women," the Marquis said. "Let me know if you hear anything, anything at all. I too will be watching her and everyone else carefully. I told you I would stop at nothing to keep her, and I meant it."

"Your jealousy is salutary for a husband but shocking for a libertine. I never thought I would see you moved to such possession. If this is what love compels, I will stay with the generous spirit of lust, which does not require ownership, just enjoyment."

"When one risks one's heart, one is not willing to let it be pierced by the blade of another suitor," he said. He tore his sword from its scabbard and held its point in front of my chest. "The gaming of the heart is the greatest gamble in life. It is far riskier than the highest wager of dice or cards, for it is happiness itself that one wins or loses."

"I would not know, having never risked such a gamble," I said, trying to remain calm.

"You must at least bet on a lady. The King's court party is tomorrow night, and he will not be put off again."

With the tip of his rapier, he pulled the handle of mine so that I had to grab the silver hilt or let my blade fall on the ground, which no caballero would permit. I held my sword in response to his as we circled around his salon. "Neither the King nor you need worry about me."

"Did I ever tell you, Don Juan, how I killed my own brother?" He thrust his sword at my heart with such force that if I had not slapped it aside with mine, he would have impaled me.

"No, never," I said as we continued to spar. Our metal clashed, and the cut that I had received the night before from Doña Ana still stung my right hand, the hand I always relied on for swordplay.

"We loved the same woman. He was older and was to gain everything, including her love."

"What happened?" I asked, tossing my sword into my weaker hand. The Marquis noticed my bandaged hand with a nod but did not stop his assaults.

"We were mock-dueling, as brothers often do, but his sword was not as quick as mine." Perhaps noticing his advantage, the Marquis wielded his weapon like a storm of thunderbolts, and I had to move my blade with desperate speed to deflect them. Sweat soaked my shirt and dripped down my brow.

"What happened to the woman—you both loved?" I said, trying to catch my breath, as was he, although he did not stop our duel even for a moment.

"When she found out—what I had done—what had happened—she became a nun—ashamed she had— caused such bloodshed. Before she left—she told me—that she loved—my brother—and could never— love his murderer—a *fiend*—such as me. And now I have become—that *fiend*."

"If you could not—capture her heart," I said, my arm growing weak under his assault, "what makes you think—you can capture Doña Ana's—now?"

"I will not make—the same mistake—of telling her—the truth."

The Marquis was an expert swordsman, and he had a younger brother's willingness to cheat. He pulled a vase down to distract me, and I was able to leap out of the way just as it shattered on the marble floor.

He smiled and stopped his assault for a moment, the professor suddenly replacing the assassin. We were both gasping for breath in the stifling heat of his study. "Very skillful—you always were my best student— almost too good."

"You have taught—me everything."

"Not everything." He slashed at me so that I had to jump into the window alcove as his blade dug deep into the soft wood of the shutter.

"Is there—something more?"

He continued his thrusting with renewed intensity, and I was forced to stop each blow as best I could, now breathless and still without any desire to fight him.

"I once told you—that the man who could win—any swordfight—was the one—who had nothing to lose—including his life. I lied—there is one man—who can—defeat him."

"The man," I ventured, pushing him off from where he pressed my sword against my chest, "who is in love?"

"You do learn fast—but not—every man. Love—you see—can make you—brave—or it can make you—a coward—and no one knows—until it is—too late."

I did not know what love would make of me, but I would not find out. "I guess—I will never know. Don Pedro—I have come—to say good-bye—I am leaving—Sevilla—forever."

At this news, he lowered his sword and stared at me, his eyes narrowing. "I am saddened," he said, regaining his breath, "but perhaps—it is best."

"I have no choice."

"You are going to the other half of the world."

"I cannot marry a woman I do not love."

"You are wise to leave while you still can."

"I have one request," I said.

"Name it."

"The penitent in front of the monstrance was a priest named Padre Miguel. He was my tutor. Would you speak to the Inquisitor and have him released from the Castillo de San Jorge?"

"I heard from the Inquisitor that you tried to free him yourself."

"I failed."

"Your love was admirable but unwise. Padre Miguel poisoned himself after you left."

"What? He would never."

"But he did."

"How would he have found poison in his prison cell? You know as well as I do who is behind this."

"Perhaps your love for the priest stoked the Inquisitor's hatred. He will do anything to destroy his enemies—and their friends." My blood was boiling with fury and the lust for revenge. "My influence with the Inquisitor is limited," the Marquis continued, "and it has taken everything I can possibly do to stop him from coming for you. It is for this reason that I was on my way to tell you to flee Sevilla and why I say that it is best that you go."

"I have always benefited from your guidance."

"Good-bye, Don Juan."

"Good-bye, Don Pedro." As I prepared to take my leave, I turned one last time to look at the Marquis, who had already turned his back. I left the room and Fernando walked me out. But something was wrong.

Fernando was distracted, agitated, and he did not look into my eyes.

"Good-bye, Fernando," I said, standing at the metal gate. "I am leaving Sevilla. I may not see you again."

"Maybe I will go with you, too," he said quietly and without a smile.

"You know you could never leave the Marquis."

"I must leave," he said ominously. "It is not like it was, Don Juan."

I stopped and put my hand on his shoulder. "Is something wrong, Fernando?"

He looked in both directions and then whispered, "The Marquis . . . he is . . ." He stopped.

"What?"

"Carlos showed me a list of names," Fernando whispered.

"A list of names?" I asked.

"For the Inquisitor."

I stared at him. "The Inquisitor?"

Fernando nodded slowly.

We stared at each other in mutual horror. I backed through the gate in a daze and stepped into my carriage. How could I owe any loyalty to this villainy, any fidelity to this evil? I had tried to persuade Doña Ana to love the Marquis, but she saw what I had not—he was not worthy of love or loyalty. I knew that it would not be long before Doña Ana would end up on that list. She would not be the first wife whose husband had condemned her for displeasing him. I could not leave her at the mercy of the Marquis. But would I save her from him only to abandon her at some point, as her mother had warned? How could I remain faithful to her for a lifetime? There was only one man who would know the answer.

The Secret of Marriage

I ducked inside the Taberna del Pirata as the Cathedral bell struck four times. The ship would be setting sail soon. I needed to be on it or risked losing the protection of the Marquis, if I had not done so already. The tavern was almost empty except for a few sailors, all facedown on the tables.

"There you are," Manuel said, greeting me with an embrace. "You've been busy."

"I have been consumed with a woman."

"Only one?" He filled a mug with house wine and placed it on the table between us.

"Only one."

"Well, this *does* sound serious."

"I've come for advice."

"Then you've come to the right place. You know I'm always willing to tell anyone my opinion about anything, and compared to the rest of the rates around here, my advice is relatively cheap."

"Manuel, I want to know the secret. I want to know how you stay content with only one woman."

"Don Juan—content with one woman?" Serena said, now coming downstairs. "That is impossible. If you could, then any man can, and any man can't."

303

"The secret is not just advice," Manuel said. "You are asking for valuable knowledge. This is going to cost you twenty escudos, at least."

"You can't charge him twenty escudos," Serena said, her sense of propriety offended.

I tossed him a purse of coins, which he inspected and with which he was quite satisfied. Serena looked on with wide eyes and then shook her head disapprovingly.

Manuel looked at his wife sheepishly and then turned back to me with his usual confidence. "Of course I desire other women—every man does." He grabbed his crotch to show that he was no eunuch. "But I don't need to lie with the girls upstairs because I can touch them all in my wife's skin. And I can know all of their joy and sorrow through my wife's laughter and tears."

Doña Ana's laughter sang its way back to me and her tear-streaked face floated before my eyes. The light of understanding dawned. "Then the secret of marriage," I said, unable to restrain the revelation, "is simply to love and know all women through one woman."

"You have figured it out for yourself," he said proudly. "Yes, all women are contained in each and every woman, as no doubt all men are contained in each and every man."

"The Marquis was right, Manuel: You are a poet, and a philosopher."

He bowed his unshaved face with a smile. "Most men take only a small taste of a woman, but to truly know one woman's body, heart, and soul is enough for a lifetime of satisfaction. What did the psalmist say? 'Thou preparest a table before me in the presence of mine enemies: thou anointest my head with oil; my cup runneth over. Surely goodness and mercy shall follow me all the days of my life.' This goodness, this mercy, is the ever-renewing Banquet of a Blessed Marriage."

"You are a preacher, too." I looked around me at the sailors, the Cowards of Love who sought solace in wine, afraid to risk the love of which Manuel spoke.

"They are my flock, Don Juan," he said, gesturing to the drunkards.

"Let me tell you another secret," Serena said. "And my advice is *free*," she added, casting a reproving eye at her husband. "The heart is forever unfaithful, and the feelings of love will come and go, but true love is not about what you feel. It is about what you do."

"And *don't* do," Manuel said with his hearty laugh.

As I looked at them and the love they shared between them, a smile broke across my face. For so long love seemed only to be madness, but now I saw its reason. I thought of Doña Ana, and I swallowed hard. Was I ready for the Wager of Love? It was still a gamble and there would be no guarantee of happiness, but I would not remain one of the Cowards of Love scattered around me. I knew that one could not be the Empire's greatest lover without truly knowing how to love. And yet I no longer even aspired to this hollow title. I wanted only what every common husband can achieve—to be the greatest lover of my very own wife. And I knew the wife that I wanted.

I heard the sound of the purple pouch of coins in front of me before I saw it. Manuel had tossed it back.

"You figured it out yourself. Payment is not necessary. I have after all become an honorable proprietor—the great majority of the time—and I cannot take payment for goods that were not delivered."

I smiled and said, "Consider it a tip, Manuel. You and Serena"—I looked at her, bowing—"have been like a father and mother to me, and for an orphan, that is priceless." I pulled my leather mask out of my sleeve and gave it back to Serena, thanking her for it. "I must give up my masquerade and my nocturnal adventures."

"I would be surprised if a man like you will be able to make such a sacrifice," Serena said.

"What is a man like me *like*?" I replied rhetorically. "The die is not cast. All men are free to choose."

"I believe he can do it," Manuel said, coming to my defense. "He has resisted the ample charms of your girls, has he not?"

I smiled at this proof of my constancy. I got up and prepared to leave. "If ever there was a woman who could make me forget all others, I believe I have found her."

At the door, Serena called, "Don Juan?" I turned to face her, and she asked me the question she had asked so many times over the years, but to which she had never received a satisfactory reply. "Why did you always refuse my girls?" Her tone was sharp, as if she were a mother wanting to know what was wrong with her children.

I took a deep breath. "Doña Serena, my mother was a prostitute, and it is in her honor that I refused them." Her face had already begun to soften, but I wanted to leave no doubt in her mind about my motive. "My mother was forced to leave me in the barn of a convent, because children 'were a liability in her profession.' I never wanted to force another woman into such desperation. She had no choice, but I do, and I have made mine today." I smiled, closed my eyes, and turned to leave.

"Juan!" I heard Serena call out. I turned around, my body feeling as if the blood had fled from my heart and head. I looked at her, and she glanced quickly at Manuel and then back at me. Her face grew calm and almost grateful. The corners of her mouth curved in a small smile and her eyes filled with love. She searched for the right words and finally settled on, "May la Santísima Madre keep you safe."

I smiled widely. "Thank you. I know I will need her protection."

Safe Passage

Captain Fadrique was standing on the bow of his ship, anxiously waiting for my arrival. Around him the ship, like the entire port, was in a frenzy of activity and hurried movement. When my carriage pulled up, his one eye glittered like a gold coin.

"You made it, Don Juan. We've been waiting for you."

"I am not going with you," I said. His face dropped. "I will instead meet you in Sanlúcar." He was relieved that I was not reneging on my investment. I knew that Doña Ana and I would be safest if we rode to Sanlúcar by horse and boarded the boat at the last moment. "We will ride out in a rowboat after the customs agents and the inspectors of the Inquisition have searched the ship." I knew that the Marquis would alert every official to intercept us.

"We?"

"I will be traveling with a woman."

"Just one?" he asked mischievously.

"Just one, and we will travel in the pilot's quarters. She is a noble lady, after all, and cannot be expected to sleep on the deck."

"Of course," he said ingratiatingly. I knew that I would need to keep my sword close at hand on our transatlantic journey. "We won't be able to wait, so don't get delayed by any other women."

"I won't," I said, knowing that we could easily ride faster on horseback to Sanlúcar than the boat could sail down the river and its many shallows. If need be we could arrive in one or two days, but still, there was no time to waste. I headed home to prepare for our escape.

As soon as night falls, I must find a way to confess my love to Doña Ana and tell her that her mother was wrong. I will not forget her when the first beautiful maiden passes by—or the last. I have until now only tasted the women I have known, and this is why my stomach has always remained empty. I hunger for a more lasting banquet, one where lust and love are served at the same table. Lust without love, I see, is no better than spice without meat, the taste without the meal. Yet, as evidenced by the bawdy kiss between Manuel and Serena that made us jaundiced libertines blush, love without lust is like meat without spice, sustaining but without flavor. The True Passionate Love of which Doña Ana spoke would be our ever-renewing banquet. But would the lord prepare such a table for me in the presence of mine enemies?

I wait impatiently until darkness arrives, and each moment feels like an age. Perhaps it is just my fear but I feel some gathering darkness greater than the night. Is it just the heart-stopping uncertainty of making the ultimate wager of love? Nothing in the casual invitation to pleasure or even in the secret trysts that I have mastered has prepared me for such unshielded nakedness.

Evening, 10 July 1593

Alma's Temptation

At sunset Alma appeared at my door, after I had recorded today's events in my diary, futilely trying to distract myself from the slow march of the hours. She wore a simple red dress without petticoats or a farthingale, as if she were in a hurry. She was fanning herself in my hot apartment. She said to her dueña, "Lenora, please leave us. Play some cards with Cristóbal or some other game." Lenora giggled and went off downstairs.

"The Marquis says you are leaving—alone," Alma announced after Lenora had left us.

"It is true. I *am* leaving."

"Alone? Have you given up on Doña Ana? Did a kiss break the spell, or did you see that there is no difference in lying with a woman you love?" Alma's erect posture and raised eyebrows showed her satisfaction.

I said nothing.

"You have not given up on her, have you?" I still said nothing. "I just don't *believe* it," she said, placing her fan on the table and, as she bent over it, arching her back in the oldest language. To leave nothing unsaid, she lifted up her skirt with her left hand so that the magnificent curve of her naked haunch was revealed. It was a beautiful sight that had the intended effect on my loins, but I breathed deeply and recalled Doña Ana's face. I could touch Alma's skin through hers, Alma's soul through hers. Alma turned her back and neck to look at me, her mouth slightly open, her eyes willing. I smiled but, for the first time in my life, with contentment and not invitation.

I slapped her bare bottom.

"Ouch!" she said crossly.

"You are a terrible temptress, but I have made up my heart and mind."

"A man's mind and heart can make up anything they please, but his flesh will always be weak," she said with triumph and some slight scorn.

"We are much weaker than women, it is true, and

neither men nor women can deny their lust. But I have made my choice for love."

"Why her? Why now? Would you have fallen in love with her if you had met two and a half—or five—years ago? Perhaps your heart has simply been cracked open, and she has clawed her way in. Perhaps Don Juan is just getting old, and the game of lust has lost its luster."

I felt the sting of her words, as she was clearly trying to sow doubt. I knew that she was arguing with herself as much as with me, since my decision called into question everything about the life she had chosen—and the life she had forsaken.

I answered her question with a question, as all professors do when they don't know the answer. "Is it the beloved who evokes love, or the lover who has love to give? Both are no doubt true."

"But do you not long for an equal?"

"I have found one."

"How could Don Juan be content with any of the shuttered maidens of Sevilla? Don Juan is a creature of the street, and only a woman who knows life at its rawest could satisfy him," Alma said.

"I warned you that I would be nothing more than your teacher."

"You think that I am here out of jealousy?" she asked mockingly. "I just don't believe that the great Don Juan would give up the world for one woman."

"A man, I have discovered, can know all women through one commander's daughter. And, I imagine, a woman can know all men through one merchant's son."

These words cut her to the quick, but with the mask that all women for hire must wear, she replied, "I at least have been able to make love without surrendering my heart."

"I have not made love to her," I confessed.

She gasped, seeing her opening. "When you do, you will see that she is just flesh and bones and nothing more. The little spell you are under will be broken, and I'll be waiting on my bed as always with all of my flesh and bones."

She picked up her fan and began to wave it, the confident Queen of Egypt once again. She stopped at the door and said, "If you wish to lie with her as a virgin, you better hurry. The Marquis is moving up his wedding to avoid any elopement. He plans to ask the King to marry them at the court party tomorrow night."

"Does Doña Ana know?"

"It is a surprise for her—and apparently for you."

She did not look back again and seemed to float down the hall and above the stairs she descended. My heart was pounding as if it might break through the walls of my chest. I had only one night and one day to convince Doña Ana to escape with me before she would be married to the Marquis. Now it is at last dark enough, and I can fly to her window, like her falcon, Fenix. But there is a knock at the door. Who else might be calling on me tonight?

Night, 10 July 1593

In the Name of the Holy Inquisition

It is hard to believe the events that have transpired since I heard the knock at my door. I will write about them as I experienced them, the greatest pains and pleasures of my life unfolding together.

I was about to open the door when I had an ominous feeling and instead went to the window to look out. There, hiding down an alley, was the windowless black carriage of the Inquisition.

The soldiers did not wait for me to open the door. Before I had a chance to get my sword, several soldiers broke it open. "In the name of the Holy Inquisition, we have an order for the arrest of Don Juan Tenorio."

"Who has signed the order?"

The soldier held it up for me to see. "The Inquisitor General himself. You must be pretty important." I could see behind the seal of the Holy Office the King's own hand and knew that I no longer had his protection. The court party was not until the following night. The month that he had given me to find a wife was not yet over, but someone was not willing to wait to see whom I had chosen.

I knocked the table over in front of them and climbed the ladder to my roof. Pulling my body through the trapdoor, I began to stand. The crushing blow seared through my skull as I was knocked senseless by a club or the butt of a musket.

In my stupor I dreamed that I was galloping on a

black horse with Doña Ana, heading to Sanlúcar de Barrameda. I was disguised in the black habit of a Jesuit priest. We arrived at the meeting place, and I helped her off the horse. I could feel the softness of her hand as she squeezed mine before letting go. The shore was covered in fog as we rowed out to meet the ship. Once within reach, they threw us a rope, which I caught in my hand, twisting it around my wrist. I pulled and pulled but could not bring us in. I looked up at the ship, and there, staring down at me, was the face of the Inquisitor.

I startled awake to find that I was tied to the rack in the torture chambers of the Castillo de San Jorge, my wrists and ankles held taut by thick ropes. I was naked except for a white cloth that had been wrapped around my loins. I pulled on my legs and arms, but they were rendered useless. Spikes from the table tormented my back. I looked around anxiously but did not see a doctor, a clerk, or any other member of the tribunal. There was only an enormous black-hooded torturer and the Inquisitor himself. His pale face with its long sideburns and small eyes now turned slowly to look at me, a smile stretching across his face.

"Ah, at last, the *question* can begin. Are you comfortable, my dear Juan? I had this one made especially for your pleasure," he said, his fingertips caressing the wooden rack on which I lay. "I wanted you to be pricked by thorns as I have been all of these years. Shall we begin?" I felt a sharp pain in my knee and then in the rest of my limbs as the cross-shaped wheel was turned by the torturer. I gritted my teeth and closed my eyes as I fought the ropes, grasping the rough cordage, my wrists and palms stinging, every moment torn into a minute, every minute wrenched into what felt like ten.

"Good enough," I heard Fray Ignacio say, and the sharp pain was replaced by a dull ache. "Now perhaps you will tell me what I want to know. The names—I want the names of the women you have defiled, the adulterers and fornicators who have betrayed the Sacrament of Marriage."

"I cannot betray . . . their confidence," I said with more resignation than courage. The Inquisitor tilted his neck and clenched his jaw. He took a folding knife out of his robes, and I heard it snap open. I saw the torturer's hooded head look up at the Inquisitor, no doubt shocked to see him choose his own instrument of punishment. This was unprecedented.

"I am entitled to a trial," I gasped in a panic.

"You are entitled to nothing!" he shouted. "If it were not for the Marquis, I would have—" He stopped, looking over at the torturer and realizing that his perversion of justice was being overheard. "Leave us."

"Leave?" the torturer said, not understanding the strange command.

"Leave us!"

The torturer now moved with celerity, and I heard the heavy wooden door close behind him.

The Inquisitor's face broke into his distended smile. He walked around my body. "It has been so, so long,

Juan—*Don* Juan," he sneered. "So many years and so many women that you have touched with these hands, that you have defiled with this skin." He held his spiderlike fingers above my chest as if trying to feel these women through me. "Tell me what it was like to possess them, to claw their flesh. What did you do to them? Did you devour them?" He clenched his hand into a fist and moistened his lips. "Did you eat their sweat and their blood and their tears? *Tell me!*"

"I will tell you nothing," I said foolishly.

His eyes widened in rage. Remembering the knife in his hand, he raised it up as if it were a holy object and spoke to it as if addressing the cross itself. "Patience, patience, we must leave Don Juan something to lose, and for a *galanteador* there is no life worth living after castration. But do not worry, I will remove them one by one, so the loss of his manhood is slow and painful." He returned from his trance and spoke directly to me. "Your death will be the end of sin in Babylon, and your burning will strike fear into the hearts of every sinner for all time." He held the ivory handle of the knife delicately, as if it were a feather, and slid it up my thigh and under my loincloth. I felt the sharp blade against my tender skin. Sweat was dripping from my temples. I closed my eyes.

"Kill me, then," I said. He looked shocked, and I continued my bluff. "You said it yourself—for a *galanteador* there is no life worth living after castration."

"All in good time," he said, as he pulled the knife out

and dragged its sharp point along my side, drawing blood from my rib cage. "First I will watch you suffer, and you will tell me what I want to know, and then and only then will I destroy the very possibility of pleasure for you." He went to the door to bring the torturer back. "Turn the wheel!" he demanded.

As my joints were slowly pulled apart, he said into my ear, "Let us begin." He spoke with judicial formality. "Don Juan, you are charged with fornication and with the heresy of declaring that your actions are no sin. Do you maintain that your defiling of the betrothed virgin Doña Ana, the daughter of Don Gonzalo de Ulloa, was not a sin against God and King?" His words were confirmation that the Marquis must have consented to, if he did not actually arrange for, my arrest. The strength started to seep from my body as I realized that no one would be coming to my rescue. I had not left Sevilla in time, and the Marquis wanted me punished, if not dead. He also would take the opportunity to discover whether his bride was still pure. This was no standard tribunal. It was the crusade of insanity in the service of jealousy. I did not answer, knowing that any words would condemn me. *"Did you defile Doña Ana?"* the Inquisitor shouted.

"I did not," I said in a breathless, low moan.

"You lie!" he shouted.

"It's true," I managed to groan.

This time the torturer did not let up. The pain continued unceasingly, punctuated only by greater torment and then momentary release when the faceless beast tried to get a better grip on the timbers of the wheel. As my mind tried to escape my body and understand what was happening, I recalled from an account of torture I had read in the Marquis's library that there were three stages of the *potro*. In the first, my shoulders would be dislocated; in the second, the elbows and knees; and in the final stage, all the vertebrae of my spine, as my body would be stretched a hideous six inches, leaving me forever crippled.

I felt as if I were being torn apart, the sharp pain turning into a searing burn in every joint, but most of all in my weak leg. I was able to endure the pain for a time, as the brute pushed and pulled, looking back to see if I would surrender. The ropes were cutting into my wrists and ankles like knives, the bed of needles piercing my flesh along my spine. I bit my tongue until it bled, but I refused to give the Inquisitor the satisfaction of my screams.

Finally, I felt my own force waning, as the pain brought me to the edge of delirium. There I saw a vision of Doña Ana descending and kissing my body, holding the cables with her own arms. In my ear, she whispered that my love would never die—that love is the only true immortality. Her words gave me renewed strength, and I strained and struggled to fight the ropes, stopping the wheel from turning. The torturer looked back with surprise and renewed determination, but even Doña Ana's strength began to slip as he redoubled his efforts. I started to feel my shoulders being pulled from their sockets. I knew there would be no chance of escape if my arms were dislocated and useless.

"Enoooough!!!" I shouted in defeat. "I'll tell you what you want to know." I felt the ropes go slack, and the clawing pain released me.

"You are ready to tell the truth and confess your sins?" the Inquisitor asked with a victorious smile.

"Yes, I will confess the truth." I knew he could have let me die in the torture chamber, but his crusade would not permit it. He wanted to use me as an example, and he needed a confession, away from the coercion of the chamber, for the *auto de fe*. He would also need some greater heresy to justify burning me at the stake, and I had no doubt that he would find one. And yet my confession might be my liberation as well as my condemnation. "But not here, not like this. Give me a proper trial, and let me tell you and the world the truth."

"There is no time to call an advocate."

"I need none. I will offer my own defense, if defense be necessary."

"There is no time," he said impatiently.

There was only one other hope. Pride, the greatest of the seven deadly sins. "Is the teacher afraid of what the student might say that the teacher cannot answer?" I challenged.

The Inquisitor's eyes flared. "Give him his clothes and lead him to the inquisitorial chamber. This will not take long." He left to vest in his robes for my trial, which we both knew would be a disputation in defense of the faith—his and mine.

As I got off the rack, my legs gave out, and I fell to the floor. I stood with great difficulty, pulling myself up by the table. It was hard to dress, my hands trembling. The plump fingers of the torturer had to help me with my buttons, which were impossible for me. I was ushered out of the torture chamber by half a dozen guards, all pointing their deadly crossbows at me.

My legs were shaking and unstable as they hurried me down the dark halls of the castle. Each step on the stone floor jarred my aching body. The dampness seemed to enter into my loosened joints, and I felt a shiver of cold snake up my spine. Torches on the walls cast shadows around us and gave the faces of the soldiers an infernal red glow.

When we arrived at the secret court of the Inquisition, three of the guards, each with a key, approached the door and turned the locks. The door swung open and revealed a large room lit by torchlight, the windows and walls covered in black drapes. I looked up and saw that the ceiling was vaulted and had once been painted with a fresco, which had faded and suffered from the dampness of the room. Yet I could still see the portraits of Old Testament kings and saints around the perimeter. In the center was a fresco of the Hebrew king Solomon, judging between two mothers who each claimed the same infant. A soldier had a sword ready to cut the baby in half. One mother was standing and gesturing indifferently to let the baby be sacrificed, while the other was on her knees, pleading to give the baby to the false mother so that it might live. King

Solomon's wisdom had welcomed death, and I would need to do the same.

As I shuffled farther into the room, I could see a long wooden table where several other members of the tribunal sat, wearing white robes and black hoods that hid their faces. A notary sat in front of a book, ready to record my every word and gesture of guilt.

In front of me on a simple wood and leather throne sat Fray Ignacio. He had changed into his formal inquisitorial black robes and wore a scarlet neckerchief. Two scarlet plumes rose from his black hat. Behind me were the six guards, all with their crossbows ready to fire at my back should I attempt to escape.

"Sit down," he said sternly, and I sat in the one wooden chair in the center of the large, empty room. "Let us be quick, since your deeds, Don Juan, speak for themselves. They are an offense against God and King. Further, you have denied that fornication and adultery are sins and have made them into virtues. This vile heresy is an affront against the Holy Sacrament of Marriage. Before your punishment is fixed, I must hear your confession and the names of your accomplices so that I can punish them as well."

"Your Reverence," I said, "it is not fornication and adultery that I make virtues. These have merely been expedients. The virtues are pleasure and lust, which I submit are as holy as your self-inflicted pain and celibacy."

"You confess that you do not believe that lust is a

mortal—a capital—sin that destroys the very Kingdom of God?"

"The lust of which I speak is nothing more than the desire and need that lead a man and woman into each other's arms—including a husband and wife. Was it not God himself who made man to desire woman— flesh of his flesh—and for a woman's desire also to be for her man? Did God himself not say, 'Be fruitful and multiply'? Did he expect us to do so by gazing into each other's eyes? He made us out of flesh."

"Our flesh is dust and ashes, corruption and worms, burial and oblivion. Our flesh is fleeting and sinful, and if we indulge its desire it will lead ultimately to eternal damnation—as it has for you."

"Why do you believe that we can know God only through pain and not also through pleasure? Do you really think that lashing your flesh with ropes pleases God any more than lavishing it with tender caresses?"

"Our Savior suffered on the cross for our sins, and we must emulate his sacrifice and his suffering."

"For you there is only the Crucifixion. For me there is the Resurrection. Our faith reveals the conquering of suffering and death by joy and new life, but you know only the path of suffering, so you flagellate yourself and torture others to bring them to your perverse heaven."

"Our faith?" he said, standing in outrage. "Your faith is not mine nor that of our Holy Church."

"Perhaps it was the faith of Our Savior. He was so loving to prostitutes and so scathing to self-righteous hypocrites like you!"

"How dare you!"

"You," I said, feeling his fury in my grasp, "have hidden the truth from the faithful. Your denial of pleasure and passion is a lie. Anyone can see in the Book of Matthew that Mary did not deny her passion, that Joseph 'knew' her, and that Our Lord Jesus had no fewer than four brothers. What a sin that you and your Church have made this greatest model of female virtue eternally chaste—branding all female desire sinful."

"*Heretic!* How dare you deny the Perpetual Virginity of Mary? You deny the very truth of our religion."

"You and your doctrine are the ones who have denied the truth of Mary's womanhood and have made the desire of all women unholy."

"What blasphemy!"

"When the truth is blasphemy, then deception becomes dogma."

"You are possessed by the Devil's own demon—Asmodeus, Prince of Lust! I should have known. I should have seen the hand of the Cunning One years ago."

"Yes, that is what you think, isn't it? You have made all desire a demon to be exorcised."

"I call on San Miguel to help me free this sinner from Asmodeus once and for all. With your great sword rescue his soul from the power of the enemy, as you did in the great battle that you fought against the dragon, the old serpent, who is called Devil and Satan, who seduceth the whole world. Cast him out." He was approaching me slowly and began to address the demon possessing me in the only language the Devil understands: *"Asmodeus! Exorcizamus te, omnis immunde spiritus—"*

I knew that what I was about to say would condemn me to burn at the stake, yet I continued to testify to the vision of God that I had seen in womanhood and to the holiness of pleasure. "In the desire of a woman is Creation itself. To know her is to know nothing less than the face, the thigh, and the breast of God—"

"—Omnis satanica potestas, omnis incursio infernalis adversarii—"

"—Is it not written that we are made in God's image—only a fool would think that the image of God is man's alone—"

"—Omnis legio, omnis congregatio et secta diabolica—"

"—It is this knowledge—that the Divine is within reach of every man—that the Inquisition tries to suppress—"

"—In nomine Domini nostri Jesu Christi—"

"—At the Supreme Moment we are released from time, from separation, from longing—"

"—Eradicare et effugare a Dei Ecclesia, ab animabus ad imaginem Dei—"

"—As eternity pulses through us—"

"—Conditis ac pretioso divini Agni sanguine redemptis—"

"—And we merge with all creation and with God the Creator—"

At this supreme heresy, he went to slap my face in a

last hope that he could offend the demon and drive him out. I stopped his wrist with my right hand and grabbed my hidden meat knife from my boot with my left. Spinning him around, I opened the knife and held it to his throat. I used him as a shield between me and the guards, who were taken by surprise.

"You cannot exorcise a man," I whispered into his ear, "from himself."

The guards stood there helpless, unable to attack, as the Inquisitor gestured for them to hold their fire with his raised hand.

"Open the door!" I shouted.

"Do it!" the Inquisitor insisted, encouraged by the sharp edge of my knife.

"If you follow us, I will kill the Inquisitor," I said as I slammed the door behind us. I dragged the Inquisitor with me down the hall and to a window, out of which I could see the dark night and, in the courtyard below, the horses and windowless carriage that had brought me here.

"Your blade is cutting into my neck," he protested.

"You don't like pain if you are not inflicting it on yourself, or blood when it is your own, do you?" I said, digging the sharp blade in further. Every fiber in my body longed to slit his throat, to avenge Padre Miguel, but I would not descend to his infernal level. I threw the Inquisitor to the ground, and without another word, dropped out the window and onto one of the horses below, cutting it free from the leather straps that held it to the others and to the carriage.

"Close the gate!" the Inquisitor shouted as I rode at a full gallop toward it. The towering wooden doors began to shut. One of the guards took aim at me with his crossbow. As I passed, I kicked him in the chest, knocking him over before he could fire. The horse vaulted through the small remaining gap, its flanks scraping the bare wood. Behind me I heard the shouting of the Inquisitor. "Fire on him. Use the cannons." I knew these small wheeled cannons could easily be aimed at me and the horse with deadly accuracy.

I rode at full speed across the floating bridge, arrows and musket shot landing on all sides. As I rode north up the riverbank to escape around the walls of the city, cannon fire began raining down, the blasts lighting up the sky like lethal fireworks. The explosions startled the horse, and I ducked and clenched the reins as each new volley fell. The cannonballs, although small, could have sunk ships or damaged the walls of the city that the Inquisitor was supposedly protecting from sin. Finally, we outran their short range, and they fell silent. I knew that the Inquisitor would send his soldiers of God to search for me, so I continued riding to the opposite side of the city and the Puerta de Carmona.

I arrived at the gate to the city and looked down the road to Carmona. I knew that I was taking a great risk by returning to the city, but I also knew I could not leave Sevilla without trying to take Doña Ana with me. I did not know how long I had been lifeless in the torture chamber before I awoke. How much time had I lost? Did I still have a chance before her wedding to the Marquis at the court party, which was to be Sunday night?

I asked a man leaving the city, "What day is it?"

"The Lord's Day," he said with a look of surprise at my ignorance, and my heart leapt as I realized that I had lost only one day in the belly of the Inquisition.

"What time?" I asked nervously.

"The Giralda has just struck ten."

The royal party had already started, but there was a chance that she was not yet married. Stealing my way into the Real Alcázar was my only hope of seeing Doña Ana before it was too late. I tried to calm my panting horse and rode it slowly through the gate of the city to avoid arousing suspicion. The guards did not suspect a noble of also being an outlaw and continued their conversation. I rode on quickly, to make the greatest wager of love. Never with dice or cards in my hand had I felt the pins and needles of desperate anticipation piercing my skin more sharply than now.

Confession at the Alcazar

I galloped down the Callejón del Agua to the gardens of the Alcázar, the horse's stride jarring my already aching joints. I stopped where the street was narrowest. After making sure there was no one in either direction, I stood on the saddle, balancing unsteadily, like a circus performer. From there I grabbed a flagpole and tried to pull myself up, my muscles trembling every inch of the way. I managed to get a foot onto a balcony across from the walls of the garden. What would have been accomplished easily before my torture on the rack now took every ounce of my strength and determination. With my hands and whispered voice I urged the horse to go away, so it might not be found. At first it just looked at me, but finally to my relief it understood my intent and walked off down a side street. From the balcony I pulled myself up, once again slowly and painfully, to the roof. I looked up at the moon, just short of full, and I prayed that Doña Ana would walk in the garden to drink in its light.

I looked across the street at the high wall. It was as if a mountain canyon separated me from the garden of the palace. I knew I could not possibly jump it tonight and noticed that guards were stationed along the perimeter. The King and his captain of the guards were not risking another intruder. I looked around anxiously for something that might aid my crossing. On the roof, I found it, a long wooden ladder that tapered gradually from the bottom to the top. I began to lay it down like a drawbridge, but it was heavy, and I had to clench its rungs to keep it from falling into the street. I did not know if it would reach as I slid it across the final distance, my arms straining like metal chains. A wave of relief coursed down my arms as the far tips of the ladder caught the edge of the stone wall, but just barely. There was hardly the width of a finger on each ledge as I tested its stability with my hands. It was warped and not at all stable. But I had no choice and placed a foot on a rung. The brittle wood cracked. I lurched forward but stopped myself from falling. I would have to walk on the long, thin stiles, trying to balance on either side. My legs were equally unsteady and shook as the ladder rocked from side to side. I slid one leg forward and then the other, for I could not lift them up without toppling over.

Slowly, slowly, I reached a quarter of the way, then half. I looked down at the street far below and decided I should not look down again. I imagined myself as light as a bird on a branch. An inch or two in any direction and I would fall.

When I was three quarters of the way across, a carriage turned onto the street, heading toward me. I froze. It came closer and closer, the coachman sitting on the horse. If he glanced up and saw me, he would no doubt alert the closest guard. I held my breath. The coachman looked up, but he must have been half asleep, or my form must have been hidden in the constellations of the night sky, since he passed under the ladder without noticing me.

I was a few feet from the wall now. Then the ladder slipped back, or the wood cracked. I leapt toward the wall, grabbing the massive stones with my arms and trying to grip them with my bare hands. I heard the guards running toward me and kicked desperately against the wall, trying to find a foothold. My clawed hands ached as my fingers began slipping. With one last burst of strength, I pulled my body up and onto the wall. The guards were shouting as they examined the ladder, and one of them ran off to alert the captain. I hid behind the crenellated wall but knew the gardens would soon be flooded with guards, all looking for an intruder. And I no longer even had my mask to hide my identity. The odds against my finding Doña Ana and escaping alive were growing every minute.

I could only rest and catch my breath for a moment. I still had a long distance to go. I leaned out for the only branch within reach but discovered too late that it was not thick enough to support me. I fell like a stone into a bush. My limbs were now not only aching and weak but bruised. I crawled and then pulled myself upright. If I was not already too late, there was precious little time left.

I stole along the stone pathways, toward the palace and the Jardín de las Damas, having to stop several times as the heavy footsteps of guards rushed through the gardens, all searching for me. The torches that lit the path helped me find my way but required me to be all the more vigilant to avoid being seen.

As I searched, I passed palm trees as straight as the Giralda, one of which had served me in my previous escape. As I peered into the dark, I saw poisonous belladonna, with its long flowers hanging in languid beauty, and flaming cypress, like pointed sentinels of the King. All of these were shadows and shades of black, since any trace of color was extinguished by the night. I smelled the jasmine that perfumed the air as I breathed deeply, trying to calm myself.

It had been less than a month since I had escaped from these very same gardens. How could it be that so much had changed in so little time? A man's life languishes in lust for two decades and then the laughter of love changes everything. Four weeks ago, I had not known there was any lack in my life, and tonight, as I searched desperately for Doña Ana, I knew that if she slipped through my fingers, I would forever be seeking her in the empty embraces of other women.

The palace was heavily guarded, but I was able to steal through the far gate near the garden house by repeating my trick of throwing a rotting orange into a bush. Once I was through the gate, my breath stopped—the moonlight revealed the long curve of Doña Ana's back. She was dressed in black like a mourner and her long hair was drawn up sternly into a knot. For a moment I wondered if this too was a delirious vision like the one that had saved me in the torture chamber. She turned her face to the side, and I could see tears glistening on her cheek. I knew then that she was real.

"I prayed I would find you drinking the moonlight," I said in a whisper.

"Don Juan!" she said, turning around with surprise and undeniable excitement. She hid her arm behind her back.

"What do you have in your hand?" I said, gently drawing her arm from behind her back. A bolt of horror racked my body as I saw what she held. It was a jeweled dagger.

"My father's," she said calmly. She looked down at it, the gems sparkling with a sinister glow.

"Would you have . . . ?"

"I would not have had the courage," she admitted.

"It is not courage but despair that leads you to consider such a desperate act."

"I cannot live the rest of my life without love."

"Nor can I," I said. She looked up into my face, trying to comprehend my words. I took her face in my hands and kissed her on the mouth, long and hard, and her lips banished the ache from my body. "I love you, Doña Ana—and I want to marry you and take you away with me to a new life far from the Marquis." Her face was filled with moonlight, and her eyes pierced me as they had that first day when she looked at me in the carriage.

We heard voices in the distance and looked to see if anyone was coming. As she slipped the dagger into the sleeve of her dress, I led her into the garden house so we would not be discovered. The only light in the dark room came from the flickering torches outside, and the only sound came from the fountain that bubbled in the center. We sat together on one of the marble window seats, and I made my confession. "I have arranged for a boat that leaves in five days' time from Sanlúcar to New Spain."

There was a flame of hope in her face, but the light dimmed as she looked down, perhaps remembering the words of her mother. "And your love, Don Juan, is it the same love that you have no doubt pledged to the countless other women you have seduced and left? I will not escape from one man to be abandoned by another."

"Not since Teresa's death have I told a woman that I loved her—not until this very moment."

"How can I believe that you are not just playing with my heart to break it once you have had the rest of me?"

"I swear to you that I have never lied to a woman to know her. For me the pleasure was not in the deception but in the naked truth. Only when a woman willingly chose to open her arms to me could there be real satisfaction. But since I met you in your carriage, there has been no satisfaction—as each woman's face becomes yours, and as her mouth is filled with your laughter."

"I don't know what to make of your declarations. They sound sincere, but no doubt so do many men's. How can I trust you?"

"The only way to trust a man is by his actions."

"Your actions would lead no woman to trust you."

"You must judge me not by my past but by my present. I did not come to you sooner because I was arrested by the Inquisition—with the Marquis's consent—as a way to keep me from you. I barely escaped, but instead of fleeing for my own life, I have come back for ours together. I swear to you that I will give you every pleasure, and I will endure every pain, as we join our flesh and our souls. This is not lust alone but a True Passionate Love that I have never known before, not even with Teresa."

"Can I have faith in the sincerity of your conversion?"

"If a pagan can discover that there is only One God, then can a libertine not discover that for him there is only one woman?"

"Doña Ana! Are you out here?" came the booming voice of the Marquis. "Commander, you should be keeping a closer watch on your daughter."

"She disappeared, Don Pedro, when I was speaking to the King," her father answered, obviously as annoyed at the Marquis's tone as he was worried about his daughter.

"The Marquis is going to ask the King to marry you *tonight*," I whispered to Doña Ana.

"Tonight?" Doña Ana gasped. "What am I going to do?"

My mind was racing, searching for a reason that would cause the Marquis to delay their wedlock. "Tell the Marquis that you want a noble wedding to celebrate your love and for everyone to witness—on Friday, before the King returns to Madrid. By that time we will be on our way to Sanlúcar and from there to New Spain." Her eyes were wild with uncertainty, hope, and fear. "I will not leave you when the first maiden passes by . . . or the last," I said, answering her mother's challenge.

"You heard? You know?"

"Yes," I said. "Everything."

"And you still want to marry me?"

"It is not your blood but your flesh and soul that I long to marry."

"Doña Ana! The King is waiting." The Marquis's

voice was closer. He was practically at the garden house.

Doña Ana got up to leave before we were discovered. "Write to me," I begged, holding on to her hand. "Use the dove. It is a messenger. Send it to me, and I will free you from your cage."

Dueling on the Rooftops of Sevilla

After my confession to Doña Ana, I made my way to the carriages. The guards did not imagine that the intruder would be dressed as a noble and barely glanced in my direction. When no one was looking, I hid under a carriage that the Archbishop was stepping into. I rode beneath it until I was out of the palace gates and slipped away as soon as it slowed. The streets were empty at this late hour and blessedly I discovered my stolen horse, hiding in an alley, before anyone else had. I rode to the only place I thought I might be safe—the Convento de San José del Carmen. It was to this new and important convent in Sevilla that Priora Francisca had been sent in the hope that she could bring to it her guidance and no doubt her discipline. I did not know how she would greet me after all these years or whether she would give me sanctuary. Yet I had no other relationship in which to seek refuge and knew no other place where the Inquisitor might not think to look for me.

I would need the horse as we fled to Sanlúcar, the black stallion being far quicker than my brown mare.

But for now it would be safer to travel by rooftop and to stay out of the streets, so I would leave it in the stable at the convent.

The entrance was much larger than the one at the convent where I had grown up, but I could not help thinking of the night when I had banged on the door for Priora Francisca to open it. That was the last time I had seen her. I banged on the door again tonight and waited nervously. I heard the sound of small footfalls on the stones and the tapping of a cane. The door opened, and staring up at me was a much older and frailer Priora Francisca.

"Yes, can I help you?" she said in a voice that was softer than I remembered. Perhaps it was the glow of the moonlight, but there seemed to be an aura of light around her.

"Priora Francisca," I said as a statement of faith, but she took it as a question.

"Yes."

"I am Juan." A shiver snaked up my spine. She looked at me, still uncomprehending, my noble clothes hiding my true identity. "The infant who was left in the barn."

Her eyebrows rose in amazement, and her left eye no longer seemed larger than her right. I thought I saw a smile almost cross her face. "I thought we had lost you, my child."

"I'm back, Madre, at least for a time, and I must beg you for your help."

"Come in. Come in," she said.

I brought the horse through the large wooden gate into the courtyard, and she closed it behind me. "I am hiding from the Inquisition." I knew I was asking her to take a great risk on my behalf, and I hesitated before making the request.

She looked at me as if remembering across the years, and before I could say more, commanded, "Come with me." After I had put the horse in the stable, she showed me to the empty one-room apartment where the gate-keeper once lived. Fortunately for me, the order's continuing poverty meant that they did not now have a gatekeeper.

"I will not endanger you or the convent for long."

"You will be safe here," she said.

"Madre, I was arrested—"

"Better not to speak about matters concerning the Holy Office, my child. God is the True Judge." She smiled and left.

I went to the window. It had been used by the gate-keeper to see who was standing outside the gate, and since it was on the ground floor, it had metal bars, several of which had rusted off. After bending one more, I was able to squeeze out. I would not have to worry about the locked door of the convent and could come and go as I must. I needed sanctuary, but I could not yet take it. First I needed to find out whether Doña Ana had been married to the Marquis, and to await her messenger.

My strength returning, I jumped from a barrel to the cool metal of a store sign that jutted out of a wall, and from there to a balcony. Once on the shuttered balcony, I was able to climb up to the roof of the building. There, close to heaven, and away from the dangers of the law, I bounded back to my home, hope coursing through my veins and dulling my pain. When I arrived at the building across from my roof, I surveyed the area to see if the soldiers of the Inquisition were watching my apartment. They had not yet arrived, and perhaps were searching the countryside, a much more likely destination for a fugitive. I descended through the trap-door into my apartment and was able to retrieve my leather belt, which still held both my sword and dagger.

I found Cristóbal in his small room, weeping, no doubt over my demise and perhaps also the loss of his employment. "Cristóbal," I whispered. He looked at me as if I were a ghost. "I escaped. I am alive." His wide eyes and open mouth were replaced by a gasp of joy and relief. I knew I could trust Cristóbal as I trust my right hand in a duel, and I told him what he needed to do. "Take the carriage with my chest and the rest of my valuables to the tavern across from the Convento de San José del Carmen and get a room there. Bring me two saddlebags of gold, fresh clothes, and my diary." I wanted to record the villainy that I had experienced and the love that I had discovered—should our escape fail.

"Yes, my lord."

"There is something else. I want you to find out if Doña Ana was married to the Marquis tonight or whether their wedding has been postponed. As soon as you know, walk down the street tomorrow singing a song, and when I look out from where I will be hiding on the rooftop, show me one finger if they have been married and two fingers if they have not."

"My lord . . ."

"Yes, what is it?" I said impatiently, eager for him to go.

Abashedly, Cristóbal said, "I don't know . . . how to sing."

It was all I could do not to hit him. "Can you whistle?"

"Yes," he said.

"That will do, and when we're safe, the first thing you will do is learn how to sing. I don't know how a man can live without singing. Now go," I said. He left to do as he had been told, and I returned to hiding.

I covered the ladder with the tapestry and pulled myself up through the trapdoor and closed it. Then I leapt across the street to another rooftop and hid there waiting for Cristóbal's whistle and for the fluttering of my dove's wings. I knew it was dangerous to remain there, but I had already risked everything and had no choice but to wait for a message from Doña Ana to find out whether she would return my love and escape with me. My hideout would allow me to watch for any soldiers of the Inquisition.

I stayed awake all night and all the next day, waiting. Lust is full of action, but love requires endless patience, and I felt trapped, like a caged animal.

Finally, that afternoon, I heard whistling. Looking over the wall, I saw Cristóbal. I waited for the longest moment of my life. He finally held up two fingers. My heart sang. There was still a chance.

It was difficult to contain my excitement in the small rooftop perch, waiting for Doña Ana's reply. My time was not wasted, as I planned and plotted every step of our escape. I would not spirit Doña Ana away unless I could ensure her safety.

Once again the cloak of night descended. I had eaten only two peaches that I had stolen from a street vendor on the way home. I had no coins with me and also knew not to let anyone see me, so I had been reduced to thievery once again. I would wait until the very last moment before I rode to Sanlúcar. Just as I was giving up hope, I heard the sound I had prayed for.

It was the flapping of the dove's wings as it landed on the ledge of my rooftop. I jumped back across the street and grasped the bird with my hand. I looked for a note tied to its leg, but there was none.

"I knew you would be hiding here like a rat in a ship's hold," a voice said. My blood turned to ice. I saw the Commander step out of the shadow with his sword drawn. "I should have run you through at the slave market. I knew what you wanted, and now I have the proof, torn from my daughter's own hand." He held up a piece of paper—the letter. Did she requite my love? Would she elope with me? I had to read that letter.

"Then you know, Commander, that I love your

daughter and have no desire to fight her father."

"I care nothing for your *desire*," he said through his teeth as he thrust at me with his sword.

I jumped out of the way just in time and said, "Your daughter will have a life of misery with the Marquis. I can give her better."

"Better? *You* who defile God and King, father and husband, with your debauchery? A man who puts his own pleasure before duty can never offer a wife anything."

"Is the hope of happiness not better than the promise of misery? I will show her and you that I will be true." The dove cooed from the wall that formed the railing of my rooftop.

"I will die before I see that day," he said chillingly, and effortlessly sliced the dove's head off with his sword. With its feathers still floating in the air, he attacked me again. My back was against the wall, and I had no choice but to draw my sword to prevent his blow from goring me like a bull's horn.

"The Marquis denounced me to the Inquisition, and he will do the same to your daughter."

"You deserve to burn!"

Our steel clashed again. With calm and calculated blows, he thrust at my heart, head, and groin. I barely stopped each blow, but I was unwilling to thrust, for fear of wounding the father of the woman I loved. He rained down blows upon me. My skills were dulled by my sleepless night, and my limbs were still weak from the rack. I barely averted his blade piercing my chest, and the hilt of my sword locked with the hilt of his. I realized how weak my muscles truly were when he threw me to the ground. As I fell, I managed to roll over backward and scramble back to my feet. I used this opportunity to pull myself onto the wall. My legs were leaden, but using all my strength, I jumped across the narrow street. I landed on the sloped roof and slipped on its curved and rotting clay tiles. The Commander watched as I struggled and pulled myself upright.

"I will not wound the father of the woman I love," I shouted back to him. "I beg of you to stop a duel that can end only in your daughter's heartache."

His face was full of fury, and he was unwilling to listen to my request for peace. He took a running leap across the steep chasm to pursue me and continue the battle. As the force of his boot hit the edge of the old roof tiles, they crumbled, and he fell as if a trapdoor had given way. He held to the slippery tiles with one hand as his feet and armed hand dangled below. I dove forward and grabbed his arm as it began to slip. I held him fast and tried to get some leverage with my boots. We began to slip together, and I thought both of us might be lost. At the edge I was able to jam the cork heel of my left boot against a low stucco wall. This stopped our slide, and slowly, I was able to pull him to safety. This kindness, I hoped, would soothe his rage as he regained his footing. I was wrong.

With my blade lowered and defenseless, he took the opportunity to cut me with the tip of his sword—two small cuts on my chest, below my neck, where my doublet hung open.

"That cross is the mark," he said with a malevolent smile, "that I give to my opponents before I kill them." Next to the Marquis's, the Commander's blade was perhaps the most feared in Sevilla, having sent many to an early grave. He thrust at me again, and this time I defended myself. I felt the sting of the cuts and saw the blood starting to seep through my shirt. We fought again, exhaustion making my sword feel as if it were made of stone. I groaned with each block of his endlessly deft and agile blade. All I had left was my mind, dulled as it was, and I read his intention before he had acted on it. I tried to steady my emotions, though fear and hopelessness coursed through my veins, weighing my limbs down even more.

I hurled my body over a smaller chasm to yet another rooftop, and my legs buckled under me. This time the Commander was right behind me. I rolled and stood up just in time to deflect his blade at my throat. As he stabbed at me ferociously, I rolled along the slanted roof like an animal desperately trying to scurry away. I crouched and then stood, regaining my full stature, and we dueled again, if you could call it a duel. Unwilling to thrust, I was always on the defensive and always within a blow of death.

We leapt to another roof and then another, moving closer to his house. Perhaps I was fleeing in the hope that his daughter might stand between us, as she had done at the slave market, and melt her father's steel heart. The Commander had the skill of a soldier who lives with a sword in his hand, but now his most lethal weapon was the fearless abandon with which he threw himself into the fray. He had only one goal—to kill or to die in the offensive. He thrust at my heart as I barely managed to knock his blade aside, and then he tried to gore my open abdomen. He was relentless in his assault, probing for any possible weakness. But he too was showing signs of exhaustion, and even more of exasperation.

At the final house, we stood on the slanted roof across from his own balcony. As always I was on the defensive, but this time I was against the edge of the rounded tiles with only the deadly fall into the court-yard behind me.

He laughed at his advantage, and our duel stopped momentarily. "This is the end, Don Juan."

I looked over my shoulder, across the small plaza at the windows of his house, praying for Doña Ana's help. As if this glance had further confirmed my guilt, he roared like a jaguar and thrust at me again. I tried to balance myself precariously on the ledge. He had me hilt to hilt and was forcing me backward to my death, my soles slipping on the tiles.

Out of the corner of my eye, I could see the light in Doña Ana's room. I knew that if I failed in this duel, not only would I never see Doña Ana again, but she would die at the Marquis's hands or her own. Love now made me brave. I pushed the Commander back and matched each of his blows with one of mine. The thought of killing me had poisoned his mind, and he abandoned his own defense, forsaking measured steps, proper times, or proportioned attacks. Recklessly he moved straight in on the diameter line and put himself off balance, overextending his step. If I had wanted to kill him, this would have been my chance, but instead I saw another opening. With every last ounce of strength and skill that I had, I twisted my wrist and my sword in Carranza's faithful coil. I wrenched his hilt from his hand, disarming him at last. His sword clattered as it hit the tiles and slid off the roof. I knew this shame would be hard for him to endure, but I tried to offer him an honorable truce. "Commander, no one will ever know of this duel, and should anyone find out, I will say that you showed me mercy and let me live."

He threw the crumpled letter on the ground in surrender. I knelt to take it. As I did, he shouted, *"But you will not live!"* I looked up and saw the shining jeweled dagger in his hand as I jumped to the side. The blade missed my chest by a hairsbreadth. Overcommitted to his attack, he was unable to stop the force of his thrust. To my horror, he fell off the roof and landed in the plaza below with a sickening sound. I looked at him lying lifeless on his back, his eyes wide, his mouth open, and his arms extended, as if silently asking, "Why? Why? Why?" It was only when I heard a man shouting *"Alguaciles! Alguaciles!"* that I remembered the spy the Marquis had stationed not far from where we were dueling. It was not Carlos. I grabbed the letter from where it lay on the tile roof. Not until I had fled across many streets did I stop and read the letter. My heart was beating as fast as the wings of a bat.

My beloved Don Juan,

I write to you with trepidation, my fate seeming as certain as that of one who has been sold into slavery. I fear there may be no escape for me from my marriage to the Marquis, which, mercifully, has been postponed until Friday. Yet I also write with some small hope that you can redeem me from my captivity. I do not know if the love you professed is sincere, but I know that what I feel for you has left me sleepless since the night of the Marquis's party. I have tried to deny my feelings, as I know have you. Fidelity, yours to the Marquis and mine to my father, requires us to, but I cannot deceive myself or you any longer. I do love you, and I have prayed that perhaps there is still time for our escape. I have begged the Blessed Virgin Mary that you might be true to your word and take me away before the Marquis discovers our plan.

I fell back, my soul shouting with joy that her love matched my own. But this joy was instantly overtaken by dread—I was responsible for her father's death. How could I spirit her away from her door with her father's body lying before it? I looked down at my clothes and saw the bloodstain on my jacket and the torn fabric where the Commander's blade had cut me. Was there any greater proof of my culpability?

As my heart ached and my mind raced with these thoughts, I knew that Doña Ana would never be able to leave before burying her father. I would need to wait, and wait I would, however long. I fled back across the rooftops to the Convento de San José del Carmen, already plotting my return to answer her letter in person and prove that my words were true.

Yet I know that tomorrow will be a bitter day for her, after discovering tonight that her father is dead and perhaps suspecting that the man whom she loves is to blame. My only hope is to trust that her love of forgiveness will be stronger than her lust for revenge.

Night, 12 July 1593

Dona Ana's Bedchamber

I approached Doña Ana's house cautiously, knowing that it would be crowded with officers, soldiers, and priests. I hid behind a wall to stay out of sight of the Marquis's spy. I wanted to be as close as I could be and to seize whatever opportunity there might be to speak with her. The Marquis's carriage remained like a sentinel at her door. He no doubt feared rightly that Doña Ana's other suitor was responsible for her father's death and was waiting to spirit her away. He would also have been told of my escape and would draw the obvious conclusion. I looked into her bedchamber window from my hiding place on the rooftop across the street and saw the Marquis pacing back and forth in her room. Doña Ana was sitting on the bed, bent forward, weeping into her hands. I wept with her and for her. How could I face her? How could I ever tell her the truth?

Yet I had to tell her. Lust may thrive on mystery, but love demands honesty to survive. Still I did not know how I would tell her. The thought of facing her piercing eyes made me tremble more than facing her father's blade. I would explain everything—how her father had demanded that we duel, how I had tried to prevent it, how I had tried to end it, how he had chased me, how he had lunged at me with the dagger, and how he had fallen to his death through his own treachery. I crouched on the rooftop all day, waiting for the Marquis to leave so I could confess the truth. The wound her father had given me stung and I pressed my fingers against my jacket, under which was the makeshift cotton bandage that I had wrapped over the wound. I knew I should have gone to the doctor to have it properly cleaned, stitched, and wrapped, but I did not want to risk revealing my identity or to miss my opportunity to speak with Doña Ana.

To my surprise, that same afternoon the body of the Commander was taken from the house. It was covered by a black shroud and placed on a funeral wagon. The Marquis, Doña Ana, and the rest of the retinue of soldiers and priests followed in their carriages. They were going to bury him quickly. The Marquis had rushed the funeral preparations to hasten Doña Ana's period of mourning and speed their marriage.

I waited until the evening, when they returned. Her veiled face and fallen shoulders were daggers in my heart. At last the Marquis's carriage left late in the night. This was my opportunity. I would slip past the vigilant watch of the Marquis's spy, even if I needed to turn myself into a falcon to do it. But how? Her balcony was in plain view of the spy. Just then I saw a pigeon take flight from a windowsill on the side of the house facing away from the plaza, a window that led into her father's room. That would be the way. I circled around behind the spy and climbed in the shadows over the roof. I lowered myself down and tapped on the window with my knee, surveying the street below the whole time to make sure I was not seen. My arm felt as if I were back on the rack, and I did not know how long I could hold on.

As I felt my fingers slipping, I heard her whisper, "Don Juan," as she opened the window and let me in. "You are safe? I thought—"

"I am hiding, waiting for you at the Convento de San José del Carmen. I would have come sooner, but . . ." She took me through the door that connected her father's room to hers. I was careful to stay out of view until she had closed the heavy red velvet curtains and bolted the door.

Now hidden, we embraced, and she cried softly into my chest, where the wound her father had given me was still tender. "I am so sorry," I said. "I am so very, very sorry."

"My father found me writing the letter and tore it from my hand."

This was my chance to tell her. I opened my mouth to speak, but I could not find the courage. I turned from her, consumed with guilt and fear that if she knew the truth, she would hate me. "What is wrong?" she asked. "Have your feelings for me changed?"

"No," I said, turning quickly, not wanting her to misunderstand, but I could still not bring myself to tell her.

"Then hold me," she said. We embraced and clung to each other like castaways clinging to the floating timbers of a shipwreck.

"Your father's death . . ." I finally began.

"I will avenge it."

I drew back from her and, holding her shoulders, saw in her face the look that I had seen the night she held a knife to my neck at the Giralda. "Let us choose forgiveness and not revenge," I said as my palms began to sweat. I stared into her black eyes, which were filled with sadness and fire.

"If you love me, you will help me."

"I do love you," I said. It was this love that had made me a coward. I could not tell her that I was the one she would need to kill to avenge his death. "Come with me, please, to Sanlúcar, before it is too late."

"My father's honor demands that I find his murderer."

"We must go in time to reach the boat for New Spain. We must leave by tomorrow night at the latest."

350

"Then I will meet you tomorrow night at midnight, having avenged his death or leaving the murderer's punishment to God."

The truth would have to wait until the fires of her passion had cooled, and we had found refuge together in the lands of New Spain. "We cannot meet here," I said. "The spies."

"Let us meet at my family's chapel. I have the key," she said, picking it up from the writing table and holding it against her chest. "I can wait for you inside and say farewell to my father. If anyone stops me, I will tell them that grief compels me to go to his side."

"Yes," I said. It was a brilliant plan. "We will meet at the chapel."

"And María—my mother—what will become of her?"

"Leave her a note telling her you have fled the Marquis but that you will send for her when you are settled. Here is a pouch of gold for her keep and for her passage. You must not tell her where we are going, or she may betray us to the Marquis."

"Oh, Don Juan, you have been true to your word," she said. She embraced me and began to cry again quietly. Her body, like soft wax, began to seal itself against mine.

"I should go," I said, as much to myself as to her.

"Perhaps charity will compel you to stay," she said, her eyes wide and her lips slightly parted. "I don't want to be alone tonight."

I hesitated, but she offered me her lips and closed her

eyes. I could not refuse her without rejecting her. I kissed her mouth gently and breathed her breath. It was as if I were sipping her very soul. She wrapped her soft hands into my hair, holding my lips against hers. She then pulled out her ivory hairpin and shook her silken mane as it tumbled down. I trailed my fingers through it and traced the soft curve of her neck down her shoulders and arms. Palm to palm, I wove her fingers with mine in a futile effort to stop my hands from shaking.

With desire spilling over from our lips, she pulled me onto her bed. We anxiously began to undress each other as the candles flickered low and our shadows fused on the wall. One by one, I pulled on the strings that held her dress closed, knowing that I had never unwrapped such a precious treasure, each new expanse of her flesh drawing my gaze and my hands and my mouth in worship of her holy body. I kept my undergarment on with the hope that it might slow the gathering storm thundering through me. She spread her slender fingers over my chest and touched the cotton bandage that covered my wound.

"You are hurt."

"It will heal," I said nervously, and took her fingertips in mine and kissed them.

She lay golden in the candlelight against the white sheet. I was flooded with the feelings I had experienced that first night with Teresa. I was terrified, exhilarated, and without any script or skill. My body trembled beside her. I gazed into her eyes, questioning, not knowing how to express the tenderness that I felt for her and that she so needed on this tear-soaked night. Her lips quivered and curved into a smile as a tear escaped down her cheek. She explored my face with her fingertips, traveling down the slopes of rough skin and hard bone. My heart felt as if it might burst with pleasure at the wonder of her touch. Her eyes were dark wells that one could fall into and never escape. I rested my hand over her heart, and she clenched it hard and drew me toward her.

"Promise me you'll never leave."

"I promise." I did not even hesitate. I would die before I would leave her side willingly.

My mind was not guiding my hands or lips. It was my heart that painted her skin in a hundred colors of pleasure. My vision narrowed as my hands and lips fell into each limb, each curve and each caress. Her flesh flowed under mine like water, generous and giving to my parched body. I could not get enough of her eyes, her smell, the liquid rush of her body against mine. I drank like a man dying of thirst who has found the fountain of eternal life. Between breathless gasps to fill her swollen lungs, she could not stifle the music of her rapture. Sound and sight, taste and touch combined into a feast of the senses, part of the Blessed Banquet of True Passionate Love.

I slowly, humbly entered her. I knew I would need to stop myself with iron chains if her face hardened in pain, but when she did cry out, it was only to draw me in deeper. We were the first man and the first woman. It was the Fall, and it was our Redemption.

We did not want to possess or to know or even to give or to receive. We shared our bodies with a fusion of love *and* lust—which I now understand is nothing more and nothing less than the holy consort of love. Lightning flashed through both our bodies, and I could not tell where my skin ended and hers began. I hovered over her, the wings of my soul arched widely as hers rose up to meet mine. I had felt the souls of many women, but never had I felt my own. We clung to each other, wet with sweat and tears, the pleasure so great it burned, the love so great it shattered us. She fell back on the warm sheets, and I fell with her. I could feel and hear our hearts pounding against each other, our bodies shaking uncontrollably. From my scalp to my loins I was torn in two, and this time I did not restrain my seed, knowing that what I felt was not just a moment of Supreme Pleasure but eternity itself.

The next morning I awoke with the sun shining on my face. I lay there like Cain freed from his curse. Never before had I been awakened by the sun on my face, still lying in bed with a woman. I looked at Doña Ana, still sleeping, and smiled with a deep contentment. It was as if we had sailed around the whole world in the night, only to find our home in each other's embrace. As I lay there, I remembered the untruthfulness that still lay between us, and I knew I could not wait to tell her my role in her father's death. Love may make us brave in defending those we love, but it makes us weak in confronting them. I needed to regain my courage. I began to kiss her awake.

As my lips left her soft cheek, a smile spread across her face.

Then a sharp knock at her door shook both of us from our dream, and we bolted upright in bed.

"Doña Ana!" said her mother's voice through the door. "The Marquis is here to see you!"

We jumped out of bed and began to dress quickly. "Mother, I am not dressed."

"He says he must speak to you at once."

"Please tell him I will be down in a few minutes." As we dressed hurriedly, she saw where the cotton bandage had fallen away from my wound. "My father's mark," she said, covering her mouth with her hand.

"Yes," I confessed. "I was about to explain—"

"You?"

"He was insane with hatred. I begged him not to duel."

"You killed my father . . ." she said as she raised her fists. I grabbed her arms to restrain her. There was another urgent knock on the door, but now it was the voice of the Marquis that forced its way through. "Doña Ana, open the door!"

"Go!" she said, whispering her command.

"I will explain everything tonight."

"I cannot," she said, shaking her head and backing away.

"I can explain this whole misery—" I was interrupted again by furious knocking. She pointed to the window, barely able to control her fury. As I opened the window and began to climb out, I whispered, "I will write to you."

I dropped down just as a carriage was passing below. I slid off onto the street and saw the people looking out of their windows to see what had fallen on their roof. I hurried back to the convent and have now written a letter to Doña Ana that will, I pray, explain everything about that tragic night. I swore to her that my love was still true and begged her to meet me at her father's chapel at midnight. I pray that my words will cut through her grief and anger and reach her heart. I cannot go myself in daylight without destroying our chance of escape, but I have given the letter to Cristóbal, who will go in disguise. I told him to give the letter to Doña Ana and her alone. I begged him not to fail me.

Morning, 14 July 1593

A Farewell

This evening there was a knock at the door of the convent. I hoped that it might be some message from Doña Ana, but I grabbed my sword, knowing it could just as well be the soldiers or the familiars of the Inquisition. I hid while Priora Francisca answered the door. It was Alma.

"Who are you?" Priora Francisca asked suspiciously as I listened through the window.

"Do you really want to know?" Alma asked, raising one eyebrow doubtfully and revealing her bodice.

"She is here for me," I said, and Priora Francisca crossed herself. "Don't worry, she won't be here long."

"I certainly hope not," Priora Francisca said as she turned to leave, showing that the sainthood she had acquired through her devotions had not completely changed her.

"I have come to say good-bye," Alma announced as I led her into the gatekeeper's room.

"How did you know I was here?"

"Cristóbal told me."

"And how did you find him?"

"Colette," she said with a smile.

"It is lucky that the Inquisition knows nothing of the heart."

"And how do you come to hide with the Carmelites?"

"We have a past together," I said. "Now tell me of your future. You said you had come to say good-bye. Will you be leaving as well? Back to Tomás?"

"How did you know?"

"Sometimes even a man knows what a woman will not admit to herself," I said with a smile.

"He came to Sevilla and saw me as a patron. I was perhaps wrong about him and my judgment that our life would be passionless. He proposed to me right on my bed and is waiting for my answer."

"Will you live in Carmona?

"Tomás has agreed to take me to Paris. We must live somewhere without the long memory and narrow world of honor and shame."

"Paris?" I asked. "They have some of the finest cour-tesans there."

"Perhaps," she said casually. "But it will not matter to me as a wife and mother."

"The end of a short but brilliant career. I always suspected that the life of liberty would not keep you satisfied forever."

"Never did I think I would be happy with a man who was so familiar, and so kind. I wanted to know all men, as you wanted to know all women, but now I want only to know one man and his good heart."

"I imagine all men can be known through one man," I said.

"I will never forget you," she said, looking long into my eyes with a combination of admiration, gratitude, and—in some strange admixture—love. She had sworn to me repeatedly that she had wanted nothing more than instruction in the decadent arts, but perhaps when the seduction is true and the disclosure honest, there is no way lust does not someday also lead to love.

"Try to forget me," I said. "All that matters is what you have learned about your own body and your own soul."

"You have taught me so much," she said, still staring at me.

"You taught yourself," I said.

She turned to me and put her hand on my soft codpiece. "One more lesson, Don Juan?" she asked. "Before we forsake all others?"

My flesh was already responding to her touch. My hands wanted to embrace her beautiful body; my fingers ached for her. But I restrained myself, as if my will were chains of steel against which my body was straining. My flesh will never die to all other women until I too am dead. No, I would always need to rely on my will. I would see all other women as in a painting, beautiful to look at but impossible to touch. I would look at their bodies with the soft eyes of an artist who appreciates each subtle curve and wrinkle, and not with the hard eyes of a butcher who looks only to consume. I sighed and said, "I cannot."

"Don Juan is dead!" Alma declared, shaking her head in disbelief. "Don Juan is dead! Long live Don Juan!" Then she said, "One farewell kiss," as her lips touched mine. I drew back but did not tear my lips away. If I were blessed to marry Doña Ana, I would never kiss another woman, and this was my farewell kiss to all the women whose lips I had known over so many years. I kissed Alma one last time.

I heard the sound of footsteps outside the window. I looked but saw no one. This gatekeeper's room was convenient but not well hidden. "You must leave Sevilla at once," Alma said with the concern of an old friend. "Every moment you stay here, you are risking your life. Is she truly worth such a sacrifice?"

"Thank you." I smiled, grateful for Alma's concern and knowing that Doña Ana was well worth the sacrifice of every caution.

And then Alma left. Neither of us needed to say another word. We knew it would be the last time we would ever see each other. I put my fingers to my lips. They felt virginal and young, as they did the first time

359

that Teresa kissed me and I tried kissing her back awkwardly. It was as if I had given Alma back every kiss and my lips were ready for a lifetime of kissing one woman. But would she still have me? I pray my letter has convinced her of the truth.

As midnight approaches, I will go to her family's chapel in the hope that I will find her there. I go to leave behind the hunger that drives a man to grasp endlessly for what he already has, and to escape the jealousy that drives a man to clutch what is not his to possess. I must lay down my quill and pick up my sword in the hope that I can use it to defend myself and Doña Ana in our journey. Whatever our fate, I do not regret having surrendered the endless craving of a libertine for the few contented moments of a lover. Fátima was right. The pleasure in a single kiss filled with love is far greater than a thousand nights with a stranger. In lust, I found the capricious nature of life as it uses us for its endless, impersonal game. In True Passionate Love, I have discovered that while our existence may be but a breath in eternity, this truth gives life its undeniable preciousness and purpose.

Now I will discover if Doña Ana has chosen love over hatred, forgiveness over revenge. I have everything to lose but even more to gain. If love is with us, we cannot be stopped—not even by the Inquisitor or the Marquis.

Night, 14 July 1593

The Last Night: A Final Entry

Editor's Note: Don Juan's entries in his diary ended here, but according to the translator, the diary contained additional pages written in a far less elegant script. It was apparently the writing of Don Juan's coachman, Cristóbal. I include it here in its entirety.

I tremble to write in these pages, but my lord gave his diary to me on that last night, so let no man say I stole it. For fifty years I guarded it in a secret hole in my bed. Now, before I die, I must confess what happened to my lord that very same night. Every moment is cut into my memory. I see it now as if it happened this very day.

My lord forbade me from going with him. But fearing he would leave me forever, I disobeyed his command for the first time. He rode the black horse to the Convento de San Francisco as the bell of the Giralda rang. I followed behind in the carriage, Bonita barely able to keep up. I stopped in front and nervously followed him inside.

The iron gate of a chapel was open, but I saw no one. I passed a confessional, its curtains drawn. The church was dark. I backed behind a stone pillar, but my way was blocked. I turned. A wooden statue of San Miguel with great wings stood over me. His eyes were hollow. He held a long, sharp spear. The metal lance looked frighteningly real as it pointed up to the heavens. I moved on quickly and nervously.

At last I saw my lord in front of the altar. His sword was in his hand. Then I saw the army he faced. There were two soldiers with deadly crossbows and six nobles, familiars of the Inquisition, with swords and daggers drawn. Behind them was the Inquisitor. Candles cast shadows across his evil face. This is what he said. I leave out not one word.

"The witnesses have been called, the testimony has been given, and the judgment has been made. Don Juan, you have been found guilty by the Inquisition of capital sins against God and man. You will not escape God's Wrath again." I watched like a coward as the familiars and soldiers attacked my lord. It is true I had no weapon to fight with, but I remain ashamed to this day that I stood there unable to move.

My lord thrust first at the crossbows. He skewered one soldier as he was raising his weapon, and the crossbow fell from his hands before he could fire. My lord withdrew his blade quickly and used its handle to knock the other soldier's crossbow. The arrow barely missed him. As the soldier tried to reload, my lord, like a cornered bull, reared up and gored him. Then the familiars attacked.

My lord knew even he could not fight six men on open ground. He ran to the covered stairs up to the balcony. The familiars chased him, shouting victory. They thought my lord was running in fear and they had him trapped. Yet the battle was not over. My lord waited for them at the top of the tunnel, where he could fight them one at a time. Just over the railing I could see the faces of the first two familiars as they fell. The third was more skillful. He fought my lord long enough for the others to escape from the stairs. My lord now fought all four at once on the wide balcony, but I could not see how. Their blades clashed and echoed through the church. I cringed with each blow.

The Inquisitor stood not far from where I hid. He growled like a beast. His face was twisted with anger that they had not yet killed my lord. He picked up a dagger from a dead soldier and crept up a staircase on the other side. I saw him attack my lord from behind, with the dagger raised above his head. But the eyes of the familiars must have warned my lord, for he turned and grabbed the Inquisitor's dagger hand before it could strike. He twisted the Inquisitor's arm around and spun him as in a dance, so the dagger was now in my lord's hand and at the Inquisitor's own neck. "I spared your life once, but I won't a second time," he said to the Inquisitor. "Stop this bloodbath before more die—including you."

"Kill him!" the Inquisitor shouted. Why did my lord not cut his throat? Instead he held the Inquisitor with one hand and fought the remaining pack of familiars with the other. I could see only the tips of their swords sparring in the air.

Seeing my lord's distraction, the Inquisitor grabbed his arm. They wrestled back and forth against the railing until the Inquisitor had my lord leaning over the balcony. The dagger was at my lord's breast. No one dared attack with the Inquisitor between them. The battle was between the Inquisitor and my lord alone. The Inquisitor pushed the dagger toward my lord's heart and with his free hand grasped my lord's throat and tried to push him over the railing. My lord could not possibly hold on much longer. His back was bent to the point of breaking. They would surely fall together to their death. I saw my lord's body slipping. With a desperate roar, he wedged his sword between the wooden posts of the balcony railing and braced himself. The Inquisitor tumbled over my lord and off the balcony. He screamed, his legs and arms thrashing, as he fell the height of three men. With a great groan, he landed on the spear of San Miguel's statue. The sharp metal blade ran through his inner thigh and out his side. A look of horror was frozen on his face.

I covered my mouth with my hand, afraid I might be sick. The fighting stopped for a moment. All eyes looked down at the Inquisitor, but soon the clash of swords began again. And soon came another scream as one of the familiars fell off the balcony and onto his head. I stole another look at the Inquisitor. His leg dangled from the spear. He moaned in pain, his eyes bulging. His mouth hung open. The other man did not move a limb.

My lord fled back down the stairs, followed by the remaining three familiars. I could hear the shouting and clashing from inside the staircase. My lord came out gasping for breath, but he had no time to recover. The three familiars cornered him in the chapel by the confessional. I ran back and hid behind another pillar.

The oldest and most skillful of the three attacked my lord. The other two stayed back, waiting. My lord and the familiar circled left and right as they looked for an opening. They continued to change the positions of their blades. The familiar thrust, and my lord blocked. Their blades struck up and down and up again. Finally, my lord drew his elbow back, leading the other man's sword. The familiar followed, leaving his chest open. Before my lord struck, he hesitated. I thought I even saw him shake his head with regret. He went under his opponent's sword with his own and ran him through. The man fell in a black heap next to a marble statue of a woman kneeling in prayer.

My lord looked down at him and then at the last two. "Has there been *enough*—enough bloodshed? Must your wives also become widows and your children orphans tonight?" The familiars looked at each other nervously. They lowered their swords and daggers and fled the church.

I couldn't believe it. My lord had won! My lord was alive! But he was not shouting with victory but kneeling next to the body of his opponent. He took off his own cape and covered the man's face. I was about to go to my lord but stopped when I saw a woman step into the candlelight. My lord saw her, too.

"You came?" my lord said as he lowered his sword.

"I had to come," the woman said, but she did not

look at him. It was Doña Ana, but something was wrong. Her face was as cold as a stone statue.

"Did you get my letter?" he asked. His voice was worried.

She held it up, crumpled in her fist, and shouted, "Yes, I got your *letter*—you *spat* on my father's grave and on me!" She threw the paper at his chest.

My lord caught it in his hand. He unfolded it quickly. "This is not my letter—it is a forgery."

"I do not need any more of your deceitful words! My life is filled with deception and betrayal, but no more!" she said. Her voice became quiet. "I could not believe the letter, so I went to the convent to find out the truth. There, with my own eyes, I saw that your words had been false and your reputation true. I saw you kissing that *whore*!" She tore a jeweled dagger from her sleeve and raised it above her head. She was going to plunge it into my lord's chest!

"Kill me if you must . . ." he said, offering her his unguarded heart. Her hand stopped. ". . . but know that you are killing the one man who loved you and you alone. What you saw was a farewell. It was the last kiss away from your lips."

Doña Ana's arm started to tremble and then to fall. Tears burst from her eyes. She threw herself into my lord's arms, their weapons falling to the marble floor. But their embrace was cut short by another voice in the church.

"I am sorry I have only one pistol shot for the two of you," the Marquis said as he stepped out of the confessional. He must have been hiding there the whole time, waiting for the Inquisition to kill my lord. He walked into the chapel holding what looked like a dagger but was in fact a pistol. "Should I shoot the one who refuses to love me or the one who has betrayed me?"

"Don Pedro . . ." my lord said. He and Doña Ana left each other's arms and stood facing the Marquis.

"Which shot will mortally wound you both?"

"Please, Don Pedro—"

"Yes, beg!" the Marquis said, pointing the weapon at my lord. "But it will do nothing for you." He began to shake his head as he held the gun up to my lord's heart. "I didn't want to kill you, Don Juan."

"With all my heart, Don Pedro, I tried not to love her, because she was yours . . . but I failed."

"You've failed me one too many times." The Marquis cocked the pistol's hammer. "I know you were in Doña Ana's room this morning. I know that you *defiled* her. *Didn't you?* You violated my bride, *didn't you!*"

It was Doña Ana who answered him. "I will never marry you—not even if you kill a thousand men."

He turned the pistol on her. She stood there without moving.

"You have no choice! Your father gave you to me!"

"My father is dead."

"Yes, *this* man killed him!"

"I refused to fight him. He fell to his death." My lord turned to Doña Ana. "You must believe me."

Doña Ana looked down but not away.

"You are not going to listen to his lies, his excuses, his betrayal!" the Marquis shouted, pointing the gun back at my lord. "I knew it was you, but I didn't want to believe it. How many nights have I lain awake thinking of killing you, but I could not? Tonight I will have my revenge." He thrust the gun in Doña Ana's direction, pointing it at her heart.

"You wouldn't kill the woman you love," my lord said. "It was I who betrayed you. Your revenge is with me."

Doña Ana closed her eyes but did not bow her head or shield her chest.

The Marquis's face was twisted in fury. He did not answer my lord but continued pointing his gun at Doña Ana. "If I can't have you"—his hand was trembling as he began to squeeze the trigger—*"then no one will!"*

My lord flung himself in front of Doña Ana as the sound of a pistol shot and its flash filled the chapel. Within the smoke, I saw them fall together against her father's tomb. Only then did I see the bloody ring spreading on my lord's back where the metal ball had entered. She embraced him, and he raised his head to look at her. I could not see his face, but I saw the look on hers.

"Madre Sagrada!" Doña Ana shrieked. My lord's body sank to the floor, and she fell with him. She cradled him in her arms and stroked his cheek. Through tears, she spoke to him. "You—saved—me."

I could barely hear my lord's whispered reply. "No— *you*—saved me."

"Don't leave me—don't leave me," she begged.

"I never will" were the last words I heard my lord speak as his body went limp in her arms.

The Marquis stood there, looking at them and holding his discharged dagger-pistol. Would he still take his revenge on Doña Ana? He still had his sword. As if my lord's spirit rose out of his body and entered mine, I found my courage for the first time in my life. I looked around me and saw a soldier's crossbow that had not been fired. I grabbed it. My hand was trembling, but I steadied it and aimed at the Marquis. He looked at me with surprise as I stepped forward. "Don't make me shoot you," I said to the Marquis. He looked back at my lord's body. I took Doña Ana's arm. "Come," I begged.

"I can't."

"You must," I said, keeping the crossbow pointed at the Marquis. Blood was pumping through my arms and legs. I pulled Doña Ana up, as she clung to my lord's body. The Marquis's expression was strange. Was it madness or sorrow that I saw? I wasn't going to take any chances. "I will shoot you," I said to him. "I killed my own father when he attacked me, and I will kill you, too." My finger pressed against the cold metal trigger. My words were braver than I felt, but the Marquis did not move.

Doña Ana was weeping and looking back. I dragged her from the chapel by the arm. As we left, I took one last look at my lord through the metal gate. I saw the Marquis kneeling beside his body. I heard his sobbed breaths and saw his massive chest shaking. I hurried Doña Ana out and pushed her into the carriage.

When we reached her house, she stepped down slowly. She was like a ghost. She did not look at me or her worried dueña as she moved through her door. The dueña and I stared at each other silently. It was then that I realized my own guilt in my lord's betrayal. Earlier that day he had sent me to deliver his letter. He hoped it would tell the truth. He told me to give it to Doña Ana—and Doña Ana alone. The Marquis had two guards at the door. I bribed them to call for Doña Ana. Instead, her dueña appeared. I held up the letter and told her I could give it only to Doña Ana herself. Her dueña snatched it out of my hand. It was the dueña, I am sure of it, who gave the letter to the Marquis.

I drove the carriage back to the convent. There I found the diary my lord had left behind. He had taken only two saddlebags of gold and had left the remainder of his fortune in the chest with me. Anything more, he said, would have slowed them in their escape. His note told me to keep his diary safe and how to order his affairs. I read every page of the diary that night. In an attempt to reveal the truth, I took it to Doña Ana's house the next day. This time I placed it in her hands myself. It was returned to me with no note. Soon after, I heard that Doña Ana had entered the Convento de San José del Carmen with her dueña.

My lord also left a letter with his diary. His note told

me to take the letter to Doña Elena, who would deliver it to the King. It was this letter that revealed the Marquis's treasonous acts against the Crown. Fernando told me later that with the royal guards at his door and execution certain, the Marquis shot himself in the face. In my dreams I would see him point that same dagger at his own head and hear an identical pistol shot from that terrible night. By taking his own life, he had committed the ultimate sin and could not be buried in his family's chapel. I did not witness the funeral but heard it took place at la Puerta Osario.

The Inquisitor survived his fall, but the horrible disease known by the name of gangrene spread from his wound. The lie parlors were full of stories about how he suffered in his bed for a month of fevers and amputations. The doctors cut off his limbs one by one. But the disease kept spreading like leprosy, reaching even his heart.

I started to visit the Taberna del Pirata in my lord's memory, and one night I met a guard of the Inquisition. He said he witnessed it all. During his last month, the Inquisitor was delirious. He saw demons clawing at his body. As they sawed off his last limb, he repeatedly shouted the words, *"Begone, Asmodeus! Begone, you Prince of Lust!"*

I was not the only one who went to the Taberna del Pirata to remember my lord. Manuel eventually turned the brothel into a *casa de conversación*. The beautiful women who work there now offer the comfort of their words. I have never partaken, so I cannot swear they do not also offer their open arms to soothe the loneliness of some of their customers. Manuel often said he ran the most honorable and law-abiding tavern in the whole of the Arenal, but honestly this was not saying very much.

My lord's body was never found. I am sure that the Inquisition feared the power of his relics. Their fears were justified. For weeks, roses were dropped at our entryway by the grieving hands of veiled women passing on foot or in carriages. Some even say one of the royal carriages passed by on its way to Madrid. No one knows if the hand that dropped the rose through the curtain belonged to a lady-in-waiting or to the Infanta herself.

Rumors circulated for months that Don Juan had been seen alive. Like Our Blessed Virgin, he was seen across our great kingdom by so many and in so many places that all could not have been mistaken. The Taberna del Pirata hosted a continual fiesta—for some it was a wake and for others a vigil awaiting his return. Guitars played and the crowd sang and danced. Even I tried to sing a little. Manuel and Serena hung a new sign renaming their tavern in my lord's honor. I was there the day they replaced the cracked wooden sign. The new one was made from mahogany. The gold letters read TABERNA DEL BUHO, the nickname he was given during his days as a burglar, when he would fly silently into the homes of the wealthy at night. But my lord never came back to us.

The note my lord left was also a will. It directed me

to give one third of his gold to Priora Francisca, for the convent broth to feed the hungry. Another third was to buy the freedom and sea passage home of the slave Fátima. He wrote, *She helped free me from my chains, and so I am obliged to do the same for her.* I took his request to Duchess Cristina. She was surprised, but for her old friend she agreed. She also gave me a good price because her husband had returned from Naples for good, with all of his servants and slaves.

I will never forget the look on Fátima's face when I told her of my lord's gift. She stared at me in disbelief and amazement. Silent tears fell down her cheeks. I drove Fatima in the carriage to her ship and opened the door for her. She was a free woman and stepped down proudly. As I watched her board the ship, I imagined my lord's vision might come true. After the long sail back to Mozambique, perhaps she would hold her husband's hands and hear the laughter of her sons dancing around them.

That was the last time I served as a coachman. The final third of the gold my lord left for me to establish myself in a trade and to become my own master. I used the money to open a bookshop and bindery, a trade I have loved to this day. Over the years I have read many books but it is my lord's diary that I return to like the psalms. And it is his style of writing I have tried, without success, to copy. I always had to watch out for the officials of the Inquisition and their Index of Prohibited Books, since I carried books for all reading interests. After the Inquisitor's death, the fury of the

Holy Office seemed to lessen, at least for a time. Sevilla was once again a marvel.

Now, as I lie on my deathbed making this confession, Colette tends to my withering body. Her own wrinkled face is still beautiful. It was my lord's diary that gave me the courage to seduce her with a pure heart and to love her for a lifetime. I hesitate to mar my lord's diary with the facts of my own peasant life. Yet I want to give witness to how reading his diary changed me forever. Colette and I have shared the Banquet of Blessed Marriage over these many years. It sheltered us and kept me from wasting my life in cowardice. Without my lord's words, I never would have had the courage to show her my undefended heart.

After I die, Colette wants to live her last days in a convent, serving our lord and tending to the sick. I did not know whom I could trust with the diary. Then the Blessed Virgin Mary brought Doña Alma back to Sevilla on her way once again to New Spain. In old age, we all return to the memories of our youth. The years had been kind to her. Her face, although lined with life, was still beautiful, and her gray hair was still long and laced with red ribbon. One could see her blue eyes, sparkling as they did the night she hid in my lord's carriage.

I hesitated before telling her about the diary, since it would reveal the role her kiss had played in my lord's death. But she is lettered and wise and married to a rich merchant who has land in the Indies. In her hands the diary will be safe. As I revealed the secret of the diary, her plucked eyebrows rose and her eyes widened. I told her that if she returned this morning, I would give her this precious treasure. I asked her to hide it until the day when Don Juan's words might no longer be heresy. She laughed and said such a time would never come but promised she and her descendants would keep the diary safe for a dozen generations.

It turns out I was not the only one with a secret. Alma revealed to me what she had heard many years before from her uncle, Doctor Pablo, who continued to care for the Carmelite nuns. After only three months in the convent, Doña Ana had, he told her, left the holy order. It was said she ran off with a priest—or a man dressed like one—and sailed with him to the Indies. Now as I read my lord's diary this last time, I imagine that it was none other than Don Juan himself who seduced her in the confessional. I can see them on that black horse, arriving together at a waiting ship in Sanlúcar de Barrameda.

Perhaps it is simply to console my guilty conscience or my refusal to accept my lord's death. Yet it is this image that makes me smile as I sit in the light of daybreak waiting for Doña Alma to return. I end with her words, recorded in this very diary: "Don Juan is dead! Long live Don Juan!"

Abandoned women According to Andrés Navagero, the ambassador from the Republic of Venice, Seville was nearly under the control of women (Andrés Navagero, *Viaje por España*, 1524–26 [Madrid, 1983]). In addition to the perils of the sea and emigration to the newly conquered lands, the continuing wars in Europe and poverty created many widows and abandoned women. By the second half of the century, 30 percent of households in the city were headed by women. See *Spain's Men of the Sea* by Pablo Emilio Pérez-Mallaína.

Alcázar (from the Arabic *al qasr,* meaning "palace" or "fortress") The Alcázar of Seville is one of the royal palaces of the king.

Alumbrados Literally meaning "illuminati," this was the name given to the mystics who appeared in sixteenth-century Spain and claimed to know God without the intercession of the Church and its sacraments. While some *alumbrados* sought only to contemplate God's love, some used carnal passion to taste Divine Love. It was alleged that some male confessors, who were "possessed by the demon of flesh," used the erotic language of mystical writings to ensnare penitents. It is not surprising that Don Juan should have been sympathetic to their position, given his own beliefs about the embodiment of the divine.

Arenal A neighborhood outside the walls of the city, closest to the port, and famous for its poor, its prostitutes, and its criminals.

Auto de fe A public ceremony in which condemned heretics proclaimed their guilt. It was followed by the execution of the sentence, and when the offense was great enough, this could involve burning at the stake.

Book of Matthew Don Juan is no doubt referencing Matthew 1:25: "Joseph took Mary as his wife and knew her not until she had brought forth her firstborn child."

Bullfights During the Golden Age, bullfights often involved a dozen or even two dozen bulls, and the bullfighters were not trained professionals but merely noblemen demonstrating their bravery. The danger was far greater than it is today. In Luis de Cabrera's *Narratives* we read: "The bulls behaved well. They killed five or six men and wounded many others." Horses at the time had little protection and were often gored and killed as well. Today critics question the cruelty of the bullfight, but at the time this diary was written, there would have been no such concern. It was seen as a brave and heroic competition between man and beast, and as Cabrera's passage reminds us, many toreadors lost their lives along with the bulls.

Caballero A knight or noble gentleman. The term comes from the word for "horse," and refers to those nobles who were wealthy enough to own horses and ride them into battle.

Cacique A term used for a tribal Indian chief. When the Spanish landed in the Caribbean, the first tribes they encountered used this word for their leaders. The Spanish used it to refer to the leaders of other Indian tribes throughout Latin America.

Calle Susona It is hard to know whether the story that Don Juan relates about the Jewess Susona, for whom the street is named, is true or apocryphal. There were many tales ("blood libels") about Jewish plots and uprisings that often justified their persecution and eventual exile. Written testimony from the fifteenth to the seventeenth centuries, however, suggests that a skull, whether belonging to a Jewish woman or not, did at least exist and was displayed on this street.

The Carmelite The Carmelite is no doubt Teresa de Jesus, also known as Teresa de Ávila and later as Saint Teresa. She was active at the time in establishing her convents, and the Marquis paraphrases her statement about Seville: "I do not know if it is the effect of the climate in this land but I have heard that demons have extra hands here to tempt men with."

Carranza's coil This secret move was some form of a spiral that was effective in disarming one's opponent. Don Jerónimo de Carranza is considered the father of the Spanish school of sword fighting; his student Don Luis Pacheco de Narváez called him *El Primer Inventor de la Ciencia de las Armas* (the first inventor of the science of arms). The Spanish school of sword fighting was based on the science of geometry and deeply informed by the humanistic philosophy and mystical teachings prevalent at the time. Carranza wrote, "The vulgar [fencer], although he professes knowledge of swordsmanship, is easy to discover when in times of anger and conflict he forgets his professed skill, committing vulgarity in his manner and action." He added, "If the skill of the swordsman is 'invented,' the swordsman in a time of danger is forsaken by his false skill."

Casa de conversación A "house of conversation" was similar to a brothel, but women entertained men with their words and companionship as much as with their bodies and sex. These were common at the time in Spain, especially among the wealthy, but apparently not in the Arenal.

Celestina A generally older woman who would help men in their seductions for a price, often delivering notes or conspiring in other ways.

Conquistadores The explorers and soldiers who conquered most of the Americas and much of the Asian Pacific for Spain between the fifteenth and seventeenth centuries, including most famously Hernán Cortés and Francisco Pizarro.

Converso Conversos were Christians who had converted from Judaism, often on pain of death.

Corral de las Mancebías Literally "Corral of the houses of Prostitution."

Deck of cards Spanish and Italian suits were different from the French and English: Chalice (Hearts), Swords (Spades), Coins (Diamonds), and Batons (Clubs). It is believed that the Latin (Spanish) suit system came first, most likely a development from the four-suited decks with court cards that had existed in the Muslim world. Card games were extremely popular in Spain, and even servants and the poor played them devotedly.

Don The title "Don" roughly translates as the English title "Sir," as in knight or lord.

Dueña A servant and chaperone for a noblewoman.

Magdalena Ruiz was the dueña of Isabel Clara Eugenia and is depicted in at least one of the royal portraits. A dwarf who was perhaps slightly retarded, she has been described by others besides Don Juan as being somewhat slow-witted.

Escudo Similar in value to a ducat (in English, doubloon), an escudo was a gold piece equivalent to thirty-five silver reales and containing 3.4 grams of gold. In a whole year, most workers made fewer than fifty escudos.

Exorcizamus The Inquisitor tries to exorcise Don Juan using the Latin *Ritus Exorcizandi Obsessos a Daemonio*. The Inquisitor's words translate roughly as: "we cast you out, every unclean spirit, every satanic power, every onslaught of the infernal adversary, every legion, every diabolical group and sect, in the name and by the power of Lord Jesus Christ. We command you, be gone and fly far from the Church of God, from the souls made by God in his image and redeemed by the precious blood of the Divine lamb."

Fans At this time, women used their fans to communicate their feelings and desires secretly to their lovers. Covering the face meant that a woman wanted to meet or talk to a man.

Familiars An honorary and, according to legend, often ruthless volunteer force that carried out the will of the Inquisition. Many nobles chose to serve as familiars because they often received immunity from the secular courts and also could use their positions to show the purity of their blood.

Followers of Luther King Philip II actively fought against the heretical teachings of Luther that were spreading throughout his Empire, and many followers of Luther were burned at the stake. In 1557 Lutherans were discovered and persecuted in Seville and in Valladolid. By the time of Don Juan, most Lutherans who were burned at the stake were foreigners, often sailors or merchants who were traveling through Spain.

Fray A friar.

Galanteador (gallant or seducer) The name given to men at the time who would seduce wives, widows, and virgins. Their success was certainly aided by the number of widowed and abandoned women.

Hacienda A large country estate or farm.

Hanging on the cross This rather extraordinary penance must have been practiced among the religious orders at this time since we have evidence from a biographer of Mother Jerónima de la Fuente that she practiced a similar devotion.

Hermana A sister (generally used in the diary with the name of a nun).

Hidalgo Literally means "son of something" and was the lowest class of nobles.

Holy Office of the Inquisition The Inquisition was established on November 1, 1478, by Ferdinand and Isabella as a means of uniting Spain under Catholicism. After the Jews and Muslims of Spain were expelled or forced to convert, the Inquisition was used to persecute those conversos (Jews) and Moriscos (Muslims) who held to their former beliefs. The Inquisition's tribunals were eventually used to attack other heretics, including Protestants, and at times to police public morality. In addition to those who were tortured or killed, generations of families were ruined by the suspicion of heresy, the guilt of which was passed down to children in perpetuity. The workings of the Inquisition were secret and people would often be denounced, imprisoned, and even tortured without knowing the charge or being confronted by their accuser. Neighbors and even family members were encouraged to denounce one another under the threat of eternal damnation. Much recent historiography has called into question some aspects of the "black legend" of the Inquisition and has compared its methods of torture to those of secular courts at the time. It seems clear that Fray Ignacio dispensed with many of the bureaucratic proceedings meant to control the abuse of power that was perhaps inevitable with a secret court. It is also heavily debated how many people were condemned and killed during the Inquisition's three-and-a-half-century existence, but there is no doubt that many thousands suffered at its hands and that its policing of the Spanish mind had a great influence on Spanish civilization. The Sacred Congregation of the Universal Inquisition, the Vatican's authority for defending the Church from heresy, still exists, although it has been renamed the Congregation for the Doctrine of the Faith. It was headed by Prefect Cardinal Joseph Ratzinger until he was enthroned as Pope Benedict XVI on May 7, 2005.

Honor "Sustentar la honra" (or "the maintenance of honor") was a central concern in Spanish life during the sixteenth century. The Marquis's words are very close to those of Tirso de Molina, the monk and playwright who made Don Juan famous: "A Spaniard will never delay the death of one who has insulted him." Honor was dependent on a man's personal qualities, especially courage, and on his social standing in the eyes of others. The Castilian book of laws described the complex nature of honor and its overwhelming importance: "honor means the repute which has been earned by [a man's] rank, by his noble deeds, and by the worthiness which is manifest in him. . . . There are two things which balance each other: killing a man and sullying one's reputation, for a man who has lost his good name, even through no fault of his own, is deprived of all worth and honor: better for him to be dead than alive" (*Las Siete Partidas,* Book II, Section XIII, Article Iv). By Don Juan's time many writers were starting to criticize the obsession with honor, an elusive goal that rested on the fickle opinions of others.

Hospital de las Cinco Llagas The hospital of the five wounds was the largest hospital in Europe at the time.

Infanta Doña Isabel Clara Eugenia An infanta is the daughter of a Spanish king who is not heir to the throne; she is typically an eldest daughter. It is not known why Philip II did not marry off his elder daughter sooner. As Don Juan suggests, it may have been the absence of the right political alliance, although her position as her father's favorite may have been a mixed blessing, causing his reluctance to let her abandon him in his widowhood. Six years after her night with Don Juan, Doña Isabel was finally married to her cousin Archduke Albert of Habsburg, and her father made them coregents of the Low Countries (Belgium, the Netherlands, and Luxembourg). She was one of the most powerful women in the world at the time, second only to Queen Elizabeth of England. It is said that she ruled her husband with an imperious hand. The extraordinary crucifix that Don Juan describes above the Infanta's bed can now be seen displayed in her bedroom at El Escorial, the famed palace-monastery of King Philip II.

Iglesia A church.

Inquisitor The Inquisitor General, also called the Grand Inquisitor, was the head of the Inquisition and one of the most powerful people in the Empire. His authority was superseded only by that of the King. Under him were numerous inquisitors, but Fray Ignacio de Estrada clearly had an authority that was greater than that of others in Seville.

Lie parlors These *mentideros* were popular bodegas (wine bars) where people went to hear the latest gossip about the intrigues of the *galanteadores,* as well as to stay "informed about the intentions of the Grand Turk, revolutions in the Netherlands, the state of affairs in Italy, and the latest discoveries made in the Indies [Americas]" (Linán y Verdugo, *Guia y avisos de forasteros que vienen a la Corte,* circa 1620).

Lovers' mail Don Juan is probably referring to the custom of having messages sewn into clothing by the washerwomen who gathered at the river, or perhaps the network of *celestinas,* generally older women, who often hand-delivered messages for suitors.

Moriscos Descendants of the Muslim Moors, Moriscos

had converted to Christianity many generations before Don Juan's time. Even after their conversion, many Moriscos refused to assimilate and continued to pose a threat, as the king worried that they might align with the Muslims in North Africa. They were eventually expelled from Spain in stages from 1609 to 1614. Don Gonzalo's nickname, "the Morisco Slayer," is no doubt a reference to Saint James, the apostle who became a symbolic hero in the war against the Muslims and was nicknamed "the Moor Slayer."

New Spain This viceroyalty was ruled from what is today Mexico City and included Mexico, most of Central America, and much of the southwestern United States, including part or all of California, Nevada, Utah, Arizona, New Mexico, Texas, Colorado, and Wyoming, in addition to the Philippines, which were named after King Philip II. Spain lost most of its colonies in North America in 1821 when it recognized Mexican independence.

Antonio Pérez Don Juan is referring to Philip II's Secretary of State, who lost favor with the King through a complex series of court machinations and was imprisoned in Castille. He escaped to Aragon and then over the Pyrenees to France. The Marquis apparently had helped Pérez escape from prison and flee beyond the reach of the King.

Portuguese Philip II became king of Portugal in 1580, uniting both empires under a single rule. The Portuguese, who had many colonies in Africa, were some of the most active participants in the transatlantic slave trade.

Priora A prioress, head of a convent of nuns.

La Puerta Osario "The Door of the Boneyard" was a cemetery outside the city reserved for the poor—and suicides.

The Question A euphemism for "torture."

Reales Silver coins equal to 34 copper maravedis. A real at the end of the sixteenth century would buy a low mass, or a short book of about a hundred pages. It was equal to one day's wages for a common laborer.

Relax This euphemism was used by the Inquisition to refer to its handing over of prisoners to the secular authorities for burning at the stake. In this way, the Inquisition was able to disavow its role in the taking of life.

Sanbenito A tunic that convicted heretics who were condemned to death were forced to wear as part of their public shame.

Secret candles No doubt these were the Sabbath candles that Jews light each Friday night. They were one of the practices that many converso women maintained after they had converted publicly to Christianity.

Sevilla was once again a marvel "He who has not seen Sevilla has not seen a marvel" was a common expression at the time. The Inquisition in Spain was abolished by decree in 1834. Its power and authority rose and fell over time and differed from place to place, depending on the convictions of the individual inquisitors and on the strength of the countervailing secular authorities.

Sopa boba The "convent broth" was brought out at the sound of the Angelus from the monasteries and convents around the city. Along with the flood of gold and silver from the Indies came an inflation of prices that put the price of bread and other necessities out of the reach of many.

Supreme Pleasure This seems to be a reference to orgasm, but the term is not found in any other contemporary works, so its meaning cannot be determined with certainty.

Taberna A tavern.

Toreador These bullfighters were quite different from modern-day matadors: they were simply nobles on horseback who rode out to face the bulls. The goal was to plant the steel point of a wooden spear, called a *rejón,* into the back of the bull. These short three-foot shafts required the toreador to come in quite close to the charging bull in order to strike it. The toreador who managed to plant the most blades (collect the most broken *rejones)* was the winner. Ordinarily, the killing of the bull was left to the commoners who worked in the corral. If the bull "offended" the toreador by knocking him from his saddle, however, the toreador was obliged to kill the bull, and the codes of chivalry forbade anyone from coming to his defense.

Tusona The highest class of courtesan. Literally, the word meant "golden locks," a reference to the most distinguished order of chivalry (Toisón de Oro [Golden Fleece]), of which Philip II was the Grand Master.

Ultimate Skill While Don Juan's secret teaching is not absolutely clear, it seems that he is able to experience orgasm without ejaculating, a practice that was well known in the east, and about which he may have learned in the books brought back by Marco Polo, if not simply through his own extensive experimentation.

Zambomba This Christmas noisemaker is made out of a clay jar covered in leather. A stick extends out of the center, and is moved up and down, the friction making a sawing sound.

Zarabanda This dance was based on Moorish belly dancing and no doubt had elements of what has today become sevillanas and flamenco. It was known for its highly sexual pantomime, undulations of the body, flirtation, and indecent lyrics. The shocking fact that the nuns danced the *zarabanda* in the Corpus Christi procession was recorded in the chronicles of that year (see Francisco Morales Padrón's *Historia de Sevilla: La Cuidad del Quinientos*).

Acknowledgments

First I must begin with my extraordinary editor, Emily Bestler, whose instinct, insight, and grace have inspired me throughout the publication of *The Lost Diary*. Her invaluable support of my fiction has fulfilled my deepest dreams as a writer. Next I must express my endless gratitude to my beloved friend, trusted confidante, and brilliant agent, Heide Lange. Her wisdom and her compassion never cease to amaze me and to enrich my writing life. Her belief in my muse gave me the courage to risk the alchemy of fiction.

Having once served as a book editor, I know the heroic effort and unflagging hope that are required to publish a book, and I am deeply grateful for the outstanding team at Atria/Simon & Schuster. Gratitude for their confidence and admiration for their creativity go especially to Judith Curr, Gary Urda, Carolyn Reidy, Michael Selleck, Kathleen Schmidt, David Brown, Christine Duplessis, and Jeanne Lee. For their gracious assistance, I would like to thank Sarah Branham, Jodi Lipper, Laura Stern, Alex Cannon, and Lindsay North.

Re-creating history requires the expertise of so many. My great friend Antonio Doblas is more than an incomparable guide to the city of Sevilla. He is a time traveler who made the paintings three-dimensional and allowed me to walk through walls into the private lives of nobles and commoners. He is a keeper of the secrets of one of the most fascinating and beautiful cities I have ever had the privilege to explore. He who has not seen Sevilla through Antonio's eyes has not seen a marvel. I am also deeply indebted to my gifted and passionate guide in Madrid, Hernán Satt, whose excitement for the novel and for revealing its every possibility has improved it in countless ways. Stealing faces from the Prado with Hernán is one of my favorite memories from the journey of researching Don Juan. In Spain I would also like to thank the tourist boards of the city of Sevilla, the province of Sevilla, and the region of Andalusia. In particular, for their creativity, commitment, and support, I would also like to thank Antonio Martín-Machuca, Fernando Hernandez, Rocío Naranjo Molina, Amanda Corbett, Juanjo Dominguez, and Beatriz Arrilla. Stateside, I need to thank my colleagues Michelle Defields-Gambrel and Jay Dautcher for their deep research, their close readings, and their ongoing collaboration.

Numerous scholars and experts of Spanish history, Catholicism, sword fighting, and the Inquisition have offered me their guidance and their deep knowledge, including Professors Sara Nalle, William Christian, Robert Orsi, Antone Blair, Paul MacDonald, Drea Leed, and William Monter. Whatever historical accuracy there is in this retelling of Don Juan's story is due to their scholarship. Whatever errors remain are completely my own. Professor Nalle in particular went to extraordinary lengths to ensure the book's accuracy. Her generosity, her erudition, and her obsession with

Spanish "material culture" enriched the book in numerous ways and also guaranteed that Don Juan ate the color fig that was ripe during the month in which his diary entry was written. In addition, journalist and literary editor Fietta Jarque came to my aid early on in the writing. It is because of her encouragement and guidance that this book is more than a mere sketch.

I would also like to thank some of my mentors, Archbishop Desmond Tutu, Yogacharya B.K.S. Iyengar, and Taoist Master Mantak Chia, who have shown me that passion and compassion are two expressions of love and that desire and sensuality must be part of the spiritual path. I would also like to thank the Esalen Institute and Gordon Wheeler and Nancy Lunney-Wheeler for giving me sanctuary to bring *The Lost Diary* to full realization. Without their generosity I doubt I would have found the time and place for Don Juan to write through me.

The book has benefited from the time and talents of incredible readers who were compañeros, collaborators, and coconspirators, including Gordon Wheeler, Hassan Carroll, Monique Scheer, Heather Kuiper, Loren Rauch, Debora Bubb, Rachel Bagby, Jessie Chaffee, Ana Munsell, Linda Acredelo, Susan Goodwyn, Joshua Leavitt, Marlene Adelstein, Phyllis Tickle, Mark Nicolson, Karen Abrams, and Richard Abrams. Also, I want to acknowledge my skillful transatlantic wordsmiths and copy editors, Ian Paten, Beth Thomas, Marilyn Schwartz, and Sybil Pincus. For help in bringing Don Juan to his readers, I want to thank Megan Beatie, Lynn Goldberg, Marc Nichoson, Rachel Masters, and Steve O'keefe. For help in bringing Don Juan to his future viewers, I want to thank Rich Green at Creative Artists Agency. I also want to thank Jim Frey for his lessons and tough love, Robert McKee for his profound insights into story craft, Pilar Alessandra for her extraordinary knowledge of narrative and the imperatives of story, and especially Frank McCourt for his unfailing support and inspiration.

Publishing this novel has become a truly international collaboration. I want to thank the masterful and delightful Teri Tobias at Sanford J. Greenburger Associates, as well as my guardian angels, Lynn Franklin and Todd Siegal. I treasure our diverse and rewarding relationships. I am honored to be working with many of the finest professionals in the publishing world (listed alphabetically by country): Roberto Feith, Julia Michaels, and Gabriela Javier at Objetiva (Brazil); Jordon Antov, Katerina Antova, and Anelia Andonova at Bard (Bulgaria); Anik Lapointe at RBA Libros (Catalonia/Spain); Wenjuan Wu at Shanghai 99 (China); Charlotte Weis at Politikens Forlag (Denmark); Touko Siltala and Kiti Kattelus at WSÖY (Finland); Nathalie Fiszman at Éditions du Rocher (France); Bernhard Matt and Julia Bauer at Heyne (Germany); Angela Sotiriou and Athanassios Psichogios at Psichogios (Greece); Judit Rozsa-Simon and Tamás Földes at Gabo (Hungary); Oded Modan at Modan (Israel); Carla Tanzi and Maria Paola Romeo at Sperling &

Kupfer (Italy); David Kim at Random House Korea (Korea); Heleen Buth and Sander Verheijen at Unieboek (Netherlands); Gerd Moss, Guri Pfeifer, and Tone Torp at Damm (Norway); Robert Chojnacki and Katarzyna Wydra at Znak (Poland); Manuela Cardoso at Presença (Portugal); Denisa Comanescu at Humanitas (Romania); Nikolay Naumenko at AST (Russia); Dejan Papik at Laguna (Serbia); Berta Noy at Planeta (Spain); Magnus Nytell at Forum (Sweden); Emily Chuang at Crown Publishing (Taiwan); and Kirsty Dunseath at Weidenfeld & Nicolson (United kingdom). Thank you all for your belief in Don Juan and his relevance for readers today.

Most of all, I must express my endless gratitude to my mother, Patricia Abrams, and to my beloved wife, Rachel. I cannot thank them enough for their profound insight into the human heart, for their intelligence as readers, and for their astonishing love. I am truly blessed to have a mother who, together with my father, has given me a love of books and the wisdom they contain. And Rachel, I wrote this book to deepen my lifelong love and commitment to you. Whatever awareness of true passionate love fills its pages, I learned from and with you.

Author's Note

The Lost Diary of Don Juan is based on the many legends of Don Juan and on the account of a nineteenth-century French scholar named Louis Viardot who argued that Don Juan was an actual noble who lived in Sevilla and was killed in the Convento de San Francisco in hopes of putting an end to his scandalous actions (see *Études sur l'histoire des institutions, de la littérature et des beaux-arts en Espagne*, p. 344n). My desire in writing the book was not only to resurrect this greatest of historical lovers and to give voice to his true motives; I was also moved to write a book that would explore the tension between lust and love and that would confront the human question of how any man or woman can find lifelong satisfaction in one committed relationship. To find out more about the origins of *The Lost Diary* and the myth of Don Juan, and to learn about forthcoming novels, please visit www.LostDiaryofDonJuan.com or www.DouglasCarltonAbrams.com.

Center Point Publishing
600 Brooks Road ● PO Box 1
Thorndike ME 04986-0001 USA

(207) 568-3717

US & Canada:
1 800 929-9108
www.centerpointlargeprint.com